WORKS

Requests for permission should be directed to 1111@1111press.com, or mailed to 11:11 Press LLC, 4757 15th Ave S., Minneapolis, MN 55407.

Cover art "Bleach Flamingos" by Samuel Robertson © 2020
Book & cover design by Tyler Crumrine

ISBN: 978-1-948687-21-8

FIRST EDITION
9 8 7 6 5 4 3 2

WORKS

grant maierhofer

for Kelsey, as ever
and for my children, Ada, Hollis and Elisabeth

with gratitude to Andrew Wilt

INTRODUCTION TO WORKS

I've been trying to remember Édouard Levé's *Works*. In that book, he lists ideas for artworks, in numbered paragraphs, of which I can describe zero. I have a copy of Levé's *Works*, but it's locked in my office, at the university. I am hectic in place in my house across town. The phone is ringing. There's a windstorm in Kentucky, and a tree toppled inches from a friend who escaped unscathed. It's windy here too. Through the window: blossoms in fleshly heaps.

Grant Maierhofer's *Works* will be published on Bloomsday 2020 and soon after Édouard Levé will have been dead for thirteen years. Édouard Levé wrote, not in *Works*, "Only once can I say, 'I am dying' without a telling a lie." Something about this sentence bothers me, the translation, or men's logic games. As though repeating *I am dying I am dying I am dying* makes it more or less true. If every living thing died at the same moment, death wouldn't exist. But that gets us nowhere.

Grant Maierhofer wrote, in *Works*, "Which came first: the flea or the plague?" When museums were still open, I saw William Blake's "The Ghost of a Flea"—barely. The canvas is dim, as though painted with oxidized blood. The figure depicted—hulking, tongue extended—rears back from the scrying bowl, as a comet streaks across the sky, presaging pestilence, drought, war, the invention of madness.

I am picturing Édouard Levé reading Grant Maierhofer's *Works*. He's wearing a pink sweater. He's not bored. It's 2003, he's alive, Grant Maierhofer's *Works* aren't yet written, the SARS epidemic is on the news, in France, in the US, people are circulating. Levé has to conceive of Grant Maierhofer's *Works* himself to read them, conceptually, perhaps at a train station, as a series of cognitive interviews with commuters, loiterers, runaways, shoeshine stand employees, track inspectors, which continues until all the language is mouthed and flyblown, collected and pinned down. Or it's 2020, the ghost of Édouard Levé is reading Grant Maierhofer's *Works*. We're quarantined together, hectic in place, with constant interruption. The phone is ringing. A friend in Jackson Heights. She heard a woman screaming, on the street, in the night, and thought, *the virus,* but her partner, often up at odd hours, explained, *no, she was screaming before. She's been screaming for as long as we've been here.* A friend in Detroit. Her neighbor went to the hospital, her guts ruined from no food, from shut inside, drinking Coke after Coke. *It's too much,* said this friend into the phone. *Who planned we're just going to get rid of life?*

Fifteen years ago, for work, I paid a visit to a homebound woman in her apartment by the East River. She managed, with obvious pain, to let me in the door. She showed me a photo album filled with magazine cuttings from when she'd been a fashion model, a farm girl newly arrived in the city. We looked at her posing with cars and watches. *Don't let them bury me in potter's field,* she said, with obvious pain. I proceeded with intake. She didn't qualify. I told myself I would remember her name. *That much I can do,* I thought. But I couldn't. Next month, or next year, when the economy opens, I'll drive to the university and retrieve my copy of Édouard Levé's *Works.* I'll find the numbered ideas I've forgotten on the page.

I have an idea about the brain. That you can open a window in the skull, and, gently, press butcher paper down inside, rub with charcoal, produce readable marks, even if the surface is deteriorated. Shadow forms of all the lost names. My across-the-street neighbor is a neuro-intensivist. We haven't discussed this idea. We talked the other day, from a sufficient or insufficient distance, about neuro ICU admissions and deaths, people in their thirties and forties, brain bleeds, cocaine or meth.

"and now it hurts to breathe..."

Édouard Levé traveled to cities that share the names of other cities, to take photographs. I am picturing a miniature painting by

William Blake: the ghost of Édouard Levé at Grant's Tomb, holding Grant Maierhofer's *Works*. It looks as though the marble has been impregnated with blood, softened, so the pillars can be drawn to stage left and stage right, in big billows of drapery. How many people could be buried in Grant's Tomb? How many could live in it, with a view of the Hudson.

William Blake saw ghosts. At the beginning of Grant Maierhofer's *Postures,* the first book of *Works,* we are introduced to the character X: *"He is a ghost of a friend."* At the end: *"…You are X, the wet sugar bled virus."*

Everything came first. Every email refers to strange, unsettling, difficult, challenging unprecedented times. A friend in Hattiesburg, Mississippi just texted, *Of the many possible things your ex is deluded about, Slugathor being awesome is not one of them.*

Grant Maierhofer's *Works* is an unsafety protocol: how to saw your way out of a head full of hells. That ex of mine moved to a radioactive canyon where the dirt road ends at a cabin, a movie set murder shack. Nailed beside the door a hand-lettered sign, the consonants' tilt indicative of pure psychopathy: *Welcome to the Gift Shop.* At the beginning of Grant Maierhofer's *PX138 3100-2686 User's Manual,* the last book of *Works,* Horace Stein, MD, praises the invention that kills him. This machine is the anti-update decompressive saw *"used to cut through fire and ore and welcome the new age when we are no longer visitors here but hosts on the shoulder of Orion."*

Reading and writing: vector-host interactions. Everyone has predeceased their last words. Language husks, heaps of pages, Earth as a comet. High winds due to a hurtling toward. The phone is ringing. On the table, Grant Maierhofer's *Works,* or its ghost. Welcome. You're here. Is there a cure for that? The rain has started, slashing leaves. Every slug rising up from the ground is tender-bodied and contains a ribbon of teeth.

Joanna Ruocco, Easter Sunday, 2020

Postures

a novel

Excerpts from *Postures* were previously published at *Delphian inc.*, *Volume 1 Brooklyn*, *Queen Mob's Teahouse*, *Berfrois*, and *Everyday Genius*.

The epigraphs are quotations from *Journey to the End of the Night* by Céline, Louis-Ferdinand; Manheim, Ralph (translator) (1983). New York: New Directions. and *A Fan's Notes* by Exley, Frederick (1968). New York: Harper & Row.

for Earl Mac Rauch and my sister C.

and with gratitude to Sean Kilpatrick

An Introduction
by Sean Kilpatrick

"Nobody seems ready to let anyone else love something for the hell of it."

We place restrictions on love because it never existed. Likewise, art regimented by currency does nothing but trend. All creative output has been demoted to the same reliant lung work of some pettier currency. That's where we stand as conglomerate peoples: likewise, and not worth being. We nametag portions of our quality flaked against time like a drive-by shooting (they won't allow us to romanticize or revel in anything selfish these days precisely because everything is selfish) and say something was achieved. Labor for the tap-dancing void. We dug our crimes a hole and the climate took a snifter of us with it. At least our measles have a niche, cave wall slash that cries "fuck procession". No, in no way will we muster a blip. There's too many of us. There were too many of us before we were mammals. Let's die sentence one, scratch out our legacy either with minor voices, innovation, or general meanness. A message to this book is: if you want to write, begin by sucking an avalanche.

You can't call someone immature just because they're living out their abortion. A somnolent amount of Victorian adulthood stacks the novel. Maierhofer has committed a great atrocity against homeownership by displaying affection for shit you can't truly buy. Meaning a book, not the humdrum commerce of infants being had. A book is only ever in a container until it rots your thought. A baby is a thing that suffers land. The worst part isn't everybody bows to money. I'm Irish enough to be practically half awake. It's that they've fashioned money into a couth plasmatic akin with manhood. Age or status are not abstract nouns to be enforced. You have to smile in the meantime, have to take pride or they lock you up. You have to stone your medium life across the less productive or you're not a citizen. Orphan others by the bank account or be stuck in a teenhood caste will smite. Then you can stand refined by the self-aware futility of your gameplay and create pariahs on the phone, the poses you can't fess up to, sneering in each profile.

Writers tribe their bottoms together and go to war for a paragraph on Wikipedia. The acerbic mismanagement of a little political marketability and your footnote is secure. Being a footnote if lucky is the deceit we got ourselves pregnant with. In that case, why not shit yourself a census. Dung accrues regardless. It's the meaning of life. I prize the pen like any toy. But a parent is someone out of touch with the arbitrariness of nature. However, alert they are comes with brackets around their young. Initially, the artist viewed your young most pleasantly as food. Keep getting by. You'll never advance from the safety of the shire. Now everything is safe enough for groceries. A birth pang is an experience point, an ambulance brag, something a father can stick a cigar inside to sustain the monopoly. Those biologically noosed from instincts equally extinct and artless, we'll take the lifeless life. We're not owed because of the sky-wide castration that is the zeitgeist, but we'll steal our two cents anyway, at the expense of everyone's dumbass property, by squatting there, nibbling familial scraps and welfare. Because we've been raised indentured by our plentitude. Say it's weak and we'll hang you by your Republican bootstraps. And if we brave suicide we should brave it so well we take our manuscripts with us. We won't, though, because a dumpster full of chapbooks shall be our single, tiny pollution. We know the big wars sucker class. We know jobs bankroll entities that hate us. It's over. If you procreate, you're obnoxious beyond a fucking painting. Let the crib you toiled to be approved about instead become a grant for a future artist or vasectomize yourself with a rag. I speak only of utopias I know could never happen. Who really wants to live in that kind and sane of a fucking world? There'd be no art to make in spite of it! As long as we clog this planet right the fuck dispensed. Even if only your bedpan gets remembered. Next, you'll excuse yourself that sports are okay. There's a retirement home you may learn to ignore the smell of. A decent writer is someone who can't ignore their madcap reek. The rest will be quirkily famous for a year. You can usually tell complacency by the groomed and grinning insert, by the voice refusing to shake. The ease by which they neglect or humiliate anything that does not resemble the proper lie. You can't embrace your puppetry with polished strings.

Any narrator for the arts is already deleted. Doubly so, as our X is quite aware. In a time when young artists are drowning in self-portraiture, there's necessity in self-touting against everyone's being vague. No one's wearing their baby like a diaper, quite this sacrificed to studying the tumor of why write. People fuck cheaper than the abortion if you pace it wrong. The only complaint to lodge against the written word is that it slows the eventual embrace of another freshly minted (and much better promoted) mass shooter. We've sat in classrooms, worked McDonalds jobs, and dated the necrotized and ambitious for the decade plus required to have a hint at how good it would hypothetically feel to be torn apart or tearing and can do it ourselves if no one's friendly, or be friendly to others if their brief blurts of chiming in continue. The secret horror of life is that there are more opinions than bullets and now we're attached to the former by so much chickenshit coaxial networking. Anyway, who can afford either, except to say read on.

When I fumbled litward, online writing was new and rife with leftover suburban Bukowskis from the zine scene who enjoyed rap as much as telling you your writing was a posture. They had scary self-confessed underground connections that never showed up and threatening first run wives or babies that brought a faux weariness to their fluorescently simpleton, meaningful prose-verse. Nothing was quite so true or cargo-shorted as the bars that bared their hearts. They took pictures bruised by homoerotic friend-manufactured fist fights and tried to be candid with their comedian-level tough love critiques, but they didn't believe their own lisps. This is why the sensitive, zombie-like selfie-monks of mock-Buddha who hop around publicly liking everything please me. Both divisions promoted themselves as humanitarian, most divisions do, but at least there's something a tad humble left behind from their paltry and meekly performed rapes. It's always only the old gorilla dynasty bullshit of miniscule dipshit John Gardner's versus linguists who enjoy what they do with religious fanaticism instead of religious shame. Even Lish is another Gardner, another man of home-lived beers, toting a standard above the technique he perfected, because the lack of a much-sought truth scars our fright. But somehow *Grendel* is great despite who it mocks and the Lish legacy (the weirder folk, not the traditional dime-tall Carver folk) is immense, etc. Of course, I talk from no position and try not to in general.

An artist is someone who bucks in the act of pissing until their kidneys leak. If some version of you wasn't always in vogue, we'd have a paycheck here. I speak of the elusive living wage my generation saw done with. You have to be a real summer house type helped into existence or study those dishes (or even stupider, born rich and doing that just to prove something to yourself about struggle), learn not to blowjob the college interest loan for White House income. I took those loans upon myself for fun. I will not be paying them back unless one of a hundred applied for jobs in my field responds. They are another mountainously declining slush pile and welcome to it. The great revolutions of our elders petered into worse. Let's take the march to our wrists. I refuse to be paid or paying. Fuck the street and fuck being a guest here. Fuck that everyone's a refugee of what shouldn't be said and fuck who says the bold thing anyway. Foremost, fuck the strong. Stand back, someone's about to be punished for their love.

Sean Kilpatrick, 2015

An Attempt

"Raising my eyes to the ramparts, I felt a kind of reverse vertigo, because there were really too many windows and so much alike whichever way you looked that it turned my stomach.

Flimsily clad, chilled to the bone, I made for the darkest crevice I could find in that giant façade, hoping that the people would hardly notice me in their midst. My embarrassment was quite superfluous. I had nothing to fear. In the street I had chosen, really the narrowest of all, no wider than a good-sized brook in our part of the world and extraordinarily dirty, damp and dark at the bottom, there were so many other people, big and little, thin and fat, that they carried me along with them like a shadow."

Journey to the End of the Night – Louis-Ferdinand Céline

X is an under-developed cancer. He walks through tunnels and alleyways and we obsess over his happiness far too much. We electrify sections of his mind and feed him vitamins. The poor little sorrowful boy with bloody hands and pupils. If he is, he is I, we are not a good person, a single unified good.

Stopping now, X falls into our peace in his forever sleep. Falls into a beginning as the specks of glass break and begin to form a desert, begin to cause a choke in the mouths of the citizens, flatten and become thick, tube televisions, and X is on all of our screens feeling bone-sick and tired.

He shakes his head and rubs his feet over the dusty floors, and we can at once feel his every fleeting memory shine through his pulsating skin.

He is a ghost of a friend.
He is a thoughtless bore.
We feed him vitamins.
He smiles, waiting.

He walked to his room, changing into this holed-up denim shirt he always wore, looking over at the shelves of books he'd yet to read. The sad truth is that buying books is almost as addicting for the aspiring young scribe as reading them. When X was younger it was all about going to the library and picking up Hemingway, or Hesse, or Hunter S. Thompson, and taking them home to devour them, write notes, then read about the figures behind them online and really inhale the literature in vacant rooms at his father's house. Then, he probably read a book a week, and bought three or four. He'd go to bookstores around the city and see names he'd never heard of, or books he'd never heard of from names he'd known full-well his entire youth. Once he found *The Black Tulip* by Alexandre Dumas, and because he'd heard so much about his *Musketeers*, and *Monte Christo*s, he simply had to pick that one up out of ignorance and the bliss of unknown work. He still has it sitting on his shelf and has yet to read it, has yet to even make a guess as to what it's about, but the fact that it's on the shelf does provide a certain comfort he cannot deny. Some people collect furniture; some collect forms of dalliance; some collect nights and nights of drinking and losing their minds in public. X happens to collect books. This tendency, this urge, could ruin him. He'd often order books instead of food and while awaiting them he'd go to libraries and check out bags of books he'd never have the chance to read only to return there late into the night to empty the bag into a drive-up book depository. He'd read one or part of one and feel compelled to buy five more. He'd sell them, get rid of them, abandon them in the street in Chicago or at home. He'd driven once from his father's home into the woods to leave a bag of books and his car became stuck in the snow. Eventually he escaped with the bag in shame only to get rid of it elsewhere. It was constant, and often torturous, and only one aspect of the ruinous obsessive nature of X.

He was currently reading *Opium*, and *Past Tense*, journals and tracts of Jean Cocteau. Cocteau was recently taking the place of his favorite author, and the more he read him—or read of him—the more X fell in love. Although he thought *Opium* a fairly minor book, and his illustrations at the end served as the most interesting content printed between its covers, his journaling in *Past Tense*, a diary he released at the end of his life, X found addicting.

His recent note on *Past Tense* read:

"No man living or dead has written more logical dissertations on the pangs and tumult of the theater, nor of the drawling and incomprehensible language of Proust's 'In Search of Lost Time,' and every night, after I go out walking, after I slow my mind enough to sit comfortably in bed and allow my thoughts to focus on one particular thing, I read him and become enamored with the world he enacts."

After ruing the very Frenchlessness of his existence X walked back out to the kitchen, where Warren was lighting another cigarette and talking on his phone in an excited voice about people coming over and bringing drugs. He hung up and looked to X with enthusiasm.

"Hey man! Few folks from work are going to come over, cool?" He'd ask rhetorical questions like this just to seem more decent than any roommate really was.

"Yeah dude. I don't care. Sounds fun." With that the front door shut, and around the corner came the clacking entrance of Emily, wearing black and high heels.

"Hey," she said disarmingly, and sounding sullen.

As was common when Emily came home from work, she walked into the bathroom, and given the laissez-faire nature of the loft, X walked in after her.

"Hey fuckface," she said, smiling up while she sat down and peed.

"Hey there, how was work?"

"Awful…" she whispered. X slapped himself while looking to the mirror, both laughed. Her presence was strangely warm. As was common she grabbed his arm, X kissed her palm.

Such intimacy is necessary when you live in a place like theirs. The amount of bodies that came through their building was sufficient to turn even the most chaste individual moronic with lust. X often felt extreme comfort, having something oddly special— strange as it was—with Emily; and she having a boyfriend back wherever she'd come from so when it came to discussions about X and Emily actually dating, there really were no discussions. She and X would sleep in the same bed when she got drunk, and they'd make out and every once in a while, X would make her come with his fingers, but he wasn't really comfortable with anything beyond that. He's never been particularly taken with sex and things like head, and going down on a girl always left him feeling separated from humanity, like he's performing some alien experiment in a class that he was never given the ins and outs of, never told why exactly such acts were intimate. So, the two had a series of nice, strange moments to keep short-term loneliness at bay.

X left the bathroom and turned right to the kitchen where Warren gave an eye roll. In the bathroom Emily coughed, flushed the toilet, went to washing her hands. She came out with her hair wet and slicked back. She looked good that way, dyes less discernible, and the loose neck of her black T-shirt showing a patch of reddened skin from the change in temperature caused real loneliness in X. Thin women in dark colors always reminded X of Robert Mapplethorpe photographs, and this unfolding sequence of thoughts briefly drove X's disenchantment with the social realm far aside.

"What's up *yo*?" Warren said in a tone that made Emily blush; made X giggle.

"Nothing, what are you guys doing tonight?" She responded, regaining her composure and sliding her hands into the back pockets of her jeans, leaning like the picture of all carelessness on earth.

"Well, some friends are coming over. Drink, maybe do a little drugs, maybe go to a bar. What about you?"

"I don't know. Tonight's my only weekend night cos I picked up a Sunday shift, probably getting wasted and fucking around with *him*." She slid her back against X. He wrapped an arm around her shoulder and squeezed close while she laughed like a wild Midwestern mother. Warren rolled eyes and took his rum and Coke towards his bedroom, X followed.

Emily almost never partook in these rituals. They sat in Warren's room watching Bill Hicks' standup on Netflix as he drank, and X drank from a rippled glass bottle of mineral water. She likely sat in her room nursing some bottle of expensive beer and Skyped with her boyfriend. Bill Hicks was and is X's favorite comedian. He always put him on Warren's TV when they sat in his room that way. He spoke ill of advertisers and god-fearing people, and at times it got to be too abrasive for Warren, but X just kept right on howling at the screen; at the now-dead southern god of American comedy.

"Where is everybody, man?" X asked.

"They were stopping someplace out by Carrie's, picking up these two guys I've never met. Half hour or something, they said."

The nature of drug users is fairly ubiquitous among the young these days. X realized it at a far younger age, that these types, and their various indulgences, were beginning to rub off on everybody he met; that the strange tendencies he saw in his own painkiller-laden comrades was beginning to take over the well-to-do; the jocks; the timid; the intellectuals; the moody; the punk; the metal headed; the boring girls that sat aching over the good-looking boys; the fat; the thin; everybody now seemed to carry a bit of drug talk and addictive behavior with them. It wasn't just for the fuckups anymore.

Several months prior it had been widely revealed that Osama Bin Laden was murdered, and the overall demeanor of American life seemed to be changing in some way unforeseen by the generations that begat these kids. X watched the president inform the public of Bin Laden's death, and couldn't bring himself to care one way or the other. Philip, a former roommate from Europe, and his girlfriend Alex, could not have been more moved, even Warren, with his carefree political attitude, was intrigued; gaping a bit at the TV, but X didn't care. He felt he came from a world in which politics are not discussed, and the only souls that become truly political do so in the confines of their own bedroom, on their own time. That was the sort of political enthusiast he was, maybe, like Norman Mailer and Jean Malaquais before the former ran for mayor of New York and the latter shut himself up entirely: to X, they seemed interested in *exploring* politics rather than *participating in* quandaries or *solving* political problems. The problem, as X saw it, could not be solved via political means but was more a question of personal human intervention; something aside from doctrine, though he wasn't entirely sure. X was, perhaps, already becoming as deluded as Mailer later did, but he did seem to *want* to care, nonetheless.

America was changing. Not in any Orwellian sense, to X's mind, although many people would have you believe it. People thought that the influx of cell phones and tablets and social networking websites, and the Internet could only be taken as Big Brother looking down over every single human being, but was it true? X thought a great deal about this. In fact, it seemed to him quite worse, they were *half*-right, but they believed in that half more than any should believe. Big Brother is watching, certainly, but X figured he must be disappointed or quite bored by what he sees: an internet filled with lonely teens, masturbating to the faces of girls being covered in the ejaculate of ramming meatheads on antidepressants to extend their endurance; and yet, more lonely teens attempting to find love on Facebook, where love seems such an afterthought that you can change the status of your relationship with somebody with a single click; and perverts on Craigslist trying to drink the urine of young boys; and people selling furniture; and people selling harder cocks; and people selling better lives; and movies; and television shows; and ten thousand ways to turn you into an interesting person while not actually prying one off the couch in your parent's basement, a place X himself lovingly occupied for many a summer after the years of his youth with that seeping regret one can only equate with staring down the face of your high school sweetheart being rammed in one of those aforementioned pornos by the aforementioned meatheads. Teenaged millionaires; teenaged billionaires; teenaged forty-year olds; teenaged icons and Cut 4 Whomever; everything teenaged. Nineteen-eighty-bore. *This is what* Big Brother would have on humanity, nothing more; a kaleidoscopic fuckscreen of bad camera angles that make mankind look like half a speck of civilization when you pick it apart for just a moment.

That was part of the joke of Big Brother X felt they were right about, but the other half, the half which they never even considered, the half that actually shows the way the world is changing, and will change, is far more dire, far more obscene, far more anti-Human. Mankind, and in particular American-kind, has chosen the quick, and the easily-attainable, over the slow and tumultuous which forges—has forged—each and every life since the origin of human beings. They have chosen the route that doesn't indicate life, but *ease*. They have chosen the route of Dick Wolf over David Simon, the work of terribly lazed, monetarily constructed musicians like Vampire Weekend over challenging minds like La Monte Young; the artwork of hacks like Damien Hirst over the blood-soaked masterpieces of Egon Schiele or Jackson Pollock. And the problem is not that these are the paramount topics of the day, but that people have been driven to choose them over a slow evisceration of intellectual and mental integrity via things like advertising, and the news cycle, and random, chaotic wars. So, did America succeed in ending the life of Osama Bin Laden? Yes. Sure. Perhaps. So what? Did America do anything along the way to encourage the betterment of mankind? Did America do anything aside from kill off that which creates hysteria—having already fed said hysteria? That which instills guilt? That which makes X and his generation frantic over what the future could possibly mean? No, America did not, it only managed to push the truth that much farther down into the ocean with Mr. Bin Laden's corpse. X's thoughts became muddy in these veins but tried all the same.

Warren's room slowly filled with humans, each with cigarettes and poses and conversations and drugs. X watched as it happened, a time-lapse of the human experience, and after a while managed to get better acquainted with one of Warren's oldest friends, a man he'd taken an interest in.

"So, Gary, how many people have you killed?" X asked. He wasn't particularly sure whether this was taboo with him but given the preceding words and its almost immediate veering into X's life as a confused and occasional drug addict/major depressive, he figured it'd be alright.

"Ah, man. Not here. Come on. I don't like talking about it here. It's sick. It's too much. I have PTSD. I'd *lose* it. I don't like many people hearing about that stuff."

"Yeah, but it's me, man. I'm not going to tell these idiots," X encouraged, and Gary smiled, letting go.

"Alright, you want the truth. I'm not sure. I've fired probably thirty shots with direct intent-to-kill, if that; but you seldom inquire further than that, let alone approach."

"Holy shit. That's crazy. Bastards!" X yelled, perhaps too loud. Nobody seemed to care.

"Yeah man, but it really becomes a sequence of actions more than anything. Your relationship is less with any perceived enemy than the sound of an adequately loaded round, or the clicks of preparation. That and sweat and months on end of discontentment, it's more like a sea of memory than one tangible bit, y'know? I dunno. I hate talking about this kind of shit."

"I hear you, but you said you felt sort of interested in that stuff, right? You know Hemingway, Mailer, *The Odyssey*, and shit. The psychology of war, or whatever, so it had to serve as some sort of fuel for the intellect, right?"

"I guess man, but I'm not like you. I can't sit down and write a fucking war novel. I can't write a fucking song. I can't paint. I can't draw. I can't even sing, and don't know if I'd want to—to process or something. I've always said that I'm like an artist without a medium, which is the most difficult thing I've ever had to endure. Constantly feeling that there was some way of speaking, something indirect that would lead right to my peace and happiness, but that the medium for said speech simply doesn't exist. That's my life."

"Shit man, I'm sorry. I don't know."

"Like I'm neurotic or insane in a lot of ways. Until I was nineteen, I didn't read a fucking thing. I'd act the part and hang around with the right people in school and play sports so that I passed. But now, it's ridiculous, I can remember everything. Like I own a first edition of *On the Road*, and I can tell you that on the fifty-seventh page Dean's talking about New York and wishing he could go back there, but I can't tell you who was in my tenth grade class, not a fucking soul. My brain just doesn't work like that. I always wished I could find the medium so people could understand. Be fucking Picasso or something. These fragmented, odd pictures of humans—the war stuff, the *Guernica*—but somehow they made sense because everybody sees everybody differently, but I can't paint."

Gary was a sort of unbelievable, exceptional person. X had seen him twice before but never really got to know him. His history with the military, and the fact that he seemed so ready for human connection—X was drawn to him. He also seemed to trust X that night, seemed to see something in him that he didn't see in the usual drunks he hung around with. And as the room spun into a real, if muted, party, and Roxy Music sang something about the hundreds of rooms in the world just like this, X began to trust Gary in turn, began to develop feelings for him as a friend he hadn't felt for anyone in quite some time. However, after they spoke, and after Gary seemed to vent much of his frustrations, he was in a conversation with someone else, some girl X'd never seen before with thick glasses and pudgy lips, talking about a new record he was afraid to listen to because he wanted to give it his full credence and adulation, and he seemed just as passionate about the music as he was the desperation of war he'd seconds ago conveyed. X became overwhelmed with jealousy and went to the bathroom to take a piss and groan like an old, bumbling fool.

When he left the bathroom, Emily was changing the song playing throughout the house on a small iPod and looking at him with a jokey seduction. She put on something contemporary X hated and came over, wrapping her arms around his waist and laying her tiny, dried-out head upon his chest.

"Whatcha doin' fuckface?" She cooed.

"Avoiding whatever's in there, slash pissing," he said, nodding at the room he'd vacated for a moment.

"Come to my room," she said it in one of those babyish tones of voice that make you wonder about the integrity of such people. She had just finished becoming aroused over Skype with her boyfriend and was looking for somebody close to give a sort of anesthetic so she might fall in a mild drunk to rest. X liked her room; liked the girlish way everything was set up, and the quiet in there from her meticulous placing of pillows and blankets. He followed.

As they entered, she jumped onto the bed and turned to face him, sitting cross-legged on the comforter making faces. He shut the door and looked around, she had no books, no films, no paintings to speak of short of these awful little things drawn on her wall from previous occupants. Her room was lofted and above the closet next to the doorway there was an empty space she stored luggage. It looked like essentially the same thing as X's room, except for hers felt lighter, flowered maybe or more at ease. She was endearing. X saw in her a comrade and an intimate, it confused him no end.

"Come here." He did. "Kiss me." He did. Pulled her frame against him, lifting her momentarily from her mattress then laying her down beneath, her thin legs tucked under his and her chest seemingly reaching up as he felt her hip bones and she rubbed the beginnings of her against his jeans. He pressed harder then, immediately slid two fingers—the middle and ring fingers of his right hand—and X lay down on the bed straddling her right leg as he moved his fingers incessantly. She opened her mouth and let out her tongue like a waiting bird and he pulled his fingers from her. She was partial to this. He began to kiss her hard and she sucked his bottom lip, rubbing against his chest and wrapping her left leg over him so that his hand was stuck. He started to lose strength or interest and so clenched his knuckles and with that she began to moan. Harder, rubbing his thumb over her as she sucked his lip until it bled, his left hand cradling her head and pulling her close. His fingers began moving so fast that brief, shooting pains ran up the arm, and she came almost too soon. Her fingernails now scratching into the center of his back; mouth on hers; her head held close. She came, vibrating against his hand and moaning long breaths into his mouth. He held her there, that way, for moments. She began playing with him.

"Want me to return the favor, fuckface?" Words against his neck, grabbing him hard.

"No. No thank you," X said. Oral sex left him feeling feeble, out of control, and despicable. He just kissed her, clenched palm against the drying plane of skin, and whispered how uninteresting his own pleasure seemed.

X stood up then, shaking his hands and letting the blood reach his extremities again. He leaned over and gave her one last kiss then walked out into the living room, leaving the door shut as he left, and Emily on the bed watching something on a tilted computer, breathing soft.

X was enrolled in a writing program at Marcel University and things were not going particularly well. Hence when the weekend came around and he could finally enjoy the company of a large pile of post-graduate alcoholics and drug addicts he welcomed it with open arms. He skipped a good deal of his classes—not out of some attempt to spite someone—simply because he felt so confused and frantic at times that he couldn't sleep until five, or six in the morning, and by then would get so scared of never waking up that he'd write his teachers these sob story letters about how he had to stay out in the suburbs to watch his baby cousins but that his homework would be in by the next day, it seldom was.

When he walked back into Warren's room X knew he wouldn't last. Warren came over to X.

"Hey! How's it going?" He beamed.

"Oh, you know." They laughed a bit, mumbled. Warren's eyes rolled, aware. For some reason the time with Emily now seemed like the funniest, most absurd thing on earth, and it didn't just strike him as some tribal ritual—their laughter—it genuinely went from being this serious, quiet moment with Emily, to some hilarious account of human comedy. Warren bummed X a Parliament and, hesitantly, he walked over to sit in a chair next to the computer, putting on a song by Link Wray and settling in with a long drag on the smoke.

More conversations happened, but X was ready to get out of there. After talking to Gary a little bit more about the military and Hemingway he went into the kitchen and fixed a tall glass of water. He drank it then went back past Emily's room out into the hallway, walking down the stairs and out the door into the cold midnight. It had started to rain a bit and gusts of water hit him softly in the face, he turned right and walked the long distance to an old theater that showed late night films, feeling with every step more like Travis Bickle, mumbling audibly what lines he remembered reading from *Past Tense*.

It was later than he'd realized by the time he was close to the theater, so X stopped at a diner and grabbed a cup before continuing on.

In the diner: students at their laptops writing important properly-cited things; couples talking about the general condition of things X couldn't understand; waiters and busboys and baristas shuffled around with drab looks in their eyes, like the end was slowly creeping up and life was now a matter of these menial actions until the rapture swallowed them whole.

In the movie theater an old man came out and played the organ before every show. The theater seated probably three hundred people at capacity, and the screen was draped in tall red velvet curtains that would be pulled back by ropes and real ushers before each movie started. The film they were playing that particular midnight was *Maniac,* by Bill Lustig. Lustig was actually in the theater to promote the movie, and before it screened gave the crowd a brief dissertation on his life and times.

The whole thing—film included—wound up being extremely touching to X. The movie would be classified as B trash these days, but Lustig himself was such an earnest fellow when he came out that X couldn't help but think there was something deeper today's audience would simply let slip through the cracks on the assumption that its themes weren't nearly art-driven enough. The movie was, cinematically at least, on the same order as films such as *Taxi Driver* or *Cruising,* lush 70s landscapes stripped of hope and duly seedy. It hardly had the content to measure up to Scorsese, but the imagery—New York as seen through dingy cameras and vile acts—reminded X of the era just the same. It traced the life of this murderer who walked the streets at night slashing people up with a knife covered in ketchup, something intended to instill fear in the audience. The audience in the theater that night found most of the film to be hilarious, and X supposed nobody's ever completely wrong in their reaction to something, but he couldn't help his sympathizing with its primary character. X was always looking past the characters into the actors that play them, and he always wound up seeming like a fool when it came to the cinema because of it. For instance, his favorite actor, had been for years and always would be, was Harry Dean Stanton. He's hardly thrown into the same lot as Brando or James Dean, or even contemporary morons like Sean Penn, but all the same X ranks him even higher than his cohorts; to the extent that X considers him peerless. Harry Dean can see that real acting, good acting, comes when you simply *are* the characters you're playing, nothing more, nothing less. Harry Dean Stanton's greatest role, in Wim Wenders' *Paris, Texas,* was X's favorite performance and film ever made. That movie changed X's life. He saw it once when he was much younger out of intrigue, and he'd probably seen it five times a year since then, mostly out of necessity because if he doesn't reconnect with those characters he feels friendless, like he's out on some island spending each day walking pathetically into the sun all by himself, alien. So as he sat there watching *Maniac*, and as the crowd howled in laughter, X was touched; touched by the same mystique such men as Harry Dean Stanton in *Paris* and Michael Douglas in *Falling Down* possess, and Charles Bronson in *Death Wish* and Ben Foster in *30 Days of Night* as well, the same quality. The outsiders trapped forever on the inside, using all their miserable chances, their long shots, to give viewers something more prophetic and human than X ever found in the Art House.

He walked home.

Young professionals would scream at him and inquire as to where he was going as he walked by, hands in his pockets. He thought about hitting just one of them square in the eyes. He thought about walking out in front of a bus and scaring them all half to death. He thought of all these things and walked on past the people that would never come to know him, never come to understand. And as he turned onto Lincoln X began to whistle, excited now that he could go upstairs and have an easy end of night conversation with a group of strangers before retreating to his quarters where he'd put on some old movie, some TV show he enjoyed, and fall into a sleep that could last just as long as was needed. Such things are seldom offered in life, such sensations are only given to the very lucky, such an affirmative knowledge that if you should choose to, you could disconnect with the world for twenty-four hours and nobody would suffer because of it. He breathed it in, slid his key into the door and turned the abrasive lock, cutting his finger lightly on the corner of the door, and as he walked up the stairs whistled "Singin' in the Rain" X could hear Warren already playing songs of the 90s, and as he opened the door to their place he never felt more at home.

The dreams he had then were largely influenced by a slew of medication X was taking, some simply to experiment, and some prescribed by medical professionals. He took Citalopram (more commonly Celexa) as an anti-depressant because he was very much depressed. He took Trazodone, a sleeping pill that initially functioned as an anti-depressant (historically), because by and large he almost never got to sleep—he hadn't taken the Trazodone for several months, however, because he no longer saw the point of sleep. He also took Melatonin, but only when five or so in the morning came around because he liked the effects it had on his infrequent dreams, and finally a mixture of multi-vitamins, each of which contained some crucial element of mental stimulation that X thought he needed. He wouldn't actually take any of these at a consistent rate. He'd walk around with the Celexa in his pocket and take one or two when he started feeling down—knowing how ludicrous it was—and took the others most often before sleep. There were however many mornings when he'd take them, knowing full well he'd never get to sleep, but wanting some natural-ish bout of hallucination to kick in out of boredom. This night no different; X ingested various materials.

Warren sat in the cool light of morning at their table with his bathrobe on; lit Parliament tucked between his pointer and middle finger on his left hand, and a weary-eyed, hung-over smile across his mouth that could break the most resilient of miserable bastards. They opted for breakfast. Warren had errands to run thereafter.

Sitting across from somebody in any diner can be a very trying experience if you don't happen to know them very well, and if you haven't negotiated just what sitting in a diner together will entail for the both of you. Warren and X had their diner behavior as related to one another down to a distinct science. The former always sat with his back toward the kitchen, in a booth tucked down past the row of counter seats and into the second dining room after you entered, to the right. When you entered you were almost certainly going to be welcomed by one of three Italian brothers, each of whom sat fat and jovial. All of this served to make dining here an easy and underwhelming experience. X ordered coffee, black, and a tomato juice and water to precede the drinking of any hot liquid. Warren ordered a Bloody Mary, as it was late enough to be served alcohol, and early enough to not worry about being cut off; slowly his hangover seemed to dissipate before X's eyes.

"God man…it's going to be a good day; I can feel it. How you feelin', buddy?" Warren asked, another smile spread across his face.

"Pret-tee OK friend. Just fine. Old Kinderhook. Do you feel like going up to Powell's before we start shopping for whatever it is you were looking for?" Powell's was one of the many used bookstores in Chicago X tended to frequent, and just down the road a spell he figured it an easy diversion before the rest.

"Yeah, but I thought you didn't have any cash?"

"You're right, I don't, but I still like looking around. Maybe I'll see something I can buy once money comes in. Never know." Mutual sips and occasional nods.

"How's this, if you see something you want that badly, I'll spot you." X knew what this meant, that Warren would simply pay for something, and that would be it. He'd never again ask for a repayment on debts, and it wasn't because he'd suddenly forget, but because somehow Warren was aggressively wired toward obscene generosity. Helpless as X was against the offering of free books and diner meals, he accepted graciously.

"Alright, but only if it's something I really need."

Mornings after an overwhelming night almost always came with a bout of over-thinking and bad food for X. He ate some blend of eggs and chorizo and relished every slow, contemplative bite. He was useless in the morning, always trying to reconstruct the brilliance he felt he'd left only hours earlier at dawn. Night tended to be his strongest time, and everything before and after was merely fuel for the fire that would rekindle when the sun went down. It was quite easy to let himself go at night; easy to imagine that the world was a loving, and just place, and somehow in the morning when fueled on cheap coffee and bad jokes about the girls who were at their place the night before, it all seemed so far off that he couldn't even recollect being a believer, being somebody that actually gave a damn about the turn of events in America, or the world, or the galaxy, or the universe.

"So, you and Emily last night, how was it?"

"Usual I s'pose, both of us just kind of looking for something that neither of us really seems to want."

"Yeah but you and her got a good thing, right?"

"I don't know man. We just want different things, I guess. I really like her though, I'm glad we all wound up together."

Warren smiled

"I just get so sick of constantly cycling back to the same shit. Even with her. I do really enjoy elements of us, but beyond that there's just this emptiness in the room, maybe."

"I hear you. So, what'd you see last night?"

"Oh man, this fucked up serial killer flick called *Maniac* from the seventies. Totally seedy, weird, you'd have loved it. I had fun. How about you, how was last night with everybody?"

"It was good, you know. A lot of talking and music and bullshit." They both nodded resignedly, a lovely old waitress named Mary brought their check out and gave a smile as she placed her hand on X's shoulder and asked if there was anything else they needed. Both replied with a prompt "No thanks," and went on sipping coffee.

X felt he was the world's most rotten whistler, but it never kept him from trying. As they walked up Lincoln, he tried belting one of Roger Miller's tunes from the *Robin Hood* cartoon, no luck. The country singers of old always seemed to whistle best; and he'd often wondered whether they had stand-in whistlers, just based on endurance; it seemed like a terribly difficult thing to do regularly— whistling those sharp and distinguishable tones.

They entered Powell's after a bit and Warren walked over to

look at the photography books, generic things that you could find most anywhere. X went over to the two towering shelves that held classics.

Enter any used bookstore in Chicago on any given day and you'll be awed by the diversity of apparent interests walking those thin rows of literature, X often puzzled over this reality in his mind. Part of it might be the public transit system, slow routes and an inability thus far to lug TVs effectively. A sense of home filled up these places as he wandered them, all over stricken with humanity.

In weeks prior at the bookstore he'd been particularly taken by two books in this section. One was a book of letters by F. Scott Fitzgerald—Fitzgerald being one of X's unquestionable favorites, having left an indelible mark on him when he'd read *This Side of Paradise*, *The Beautiful and Damned*, and *The Great Gatsby* in succession the Christmas prior. He looked at its green cover, now devoid of its dust jacket and carrying a certain level of timelessness. He opened it up to some letter he'd written to Hemingway about the pain it caused him to read of Ernest's opinion of him in certain of his stories, and that he hoped Hem could please stop slandering him in the public eye. That brought X down. Both were Midwesterners, occasional expats; both hard workers. Both of them believed in the Art of Writing more than anything in this world, and yet Hemingway—because he'd spent too much time watching bull fights and drinking wine with Ezra Pound—felt that for some reason he'd exceeded Fitzgerald as a man, and a writer, which X couldn't see as anything but piddling rivalry. Ernest notes that Fitz once asked him to measure the size of his cock in a Spanish café, and that very likely was the case, but wasn't this sort of paranoid neuroticism at the root of all writers? All creators? Didn't that challenge Hem's loyalty? X didn't care much; Nobel laureates are mostly dull.

The book was now marked down to four dollars, so X grabbed it; holding it while eyeing up the novel he couldn't take his attention from any time he entered the store.

Its author was a man named Patrick White. X had seen his name before, even seen the only interview available online of the man upon his being informed that *he* was going to win the Nobel Prize (when X becomes interested in an author/artist he begins a long process of researching their work and their lives with a severity that is unlike any course of study he's ever experienced in, or out, of academia). White seemed like a funny man, he told the interviewer that the night he received the news he'd already taken his sleeping pill, so he went to sleep just as he would've any other night. X liked that. The name of the White novel he'd so come to adore was *The Vivisector*. On its cover was a man with a delusional look in his eye, and above his head was a sort of Eye of Ra drawing done in blood red paint. X opened it, as he had many times before, and began to read of Hurtle Duffield and his journey from bleak Australian indigence to the life of an artist.

Both books came to nine dollars, and Warren again opted to pay. X let him, smiling and welcoming the arm Warren reached out to wrap X up with. He paid the girl; dressed in a torn yellow sweater with dyed black hair. X took the bag she offered with both of the rather heavy books and they walked outside into the day, sun shining fully down on them as they turned right and continued to consume.

The summer prior X had done two unchangeable and pivotal things. The first was the writing of his first—at least he considered it his first—*real* novel. He'd written a novella the winter before entitled *Ego Wilts to Sunday* about the life of a young blind boy who's suddenly lost all his family and is required to spend his formative years in a group home; but that never felt real enough to X in terms of length, or even a book worth publishing. The book he wrote that summer was called *The Debauchery of St. Vitruvius*, and it documented the life of a man who works as a lobbyist for Atheism. He writes entire books, volumes on all things anti-god, and he functions as a generous and well-respected member of society. He speaks at the White House and is given an honorary mention in one of the Presidential Addresses—to be sure, will always be seen as a bit of a novelty in the press. Eventually, a group of maniacal pro-religion goons start stalking him, and when one of them finally—

after roughly 300 pages—holds a gun to the back of his neck, his last words are, "Thank you" before the trigger is pulled. X wrote it in a fury after watching hours of conspiracy videos on the Vatican and its functions for the last two hundred years or so online, and he had finally completed what he thought was a book worth reading.

The second thing X did was print *Ego Wilts to Sunday* as a chapbook. He'd read of Fernando Pessoa and Pier Paolo Pasolini publishing certain things as chapbooks and was so taken with the romance of it that he managed to cram the roughly 50,000 words of *Ego* between the pages of a small hand-sewn edition. He printed 50, with artwork done by him, and handed them out all over Chicago.

This was on his mind as X was walking by an M. U. building, at the door of which sat a small display marked 'Free,' where students could place their work. Two copies of *Ego* sat there, and although he knew they'd be there—given that hardly anybody really seemed to want to read the novel—it struck him as one of the more moving images he'd ever seen. X then felt much like Windham, the man from *Debauchery*, who walked the streets of Milwaukee in his youth trapped in the paranoia that one of the men who took his father away—men, it would later be revealed, who had met Windham's father at a meeting of Scientologists—would come to take him. Windham lived his youth on the street, drunk and trying to make ends meet, and finally he walked into a building where this man was talking about Nietzsche, himself rather drunk, and homeless, it appeared. The two of them developed a friendship that would change Windham's life, and eventually all of Windham's work would be dedicated to this man.

Throughout one's life, X figured, every human being develops certain avenues, buildings, or frames of mind that resemble the womb. For a while in his younger years it was always the shower, or the bathtub. X would sit in the shower for roughly an hour each night, masturbating, sometimes even falling asleep to wake in cold. Then in his senior year the bathtub became highly important because his bedroom at his father's home did not have a couch, nor was there a couch in the entire place that he was comfortable sitting in, and accordingly the bathtub became his place to read.

In recent years, X's womb had been the movies.

He walked to the train, rubbing his hands together, anxious. The train was largely empty as it was a Sunday afternoon, and he took Chicago's Redline into the loop, where at Roosevelt he exited, and walked quickly in the sun to a theater tucked back in a clandestine village of condos just beyond a Target; his recent hiding place.

X paid to see something new with Christian Bale, then bought a large popcorn, a large Diet Coke, and two boxes of Milk Duds. X went to the theatre—the largest one in the building, as this was the newest film to date—and walked up the steps in the back to his seat. X always sat in the back, on the far left; as far back into the left corner as you can possibly go. He set down his stuff, buried the cell phone, and keys, and wallet beneath the sweater he took off to take a breath. Then he went out, walked to the bathroom, relieved himself and washed his hands with severe fastidiousness, and walked back to his seat in the theater. He took off his shoes, as he often did, and drifted into the waking sleep of the next two hours, enjoying—even relishing—every minute of it, but knowing all the while the pain he was escaping, the reality he then needed to reject.

It is rumored, and who can say whether this is true, that Andy Kaufman—the comedian that "Man on the Moon," the song by REM is based on, dedicated to, etc.—in the height of his career, when he was an icon, when his stand up comedy was the sort of thing kids hung on the very edge of their seats to indulge in, had a very particular way of surprising his crowds: He would walk out, clad in his trademark suit with parted hair and turtle neck beneath, holding a copy of *The Great Gatsby*, and for the next four hours or so, however long it took, would read the entire book to the audience, not exaggerating any more than was necessary, and not giving any indication that what he was doing was supposed to be funny. Now that's just a rumor, something X heard from a friend on the train one night, but he's never heard a more perfect example of what the artist should do for society. THE ARTIST

NEED DO ABSOLUTELY NOTHING FOR SOCIETY. Society begat the artist, and very much like the Engineer, or the Construction Foreman, he accordingly only owes his life to the shit and nothingness of being, perhaps a cat.

After the movie he was drained; went into the bathroom and took a long shit, reading the AP on his cell phone and texting several girls, and Warren about plans for the night. X looked forward to going home; looked forward to watching TV or something with Warren and getting into something; likely he'd just masturbate and get to sleep.

Returning then, his roommates—Emily and Warren—were watching *Closer*, a film he'd seen once and moderately enjoyed. The minute X walked in his favorite scene happened, which plucked an eerie note. The scene was the only moment he felt truly engrossed from the beginning to end of that movie—it featured music from both Damien Rice and The Smiths, two of the musical projects from the last fifty or so years that X detested with a vigor bordering on bloodlust—and in it Clive Owen and Julia Roberts are having one of the greatest arguments he's ever seen, a fight, and Julia Roberts is asking Owen why he wants to know something about fucking somebody else or whatever, and Clive Owen screams "COS I'M A FUCKING CAVEMAN."

They both looked up at X when he entered and gave the appropriate nods, but the mood he was in that's all he could stand for. He walked straight for his bedroom and sat at the desk—really just a circular glass table with his computer, and several books atop it—pulling the manuscript of *St. Vitruvius* from behind the laptop and setting the parts he'd finished transcribing to the left of the computer—probably only thirty double-sided pages out of a hundred and fifty or so—and put the much larger stack of work still needing done on the right.

The work of writing a novel manuscript at first was always rather sweaty for X. During the summer, tucked away in his father's basement, he worked on an old typewriter and could let himself become a bit manic, to the degree that at times he would have his headphones on, and his body would dictate its own actions and he would sit there moving around and hovering closely into the page he worked on to scrutinize it terribly, then pull back when he'd added another page to the mounting pile and take the biggest breath of his life, feeling full again. Those were the pleasant days and nights.

Often, he preferred to work in the dead of night, from around eleven until four or so in the morning, at those points where there's a stretch of darkness so apparent that nobody—but the off— dare stay awake. He'd listened to The Doors mostly while writing *Vitruvius*, and other melodic music like Debussy and Faure to calm the nerves when things became quite hasty. After work he liked to really deflate, so he'd either go upstairs, fixing himself a gigantic plate of food, bringing it down to watch hours of boring TV to completely zone out; or masturbate, then take a nice long shower muttering virile nothings to the darkness of the bathroom; or finally, when things were perfect he would walk outside, barefoot, often only wearing underwear—his father's neighborhood was very stuffy, and rich, and nobody save for X would be out at this time— and he'd lie down in the middle of the pavement with "End of the Night" or "The End" howling away on headphones, then standing at odd intervals to dance violent on the empty road, and at those moments—not every night it happened, but some—it would rain the cold rain he'd felt as a young boy and his family took a trip out east to a place in the woods where the rain never stopped, and X would be at peace, staring into steaming midnight, lost at that apex where nothing but belief and love exist, and death is an empty threat.

That was the initial draft; editing, however, was a sour possessive thing that never let go of your throat until you cast her lifeless into the sea. You have to understand certain things about X's psyche before this last claim can hope to take real effect. When he writes, at best he's like an abstract painter—romantically he thought Jackson Pollock; realistically more like a middling graffito—where the only possible thing he can convey is that odd interpretation he sees somewhere buried in the confines of his skull, and writing that first draft is much like splattering a gallon of red paint across a canvas and dictating its actions with a drunken euphoria until it seems complete. Editing, however, is like staring at said painting with every painter in history who ever picked up a brush then staring at him. And the goal of this editing is not to make the work more like theirs, but to do quite the opposite and push it as far into originality as he possibly can before X tears his hair out and smashes his face against the glass table; winding up derivative anyway. That's how it is for him, anyway. X knows of the naturally literary types and their easy revisions; he's heard of the gals and fellows that send off their manuscripts in one go—Kerouac, for instance, another whose writing X ignores—and frankly cannot believe them. The first fools, he figures. The students early to class. X simply lost interest.

As he wrote—or rather, mumbled through nearly-dried cement—X often thought of things like that, aggravating notions that could push him that much further through the work. For indignation, he felt, is the only true quality any real writer should hope to possess if he's to succeed. Hemingway noted that a bullshit detector—a built-in, shock proof shit detector was his wording in X's mind—is more desirable than anything else, but then haven't we heard the tales of Hemingway's coming-of-age as a young scribe? Didn't he seemingly fall into fame with his *Three Stories and Ten Poems*? And after that did, he'd never have to worry about sending out a veritable fleet of submission letters, only to be rejected? No; likely not. Hemingway did not have to endure the things contemporary shit-peddlers have to endure (and wasn't that collection his father used to own of Hem's entitled *The Enduring*?). Even Didion, even DeLillo, even David Foster Wallace did not have to endure the monotony of sending out hundreds of submissions only to receive that many kindly-worded rejections. X fondly acquired histories like David Markson and his fifty-plus submissions of *Wittgenstein's Mistress*, as armor for these moments. These publishers will not break your determination with hammers, they'll break it with thousands of little pricks from all directions, and slowly you'll begin to fade, and fade, and if you cannot fight your way out of this misery, you'll wind up locked away in madness and obscurity. Unwilling to accept it, X also began assembling lists of authors he despised, of *lucky* little art school brats that he would soon eviscerate, and with every submission letter rejected gained more and more fuel. He worshiped failure. And with every miserable page of that manuscript turned over, it became yet more and more alive, and with furious hatred and indignation now at its peak X felt ready to shatter his skull in that tiny space in Chicago and let the world feel the blood of his measly existence. Thus, that night, as X turned over the fifteenth page of a good day's work done and done, he felt affirmed not only as a young and angry human being, but as a writer. For X, he felt the need to be a writer more than anyone he knew needed anything, and to this day has not met a soul whose eyes seem brighter with the anxious hope of turning that one success into enough to sit and write more, and more, thus having *made it* into the existence by which he feels so unrelentingly called. Perhaps it's only voices. He never remains sure for long.

The necessary horror it seemed to take to write anything worth its salt could never quite deter X from trying. Yet still, after finishing work—every time—a slow, creeping, always unexpected depression befell him, and he seemed to have no choice in the matter or its possible resolution. He'd heard of artists with apparently good lives—Stephen King came to mind, maybe—and couldn't conceive how to manage it. There is—and this has been proven through years of the same, same, same—an inherent abrasion with real substantial creativity and living a wholesome, well-wrought life among the people you love. Does this mean that art equals misery? Perhaps not, but when Elizabeth Gilbert publicly denounces perceived flaws in the lives of artists like Norman Mailer, or Fitzgerald, because they were so laden with sadness, she also disregards that their legacies have already—in only a half a century for Fitzgerald, and less than half a decade for Mailer—paid for themselves twice over. Does art require one to be hurt, and shat on one's entire life? X doesn't necessarily think so, but does have an inherent ability to endure the blows life tends to dish out to those that challenge any and all social norms to create real work heighten one's chances for longevity? Again, perhaps. He's no longer sure about much, but X would like to believe.

In those days, to be an island was a near impossibility, though. And as such X moved through life, and moved into the living room, to watch several episodes of *Californication* with Warren and Emily, while they all talked and joked about the nightmares of their days, and the severity with which they all planned to approach points of escape the following weekend.

Classes that semester started with Nabokov—more exactly a book of his letters, *Lolita*, and *Invitation to a Beheading*. It was largely an introductory course to M. U.'s fiction program, as Nabokov was one of the poster boys for the program's overall oeuvre, and the patron saint for their notion of good literature. X hadn't read *Lolita* in total, but had read *Beheading* that summer anticipating the course, as well as several of his letters documenting one of his book tours and the tumultuous—and rather needy, on his part— relationship Vlad had with his wife. X preferred the bent reality of *Beheading* far more than the stumbling he perceived in *Lolita*; although, to be sure, his bias resulting from having seen Stanley Kubrick's adaptation to the film many times prior to opening the novel warped his interpretation—nonetheless it left him fairly bored.

He walked in around eight fifteen AM, and the class was to start at eight thirty. Kids spread at different corners of the room; one young guy with generic-looking Led Zeppelin and Pink Floyd patches on his bag; one girl, tall, dressed in average bulky skateboarding shoes and thick dark jeans that covered an unwieldy frame, unwashed hair and an ill-fitting pair of glasses covered her green eyes—she jabbed at her cell phone accusingly; one rather voracious looking young brat reading a copy of *The Stories of Peter Taylor* who immediately seemed to fall in love with X and, accordingly, X sat as far away from him as possible; and one fat girl, who sat by herself reading a paperback copy of *The Fountainhead,* scowling.

As the room began to fill X realized what he was in for. Certain students would seem to show such interest that the teacher would have no choice but to pass them; certain others would be hopelessly confused at the Russian wizard's synesthetic masterpieces and would simply tell jokes and goof off for the duration of the class, and others still would fall right between the previous, showing interest, but ready to leave the second the clock moved past the three hour mark and they had only an hour left. Then there was X, not exactly desperate to listen, but not exactly rejecting and fucking around either. He cared for the classroom setting and sought to project this level of compassion for a seemingly endangered academia as much as possible that year. He hoped to join up in protests—*Occupy* was beginning to permeate things, or rather, what would soon be officially-termed "Occupy" and thus almost immediately swallowed by too much feeling, as X observed it—and start magazines, and really stare dumbly at the unbelievable knowledge of as many of his professors as possible. He figured this was a point in his life when he was at his most earnest, and thus refused to let any of the creeping cynicisms common in all college classrooms stay his desire to consume, and be taught by the "best" (and most expensive) college in the heart of Chicago.

After his first course he left the room and his previously noted leech (the boy who loved X) immediately chased him down the hall.

"Hey, hey, are you..." he mumbles something like the name X gave in class: an attempt to seem clueless or blasé so that any relationship could start then, fresh, and free of the petty introductions and name-games.

"Yes, what's up?" X wasn't enthused but wasn't entirely harsh either. To reject him based on the notion that he didn't like looking at him, didn't like what he had to say about 20th century Russian authors, and didn't generally like the idea of *making friends* at that particular juncture seemed a bit steep.

"Hey! I happened upon your, uh, novel!" He sounded off, cloying—like drying paint in the corners of some museum.

"Yeah?"

"Yeah! Really good...*Ego Wilts to Sunday*? How'd you come up with a title like that?"

"A dream I had..." he mumbled.

"A dream? Hey man, what do you have going on right now? You want to grab a coffee?" X had nothing going on but felt like experiencing it alone.

"Yeah, nothing… Sure man, whatever, let's go somewhere."

They went to sit at one of M. U.'s cafes and Paul, X's company, began telling X about the course of realizing his potential as a prodigious author.

Apparently, he'd once wanted to be a rapper and when the *game* (his phrasing) proved to be too unaccepting he decided he wanted to write poetry. After writing poetry for a while he started reading Chuck Palahniuk, and because of his *Invisible Monsters* Paul decided he wanted to become a novelist. Considering X'd been editing, and working over manuscripts for some years at that point, and had dealt with the obscene rejection of nearly every publishing house, literary agent, and novel writing contest in circulation, he probably could have told him things to settle the pain as time wore on and he completed the draft of his first, boring novel. X did not do this. Instead he avoided nearly everything as Paul rattled on about Mobb Deep in the *old days*—he was nineteen, so would've been around six for Mobb Deep's *old days*—and all the women he'd been with back where he was from in New Jersey. Eventually he started rapping, actually rapping these lines from old 90s tunes and feigning a seriousness that was more depressing than anything. He seemed to hit his stride and gestured emphatically with sweaty fingers. X decided to take his leave.

"Listen man. I can't hang out with you. I'm dead."

"What? Huh?" Paul was confused.

"I do not ever want to speak with you again. Bye!" X said, smiling in a very demented way, and turning around to leave. He didn't look back, didn't care what expression Paul chose to send to the back of his skull at that point, he simply needed to fucking *leave*—before the previous faith in university settings completely dissipated and he was left as disenchanted as ever.

Medication.

X ran into an old friend from the writing program named Carl before his class one afternoon, and the two of them had a discussion about the arduous nature of X's mental state.

"It's just tough to see, man. It's almost blinding, thinking about life that way—life without 'em—but even the doctors gave the stuff a shelf life…I'm just starting to think maybe I'd see *more* if I weren't taking anything." They were sitting beneath one of the statues in Grant Park, it depicted a man atop an angry warhorse, and above his head he held some country's flag or other. Carl had long hair, ponytailed—was a poet, primarily—and dressed how you'd imagine a deathly-skinny college-aged coffee shop waiter in 1995 dressed: baggy pants with rips in the corduroy, band shirts depicting such groups as *Circle takes the Square* or *The Mars Volta*. He was good, an earnest fellow, and though at times his passions ran deeper than X was willing to go publicly, he still admired Carl a great deal.

"Shit man, I don't know. It's up to you, you know? For me, I've always been kind of hesitant to advocate medication as a treatment for depression. But I know you, I know that you've dealt with this stuff before, that you *know* yourself—hell, that you know more about depression than I might ever want to know—so all I can say is that either way, I hope you keep your head afloat. I hope that whatever decision you make feels like the right one for you, because that's what matters, not my opinion on behavioral meds."

"I guess I'm just scared. My family doesn't really have anything to do with the decision anymore, you know? They're all in different places, dealing with different shit, and for once the decision regarding this stuff is kind of up to me. I mean I've been on this medicine for what, like three years now or something? At least on *some* kind of medication for three years, and I sort of wonder what life would be like without it. I'm interested in breathing once as *me*, you know? I mean shit, I guess I believe in anti-depressants, and like you said, I don't want to get into a debate over whether or not they work, because I think in the severe clinical cases they serve a purpose; but for me, as a writer, as a fucking student, as a human animal, I really worry that I'm overflowing my head with these chemicals and I'm going to come to regret it…"

"Well then, do what you want to do. But you promise me something, okay?" He looked at X with large, emphatic eyes.

"What's that Carl?"

"If you start thinking about killing yourself, or about leaving, or about stopping caring or any of that shit, you call me first, alright?"

"I can do that." And already the seed was planted. Already X knew that he wouldn't call him, or anyone, should anything come up that left him despondent all over again. He knew it; knew the likelihood of his forthcoming misery, however X also knew that somewhere inside, what he was doing was right, and it was all enough to keep him going that afternoon, keep his mind reeling and thoughts afloat until he was able to go home to flush the drugs.

Downtown, around him, X observed humans blindly needing to associate themselves with a perceived high echelon of society based entirely on some notion of what's *cool*. He slowly came to detest any person that could be defined as stereotypical and rejected them with much vehemence. He had, however, also seen the opposite individuals, those characters that chose to differentiate themselves from all stereotypes by merely being assholes and wanted to abstain from each side of the spectrum. Lars Von Trier had recently discussed his feelings on Hitler, his sympathies or something at the Cannes Film Festival in France with Kirsten Dunst (who looked ridiculous) and Charlotte Gainsbourg (who is incapable of looking ridiculous) on either side of him. Everyone seemed scared of not fitting in, X felt, and on college campuses you might multiply this fear ten-fold. However, he felt it should be rejected: this opposite notion of the young covering their fear with monetary prizes and symbols to associate with all the friends they'd never meet in the flesh anyway, not anymore—and somehow he connected it to the three faces of Von Trier, Gainsbourg, and Dunst on stage at Cannes, the one wholly rejecting acceptance and pushing some public away; the starlet timidly nodding, *trying*; and the daughter of Serge apparently in the center of the spectrum where X might like to live, beyond the reach of *nice* and its opposing fascisms. America was excellent at rejecting the things that mattered, like books; like films; like art; like empathy; like love; like strength; like weakness; like anxiety; like truth; like substance; like honesty; and America was quite equally as prolific at accepting the things that couldn't matter less, like rudeness; like T shirts; like the way you smell; like Nickelback; like Coldplay; like Lindsay Lohan; like *Avatar*; like

Social Networking; like Mark Zuckerberg; like HOLLYWOOD; like Reality TV; like the Playboy Mansion; like whether or not to eat wherever; like more war; like politics; like political figures; like abortion; like God; like everything on the news. And at times it became too much, at times—such as that day, sitting then in a darkened classroom looking at Edison's footage from *The Black Maria* and swallowing bits of Cinema History 1—X wanted to burn it all down and begin again. He wanted to watch his foolish brothers and sisters burn in a cloud of digital smoke. He wanted to end the life that begot him, start anew on some astral plane of heaven, left to spend his days staring at the sun and measuring its size for nine hundred years.

But X liked Edison, liked sitting near the front of that classroom, on the aisle on the right, while the teacher—a plump, bearded man who wore sandals with his khakis and a blue baseball cap over a balding head—told the origins of film through certain inventions as the Zoetrope, and the furthering of this dream world by the minds of silver screen gods: Georges Melies and the brothers Lumiere, Eisenstein and Edison, D.W. Griffith—and his racist debacle—and the forging of such epics as *The Great Train Robbery*, *Intolerance, Man with a Movie Camera, A Trip to the Moon*, Fritz Lang's *Metropolis, Nosferatu, The Grand Illusion*, Charlie Chaplin's *City Lights*, Buster Keaton's *The General* and *Steamboat Bill Jr.*, and more. When X was in there, listening to the slow drone of the projector and watching the beautiful, anachronistic on-screen beauties make horrified faces at the men vying for their love, it didn't seem so bad, didn't seem so insane to want to keep on living.

X rode the train home in an empty car and exited at the Wellington stop to an empty street. It was late, and that part of the world went to sleep early during the week. A few stragglers ambled down the street past him with hurried expressions on their faces and heavy bags on their shoulders. He ignored everything; held a long conversation with himself instead.

"You know, it's like I've spent my entire life leading to this empty plateau, and I can't decide what to make of it. Obviously, I've *endured*. I've fought and earned a few things that make me feel good about being alive, but there are other, simpler elements that leave me feeling further away from some *happiness* than I ever imagined. Sometimes I think it's relationships. Like I just need a girl, but then I figure how fucked up I actually am. The things I do. The thoughts, I think. All of it compounds on itself over and over again the second any notion of becoming normal comes to light," X held these interviews with himself at low tones, nearly every time he walked around the city or went from A to B, "the sad truth is, I think I'm doomed to be this way my entire life. And that doesn't scare me really. Doesn't make me feel like I'm going to topple over some prophetic edge and suddenly change or anything, but it does confuse me. So much of my existence has been about moving forward. Moving away from things in my past. Moving toward some future that's so *other* it will blind me, but now I'm not so sure. All I want is some quiet place, it's like that line, 'A writer's life is, at best, a lonely life,' who said that? Gotta look that up later. That's all I really hope for. Give me a couple good slobbery dogs and no other fucking men around and I'll be good." At that point some young guy walked by him, obviously hearing. They bumped shoulders, and X continued on, jeering, "Who's this fuck? Fuck you. Fuck you guy. This fucking fuck, people always have such bad attitudes when they walk by. Why? Am I a fucking loony? Am I some fucking mad man? I don't know. It's all so stupid, this guy's so fucking stupid. I wish he'd come back here; I'd stick my thumbs in his eyes. Stupid fucking piece of shit. Fuck him." X held his hands in the jacket's pockets and imagined himself as the butcher in *I Stand Alone* when things became tense in public. Useless endless thoughts and occasionally he slips or realizes he's walked the wrong way; his mind is full-up.

Nobody was home. X threw the mail down on the kitchen table and turned on some music. He went into his bedroom and grabbed the four or five bottles of pills and vitamins from the dresser, holding them to his chest like a kid. He went into the bathroom, locked the door, and listened as the music took hold, knowing again he was more right than wrong for whatever it was.

First, he wanted to get rid of the sleeping pills, and with a small *plip* they hit the water. He wondered what would happen to them if he'd simply let them sit, if they'd turn inky reds or something. He couldn't worry about such things. He poured in the rest, until a final pile of chemical shit mounted in the bowl, bright reds and oranges and whites; and X laughed, thinking how good it all was: the pills being at the bottom of this quite human item just then, being turned to the shit they were. Destroying them for all they apparently were.

He started to hurt a bit; hands started to sweat profusely, and he didn't know what to expect next. The act seemed to have immediate ramifications, a withdrawal all its own. X flushed the toilet and just to ensure it all went down put a few sheets of toilet paper atop the capsules and tablets. It flushed. They were gone. X watched them spin down the bowl and felt a weight lifted from his shoulders; but there was that coldness and sweat dripping from his hands. He started to worry that a certain state would overcome him and decided he'd better plan ahead in case the next few days gave any trouble.

First, he masturbated, figuring there might be a bit of the medicine in the murk of his groin. X went into the bedroom and watched some strangers fuck before coming into one of his dirty socks. The setup for masturbation in X's room was simple, he had a shelf in the closet as far from the doors as possible, so he'd lock everything up, go in there, put on headphones and take off all his clothes, sit in a leather-backed—pertinent because it gave a terrific chill on first acquaintance of skin and seat—computer chair to sit with his head in close vicinity to the screen—as his headphone cord was short. He realized in the moment how pathetic it was, but didn't care, what X was doing was precautionary. What if he went insane? Wouldn't it stabilize his thinking to masturbate? Wouldn't it suit to get rid of any possible loneliness, or prurient thoughts so he could avoid the embarrassing debacle of writing old girlfriends looking for *real love this time*? Of course, it would! X was saving himself and the world a great deal of trouble. He was becoming heroic. Turning himself into a futuristic organism who'd come back from the wars of anti-depressant medication to better himself and move further down the line of history than all his predecessors. He was becoming saintly!

X finished and his hands still felt chilled. He worried about the contents of his section of the kitchen—as he would likely become gastronomically confused in the coming days—and had to check over everything several times before deciding he'd live. Then taking that celebratory post-come piss in the bathroom and sitting down to a few pages of Fitzgerald's *Letters* before a shower and the night bullshitting and playing guitar with Warren in a pair of gym shorts and sweatshirt.

They are young and at a carnival. Bea tells X all is fine and he believes her, she and X sit far above it in white and red seats smiling at the animals. They feed them peanuts and X marvels at their strength, the bright lights above teach him something, carry him somewhere away from crying.

A trumpet sounds, and real men and women fly high and away from them as she holds his tiny hand.

"The king, the king, bright as the sky as the dandelions sing!" Bea's voice, here and far away, covers X like the leaves parting between their fingers in piles on the ground. An odd song he never understood but hated. He never knew where it came from.

She writes X letters, tells him stories in them about her home away from him, and he listens and tries to understand too much.

The onset of neurosis is like the time-lapsed bloom of a rose. The things X begins to believe then will be the things he believes forevermore, and at once he is a small, unique, King of everything he sees.

They feed him cereal and on May Days he tries too hard to kiss the neighbor-girls. X is damned and smiling on Halloweens in droves of apprehensive, deceptive children.

X is teary-eyed by the time the elephants leave, wanting to fly away on their backs, wanting to swim in their huge black eyes, wanting to place his tiny hands on the back of the mother and fall asleep as she trundles along to an oasis in the fog.

When he was younger X felt certain he'd become a painter. His younger sister, Bea—short for Beatrice, abbreviated by X since they were children—was constantly sure she'd be the writer, and he'd be the abstract artist, both of them to wind up living in New York City somewhere mythic like the Village, and they'd somehow become real artists.

They grew up in St. Paul, Minnesota, were born there, and lived their entire childhood in houses (two, parents divorced when X was ten, and Bea was nine) that lined the same lake. His father was the manager of the Fitzgerald Theater, which put on Garrison Keillor-linked events for much of the year and gave the most fantastic performances of plays and concerts he's ever seen through those falls and winters of their youth. The staff actually vouched for his father in the recent economic downturn, telling them explicitly that he was worth every bit of money made at the Fitzgerald, and that if his father were let go due to a decline in ticket sales, they'd be leaving with him. They kept X's father on. X loved telling that story.

When they were babies their parents were in their mid-thirties and thus their lives were rather art-driven from as young as X can remember. Bea was always writing something down, or reading some book of adventure stories or romance, her favorites were the Brontë sisters. And X, since he was very young—perhaps five or six—was constantly flipping through his mother's books of paintings, staring wide-eyed at the world existing beyond them. He was particularly fond of this edition of the works of Albrecht Dürer, though not then knowing the significance of any of it—and neither registering that each of their favorites were at least in part their favorites as a result of umlauts.

Their mother was a painter and had succeeded in creating a small store with several other local female artists in the heart of St. Paul. Every day that X didn't have school he spent down there, helping out putting up work, having his cheeks pinched by the strange old hippies that took care of the building, falling in love with all the colors they used. He couldn't dream of a world in which something like turquoise could exist, and yet it was there, on all the paintings, on all of their dresses, begging to let him throw it all over the walls.

X and his sister have always been close. He's taken care of her since she was a little girl and to this day, he'll receive calls at odd hours of the night in which he needs to console her. She's the only sibling he has, and could ever dream to have, and he'll always protect her, no matter what. Recently she'd been in France, having taken a job with an interior design agency that specialized in creating fantastic homes for people living along the Champs-Elysees or something, making nearly ten times what X will ever make in his life.

When they were younger, though, for a time they were entirely separated. After their parents got divorced there was an ugly cast overtaking the city for X, and he started to have crying fits where he'd sit in front of his door—allowing his father to attempt to nudge his way in, only to cause bruising along X's side—for hours unable to move. He lived with his father, and Bea stayed with their mother. He can't remember those years much anymore, and the time he spent at his father's house always seems unreal because of the way things wound up, but he knows for certain that in his youth, in several of his most formative years, X was completely separated from his sister.

This, incidentally, was when X started to read more voraciously. He was around twelve years old when it happened, making Bea around eleven, and they hadn't spoken much beyond the telephone and the occasional weekend when all that would happen was their sitting around watching Disney movies, the world devoid of all its usual color.

X started to read because he was scared, scared of losing his sister. He started to read thinking that he might reconnect with her, thinking that if he did the one thing she loved so much they would somehow come back together someday and their parents, and all the crying, and all the time apart wouldn't matter anymore. X read the adventure stories, *Robinson Crusoe* and *The Swiss Family Robinson*, and even tried once to make it through *Jane Eyre*, failing then as he's still failed today to make sense of what he then deemed "too damned wordy." But it didn't stop him, he read old paperbacks of Ian Fleming's *Bond* novels and started reading newer authors who talked about kids like him, like Stephen King, and moment after moment, X learned what he'd been missing all those years, learned what Bea had that he could never have dreamed of, looking at paintings.

And coincidentally, during that time, Bea was looking through the books of Albrecht Dürer, and drawing in the margins of all her writing notebooks and attempting to reconnect with her brother.

X learned this over coffee one day when Bea had come to visit Chicago. The two hadn't seen each other in quite a long time and she was just getting ready to leave for France out of O'Hare. X suggested they get a hotel on her company's dime, and they stayed at The Drake on Michigan Avenue for two nights talking and recapitulating everything that had happened until now over bottles of wine, and intermittent old movies with characters he told her all about.

Funnily enough, she'd used her savvy with drawing, and her interest in the arts, to get a degree from a prestigious university out East in design in a matter of only about two and a half years, utilizing the school's summer and winter terms to get ahead. And here X was, the lonely writer, still having failed, still in school, older than her, much more lost and despondent than he'd ever hoped to be, and both of them careless, blissfully drunk on cheap red wine from the hotel bar downstairs, trying to reconnect, trying to find something.

He was fourteen when they put him into the hospital, finally forcing their family to reconvene.

In a matter of days X had fallen into what would be deemed his first official depression. Skipping school, he'd hang around underneath the bridges of St. Paul by himself, talking aloud and trying to hold conversations with Bea that simply wouldn't come, and he'd felt all the worse for it. His father became concerned when one day his razor was missing from the medicine cabinet and, reluctantly, X brought it back to him, having removed any remnant of blood from it fastidiously only hours before. X wondered in that first moment of confrontation between them what he actually thought *had* happened between the blade and X's body, unsure. X denied anything severe, told him nervously that he wanted to learn how to shave or something. X went back into his room. This time he brought with him a small knife from the kitchen, sharp, thin, and went back to sitting there in darkness dragging the thing exploring across his thigh.

The depth X was able to thrust the blade before any lucid thoughts started to kick in and his pain outweighed the desire to do something rotten to his body surprised him. This aspect—being the depth of X's wounds—was what concerned his parents the most. Strangely, X could enter it into the meat of his thigh and drag it across with an ease that was almost procedural. One day, with the tip of the knife, he'd actually felt it press against what seemed to be bone, and still to this day X feels certain that this was what caused the biggest change in his life; a minor, almost impish little scratch against the femur that changed the course of history for X, and all those involved.

It fucking hurt—and by then X was fairly acquainted with pain. Hurt beyond you've stepped on a tack and it's gone into your heel and like a fool you've continued stepping; rather it hurt like you'd imagine a barbed arrow, covered in rust, shoved through the fat on your arm and pulled back constantly by a rabid Rottweiler might hurt. He didn't scream on the initial scrape of bone, however the next few days—dried blood, bedroom dust, and dirt can cause a rather awful infection—when X was walking along in the first year of high school, his thigh distended to the size of a bag of vegetables in his pocket to an onlooker, it hurt so bad that X fainted in the middle of the school's cafeteria.

X remembers the same things everyone who's ever been in an ambulance remembers. He remembers lights, and the one nurse who seemed nice enough that he clung to both figuratively and physically once he woke from the lapse, and finally, the rushing sensation of marble under his body as they wheeled him into the hospital's ER, and the naked cold once they cut off his clothing.

There was then a numb relief that is better than any emotion X recalls. They numbed his leg with painkillers, strong, and gave him Morphine and Ativan so he wouldn't lose his mind when he realized what was being done. The infection had grown so quickly—he'd been cutting that same area for some time, and it's clear in retrospect that an infection had begun mounting prior to the scrape—that they needed to slice open the wound and drain it the moment X arrived in the hospital. They mumbled a wall of sound at that point, told him the infection was the worst thing they'd seen in months, and asked, accordingly, just what he'd done to himself to create such a horrendous wound.

X told them—his sister, mother, and father were all present, in tears—in essence every single thing that had happened. How initially he'd burned the skin on his calves with old lighters but that it got to be so bad that he'd just burnt blister after blister. How after that he started taking the razor and dragging it across the skin on his legs, already burned, but that they didn't bleed much so he dragged it across fresh skin, on the thigh, and finally told them about the knife.

"But why did you do it, honey?" His mother asked, frantic expression, tears in her eyes. His sister came to his side and wrapped her arms around him; X held her and kissed the top of her head.

"I don't know. I'm sad. I'm *sad*. I don't understand..."

"The doctors are saying you might have to stay here a little while, honey, until we get things figured out. Are you OK with that? Me and your father will take turns being here every second we can and will bring Beatrice in with us as much as possible."

"I won't leave you," Bea said, her head burrowed into his shoulder. X could tell that she was crying, and more than anything wanted her to stop.

"I don't know. I mean, I don't see. I mean what about school?"

"I wouldn't worry about school for a little while, honey." In his adult years he's often thought of his mother saying those words, how determined she looked, how strong she seemed in wanting to nip this depression in the bud before she had to worry about her son chugging bleach. X felt sorry for her, felt sorry for his old man standing in the corner, confused, with tears on his face—not knowing what in hell to say—and his sister, her head buried in the blankets around him. Tears running her cheeks in warm falls, all of this overseen by an old man in a white coat with silver hair and a clipboard.

X witnessed the rather impossible nature of a fourteen-year-old boy becoming depressed. He wasn't certain that fourteen-year-olds have a great deal to be happy about, but became certain that, should they become depressed, they'll be doomed for some years to find some way of actually talking about it.

He was in that hospital, in those rooms, unwillingly and finally willingly for just under a year and a half. It was in a way the most definitive point in his life but does not feel that he was necessarily taught a great deal about the way things are going to be. By recalling time in a place with rooms full of strangers and soft-voiced therapists and nighttime visits from his mother and sister and father as *definitive*, X feels that it was really the only place in all his years that he's ever been able to know just what would happen the following morning regardless of how he felt falling to sleep.

You develop habits. You learn to relish your time in the shower because it's the only place you truly feel alone. You learn to relish therapeutic techniques like writing or reading time because those are the only times you feel truly free with your ideas. You learn to enjoy the rather drab elements of evening television and movie nights because as entertainment alongside one's kin it's simply all you've got. You learn to get past the emotion in your sister's voice when you speak over the phone about all your friends, about how they're worried about you and they wish you would come home, about how mom and dad told them you were getting special eye surgery and were spending time with a tutor so you could learn how to write properly again. You learn to fool tutors, learn to test quickly out of subjects because you don't want to exercise your mental faculties with them; you want to do that alone. You learn what it means to lie and to be lied to, learn just what medication is capable of. You learn from other occupants that drugs might be the ticket to a better and more interesting life. You spend hours staring out the window at one bird on top of one tree and you wonder if it's the same bird from a day ago, from two days, from three. The bird changes its habits, some days it's on a wiry branch taking all the risks in the world, and some days it's on a good firm branch because the wind is causing its feathers to ruffle horribly. You learn to appreciate those black birds, and you learn from certain writers that sadness doesn't always have to be bad, but that it does have to be. You develop a habit of masturbating quite often and this in turn mellows you out that much more. You get good grades, invent craft projects, listen to the music on the radio and even sometimes sing along when you and the van full of kin go to the YMCA. And when you're finally ready, when it's finally time to leave that place, you don't want to go, and you wind up staying another half a year because you're too scared to see what the outside will look like. You're too scared to see the movies or what your friends will now have in their lives. You're too scared to eventually be honest with the friends that matter about your misery because you think they'll think you're a freak. You're beginning to obsess over little, trivial things like what color your mother's car was before you came in. You're wondering what a Frosty from Wendy's would taste like on a hot summer day, wondering what your father's voice would sound like when he calls from the living room that something interesting is on TV, and all of this slowly plucks, and plucks, and plucks at you until finally your parents tell you it's time to leave, and you do, and nothing in your life can ever remain as it was before you stepped into that cafeteria—blood dripping from your leg—and keeled over in awful submission to the spectacle of the world.

"Oh, come on, I just wanted my fucking coffee topped off, I wasn't being a dick." X sneered.

"Yeah but she's just a waitress, she doesn't need to be heckled by some asshole…" Bea was just as patronizing as death. They were drinking red wine in the restaurant at the bottom of their hotel and she was smiling incessantly. X was having some coffee as the wine was cold and running straight through to his brain, and he was trying to get the waitress's attention when finally he let loose an awful, breathy whistle.

"Yeah, yeah… Look, over here! So, are you excited sis, France? That's fucking huge!"

"I am… I mean I'm really nervous. I've only been to Spain and that was when you and I were a lot fucking younger. This is a big deal."

"But don't you know the people? Didn't you say you were moving out there with one of the women you've been working with?"

"Yeah. Delia…"

"*Delia*. O, Delia's gone, Delia all my life!" He was feeling excited for the first time in months, finally at peace with the situation in Chicago. He'd met a girl that seemed kind and was comfortable at their place with all his roommates.

"Yeah, so she's coming. She'll be there with me, the whole time, which will be nice. I'm actually just starting to get excited. I'm finally going to be doing exactly what I've wanted to do with my life, you know?" Her eyes glistened in such a way that X couldn't tell her that he hadn't the slightest idea, that he'd fought for it, but had yet to be granted such a prize.

"I know, sis. That's great. I'm really happy for you."

That night they sat up in their beds at the hotel watching *Breathless* on one of the movie channels. X's sister lost it when Jean Seberg was selling newspapers, going around cooing, "New York Herald Tribune! New York Herald Tribune!" and he looked over at her amazed, seeing for what seemed like the first time his sister smile, and hearing for the first time her laugh. There are two moments in American literature that came to mind, which X mentally paraphrased by imagining Exley reading Salinger—and both of them witnessing Holden Caulfield watching Phoebe on the carousel in the rain, all of them caught up and stuck, saying: I wish you could've been there. *God*, I wish you could've been there.

Over the next twenty-four hours X watched her assemble what seemed a brand new wardrobe for the City of Light. They went to his favorite used bookstore and she asked if there were any books he could suggest for her to read connected with Paris. He went to the shelf where he knew sat a copy of Céline's *Journey to the End of the Night* and handed it to her. He then grabbed a copy of Rimbaud's *A Season in Hell*, and a book of the poetry of Paul Eluard. He hadn't read that particular collection of Eluard, but didn't care, thinking more of Godard's *Alphaville* than anything else. Finally, he grabbed something on early 20th century art movements centered in Paris, and Michel Houellebecq's newest, realizing his earlier choices were simply the closest thing to Paris he could call to mind, and not wanting Bea to later call him out as entirely clueless. X understood from enough perusing of those shelves and the vistas of the Internet just which literature might somehow be appropriate in nearly any city on earth. He didn't feel particularly sure in giving his sister a copy of *Journey,* but also knew her capacity as a reader and that she'd understand where he was coming from in giving her that scathing tome, considering she'd read X's newest efforts.

They rode together out to O'Hare after that day together. She rested her head on his shoulder as the train plugged along endless stretches of Illinois interstate. At times her hands would clench his sleeve in brief, fleeting moments of fear, and he'd in turn rest his head against hers and assure her that everything was going to be just fine.

X's time in high school was like yours, and he was miserable. Like you he remained separated from everybody as much as possible, only coming along for nights in the country when there were enough weird drugs, or booze for him to forget just how painfully normal they all were. And like you he obsessively began to watch movies about punk rock, and alternative cultures, trying to find exactly how he fit into the gigantic melee of confusion that was the United States. Like you he made it a point to damn his parents and everything they believed in, and living in St. Paul he spent a good deal of time driving around on Highway 94 to the surrounding suburbs with his sister and their friends getting high and drunk and being careless, maybe free. X enjoyed danger, enjoyed the sensation of being on that edge he'd heard described by men like Hunter S. Thompson, wishing he'd been born years earlier, so he could've been a Hell's Angel or something. He tried most of his drugs in those days and has slowed down since out of sheer boredom with that world. He drank enough in high school to satiate the tongue of any fifty-year-old war veteran. He'd to go punk shows in Minneapolis and wind up passed out on some couch next to some twenty-three-year-old girl with tattoos honoring bands like Joy Division and Black Flag and he'd playfully suck on her neck when four in the morning got too hellish. He cut himself a bit more but was taking anti-depressants and thus didn't get too down on himself for those slip-ups. On occasion he got in trouble for drinking and received various admonitions from police and parents by the time he was eighteen. He spent one night in jail on his nineteenth birthday and that night was one of his final bouts of real drinking; all indirectly related to a mood-shifting breakup with his high school sweetheart. He enjoyed the hell out of himself, much like you, but remained convinced all along that this was probably the worst place in the world to grow up. He went to see Garrison Keillor's show with his father and his rebound girlfriend, Ella, and had an OK time. Went to see his mother after that and spent the evening watching Audrey Hepburn movies on her couch with Ella and his sister. He spent many nights alone in his room listening to Iggy Pop's *The Idiot*, and Elliott Smith. Somehow the two seem to signify his youth better than any description could do. Smith's work has always connected X with that miserable core we all possess. Misery is humanity to X, and out of that misery came a profound change that he kept running back to time and time again with his rendition of "Figure 8," and songs like "Needle in the Hay," that described pain better than everything else. With Iggy Pop he felt connected to the *weirdness* all possess at the very core, the absurdity, and on that record in particular Iggy Pop had accessed something that went largely unnoticed by the rest of the world. X thought endlessly about the whys of Ian Curtis's choice to play *The Idiot* prior to ending his life and this by itself became a sort of therapeutic exercise in considering a life as an artist. No clear answers ever presented themselves and perhaps this is what so settled X's mind about these thoughts: he found no answers because there *were* no answers, only misery and resultant absurdity, perhaps.

X enjoyed going to several museums in the city in those days and as a result became acquainted with the works of Jackson Pollock, who became his favorite painter. When he was nearly infantile it was always Dürer, and that still goes unexplained in the confines of his skull, but now, and forever more, it's Pollock. Pollock. Pollock.

One of the most discussed drunken self-destruction artists of the last three hundred years, Jackson Pollock influenced X because he seemed more human than any painter before, or after, his time. Boring art school types enjoy citing the works of Warhol and various conceptualists and are often quick to dismiss Pollock as too scatterbrained, with too much emphasis on the bizarre and nonlinear. However, even as a teenager, X put it to them that his work not only chronicled the American Mess in such a phenomenal and groundbreaking way that it defies petty judgment or mere *criticism*, but that as a man and an innovator Jackson Pollock was and remains the most influential abstract artist to come from this country's soil, period.

But that isn't what X liked about it. He didn't like those conversations, didn't like having to prove why he liked somebody. It's become a reflex to try and articulate it now; nobody seems ready to let anyone else love something for the hell of it. What X liked about him as a teenager was that he'd never seen thoughts conveyed that way before, and the way Pollock did it, hadn't seen it since. He'd stand there staring at every inch of his paintings from the opening to the closing of the museum, and he'd go home trying to write expressionistic poems in homage to his work. X realized through looking at his work that he could never and would never want to be a painter, or even a sketch artist, because everything Pollock was doing with paint, X seemed to want to then be able to do with the written word. Somehow the channels just made sense to him. So, he'd sit in his room, watching that Ed Harris biopic *Pollock*, over and over and write long, bizarre pieces in which the characters found interesting ways to scream "BITCH. BITCH. BITCH. BITCH. BITCH. BITCH. BITCH," at one another before painting chaos.

Thus, X was not taught to write by the works of another writer. He did not look up to Hemingway. He did not find a copy of Fante in the back of the Los Angeles Public Library like Bukowski and he did not seek to emulate Joan Didion like Bret Easton Ellis. He did not read Faulkner or Tolstoy or Dostoyevsky in his early years and find that he was compelled to tell a story. X learned to do what he now does through the process of negation. His desire to write came from the crushing *non-desire* to paint. He looked at the works of Jackson Pollock over and over again and, realizing he could at best hope to paint like he did, knew that he had to find some other form, some unprecedented way of approaching the medium just like Pollock; and that way could carry on his legacy without simply using his aesthetic to feel closer to an idol.

After X realized what he wanted to do he approached books with a new awe that seemed to come from nowhere at all. He'd sit up nights on his father's couch, having to wake for school the next day bright and early, tearing his hair out over copies of books like *American Psycho*, or *Garden of Eden*, or *Ask the Dust*, or *Speedboat*, or *Journal of a Solitude*, or *The Killer Inside Me*, or *Carrie*, and he'd leave the paperbacks read, and reread, in piles next to the couch when he finally fell asleep. Sometimes he read five or six books at once, plowing through them in various locales around the city, riding the Light Rail out to the St. Paul Airport and back just for a little extra time in each of his fantasied lands. And it was through all of this that X slowly learned to write his way, and thus became obsessed with the thought of when he'd finally be able to write that first novel.

Ego Wilts to Sunday came to him in winter out of sheer luck, and X sat down with it on an electric typewriter, only getting up to celebrate Christmas briefly and thank his parents for their generous gifts. He sat down in a concrete room in the basement and wrote as passionately as he could for the following six days. What he wound up with felt surprising. He held it in his hands, that foreign stack of white pages, those words compounded atop one another like snakes across every page, and realized he'd done something. He'd created what wasn't there before: conveyed perspective.

That book might've never seen publication, but all the same X can't recall being more proud of anything he'd done than that soft winter morning when he finished the work. He would remember it like it never stopped happening. He came out of the basement with the writing in his hand, held it together with one of those massive black clips, and walked outside in sweatpants to feel the trite crunch of snow beneath his feet in chilling waves. His father was busy at work setting up for a holiday showing of *A Christmas Story*, and X had the house entirely to himself. He wasn't wearing a shirt when he went outside, and rather uncharacteristically he turned around and fell backwards into the snow without bracing his fall in the slightest. He'd luckily chosen a tactical spot for this brief slip into insanity and thus the extent of injury was a very cold back and a few scrapes on his arms, but in those seconds, he took a breath that seemed to alter him. He looked up into the bright Minnesota sky and knew something natural; knew wholeheartedly that writing was not a *craft*, a *job*, or a way to kill time anymore, that it would be his *calling*, his connection to the humanity he felt so inherently alienated from. His only lifeline to this world and to maintain it X would need to write, and read, and write more and more if he were to remain sane and human.

He walked inside that day, fixed himself a tall cup of hot apple cider, and sat in the living room with the dog at his feet, manuscript to his left, and reruns of old James Bond movies playing out in some sort of holiday marathon. Later that night his father came home, and when X told him the news he dropped his keys and cell phone on the floor—X hadn't even told him he was working on anything—and when he gave him the manuscript to hold his father actually cried, pulling it to his chest then reeling X in close to him for a long embrace. He kissed X on the forehead much in the same way X would kiss Bea when she was scared, and told him that no matter what it took, he would help X in any way he could to make him the writer he wanted to be.

His father wasn't a particularly sentimental guy, but when it came to books, and writing, nothing touched him deeper than to see his son working at it that way, excited to share with the world. That night they watched *Diamonds are Forever* on cable, sharing glasses of red wine and taking turns snuggling their dog Jessie as she lay there on the floor, oblivious to it all. That was the greatest Christmas of his life.

They were attending an art showing a few days later and X was feeling good and settled into his classes, mostly. Warren was making jokes about everybody they passed on the street, already a little drunk. When they came inside they didn't really know what to expect, Warren knew some girl that attended the school in which the showing was being held—one of Chicago's more pretentious art factories—and while half the walls looked like they were covered in pretty genuine pieces of artwork, the rest looked like some bad wet dream conceived by Andy Warhol in an attempt at waxing interesting four generations too late.

"Art: the absence of the absences within the absence of the absent, ah…" X slurred in a garish gesture as they walked through the sliding glass doors on the fifteenth floor of some generic college building off Michigan Avenue.

Someone mentioned the Internet/conceptualism/Dr. Oz/ Johnny Depp/P.T. Anderson/feminism/dead cops/Martin Luther/ stick and poke tattoos/Keanu Reeves/fashionable backpacks/student loans/television/the death of the author/*Repo Man*/Paul Rudd/*The Wire*/pierced parts/streaming pornography/artisanal cheeses/Whole Foods, and everything else. Someone mentioned something.

"How are you?" Warren's friend asked X. She was a lovely girl, and that night—for the showing—was wearing a neat black dress. She possessed a certain suburban air that—commingled with her obsession with Matthew Barney and half-wrought feminism— left one feeling nagged by not only the most obnoxious presence at the party, but the most obnoxious presence who happened to understand certain elements of the life of Yoko Ono.

"Alright, you? The show looks great." She placed her hand on X's wrist then, a gesture he never processed well.

"Thank you so much! It means so much for you to say it! I've had *such* a hard time with everything this week, that to be here, *ugh*! It's just so good!" X shared in the pleasantries as they stood in line waiting for a slew of high-priced eats. He filled a plate five times as high as any of the plates he saw around him and, when he reached the drink vendor, made him fill a tall soda glass with ice and red wine. Warren and Co. stood along some wall with a window that looked down on Chicago's State Street. X noticed across the way an Old Navy store whose lights were brighter than any building on the street. *Waste…* X thought. *Glorious waste.* If you were going to give the aliens one indicator of our humanity on their first descent into the atmosphere, would you want them to notice the Old Navy?

Their night in the center of the earth rattled on, and X began to imagine himself as some celebrity, worth his weight in screens and gold. He was wearing what seemed to be an aesthetically pleasing ensemble for this crowd—pants and a T shirt, but fitted *just so*, it made him smile—and as Warren followed him around in X's lightly drunken miseries he knew he started to feel it too. They were lucky. They were young, were ambling around rows and rows of tired-looking students so obsessed with images, and statuses, and labels, and none of it was hitting them! In fits of buzzed reverie they examined this piece, and these performance artists, and if they felt an urge to laugh they didn't hold it back but put it forth that much more severely because they seemed to sense the harm which could be caused if these students were to take themselves seriously much longer.

X seemed to comprehend all of this and more, talking in idle tones to girls about how distasteful he thought one drawing was; how genius he thought Iggy Pop was; or how much he enjoyed writing things on broken old typewriters to ensure the work had *integrity*—an elusive word which, had he not been entirely drunk by this point and enjoying a moment of pure dishonesty with his cohorts, X would not be caught dead uttering—and all nodded, spoke up, posed accordingly.

Down on the street below the gallery, as X walked, he observed: you didn't see happy, awestruck tourists with stars in their eyes. You saw homeless people. You saw the tired eyes of college kids looking out before a night of drunken slurs. You saw monotony. You saw sales. You saw bookstores that made it impossible to find the right books. You saw clothing stores that turned currency into some obscure piece of child-sewn fabric, which in the end only brought you further away from the life you wanted to live. You saw nightmares. You saw sleepwalkers. You saw an American Middle-West on the brink of being completely bankrupt, completely miserable, and completely nameless in the battle for the future which all were running towards in madness. You saw yourself, reflected in the bottom of a building and miserable. You saw those green eyes that stared from behind a face that seemed entirely foreign, and at the moment it was obscured you were thankful. Thankful that you'd no longer have to see yourself cast into such shadow amidst all these tired patrons of Hell City. You prayed wholeheartedly to the devil that something would eventually change, and finally you stopped, life slowing to the speed in which Jimmy Stewart finally kisses Kim Novak, or Norman Bates is taken and in an existentialist plot the murders have still happened, and fear is still cast across the audience, and life has reached a cinematic peak you cannot capture on your cell phone. Existence has ascended to a new sheen of brilliance that cannot be summed up in anxious blips of thought, cannot be transcribed in some digitized note, and hesitantly, with a stomach now devoid of food and those anti-depressants you've come to rely on, you begin to weep, and night becomes the only guide to turn you back the way you came.

They rode the Redline that night as Warren's friend drove to their place to meet. When they returned home, Emily was nowhere to be found, and the other roommates were locked up in their rooms, likely masturbating with their headphones on like all are wont to do when they feel alone with their computer. X turned on the score to *Taxi Driver* by Bernard Hermann and the night became soaked in rain and light that seemed to wash away all of X's discontentment at the prospect of surviving his own existence.

Warren's friend came upstairs, and they spent the next hour or so watching videos online of hilarious, completely fucked, things. They drank a bottle of red wine that Warren's friend had managed to swindle from someone who organized the art showing. Eventually Hank came out of his room and Aaron after that, both were in horrendous moods and Hank took his out on Warren's friend, saying offensive things about the art she was admiring aloud on the laptop. Aaron took his out on Warren and X over the dishes left in the sink. Actually, Warren left the dishes in the sink. X never left dishes in the sink because he immediately washed his dishes upon eating his meal—a nervous tick he picked up when living in studio apartments by himself and having nothing to do—so when Aaron aroused a bit of fury in Warren and he looked to X to join up and throw Aaron out to the wolves for heresy, X simply sat there smiling, acting as though he hadn't heard a word the boys were saying. Hank's remarks were against Andres Serrano's *Piss Christ* and eventually X spoke out in defense. Urine, X felt, held an untapped artistry that Serrano was brilliant for bringing to light, and though all were drunken fools by this hour an entertaining stint of anger passed that ended with X howling odes to "piss in the arts!" that quieted Hank's criticisms.

That night was the first time he did it. Perhaps it was a joke initially, though it became serious almost at once. He had friends back home that would go onto Craigslist and respond to personal ads in an attempt to engage in lurid conversations with young coeds or some such rubbish, but X hardly felt connected to them when he began scrolling the rows of requests for odd sexual company and *real love*. He felt more like a leper, separated from humanity in his dark room while the planet sleeps; searching to connect sexually with some total stranger out of no want beyond the destruction of boredom.

He wrote an ad that night. In his ad X conveyed that he wanted somebody older, however did not want something Oedipal—though at the time he wrote 'Oedipisinal' as he was too excited to consider Freud—and that though his interests at the moment were primarily sexual, he was more than open to a real relationship with somebody should they feel apt to take on a neurotic mess.

He responded to several as well.

He found an old businessman that night, who was visiting, and quite interested in X coming to his hotel for sex. X told him he could never come to his hotel, at which point he offered to pay X two hundred dollars. X still declined, and he asked whether X would be interested in a sort of mutual masturbation thing. After some convincing, X agreed, and allowed him to call.

"Hello…" his voice was disgusting, grating, as though he were eating a plate of chips between each syllable.

"Hey. Uh. I'm not gonna say anything. You say whatever you want."

"That's fine…you're my timid little boy huh?

"…"

"You want me to do things to you little boy?"

X became a bit scared at that moment, knowing he wouldn't be able to masturbate; but allowed the man to continue on talking out of interest in the despicable nature of America's traveling salesman.

"Yeah. I wish you were here so I could show you what I have for you.

"Make you lick it.

"Pay you like a whore.

"I could do anything I wanted then."

He started breathing oddly, more like he was bordering on a heart attack than he might actually want to make X taste his own blood, and he listened, more alert.

"I've had other boys and girls come to my place while I've been here for business this week.

"I made them bleed, made them taste each other's blood.

"One boy even let me hit him. *Would you be good like that?*"

He asked then, waiting, and imploring X to answer with subtle groans and slapping sounds.

"This is so fucking boring. Are you serious? You're so fucking boring!" X yelled and hung up the phone. He laughed then out of nervousness. The Internet seemed to make being alive impossible. X wanted to empathize or understand but all he saw were the bored actions of a bored individual and he felt miserable.

He fell asleep hours later, after editing a while and trying to piece together the one thing in his life that seemed to make sense. The sun was rising when his eyes finally closed, and bitterly, X buried his head in his pillows and began the road into sleep before the redness of morning broke.

X was in the bathroom and not thinking about anything at all when a bug started crawling on his shoe. He picked up the bug, looked at it—some sort of forgettable beetle—and with a small crunch mashed the thing between his fingers. X could give no acceptable reason as to why humans initially wish all bugs dead—for humans seem to kill them as a reflex unlike anything else in life—but this, this *reflex*, was one way in which X was painfully human, and wiping the guts on the sole of his right shoe he smiled ruefully at the loss of yet another plague, another annoyance.

X liked the bathroom on the 9th floor of one of M. U.'s buildings because in the rather spacious stall you could open up a window that gave you a view of absolutely nothing. After he finished, he enjoyed leaning out onto the window frame and looking down and up—it was really just a rectangle, sectioned off by four separate buildings and a roof on top—at this complete emptiness. There were no doors at ground level, and as far as he could see, the window he peered out of was the only one looking out into this brilliant metropolitan crawlspace, but it was his portal. His doorway into something highly purposeful and terribly *his own*. X supposed that other students were less likely to open up the window than he, and this too made him feel vindicated. On leaving the room he left the window cracked, though, just on the off chance that someone in this world was in the least bit like him.

Class that night was one of few real writing workshops that semester, and he'd become generally hesitant the moment he walked in the door. His hope was waning. His teacher was a pleasant woman with a long, black, braided ponytail that she draped over her right shoulder. She wore an olive khaki shirt with sleeves rolled up, and dark jeans rolled atop a pair of black Vans topsiders. She looked hip, if not in that moment entirely severe, and it was she that gave X reason to retain hope in the class, nobody else.

These classes had tried to sway X for some time. Hours had transpired in those rooms. And X surmised that any hopes of teaching, or being taught, how to write, are simply not worth harboring and if he'd waited for the day somebody would sit him down and convey just exactly what it takes to write a novel, he'd sooner consider the dream crushed, and get a job somewhere as a gas station attendant. X sees himself already making certain contradictions theoretically, however, for he felt he could give advice gleaned from others that kept him from burning it all like Max Brod, but then again if it isn't already apparent—even a sliver, a modicum, of hope—then advice or none it doesn't matter. He'd zone out, ignore the teachers, weigh in when it seemed to matter, but something about those rooms frequently *crushed* him. X looked at his classroom of strangers, more concerned with things X never understood than what constitutes a good book, and couldn't help but feel that you'd do much better to take on some severe part time work as a way to learn to write than you would be sitting in there with them, the privileged, the docile. X hated himself, in short.

Perhaps it comes from reading—and loving—Henry Miller types at a young age, perhaps Hemingway, almost certainly Fante. But writing about your life as a miserable fucking employee seems to work, and anybody to deny this would simply be doing so out of some academic notion that only by living betwixt real Artists, and real Creators, can one hope to create art.

Running through the exercises, taking certain images and trying to harness within them the story that the New Yorker would finally accept, X began to simply fantasize about murdering, or fucking his idols. Such is life for glum bastards. Either he's entirely engrossed and feels it's a worthwhile time to speak up about all the things he'd so valued learning, or he wants to chug bleach and lose his teeth.

X was the bastard of that classroom, it was apparent. Kids were exchanging numbers and laughing about stories he didn't care to understand. The teacher was laughing and relating with everybody on a level he seemed far below, and X sat there trapped within himself, nearly crying out to his fellows for some sort of helping hand out of not only the classroom but of the core misery. But no, only more funny stories, more classroom politics, more favoritism, and more name-dropping of the favorite films and authors and artists and musicians of these hopelessly hip individuals. It was only in the small glint of compassion the teacher conveyed that X felt some comfort, and never apparently enough. He'd take those images home, however, he knew the sorrowful ambitious teaching attempting too well, and doubtless they had their effect.

He left with an assignment to create a six or seven page story of a memory from childhood. He chose to completely fabricate a story about a boy who fell in love with his neighbor, and best friend, Michael, after the neighbor's home had a fire and they spent their entire Christmas together.

Lying that night when X sat down to scribble out the story was the first edifying thing he felt he did in college. Not only was it edifying, it was calming. He made himself separate from the world in ways that could not be taken back. He lied outright and when he came into class the following week realized that everyone else had told the truth.

X had to fight to believe in that semester of school. The only relief, inevitably, came when he would sit at the computer nights and revise the work done the summer prior. At times he'd open emails and find responses to his ad on Craigslist but, caught up in such a fury of editing and revising, he simply couldn't give anything else his attention. He hardly ever read another writer while he wrote, and this go round, the same was true even for revision. The process of taking one's words and shoving them through the filter—a terribly miserable and suicidal filter, what's more—after you've only recently spat them out is a difficult task. As a result of all this, when X received one particular letter those nights, he couldn't have needed its contents more.

One of his submission letters had worked. He didn't get the brilliant news of *Yes, we are going to publish both of your novels at no cost to you and, what's more, you're now a famous Enfant Terrible of American Letters!* He did not receive this letter. But one man, so taken by what X put down—a letter he'd almost totally forgotten writing by that point—decided that he was willing to edit X's work for a small fee, and X would in turn receive his every suggestion on each page of the manuscript to bring it to a publishable state. He—the editor—had garnered small amounts of fame as a poet in Florida and had under his belt two books; one a tome of nonfiction on the immigration flaws in that area, the other a collection of poetry. X scoured the Internet for his credentials and found them reaffirming. This was his Mencken… His Perkins… His Hackmuth… And after working with him X just might have a real shot.

The second was a letter from an older woman that had seen the ad. X had neglected it because for some reason it went into a junk folder in his inbox but when he read it X could tell she was earnest, and seemed to want what he did. In fact, she spoke of feeling shocked at finding somebody professing exactly what she was looking for. She asked X if he was real—a strange thing to ponder, in his state—if it was even possible to find somebody so obviously meant for her. He responded telling her that he now felt equally as shocked, that he was very much real, and that it did seem possible if you looked in the right places, to find that person. He sent along a picture of himself sitting there in his lamp-lit bedroom with books scattered about. Told her of the news he'd just received, and that he was now a writer. She put at the bottom of her first letter that her name was Marie, and that—post scripted—she was unmarried, wealthy enough because of it, and happily living in one of Chicago's Northern suburbs. X rambled on; telling her of discontentment at starting another semester at college with no real faith in the crux of the college's message and even going so far as to damn the notion of a person being taught how to create art, hoping that she'd agree. He told her of the roommates, that he loved living in Chicago for the most part and that he felt himself a particularly abnormal young man. He told her that he only lightly drank, that he didn't smoke or use any drugs, and that when presented he would smoke cigarettes. X told her what he was working on, publishing his own work, and that he'd love it if she'd read what he'd written, and at the end noted how eagerly he awaited her reply.

Breathing a bit, settled deeply into the chilling fall, X sent off replies to the both of them. Feeling good and calm, he walked out into the living room to Warren smoking his bong, and Hank sitting there, sipping beers as they watched videos on one of their computers. X smiled at it, grabbed a beer from the fridge and began to feel overcome with the sensation that life until then had been a sort of fugue, that in moments he wouldn't remember any of it, and would start something entirely new, like Marcello in *La Dolce Vita*, he'd begin a new life, his good life, and all would finally be well. At that his roommates were laughing at some video of a girl sitting in her college dorm room recounting the evening's events and interspersing brief chants that made her look potentially insane.

Such was the status in the minds of young ones. A season of laughter; laughter at the expense of anyone and everything that could possibly evoke even the smallest chuckle. They were all likely depressed, all dealing with things that made the days harder and harder to face, but somehow that didn't stop it, and at times like that X gave whole credit to ridiculous contemporary innovations that allow mankind to watch stupid morons just like them do stupid, moronic things.

"God, I am so fucking sick of hearing about David Bowie. Don't talk about it…" X said to her. Bowie'd apparently released some video or statement and it was on her mind and bringing X down. It was after class and seemingly, neither of them had anywhere better to go. They sat in a Starbucks at the bottom of one of Chicago's many hotels, sipping espresso and looking at each other—strangers—with an odd fascination. Her name was Kari, and she had short blonde hair, not mid-length and punky like so many girls then, but shorter than Mia Farrow's in *Rosemary's Baby*, without being buzzed. He'd stared at her most of the class, so much that eventually the teacher called on X to answer a question and he had nothing to offer in reply—he mumbled something about postmodernism. She laughed, and X took it as notification enough to approach her after class.

"How can you even say that? How can you be so fucking terse about David Bowie?"

"Because, first of all, I spent my childhood—teen years, I guess—in love with Iggy Pop. Iggy always beat him, even when they were together. I like my weirdos just *so*, homespun, draped in their own shit when they pole dance on stage and spit at the crowd. *Metallic K.O.*, whatever. It's just the way I was raised I guess…" Both laughed at that, started to sink into the evening just a little. Whenever a Starbucks put a café in the bottom of a hotel, they seemed to give it more attention than the quick locations scattered randomly all over the city, and this one had a nice mood. Young kids behind the counter, their arms covered in tattoos, and some calm, airy sort of jazz seeped out of the speakers with an inexplicable assurance that this was the right place for now.

"I guess. But then how do you rank Serge Gainsbourg? You can't tell me you don't like Serge Gainsbourg. *Everybody* likes Serge Gainsbourg…"

"I do, however with one very important distinction: Gainsbourg *feels* homespun to me, local, at least in the ways it matters. The French typically personify a level of Americanism more than most Americans; they're more secular than us; more outspoken than us, and whatever else. So, by definition Serge Gainsbourg is homespun in the way of James Osterberg, if you'll pardon my total ineptitude and absence of authority in these matters."

"Well that's not the usual bullshit then, is it?" Smiling like that she looked every bit as cinematic as death. X felt touched.

"How do you figure?"

"This is our first time meeting. And you've posited theories on what it means to be an American, pray tell, monsignor, what is an American in your eyes?"

Hesitantly, he attempted a reply, "I saw an American in that video of the senator—or whatever he was—shooting himself in the head on national news at that press conference. That man was more American than any blip or fart we've fashioned: he did everything he could to make his life work, and when it didn't, he turned around and died the exact way he wanted to. He stands there, calm, appeasing, and finally takes a small revolver from a larger manila envelope and when he's attempting to give his speech—and what a painfully American speech it might've been—the response from the crowd is panic, and before he can soothe them enough to speak, after he tries to calm them, telling them he doesn't want to hurt anybody—they're simply too rampant—and he puts the gun to his chin and pulls the trigger. I see something oddly American about death by stubbornness, I don't know. I hate this place most days. I hate its history, what it's come from and what that implies for the here and now, but I've got to try. I'm not ready to kill myself in public just yet, or likely ever. It doesn't make sense but it's the best I can do."

"Wait, what the fuck are you talking about?" She looked incredulous, and X saw that he'd become too comfortable with her.

"I'm not sure, there's something suicidal about the founding of a country maybe. I don't much like to think about this stuff, I just like to ramble over abysmal cups of coffee."

"We're all fucked, amen."

X hadn't really spoken with anyone like that since he'd stopped his medication, so it was certainly nice, but still he looked forward to an evening's solitude. X was destined to be a certain way, to be the guy more bizarre but less appealing than the beloved. To be that guy who was stuck in the corner of the party looking at more and more couples come together as he fantasized about that story in his youth of the world record holder who ate an entire plane. Bitterness is never inherent, X let thoughts tack onto thoughts. Neither is sin. God-fearing folks have it wrong that way. X couldn't offer a guess as to what was right, though.

The hand is cut in the loose gravel on the sunstruck road. The piece of gravel has moved up into the wrist by the time the parents return. Screaming. Pulling. A cool slide into the worm skin with a tweezers and a rock the size of a nickel is removed.

Staring into the hole, the blood teeming like syrup, the skin starting to close, the top of it starting to harden in one glowing line. The boy (X) taking an unnoticeable sip of his own flesh as the mother collects rolls of puffy white gauze to tend the wound.

Out the window a Cardinal flies, red and sharp to the top of a Birch tree, staring into the face of X. Beating him with its eyes, it whispers inaudibly to him, and flutters away. Not a soul but X knows the words.

X began exchanging messages with both his editor and his newfound Craigslist mate. He finally came out with it that his second rewrite was not yet finished and that he'd need a few more weeks before it was ready to send over. He assured X that this was fine, that based on his letter regarding *Vitruvius* he was interested enough, and they already started toying around with phrases on X's apparent merits as an author—based entirely on emails, alas—and X felt better after every word. He'd write him these long tomes about the years up until that point, about what he believed regarding literature, about how he'd read a good deal, and wanted desperately to rank with his favorite authors someday down the road. He'd ask X who his favorite authors were, and X would respond with: Fante, Fitzgerald,

Baldwin, Adler, Didion, Cavafy, etc. He'd tell him that these writers raised him more than his family had, that he owed his life as a writer to them and intended to sit down many more times to write much bigger novels as life wore on. He gave X nice cordial replies about how it all sounded well and good, that he looked forward to reading the work, and assuring X finally what a good deal he'd be able to provide as an editor. X relished those nights, coming home to an inbox filled with yet more rejection letters and finally those from his first acceptance, first "yes," seemed conducive towards the better life which he so desperately sought.

The letters from his Craigslist mate were becoming more frequent as time progressed that fall. They spoke about meeting eventually and started exchanging pictures. With the first night of pictures X decided to shift the conversation toward things more sexual. The response he received was shocking. She wrote these long fantasies about letting X drink her urine, about his eating her out while she was in fact menstruating, about her tying X up. That she knew he said he wanted nothing Oedipal but that she knew the truth. Apparently, he wanted a very particular relationship and by the time X ended things they were having nightly conversations constantly referencing how much they loved each other. X had feelings for her, however he was also deathly afraid of what would happen if it went any further than that.

She responded, insisting he needed medical help—he couldn't disagree—and they didn't speak for several days. However, horniness crept back in, and X sent her this poem about his undying love for her, along with four pictures looking terribly emaciated and afraid, standing there naked with imploring eyes as though a fawn. She accepted him, encouraging that they meet soon, and X developed this haunting image in his mind of her stabbing him repeatedly in the kidneys. Accordingly, after another week or so, he told her it wasn't possible, and stuck by the words this time.

She sent him terrible threats, telling him that nobody would get away with treating her such a way. He tried to laugh it off, though admittedly he became paranoid. He tried to change the subject, so to speak, sitting there in the fall with windows open and Hank and Warren laughing, drinking beer as football season seemed to swallow Chicago. Oddly, romance seemed to only register as romance if it was slightly terrifying. X lost his grip with growing frequency.

They started having to wear flannel shirts. X enjoyed classes less and less but continued going. He'd have brief laughs here and there and learned a great deal from his class on Cinema History. Fall was coming to its end, though, and a Chicago winter came creeping in with typically horrendous intent. X left behind his relationship with the old woman, finished revisions on the manuscript, and had his father send off a physical copy to the editor out East.

He told X in late November that he'd received the book, and he began to feel good again. He took long walks through Grant Park staring at the almost entirely absent leaves in long rows of trees. He saw movies roughly every Friday, and afterward spent each weekend with Warren at the loft drinking and socializing with various girls. His sister and X exchanged emails every couple of weeks and he learned that she'd met somebody over in France. She would apparently be home that Christmas and was looking forward to seeing X. He finished out that stint of classes with decent grades and prospects higher than they'd ever been. He hadn't told his family about the editor and was planning to do it the moment he returned home by train.

Eyes adjust, you know? This is the thought that passes over his sleepless brain at five AM as he rides the train downtown to Quincy and walks across the Chicago River to Union Station for a train that would leave at eight AM. X has always been concerned with time, and typically figures that if he has nothing else to do he might as well be someplace well in advance rather than sit around trying to fill the hours with monotonous nothings. To be sure, he's aware how foolish it might be, how utterly devoid of logic it is to forgo several comfortable hours at home perhaps sleeping, or watching TV, or reading, but even still X was on the train, stomach full of bad diner food and hot coffee, a paperback copy of *Hannibal* by Thomas Harris clutched in hand, several men in coveralls obviously heading to work seated around him, and that fleeting thought, that *eyes adjust, you know?*

Two things first: X was taking the train out of Union Station to return home to St. Paul for Christmas; was feeling rather flat and uninspired about the whole ordeal. He'd recently watched a batch of Christmas movies in an attempt to refuel his interest in the season, but after a fall comprised of no real connections with anyone, yet teeming with people, all of which evoked in X some drastic emotional response (the woman; the friends; the drunks and talkers; the editor) he was simply tired, and wanted to go home for a nice long sleep with pup curled up on the ground before him. The second thing, recently the lack of medication, had fully settled itself on his brain and he was spending days pacing the wood floor of his bedroom rambling aloud about nothing in particular. He became obsessive about knowing the definitions of certain words that he'd come across and couldn't immediately recall, and every day seven or so new words would arise in his brain and he'd challenge himself by walking Chicago's downtown saying the words over and over with their definitions out loud. The funny thing of it all was that the words seemed to get less and less esoteric; initially it was more difficult words like *penurious* or *recondite*, but as time wore on into fall X found himself needing help to remember the definitions of words he was certain he knew like *impregnable,* or *perambulate.* To be certain, the human species obsesses with all kinds of things, and with a lexicon such as English so overfull with words hardly used except by dead souls like Herman Melville and the like, X could hardly deem himself stupid, or idiotic just because he couldn't remember, and yet he did. He felt *slighted* whenever reading something—even as basic as Thomas Harris—if a word didn't immediately define itself in his head. He felt moronic, as though he was losing his edge; and *that,* on top of everything else, X hoped to reconcile with several weeks on his father's couch, with sister and mother, sitting around drinking wine and eating plates of good food.

"Iridescent of or characteristic of a rainbow," X muttered on the train as they neared Merchandise Mart, "Contrived, obviously planned or forced, artificial or strained. Distended, *swollen,* distended. Dusty Springfield's real name is Mary Isabel Catherine

Bernadette O'Brien," for it wasn't limited merely to adjective or verbs, but to nouns—even proper nouns—if they so perplexed or fascinated him, "Bibulous, of or characteristic of a person indulgent in alcohol. To be imbibed means to be drunk. The proper spelling of discreet, when meaning quieted, or sheltered in social interactions, is d-i-s-c-r-e-e-t. Discrete, spelled d-i-s-c-r-e-t-e, means to be separated, to be on one's own or insular. Insular means characteristic of an island. Peninsula, penultimate—the moment or scene before the last—Pen-insula, before the island, insular." Such was the way his brain began to function, and he'd become so attuned with needing to live this way—to recite things aloud etc.— that X learned to hide in particular corners of trains and classrooms, wearing the proper garments—layered with hooded sweatshirts—so that if someone should feel the need to intrude upon his intellectual ponderings he could merely put on a face that would leave them feeling out of line, and would thus continue.

Eyes adjust, you know? And that was the thought that stopped him on the train as he exited and began walking up the darkened street to a right where he would cross a bridge and witness the Willis Tower—formerly Chicago's Sears Tower—in all of its obsidian spectacle against the gray blue morning sky. A man asked X for a cigarette, he gave him one because he often purchased a pack before these long train rides—as well as a tin of Citrus chewing tobacco—and when he asked X for money he told him "No," that he couldn't be bothered because he had a train to catch. He insulted X's intelligence, telling him there were no trains at this time of day, and X told him he was to catch the Amtrak, to fuck off. Being larger than the man—who was a hunched over five foot, maybe, he hassled X no longer, and he walked on as the morning got lighter and lighter, thoughts less and less morose.

Thinking of eyes, and the fact that they adjust to whatever light should possibly befall them, X was always quite overwhelmed. He saw his kin—the lonely, the depressed, the moronic—as sort of *shadows* to the light, and that image in his head, pressing, when he was much younger, only served to enhance interest in the correspondence of light and dark to the human eye. People are scared of caves, scared of darkness, scared of the white light at the end of their lives, scared of having a policeman's flashlight shined into their eyes in the darkness of a lonely night on the highway, and yet, their eyes adjust, accommodate them to whatever possible tortures the shadows, or lights of the world could inflict upon them. X has decent vision, though at times it's rather terrible and he has to stop momentarily to laugh at his condition—a bit near-sighted—and allow blurry sight to adjust to the world, yet another way in which humanity has evolved to allow living in such mirrored, digital times. The streets are often coated in neon, the people today holding up beacons of light to the world and all of it can be dealt with by a simple adjustment—totally unconscious—of one's sight.

Tangential modes of thinking are ideal for somebody that prefers to live outside of social structures. And X relished those moments of almost microscopic thought regarding the nature of the human race, its makeup. As he walked down into the empty hulking marble hall of Union Station and descended further to slide a barcoded piece of paper beneath a scanner to receive his ticket, X almost started laughing in great fits at how brilliant it all was. Nights, or mornings such as that one, were and are the only things that have kept his head afloat with, or without medication, vitamins. At times you needed to dance on the fringe of the world inside your mind, at times you needed to take long baths late into the night and read the works of Frederick Exley only to stay sane and laugh passionately when Ex tells another tale of some New York Fans and Rudolph Valentino's armpits, at times you needed to be alive—really *alive*—without the world's permission, without anyone's consent, and by your own standards. That sort of propriety is the only sort X maintains any interest in.

Waiting with others for the train that would headfirst to Milwaukee, then to a wide range of snowy Wisconsin towns, he felt at peace with all surroundings. Men and women obviously traveling on business began to fill the small corridor and gave the appropriate nods so as to assure one another that the train would be a unified front of travelers all merely interested in getting from A to B as easily as possible. The news on the TV set in that room was not particularly congenial, however. Men and women sat over their morning coffee with scowls on their faces talking about money, and crime, and religion. An endless cycle of all these things commingled at times and at others set apart as their own issues, the most important issues of today. The money almost always belonged to some celebrity who'd committed some terrible crime against humanity by having sex or causing a domestic disturbance. X enjoyed watching the dismal morning news circulation; however, it was only enjoyable as an act of voyeurism, watching the annals of humanity in his lifetime. He smiled as these moneyed, bubbling psychopaths talked about Mel Gibson; and Gaddafi; and Obama; and Paris Hilton; and Lindsay Lohan; and Oprah; and Michael Moore; and Larry David; and Mark Ruffalo; and Quentin Tarantino; and the Coen Brothers; and The Underwear Bomber; and SpeechGate; and the end of times; and the beginning of times; and some religious protest against another church; another burial; another chance for humanity to move forward by supporting some date on which all will be burned alive they referred to as *The Rapture*. He smiled, and even further, began to laugh. He laughed because although they insisted these psychotic delusional parasites impacted daily lives far more than he'd care to realize, X knew the opposite to be true. He knew that he was just a young man, about to board a train, with a bag at his side and one on his back filled with snacks and books for Christmas break. He knew that the train would not be bombed today, that god would have no say in the end of his life, and that his kin, the shadows, would always have their say in a world so drowned in the horrendous lights of Celebrity, and Fame, and Murder, and True Love, and Art, and whatever other rubbish they cared to fill up the hive mind with. There is a sense of true faith one feels when staring down the gullet of a society that has, in many ways, let itself go to shit, and that true faith is, and always will be, enough for the believers in a betterment of our world to go on.

So, X chuckled, stood, and went to the bathroom several times, read a magazine about today's fashion that was actually quite interesting and beautiful, and read more of his book—one of his favorites of pop fiction—settling into a world where morality was as obvious as the *Goldberg Variations* of Glenn Gould, or the slicing of a thin, artful blade over the skin of some wrongdoer. Hannibal

Lecter was, in many ways, X's introduction to the more serious side of art and literature, watching *Silence of the Lambs* when he was a boy was one of the first times he can remember having a vision of alternate humanity. And years later, reading the masterful—if not rather unbelievable—works of Thomas Harris over and over, X began to see Hannibal as more than a fictional character, as a hero, as somebody who sat in the confines of the skull urging him to continue on; that life would get better, if only he could believe in his art, in his purpose, that life would get better if only he could endure long enough to not succumb to Lecter's approach of murdering and killing to appease the terrible hurt all must feel. That life would get better if X let it.

The grays become deep blue. Blues turn orange, fading into yellow, and finally blurring towards red before burning off into the finger rubbed sky. That snow, that milky plain of solitude, running randomly between the farmhouses and street ways of Northern Illinois, all the way into the nest of Milwaukee's downtown. *You watch it, not believing in it at first, you sit with your head against the window and a hooded sweatshirt you've mounted there. Nobody sits on your right for the ride into Milwaukee, but you don't hold your breath in the hope that you'll be lucky enough to ride the entire way alone. You light the small lamp mounted into the ceiling and it causes you to feel more and more immersed in sleeplessness. Your stomach loses its constant chiming vigor, your throat becomes coated in subtle pain that brings a smile to your lips, your eyes become coated in hot, slow tears as though you've eaten an enormous dinner. Beauty rests in that tract of land in Wisconsin's heart.* A beauty unlike anything he'd seen in the world, trapped somewhere between the Iron Range of Bob Dylan and *Nanook of the North.* The sort of quietude in which men grow beards depending on the stretch of months ahead. Women cover their children in heavy winter coats with big pink boots for the girls and tan leather minis for the boys. Kids play on mounds of snow as though conquering entire civilizations, teenagers make out in backs of cars with engines on and heat constant. Families cuddle up in small homes to commemorate a year's good work. An anachronistic stretch of humanity which will never advance further than it has to;

a sort of nowherescape where nearly every thought felt permitted, every emotion prophetic.

X stared out at the place of his youth then, thinking of Nick Carraway near the end of *The Great Gatsby*: he's realizing how important those train rides back from out East in his younger years were; he's talking about *his* Middle-West, about the small structures and the snow like tufts of angelic pillows—though X can't recall his phrase exactly—and all of it settles down the torrential stirring of emotions he's recently incurred as a result of meeting Jay Gatsby. That's how X felt that morning, connected with the landscape, thinking heavily about what it meant to be going home, what he wanted to get done, how he'd need to print out more copies of the novel, and send out more submissions, and finally X recalled an email a few nights prior indicating his editor might be done in a week or so, and at that moment X wrote him on his cellphone with his father's address, so that in addition to the other work he might start on that final rewrite of *Vitruvius*.

Amtrak trains are all the same. This, sharing obvious similarities with planes and cars, has a very distinct purpose. If there were much difference between each train, or plane, or car, meaning a difference beyond having sleeping cars, or first class, or SUVs for families and wealthy travelers, then people would lose their minds over traveling and either stay at home, or blow up every train station and airport from here to Florence until they got their way.

Sitting there in that generic bluish seat, he was thankful it was exactly the same as everyone else's. He was happy to share it with the college girl traveling to Portland, her with the laptop open watching episodes of *Dexter* with sweatpants and a sweatshirt on and a tired look in her eye; happy to share it with the old man and his miserable gait as he moved from seat to seat all morning looking for just the right amount of sunlight; happy to share it with the mother and her child, obviously heading someplace close to Minneapolis by the nature of their clothing and bags—red U of M hoodie, North Face track jacket, etc.—X was happy to share it with all of them. Sometimes conformity has its benefits, and X embraced this, didn't want a sense of individuality when traveling by train for seven or so hours. No person—short of the conductor, X guessed—spends enough time on a train, or plane, or what-have-you to feel the need to affirm their individuality by demanding some higher level of service. It's the same thought process applied to militaries the world over: everyone traveling has but one function in the interim between locales, to moderately enjoy themselves—at least enough to not feel miserable or aggressive—and to sit in one designated place that isn't terribly uncomfortable. There are people that reject this basic truth, assuming that because they are who they are that it suddenly means they deserve better service or more attentive service or whatever; and conversely there are those who assume because they work for the railroad or the airline that they have seniority enough to be an asshole. Neither of these seemed valid to X, and he often guessed who'd fit this role. It's a shame, he felt, that the assholes on each flight, or the asshole flight attendants, can't simply be ordered to only discuss matters with one another, that way all could have the freedom to travel in peace. This was not the case, and thus, a few obnoxious patrons were to be expected when making a day of movement, but X didn't particularly mind, nothing got under his skin, his only desire was getting back to the old house, to the couch, to pup, and family.

X took a good long shit and read forty or so pages of *Hannibal*. He liked to relish it as long as he could and then just sit there, flushing the toilet every five minutes or so to feel clean, and read something, maybe write a little bit. The bathrooms on trains might make most people feel claustrophobic: they're pretty tiny, and there isn't much room for comfort, but X liked it in there, like anything extraneous simply couldn't fit, like you had to make do with what you had otherwise you simply weren't going to enjoy yourself. He enjoyed himself. He read of Clarice Starling and Hannibal Lecter's comeback after so many years and for a moment became lost in that world, lost in the cops and robbers of it all. Then the announcer notified over the intercom they were nearing on Tomah, Wisconsin, and X realized how long he'd been shitting—through roughly three or four train stops—and decided he'd better get back to his seat.

When X walked up the tiny stairway and out into the hallway

of seats his light was still on, but some man was sitting in the aisle seat next to his. He looked older, perhaps forty; like he'd worked out most of his life. He had the strong features and short haircut of a soldier.

He sat down, nodding to his new seatmate, and got acclimated so that he didn't have to worry about his legs—now asleep—from getting uncomfortable.

"How ya doin?" He asked, his voice was gravelly and comforting, a Midwesterner.

"Alright, man. You?" X opted hesitantly; he didn't much feel like starting conversation.

"Good. You know it's the damndest thing, every time I get on these trains, I get sort of like an anxiety, but it's passing. I'm good."

"Good."

"Where you from, man?" He was becoming more relaxed; you could see it in his face that talking might help him out of the worry.

"Well I'm coming up from Chicago. I go to school there. Originally, I'm from St. Paul. You?"

"Chicago? Man, I love it there. I'm headed from Wisconsin Dells—where my sister and her husband live—to Minneapolis where me and the wife have lived for the last fifteen years or so."

"Oh yeah? Didn't the family want to get together for Christmas?"

"Ah well, my sister's husband wanted to spend it with his parents, so it's just gonna be me, the wife and our daughter—Natalie—this year."

"Sounds nice."

"Yeah, should be."

"Are you in the military?" X wanted to change the subject. He wasn't acting particularly timid, so X just went for it.

"Was. *Was* in the military. Yep. I served in the first Desert Storm missions back in the nineties. Trained in basic for ten years or so after, that just south of the Twin Cities."

"Wow. That's pretty amazing."

"Yep, I guess so. Actually, I wrote a book about it. That's why I was able to quit my training gig. Well, not exactly. The book has sold OK, but the real money's come from speaking events and such.

I've done alright I guess."

"So, if you don't mind my asking, what was your book about? I mean I'm sure all soldiers have an interesting story to tell, you know? What was yours about?"

"I don't mind. Hell, I wrote it. I was in a particular troop that went in before most others in Kuwait in those days. We were referred to—without our knowing—as *cattle troops*..." He let it fester. X understood.

"Oh yeah? I think I've heard about that..."

"Yeah. Well anyway, they'd send us in there before anybody else to inspect really high-risk scenarios: buildings that were believed to be strapped with explosives top to bottom, any hairy sniper situations. Pretty much any time they couldn't trust a group full of grunts to go in first they'd send us in. My particular group— about five or six of us to start—was sent in to inspect one of the initial buildings where they thought some of Saddam's people were hiding with an entire arsenal of weapons. I'm not just talking about truckloads; this was supposed to be a warehouse *filled* with explosives. We went in, doing everything that was expected, and all of a sudden one of my guys gets shot. Another's hit. Within five minutes this building's lit up from here to eternity with bullets from both sides. I've never been more scared in my life. Five or six of us to start, and I was the only man to survive. After about an hour of back-and-forth gunfire they assumed every one of us was dead. I radioed as quietly as I could. After another hour or so of hiding in the dark beneath these bodies, footsteps all around me, the place was lit up again, and I was able to crawl out."

"Oh man, that's crazy." X couldn't muster much more than that, felt shocked.

"Yeah, *heavy*. And so, when I wrote the book, initially I was incredibly angry. I looked into the way certain soldiers were being sent in first and I just thought it was all backwards and a terrible way to do battle. And it is. It is. But by the time I was fifty or a hundred pages into it I lost my nerve; wound up doing what I could to commemorate those I served with. In the end, their stories seemed more important than anything else."

"That's unbelievable."

"Yeah, well. It definitely was. Hey you know what? I've got an extra copy if you'd like." He reached into his duffel and pulled out a paperback with American flag imprints all over it. X graciously accepted.

"It's just crazy. I mean, like Iraq today. That was the cradle of civilization thousands of years ago, and now it's the place young men go to die. Thousands and thousands."

"You're not wrong. But soldiers don't go there to die. They go because they believe in something. Some know it better than others. Some may just feel like killing. Some do genuinely want to die. But I'll bet you seven out of ten out there want to fight for something. Something real, you know?"

"I think so, yeah. I guess so. Man, I'm excited to read this. Thank you, man. Thank you."

X became genuinely invigorated then. Soldiers often had that effect on him. He'd always wanted to serve, always wanted to fight for something, but he'd also been raised into a family where it simply wasn't discussed as an option. His parents were too far-gone into the left with so many other Midwestern mothers and fathers. It was understandable, and he didn't hold it against his parents in the least, but he'd always wanted to know what it felt like. Maybe it all boils down to the male writer wishing he were Hemingway at some time or another; but X hated that idea.

After that the ride was better. They didn't speak much beyond that conversation, but the rest of the ride seemed to have some connection. X didn't tell him about his own writing, or how he wanted so desperately to be published like he was, because it didn't seem to matter. His writing would never be X's writing, nor X's his. They were on different planets in a great many ways, but that winter evening sat together, staring out at the cold windows with paperbacks and mild grins across their lips. X pulled on the hooded sweatshirt he'd been using for a pillow and began to brace himself for the abrasive cold of Minnesota's winter at night. They were just stops shy of St. Paul, where his sister was scheduled to pick him up.

Leaving the Amtrak station, he felt a certain sensation of letting it all go. X's sister stood there clad in the parka she'd worn the last five or so winters. She didn't move from the car's headlights and somehow, they both knew why. He was to walk through the snow to her and give her one of those long hugs where neither soul says a thing, and everything is insinuated at once. X breathed in the cold Northern air and smiled at her as she gave yet another hug. He was home.

"How was it?" She shouted over the wind.

"Ah, you know. *Long.* Let's go..." X said. They slid into the car, she in the driver's seat, him the passenger, and he looked back to find his pup Jessie nestled into the backseat. He immediately climbed over the seat and wrestled around with her back there while his sister drove on, playing Elliott Smith and humming softly.

The dog slobbered all over his face. A Newfoundland, and every bit as massive as her kin. She had a thick black coat, which only let up in the center of her chest in a small tuft of white.

"How long was the train ride anyway?" Bea asked from the front seat as X settled in, Jessie in lap.

"Oh, I don't remember. Maybe six hours? It went by pretty fast. I met this soldier who wrote a book about Desert Storm. He gave me a copy."

"What? Really?"

"Yeah. It's in my bag. He was one of the soldiers that went into hellish situations first. A nice guy. A real nice guy."

"That's sweet. Yeah, I think my plane ride from France was just over eleven hours. Maybe? I don't remember. I just watched *Curb your Enthusiasm* and slept most of the way. Have you watched the new season yet?"

"Yeah. I downloaded it just before I left. Then I watched it cos I got so fucking bored. God it's been a weird semester. I'm so fucking relieved to be home..."

"Bad?"

"Nah, not particularly bad. Just not particularly good, either. I'm sure we'll talk about it. For now, let's just get home. I'm starving! Did you guys eat already?"

"Nope. We've been waiting for you, idiot."

"Yeah well. Merry Christmas to alllll." She drove along

humming to "Needle in the Hay," and X marveled at all the buildings of his youth. Things started to fall into place again. Cities like St. Paul may certainly be lacking in many respects, but they were comfortable there. X knew every street, every spread of land or field, and it was a relaxing thing to witness.

Seeing his mother again was odd after the brief cyber affair with the older woman. X kept thinking bizarre things and feeling terrible. Strange stomach pains. He could never admit to his family a great deal of the things he'd done—or might do—in life, and was mostly OK with that, but certain instances like this brought him face to face with an addled mind and made him feel nauseated.

Coming inside at first though, things were hardly terrible. Jessie ran up to the door as though she were guiding them, and the dark wood structure that was his father's for so many years looked as though it hadn't aged a day. His parents wrapped X up in their arms and all walked inside, immediately sitting down over glasses of wine to discuss the day's travels and postulations as to what in hell they were going to do with one another for the next month.

"You look tired. Doesn't he look tired?" His mother asked the room, "Have you been getting plenty of sleep, honey?" she asked. Little things like that, simple things which every mother asks every son, seemed alien, and X had to hold back the rush of nervous emotions that plagued his brain.

"Yeah, I guess. I mean, what does that mean?" He smiled. They laughed a bit and whatever tension might've existed seemed to flee.

"I don't know about you guys, but I want to hear about France!" their dad opted, obviously sensing the subtle discomforts and lags in conversation. He was good that way, a good man; never particularly outspoken, his father, but he made sure to speak up if the moment called for it.

"Yeah!" mom chimed in; her grin spread now beyond what's accepted as natural human facial function.

"Yeah. Totally!" X agreed, looking at Bea. Now it was *her turn*.

"Guhh, fine. I guess I saw this coming. I've been avoiding this conversation the last few days because I knew how badly mom and dad would want us all to be together when I told it. They've been ransacking my computer looking through all the photos and whatnot though. But yeah, I'm working at what I started doing there; designing apartments for a few clients consistently right at the hub of Parisian culture. What I'm really taken with, though, is blogging. Don't look at me like that, X. I'm serious! I've been taking photos of everything, and I have a decent enough camera, and I've been writing about it pretty seriously on there, like every day. It's a good feeling you know? Having an immediate audience like that? And I do advertising stuff online for the company I work for, so they've paid me a little extra to put their houses and apartments on there any time a photo really fits when I'm working. I've got a decent little following, you know? It's pretty cool." His sister sat there beaming, their parents rapt and not understanding a word she was saying. It was an image to make you weep, an image most people let pass as something Norman Rockwell might think up regarding the American family, but X knew better. Bea was an impressive girl. Impressive in ways he could never be. The Internet was a vile beast that continued to evade X. At times he bought into it, at times even genuinely tried to make something of himself using it, but he always came up short because at the root of X there is absolutely nothing but a human attempt and a sense of failure; while the Internet smacked of success. She was a good sibling, then, and he enjoyed sitting there fading in and out, imagining the couch beneath him melting away, and the dog slobbering on his right hand as it hung precariously over the couch going along. He enjoyed it because she knew X didn't have the capacity then to give full attention, and through some divine connection between them as kin, knew to carry on long enough so that Ma and Pop had their fill and they could peacefully get to sleep that evening without worrying over what time they'd wake up.

X felt a sense of something like sweet victory, the feeling of lying back down on his father's couch in the basement where he'd slept so many nights before. He thought vaguely of warriors in Ancient Rome, how they must have yearned so long for situations like his that wintry night, how they'd embellish every stretch they could possibly come up with on that well-sized sofa—draped in comforter and blanket, with several pillows, exactly how he'd slept so many nights in the past. He then thought of Frederick Exley, and his perpetual return to the *Davenport*, that tiny symbol of sanity for the man who'd seemingly lost everything, and as he turned on the television, heard the droning noise of Larry David's whine as the dog came into the room—an excited look in her eyes like always— he felt more connected with Exley, with genius, than he'd hoped in the earlier, passing familial mood, and something clicked. People will often surprise you that way, alive or dead: just at the moment you feel completely separated from humanity some tiny image will bring you right back to the center of it and you'll wish you were watching the Giants trounce some other team when you've never cared a lick for football. That was X's night of reconnection, and as he fell asleep with the warm breath of his sleeping pup and the tunneling monotony of midnight TV playing out away from his eyelids, he developed at first an urge to jump and sing his great fortune, and then that cold, sweet, burrowed taste of darkness crept over him and X submitted to rest.

After several days of essentially the same thing—TV-Sleep-Dinner-Deep Conversations with Bea-Browsing the Internet-Helping Bea with her blog-Walking—X received the manuscript in his father's mailbox. It was in one of those big yellow envelopes, nice and thick, with plastic bubbles to protect its contents. It was larger than he thought it'd be—the original draft was typed up on both sides of the paper on a typewriter—and when X lugged it inside, he felt a grand sense of accomplishment. He took it into his father's basement, cut it open with a Buck knife, and pulled out the novel.

The editor had written him a letter, which apparently listed any major flaws in the manuscript outright, which he ripped up into little slips of paper after reading the first line. Looking through the entirety of the work, he'd written notes along the sides of nearly every page and corrected any slip-ups with small notes atop the double-spaced markings. A sickness came over X, not because of how profuse the editorial marks were—that much he'd come to expect—but because he'd written his corrections in *purple* ink, and

X realized how horrid it all was. He wondered, was this some sort of comment on the frivolity of the work? Did he not warrant some glaring red markings throughout his opus? His heart sank.

His father had a small cedar closet in the back room of his basement, and X knew then just exactly what he'd need to do. He carried the pages and walked down the darkened hallway to that closet, opened it, and set the pages on the floor. He couldn't give some logical dissertation as to why the following made sense, as he was overwhelmed with horror at being exposed. A primal ritual, something that indicated X's full connection with the lesser species of this planet, something that made him feel virile, and that much better as an artist because of it. He pulled out his cock and, eyes closed every second, let go, covered the manuscript in piss. He opened up the pages with his left hand as he did it—in turn covering the left hand in urine—just to ensure that every single page would carry markings. The piss turned the manuscript into a swollen pile of rubbish momentarily, and X shook off the excess onto the carpet just to ward off any pages sticking together. After doing so he watched the brief notes his editor had inscribed on the front of the manuscript—the title page—drip down into obscure watercolor trails. X felt grateful, because you could still for all intents and purposes read what he had written, it now just took real effort.

His thinking was such: he didn't want anyone else to feel connected to this particular pile of pages. He wanted this urine stain to deter anyone from looking at the words as they stood. However furthermore, he wanted his connection with the manuscript to be that much more primal. X figured that when you're writing a novel it's typically your first draft which feels visceral, and the edits to follow measure up as merely little blips on the radar of having a final product that's worth reading. He didn't want this to happen, knowing his current mental state and that if he were unable to feel fully connected to this writing then he would be hopeless in trying to squeeze any merit out of the text.

He left it to dry there in the room and felt much better when it was over with. He felt grateful for the help the editor had given, at times even believed he had saved X's life as a writer for good, but this was *his* book, and he'd be damned if any stranger would give advice without X's own declaration of war, at the least some abrasion.

"Hey kid, how's it going?" His father was home.

"Alright, I got the manuscript back from my editor…"

"Oh yeah? He give you some good notes?"

"I guess so. We'll see. I can't really get into rewriting it just yet, it's too close to the last draft, you know?"

"I think so. What do you feel like doing tonight?"

"I don't know. *From Russia with Love*'s on."

"Yeah? Hey, wasn't that the director who did *Wait Until Dark*?"

"Yeah, I think so. Terence Young. That's probably my favorite Bond movie."

"Hell, you know mine. *Diamonds are Forevaaah*," he tried to belt it like Shirley Bassey.

"Hey, you know what I read? At the *Wait Until Dark* premieres in the old days, they would bring the lights in the theater down to 'the legal limit,' at the last twelve minutes of the movie, for dramatic effect or whatever. Do you remember when we used to watch that with Aunt Kay?"

"Oh yeah. Those last twelve minutes used to scare the bejeezus out of you kids. Uncle Bill would come in grabbing your ankles when Alan Arkin jumped across the screen. He used to scare your sister out of her seat!" Both laughed at the memory. The sun was shining through the iced-over windows and his father was dressed as so many other Midwestern fathers were dressed, in reddish flannel with thick tan cargos that held all his worldly possessions in them. "So, your mom and sister are out shopping. What should we do?"

"Um, I don't know. I kind of felt like taking a bath and reading a bit. Is that cool, maybe after we take Jessie for a walk?" At that the dog raised its head in the adjoining living room and walked over to join them in the kitchen.

"Yeah. Sounds good. What are you reading these days?"

"*Hannibal* by Thomas Harris. The last in the series. Well he's got the prequel, but who really cares?"

"Oh, I love those! Yeah, you take a bath, enjoy. I'll play piano a bit or something." Both went their separate ways and the morning that started with X's urinating all over his most prized possession culminated with him in the bathtub reading about murderers that love Bach, and his father playing Mozart's piano pieces through the floor below.

In X's mind, the trip got no better; the days became obstacles on the road to sleep. This sort of thing was always happening to him. Expectations ruined X. At one point over break he stayed up all night watching some fourteen hours of television before his brain started to feel what he termed *radioactive*. He felt afraid of telling his family anything about quitting the medication and as a result a sort of regression took place, he hid from them most of the break and nothing much occurred. He probably masturbated too much but what was too much? He walked around angry and listened to Ceremony's *Still Nothing Moves You* on headphones while violently punching the air. He enjoyed moments with the dog and read some paperbacks and watched films. He ate decently which was probably the greatest aspect of the trip, eating decently. He started to imagine having to travel back to Chicago about halfway through the break and this in turn seemed to speed up his time at home. He wasn't ungrateful for his time but seemed unable to appreciate it fully. He saw old friends, but this made things worse. He had a few decent conversations with his father, his mother, or Bea, but nothing seemed to really *strike* X during this period. He couldn't place it, a mixture probably of the loss of meds, his relationships, and constant consideration. He thought of the soldier on the train, of Gary, and realized why he'd always had such a fondness for the military life; his was such a directionless blur, to be forced to wake up at such-and-such an hour didn't seem half bad. He just sat there, pale. His family might've been concerned, he's not entirely sure. He started to see even this vacation as something to endure until something else presented itself, when suddenly it was over. There was no *Less Than Zero* chaos and he surprised himself through waves of unexpected comfort or contentment in what seemed his allotted misery; a cold, long winter away from applying himself, he slept and nearly never pulled aside the veil.

He experienced no great becoming on that trip and his parents only seemed to distance themselves more and more from whatever it was X turned into in Chicago.

X rode the Amtrak home on a cold Sunday morning, the sky was gray, his bags were heavy, and he felt just as miserable as he had the day he left, perhaps more so.

The ride was long, X met no exceptional human beings, and unlike the way home couldn't muster the energy to read a novel so he simply sat in the chair staring off into space most of the ride. Finally wilting he turned his laptop on and watched episodes of *Curb your Enthusiasm* he'd saved just for those lonely moments.

The train's monotonous drawl brought questions of sorrow to X's mind. Misery was like that of late, unexpected and industrial. No frills. Misery is the most furtive thing yet expelled on the people of this world. Misery is the end-all-be-all answer to those worthless questions all ask themselves on lonely days, through lonely trips home. Lonely, lonely, lonely. Creeps, creeps, creeps. You become drunk, and somehow this changes things. X knew this to be true. The first drafts, or the first meetings, whatever it may be; it gets you drunk, and somehow this changes things. He was lost there, lost here, lost anywhere. He was lost trying to sort out the good memories from the bad in an attempt to assemble a narrative, but he had that naïve self-assuredness of the promising novelist to back him—he paged through the dried editor's notes in fear. X became drunk on the train ride home from Union Station. Drunk with an ambiance of absolute terror. X looked at the metal buildings, dismayed by their obscene glory, and somehow out of this a sensible drunkenness came. He slumped down in the seat on the train as low as he might go. Several girls texted him, several lovely lovely girls. He told them they were lovely. Told them he wanted to marry them. Told them he wanted to fill homes with their children. And they all laughed in reverie, knowing he's just as drunk as he has been every time they spoke. Knowing that it's all fleeting, nothing will last, nothing ever does. He's tried to make it all last, tried to make the writing and the loving and the women and the drinking and the sex and the books and the movies all last, but it's all fleeting.

It all comes down to the things that stick from that onslaught of information and absolute lucid thought, those are the things that matter. Mark Twain wasn't a brilliant man because he wrote one book, or two, or ten; Mark Twain was a brilliant man because he remembered through the flux of his life those things most Americans choose to forget. For what is a writer if not a glorified *rememberer* of things come and gone? Or things *past*, for the Proustian knobs. X could taste it on that train ride, taste a new life, a new verve having left home yet again. He became drunk off of it, wanted to write symphonies. He wanted to sit down for coffee with Mahler, and Mailer, and Monet. He wanted to pull the bullets from van Gogh's chest and suck the soot from their blackened backs. He wanted, wanted, wanted. And for his want received a train filled with college students returning from breaks with that dead look in their eyes like they've just witnessed their parents fucking. Like an omen, some curse, X was to enjoy his life at its most when these glum fools were miserable; and the following weekend, when they'd fill the train with seeping pores of idiocy and lust, X would be Mr. Miserable off in the corner sulking and wishing them all death, permanent.

The girls sent messages, often laced with sexual innuendo; sometimes there were explicit sex scenes. While he rode the trains, he acted as though nothing much was happening in that tiny device at his fingertips. All forms of modern technology really just wind up being glorified ways to masturbate for X. He was OK with it though, enjoyed this new realm of sexuality. X was on Craigslist having chats with all sorts of weirdos. He didn't mind them; he was *of* them. He was their young son and they were teaching him all forms of lecherous perversion that he could carry into old age as a veteran pervert. X was filled to the brim with sexual thoughts on an almost daily basis and what something like sending a *sext* does for people like X is give them a quick fix right in broad daylight. It was like Cocteau's *Opium*, sitting there on the train as they moved fast, everything fast, to where he lived. He was getting away with the murder and assault on decency, he imagined, and was doing it with the click of his finger. *What ambition!*

Nurse Nancy has small firm breasts and beautiful little brown eyes. She looks like a squirrel. She brings X his vitamins and without water he gulps them and subsides back into his bright white hole.

The walls never stop talking. The faces never get any better, and the morning inches that much closer with each terrible night.
Friends do not exist, and this may likely be the best it will ever be for X.

X presses his temples together and implodes upon himself, feeling instantly better, instantly more alive. As X stands to rub his skin against the coarse fabric they provide. It's all a symptom of their vitamins, making X better and better at being himself every day.

X is smiling over the corpse of all his memories. A former self is forgotten and in its place is a flaming orb of sunlight, though no one knows the evil the sun possesses.

X stares through the eyes of Bea, a boring calm he cannot contain.

X stares through the eyes of his mother, and everyone is suddenly far too necessary.

X stares through the eyes of Emily, and soon cowers and runs.

X stands alone on a cliff above humanity, wilting to the lefts and rights of her confused mishaps and forgetful nature.

X jumps to the waters below only to be hoisted back by their waiting palms.

X crouches and accepts oblivion, cringing and wincing no more, he breaks and flies again.

If nobody kills me or thrills me soon. I'll die in your arms, under the cherry moon… X let the lyric pound through his psyche like some koan of modern discontent against the pangs of such an ugly world. He wrote and rewrote and turned the urine-laced pages one-by-one and still he was left with more. The stack was insurmountable, unbelievable, aggravating beyond discussion or logical discourse. He sat in his room naked with a towel beneath him on the bed working through the writing and alternating between the Microsoft Word document entitled simply *Vitruvian Nightmare*—as some sort of comic relief—and pages of 70s pornography when comic relief simply wasn't enough. X enjoyed listening to Prince, particularly the score from *Under the Cherry Moon*, or *Controversy*, or *Purple Rain*, because he knew what it was like to grow up in the middle of Minnesota with a head full of hells wanting to get away from it all. And so, under the cherry moon, X continued on through the manuscript several days after returning from the cities in his room, the door locked.

When strained, X needed a special kind of quiet to get any real work done, and his loft was so loud that any quiet that severe had to be accompanied by music at full volume. He was useless without it. Warren had already texted several times telling him to stop jerking off so that they might go grab a bite to eat, but X was into the work for the first time in what seemed like his entire life, and couldn't let it slip quite so easily.

Again, he faced those characters: the atheist, his family, his city, and all of it told in a functional way that let X feel connected; it left him feeling free to emphasize any particular point or go off into a world of tangential thought if his dissatisfaction called for it.

As he observed it, when you're writing the first books, you almost always imitate your favorites. This is a phenomenon that cannot be avoided. Even the best—the absolute *best*—were imitators at first. Mailer couldn't have more obviously sucked the marrow of Dos Passos and Tolstoy with his first novel. Even Céline—when one picked apart *Journey*—could be seen emulating Kafka, or perhaps Conrad. But it is precisely in the choices of who you emulate that you distinguish the ways you'll redefine *your* literature in your own way later on. X chose early on to emulate those like Fante, and Baldwin, and Sarton, and in his own hopeful way often thought of Pollock paintings as he wrote, in a perhaps futile attempt to create that literary answer to the painter he saw as God.

His mind wandered: *Sometimes it Snows in April* might be the best song ever written about human suffering. Prince went on— much like Bob Dylan—to proclaim his love for Jesus Christ in his later years, if X remembered right, and it's only when you look at his body of work that you understand just why somebody would do such a thing. Judging his actions based on the presumption that he was at least an agnostic in the days of his highest eminence, of course. When you listen to a song like the aforementioned, however, something so striking, so emotionally sincere, and yet so obscure and abstract that it can only be taken as personal, you understand with what depth it was created, and thus can forgive the moments when even the greatest artists move from devout atheism—or whatever—to Christianity. It cannot be avoided for those souls—brave enough to live on the fringe of society for the most pivotal years of their life—to at some point, no, they most simply must go back, the Christian faith is—among its slew of shit and hypocrisy—a widely-known and apparently enticing organization.

Even X at times felt the fight to run back to church, to be back under his father's arm like when he was young. X resented god, *hated* god, but still there were days when those churches seemed warmer than any place on earth. When he'd finished writing that night, finished bleeding out over the laptop and those disgusting smelling pages, he walked outside his door with that in mind, with the knowledge that he could find comfort in something he also despised. He was primed and ready for the onslaught he would undoubtedly receive from Warren, and the following hours they'd spend out eating, or drinking, or whatever.

X saw the new Woody Allen movie then walked home. The theme of the film was obviously terribly important, and it left a grand impression on him by weakening his hesitation toward acerbic comedy; however, it could not be recalled easily, and X just didn't care. Anyway, he was walking home. He took the long way so that he wound up walking down Belmont passing bookstores and record stores, little shops selling pipes et cetera; little cafes and Jimmy Johns, Starbucks, and everything else. *That area of Chicago is a good place to spend your twenties*, he figured. There's a good element of weirdness to it, plenty of free spirits and crossdressers, queers and indiscernibles, and every imaginable race as X could guess, all walks of life came together in that place and neither had too much more, or less than any of the rest. It was a good place to think, the noise of it all brought thoughts closer and closer together and the lights above encroached in such a way that one was left only to stare at the stretch of sidewalk directly in front, or else be dumbstruck and sent into a spree of consumerama.

He'd developed several entirely different obsessions in that second half of winter in Chicago. The first was an appreciation and level of fascination for the trans crowd both in the city, and elsewhere. Somewhere reading an anecdote that Serge Gainsbourg spent his nights at trans clubs in Paris made this lifestyle grow in romance and importance. This may be true, X couldn't really say, but of the various individuals on that stretch of Belmont, X seemed to see the heart of humanity; all drew his eye. He figured he came to appreciate them because of how terrifically enigmatic they were. He'd spend evenings staring at Duchamp done up as Rrose Selavy attempting to access that tendency in himself. X always envied those persons so apparently separated from society in some taboo way. He'd always felt his separation deep in the gut, buried, so people with apparent physical differences that made certain unwise/ ancient bigots cringe always seemed to have the upper hand in life, to X. He came to sympathize with them for a different factor of that very same reason. When you're separated that way, X observed, strangers will only acknowledge your existence at times when it serves them. For transsexuals it was the businessmen visiting from out of town and they'd have to sneak up into their hotel rooms for odd fees and skitter off into the night as though the moment never happened, the businessman going back to his family the following day. That isn't right. That bothered X a great deal. He found the whole world of transsexuals to be endearing, and even touching in many ways. He'd wound up wanting to stab himself over most of the women he'd dated for some reason or other, so when he was able to look at these individuals that drift on the borderline of society and gender, he couldn't help but feel drawn. Most of them struck him as gorgeous human beings. Most of them seemed to be awfully kind. X welcomed their unconventionality and resented their stigmatization. After all, America was entirely absurd of late, entirely alien. The orange skin. The earrings that cause your ears to turn green. The tattoos on lower backs of the biohazard logo. The haircuts. The constant attempts to revitalize with surgeries and injections. Gender had become something vague, and illusory. And as far as sex, X really couldn't bother with what anybody wanted anymore in the bedroom. Couldn't it all be *different* each night as well? Couldn't we want men some nights? Women others? And some sort of combination on the weekends? X welcomed ambivalence, detested normalcy.

Another obsession was a pounding desire to fall in love with some fully established member of a prestigious foreign ballet. Somehow there was etched in his skull a memory of the description of what ballet dancers endure; their feet, their bodies crippled by the endeavor, and it was from this place of empathy that he developed a fondness for Sylvia Azzoni, and watching her perform seemed to tear holes in his heart. Often, he found those artworks he only rudimentarily understood the most moving, and while he'd read biographies of various dancers and attempted to understand the mechanics of their work, he retained a distance that seemed to amplify what these individuals put forth.

It wasn't working. X was trying to write the story of a man he met one day on the train—they'd discussed Céline, and other things, and wound up spending the evening drinking wine at a small café near his place. X kissed him after their night, which is why he tried to write it, tried to convey his thought process regarding the opposite sex et al., but it wasn't working. He simply could not *write* certain elements of his psyche without feeling he was lying to himself, lying to all. To explain this would be to explain the secret of every liar throughout the past hundred or so years, he figured, and so abandoned his efforts, simply noting that he did enjoy the hours with that man, and he did not regret giving him a rather long, drawn out kiss at the end of the date—for that became what it was—and went home feeling good to have yet another secret under his belt.

Anyway, another day probably started, and X was probably being some pervert, trying to assemble his manuscript and beginning a reflection on his own upbringing. At best he would assemble shoddy recollections here and there, while continuing his revisions, attending class, doing little else but masturbating and watching the films of Gaspar Noe, reading Renata Adler.

Emily was packing up her things to move home one evening. X was sitting on the couch watching *The Simpsons* when suddenly she drew him into her bedroom. They pursued one another's deviance, wore one another out in sweat and mindlessness; she, at times, employing items apparently scattered around the bed; he submitting to her and welcoming this mania. She was leaving soon, and they fucked as if all was lost. Suddenly the intimacy struck him as terribly sad, nonetheless they continued. X hated saying goodbye and laughed to himself after they'd finished, wishing his various miserable goodbyes and the resulting daylong pallor could've felt as exhausting as sex with her. He realized he possessed a sort of love for Emily. Nothing too substantial, to be sure, but they were similar in many ways. Both had lives elsewhere, both harbored small hatred in their guts that came out in morose comments and long nights, both were secretly apparently quite sexually endless, and he noted—as she lay across his stomach—that in another life they might've been quite happy together. Her sweat met his, quite silly and childish, the whole scene.

After a shower they toweled up, and Emily went to her room to put on the traveling clothes she'd saved for the plane tomorrow. He put on shorts and a shirt and walked back out into the living room to watch *The Simpsons* until she came out again.

They watched *Finding Forrester* that night, under a heavy afghan of his he'd stolen from some summer camp in his youth. The film typically gets a bad rap, as far as X could tell, and that night was the first time he'd ever seen it. Perhaps it was their sex— or the blissful illusory moments that followed the sex, rather—but he saw a depth to the film that evening which could not escape his memory. X observed it thus, you have Sean Connery, a man not typically sweet or genuine, playing this disenchanted, brilliant writer in a small neighborhood in New York City now filled with young mostly black guys who like to spend their days shooting hoops in the courts adjacent to his top floor apartment. He never leaves his home, and by cinematic happenstance one of these youths winds up inside it. Not only is this youth also a bit disaffected by his circumstances, he also happens to be a budding young scribe who's—again, *cinematically*—read all the greats at the young age of sixteen or so and writes these long journals dictating his life and times. X couldn't accept the movie geniuses, however, the *Good*

Will Hunting trope. Nobody—nobody worth reading anyway—reads *everything* by the time they're sixteen. It simply doesn't happen. Tolstoy *maybe*, Dostoyevsky *probably*, if you're particularly precocious and literary, but to quote Shaw and Twain and all the other romantic poets in a single breath without thinking seemed too perfect. He thought of Caulfield's anger at the movies. The memory, for writers, is not like the memory of, say, chemists. As a chemist you may feasibly memorize all the elements by such an age and be able to rattle them off with terrific speed, however as a writer if you can do so you've merely scraped the surface of what is really going on—in fact, you've approached writing with a mind better suited for chemistry, to X's mind—but still, the movie was deeply effective at being a general encouragement to young promising intellectuals, and it gave a portrait of alternate worlds closely set that should always be remembered, but as X figured, sometimes unbelievable.

As the film transpires, the young man and Sean Connery wind up vouching for each other and in their respective ways begin writing masterworks of entirely different caliber. Connery's Forrester winds up having been quite sick for some months, and by the film's ending he's dead. Connery is a sort of Salinger type, who's written a masterpiece at a young—Salinger wasn't young per se, but nonetheless—age, and thusly drifted into personal exile. He's apparently written other things, but only the one was published. This other work, and the initial novel, weave their way into the themes of the film, but it's only worth mentioning at this late state because with the movie's close the young man receives a package from the then-dead Connery containing the draft of his second book—dramatically titled *Sunrise*—the foreword to which is to be written by our disaffected youth.

Perhaps it isn't as good as X perceived it post-coitus, but as a movie to inspire it still remains top in his mind. That night when Emily went to sleep, and his roommates had all returned and gone to bed themselves—likely at four AM—he walked up Belmont all the way to the lakefront talking with himself about the nature of being a writer and believing in himself, coming to a personal consensus that there truly was nothing else in the world for him, and that if he hoped to make it he'd simply have to endure and wait for some sort of understanding to reach him, at which point he'd grab hold and never let go.

X was being interviewed by Charlie Rose in his head and extolling him for being so gracious in accepting X as a patron of his fine TV show. Really X was walking down Wellington Avenue on the Near North Side with a sneer and the side of his mouth perpetually murmuring the following conversation, on the way to some movie at the Landmark Theater on Clark: "No, you see, the method is absolute and total madness. Or is that the message? Well anyway, the method to the madness, or the method to the message, or whatever it is I'm trying to convey when I sit down and write a book is that of Total-Uninhibited-Madness. I prefer it. Hell, I *love* it. I worship madness. I adore it; I treat it as though it were the only woman I'll ever love. You understand what I mean, don't you? No? What I mean, Charlie—what I *mean*, friend—is that at the root of every man and woman, when he or she is truly staring into the depths of his or herself, there is a chaos so profound and acute in its message that most people spend their lives on one single trek attempting to evade this fact, while almost none are successful. Madness is the thing that drives an alcoholic to relapse after months of sobriety; it is the thing that causes us both to murder, and to love; it is the inherent anxiety we feel at the bettering, or worsening of our lives; and it is the one element present in all truly worthwhile fiction ever written in this world and it will remain so until books are entirely burned by things like Kindles and bureaucrats with lazy dispositions. The book—or the painting, or the album—is essentially an act of madness personified. We do not seek, when creating art, to make something that is entirely sane, or attainable for the general public. We, as artists, seek to create something that is unforeseen, that is unbelievable, and that is accordingly sought by enough of a public to keep our miserable selves afloat! And that is why I'm miserable, I suppose. It's probably why Hemingway killed himself, and why most others will kill themselves, because the very act of confronting this madness—this *chaos*—for one's entire life is not only draining, it's a near impossibility. So yes, the method is madness.

"As far as influences are concerned, I've taken both stances in the matter; that of Salinger—that an author should simply stand in a room (was it a room?) and shout their favorite writers at the top of their lungs, for the world to record; and that of whomsoever else—that one should carry one's influences close to one's heart and unveil them at small inopportune times for the public so that if they're truly dedicated they can pick up the scraps of the writer's incessant searching for more and more interesting and recondite scribes throughout the centuries. For practicality's sake, I've decided to take the former stance, Chuck. And I'll do this here for you now, for only the cameraman and us, and fifteen million people in the world to hear: FANTE, SARTON, EXLEY, BALDWIN, ELLIS, HEMINGWAY, THOMPSON, CAVAFY, NABOKOV, PESSOA, ADLER, DIDION, TARTT, COCTEAU, and, for my sanity, EARL MAC RAUCH. Those are the bastards that have stuck with me the longest and will likely stick with me until my last breath of life in this miserable world. But I must also note now that such things are ever-changing. To assume that a writer should only ever be influenced by those authors he or she read when he or she was sixteen is as egregious as stating that an author should only ever hope to transcribe the trials one faces when sixteen, and it won't do. For instance, lately I've taken to reading Céline over again and it's striking me as it often does—terribly Célinean and misanthropic and decaying and dead—but that may change. I also recently picked up more Patrick White—in addition to the *Vivisector*—and it may happen that in his way he's the writer that carries me through another year of misery. You see, Charles, this is the benefit of picking a field such as literature as your life's blood: things never get much better or worse than they already are—which is pretty bad—and thus you're always looking for that one book to pick up at a used bookstore which will save the day, and you're always hoping to write that one novel which will forever quiet the thinking that fills the pages."

He was too close to the theater to continue on having the conversation. That particular Landmark was, on the outside, a beautiful sight. Inside one must ride several escalators before you even reached the floor which shows films, but outside it was lit up in all the grandeur of a movie house in the days of John Dillinger—the *Biograph*, where he was gunned down, was mere blocks away—and X relished those few moments on the sidewalk lit up by the glow of Hollywood from all the way here in Old Chicago. Inside, as noted, it was perhaps less breathtaking, but once you were upstairs, had purchased your ticket, bought popcorn and a Diet Coke—large, no ice—and you'd set everything down in the theater where you were to see a new film featuring Lambert Wilson, you decide that things could certainly be worse.

X liked to set down various possessions and food products before going to the bathroom before the film, and so did. Lambert Wilson was the man who played a rather satanic figure in one of the *Matrix* movies, with slicked back hair, and an unbelievably sinister demeanor. The movie X was seeing showed him as some sort of priest, and he felt vaguely interested. That sort of interest, though, is not important in retrospect, and thus went largely forgotten. Like the Christian Bale, Andy Kaufman debacle, X felt strangely suspended above himself in the theater, sometimes falling into the land of fleeting memories. All he retained was a moment when, briefly lost, the soundtrack of the film drifted into a piece of Swan Lake that brought tears to his eyes. X almost never cried, especially after his body's response to the absence of medication—a sort of retaining wall against real emotion, it seemed—and this stood out to him looking back, a turning point perhaps.

After the film X went to the Sedgwick stop on the train and walked through the Lincoln Park Zoo until he came out to these jagged concrete piers that jutted out into Lake Michigan like rusted knives.

The night was cold, several runners passed, and X hunched deeper into his hooded sweatshirt, his jacket surrounding against the weather. Chicago's skyline from the north was quite heady, you could see it extend all the way out to Navy Pier and back again to various hotels and skyscrapers. No matter X's mood, it stopped his breath.

The ice cracked beneath his feet and X put his hands into the pockets of his coat and looked up at falling snow. Chicago winters could be horrendous, and that one was certainly awful, however X hardly noticed seasonal shifts and meteorology in his current state. Then, and occasionally in bursts of wind-blown snow, it struck him. It was cold. One of the coldest winters in recent memory and he was constantly wearing heavier and heavier clothes to ward off the climate. Still, X tried not to notice and certainly not to care enough to wander, lamenting these conditions to neighbors. He became an *emotional* scape and as a result not one to notice physical surroundings beyond draping extra woolen shells on walking out the door.

So, he walked across the snow-caked beach, gazing stupidly at Chicago's towering heights and feeling all of a sudden like a terribly insignificant fool in the grand design. When you walk that way, when you let yourself drift into the drum-drum-drum of your footsteps and thus forget that other people are mere yards away, you tend to address such existentialisms.

X sat down on the beach, his ass and legs nice and cold on the noisy let of snow, and instantly felt better. Stupid actions, really stupid actions, he observed, can sometimes pay off in the end. You've got to let yourself fall into the cold snow of a Chicago beach on a cold February night to truly understand just how absurd it all is. You've got to slap yourself in the face in the mirror every now and again if you ever hope to look in the mirror and seriously find yourself a human being.

So that's what he did. He sat down in the cold, now contoured, snow and didn't worry for a minute about catching a cold, or pneumonia, or even what his mother would think of her son in such a stupid situation. She'd probably give him hot chocolate, probably try to make the bed for him, that sort of thing, but she wasn't there then and somehow even thinking of her made him lay back on the snow and look up at a starless night and start howling in a foolish stint of laughter and he didn't let up until he'd punched both hands down into the white and let them turn a good beet red and swell up just a bit.

He guessed that he had to go home, that it was getting late, that he might even be raped, or stabbed, in the Lincoln Park Zoo on the way back by some horrendous meth head, but none of it seemed to really resonate that evening. Perhaps it was the movies, perhaps it was that delusional state one sometimes drifts into after being so immersed in the lives of others, perhaps. X didn't care; he was sick of self-analysis and condemnation. X was dancing. X was writing a love letter from his gut in the air facing him. X was delusional, maybe, but he felt free.

He walked to the train station with cold haunches, and the park was nearly pitch black. He was certain at every corner of that long and winding place that he'd be stabbed, that at any moment the aforementioned meth head would come out of nowhere and tear through X's revelations and woolen cloaks; leaving him cowering in the park, moneyless, with the unrelenting notion that freedom is an impossible state to maintain in this place. As it actually happened: X walked to the train, saw a few friendly faces, and made it home, where Warren and he began discussing the interviewing process of bringing in a new roommate to replace Emily.

Emily was eventually replaced by a mid-twenties quasi-professional named Elena, who rather quickly went to bed with Hank, and prior to total indifference to the shifting roommate landscape X felt relief, realizing he could comfortably cease thinking of both of them.

While his roommates fucked each other and the world as he knew it seemed to otherwise fall apart, X felt compelled to write down a sort of statement of purposes—a Charles Foster Kane, so to speak—as to why he wrote the way he did, what writing might come next, and furthermore, why anybody should ever be interested in reading it.

He scrawled one night in long, manic pen strokes:

"I am a failure. Not just in the Beckettian sense, nor even in such a dire sense as Céline, but in a much simpler, more loving way. I have failed at almost every form of human interaction there is. Even sex with Emily was a failure. My fighting with academia is a failure. Everything I do is geared towards my becoming the nothing that I am, in my heart of hearts. This notion makes my failure that much more incessant and

glaring than the failures of the homeless or the drunk, the weary or even the lonely. For in my heart is failure at its most fundamental, just raring to unleash itself on this world, and my existence as a human being is basically the slow chipping away at this edifice of marble failures, which only lead to a core comprised of the worst depths of human failure in existence.

"But, wait, you got an editor, old boy! You pissed on your own manuscript; you must care! And to this, I can only counter that I do care, and caring, in itself, is an act of failure. Giving credence to some possibility of anything ever working out for you is an act of failure. Hell, look at these pages! It isn't a novel, it isn't a memoir, it isn't a biography or autobiography or work of non-fiction! It's nothing! A failure! The grandest failure any writer could ever hope to put down on paper. I give you little tastes of my real life, give you those scenes and then I take it upon myself to scream into your ear about absolutely nothing at all! My fake interviews with late night pundits! My dreams of the city! My ass plopped down on the snow-covered beach! All of these things are merely personified examples of my failures! With a capital F! And yet we've finished nothing, have we? Have we reached some sort of close? I should think not, you aren't satisfied, are you? I'm left ready to scrape hundreds more pages of that year in the failure's city, Chicago. It's a grand tale, a brilliant affair, and I'll do everything in my power to turn it into the massive pit of failure that it really is! I'll give you the existentialist rut we all seek to rot in by the end of our lives! I'll give you a taste of the medicine we all seek in drugs, and sex, and days and nights spent in the backseats of movie theaters! And, O loving reader, someday you'll pay to hear about it! That day won't come until long after I'm dead, though, and because of that my manuscripts will tend to be long and ambling around nothingness very much like this particular treatise, which I've come to call Shadows to the Light, the closest thing to my real life I'll ever wish to give to the world."

X was losing perspective, though he continued to write in this way.

Stranger things started happening that spring semester. The first thing was, X began swallowing every single heads-up penny that he came across. The second was, he began drinking tall cups of his own urine every evening in the loft in the quiet of his comfortable white room.

The first penny he swallowed came on what he remembers as the first sunny day since winter had ravaged the landscape, it might have been in late March. X was walking downtown, and the first thing he noticed was a small bird—dead—on the sidewalk in front of him. He picked up the bird and put it in the zipper pocket of his coat. Then, several steps forward, X noticed a heads-up penny and, remembering those incessant lectures of his youth, picked it up and put it heads-up into his mouth, utilizing throat muscles to give it a slow chug down into his stomach. The penny went down without much of a struggle, and X began playing with Peter—the name he gave the little bird—in his pocket as he walked along the sunlit afternoon streets of Grant Park.

Eventually he came to a bridge and, deciding it was best, pulled Peter from his pocket, gave him a minor vigil, and pulled his head off. That was the first head he'd pulled from an animal, and it came off without much resistance. Minute entrails followed with the pull and, feeling rather rotten about the whole ordeal, he threw the bird into a bush and gave it a lofty air kiss goodbye.

The penny sat in his stomach though and gave X no gastronomic problems that he could discern. He walked along then, knowing he'd likely swallow every heads-up penny he came across for a good long while, all the while rattling off the definitions of words that were giving him trouble. "Amanuensis: the transcriber of one's dictations. Satyriasis: the male equivalent of Nymphomania, or hyper-sexuality, being *overly* sexual. Karl Marx coined the notion of religion being the opiate of the masses. Freud was a pop psychologist, an asshole. Peremptory means certain, as in a judge; *he made the peremptory decision to jail the crooks.* An Arbiter is the overseer, or judge, of any society." Oftentimes one definition snowballed into the other, and it became a sort of word association game of obsessing as to whether he knew enough just yet.

The urine drinking was less frivolous in the ways it came about. X was sitting in his room one evening after working on the manuscript for several hours, watching pornography in a perfunctory way and sort of upping the ante with every search entered in. Starting with something more every day, say, eventually winding up with poorly lit rooms and men or women producing then tasting their own urine. X thought of rumors he'd heard of J.D. Salinger and this tendency; thought of stories of friends and their more wild better halves—it was always their boy/girlfriend who suggested they try something like this, something unconventional, always the person not then in the room, X observed—thought of things like the oft-mentioned sterility of the stuff, and became so convinced watching an anonymous German woman sitting out near a garden, apparently all by herself, when she drank the urine, that this was a *valid* act, a *human* act, that he must then try. He thought of that passage in *Jernigan* when its protagonist shoots himself in the hand, how he justifies it by saying he wanted to do *something that would be hard afterwards to pretend I hadn't done.* X liked this sort of thing, a limit-experience in a way, something to separate himself from the drone of humanity.

And he did it. He had a glass in his room which was previously filled up with beer, and X pissed in it one evening—making sure he wasn't going to masturbate for some time (at least a night's sleep) before or after, to ensure the integrity of his decision, the *un*sexuality of it—and swallowed it up rather fast, plugging his nose. It wasn't particularly awful, however X soon ascertained it was best to drink one's urine *cold*, for the body temperature at which he drank it made it taste of some odd mixture of wheatgrass and milk, not particularly pleasing. But he did it, tasted his urine. And felt all the better for it, felt ready to sit down and edit more of *Vitruvius*, and so he did. A stomach full of pennies and his own piss; X sat down and transcribed thirty or so pages that evening as *The Zombies* played their greatest hits into his headphones (X's favorites being "Butcher's Tale," and "Beechwood Park"). The editing came easily then, and thoughts of *making it* in the world had completely left him. When he finished and walked out into the living room, Elena and Warren were watching some Glenn Close film and X fixed some food, brought it back over, and sat there on the couch with them feeling entirely normal as they all sat there exchanging laughs about the movie and talking bullshit. A nice night.

When he was a boy X's best friend's name was Will, and he was originally from Alleston, Wisconsin. Alleston, Wisconsin is a tiny place, its only lake is filled with dead fish and the contents beyond that are mostly gas stations and churches, small apartment buildings. Will liked it though, spoke fondly of it. They were in class together in elementary school, some public school on the outskirts of St. Paul. Will moved to the cities to be closer to his father when he was six. His father was a truck-driver, drove all over the country, and Will's mother was able to take over the home activities while he was out on the road, this arrangement resulting in a trial separation for a time. After a while the family was brought back together. Will had a younger sister, X can't remember her name now, but she was his first crush. He was seven when he started really hanging out over at Will's place, and she was a year younger. Her and Will were obviously close, even then X knew how wrong it seemed. X used to do stupid things, like kiss her on the cheek or hold her in his lap like they were husband and wife. One time he kissed her hand and she went down the stairs yelling about how he'd kissed her. X bit his hand and ran down after jokingly saying she bit him. The family believed him, and nothing ever came from it, but it was largely those moments when he first realized how guilt functions in a person. They were just kids, but he felt manipulative, strange, like he was lying to Will and being bad all over.

X had a penchant for collecting basketball cards, as did Will, and after school they'd walk to a store that sold packs for around two bucks. Each pack had one extremely good card, and about fifteen less-than cards. They'd open up the packs, go straight for that card in the back— sitting on the curb around the back of the shopping center—usually pulling out a famous point guard or the like and exchanging cards with never-ending smiles across their faces.

Will was always interested in the military. In fact, as far as X now knew, he's currently serving overseas; but they haven't actually spoken for around fifteen years. He'd collect little knives and Zippo lighters and when his parents were gone, they'd sit in his room playing with the cards they didn't care about; lighting them on fire or throwing knives at them tacked up on the wall.

X once visited Alleston with Will and his mother. Will's younger sister came along, but she spent the entire trip with their grandma sitting on her lap and watching *The Lion King* over and over again. Will and X spent the trip walking around a pond full of dead fish. He pulled dead fish from it and Will handed him a knife, egging X on as he stabbed its eyes out; cut out its guts, things like that. They'd throw the fish back into the pond afterwards and X would constantly be asking Will whether or not he thought they'd get in trouble for stabbing the fish, whether they'd think he was crazy or what, and Will always replied really coolly, saying how X was crazy, how he worried too much. Most things never change.

They went to a church in Alleston because that's what was done over the weekend. X didn't usually go to church with his family and it was the weirdest thing he could remember. These were bizarre, diehard Christians. They wore shirts with large numbers indicating favorite NASCAR drivers into church with gigantic 32 Oz. cups of coffee to sit with as their wives—all prettied up—would worship by singing and listening to a preacher who basically served as the town crier, giving everybody weekly updates on things, talking about AA meetings and such. It was a wild time for X. They sat in the back, and the room was painted this bright, amazing blue. Will's mom wasn't too strict about each of them paying attention or even standing up, so they wound up having thumb wars and talking about disgusting, playful things.

One summer day back in the cities Will was over at X's place. He suggested they do something X had never done before.

"What are they gonna care? We're kids! They aren't even gonna catch us!" He'd suggested that they break into one of his neighbor's houses and look around for criminals.

"I don't know, what if we get caught? That'd be awful!" Was all X could say to deter him. It didn't work.

The Bentham's lived a few houses down from him. To X, Will's parents never seemed happy when they were together. He knew from their cars that nobody was home but something about it made him feel pretty terrible. They walked around the back of the house, the grass was dry beneath their feet; it cracked and crisped as though it were the dead of winter. The hot sun seemed bright as death when Will egged X on to slide the glass door open at the back of this quiet home.

It gave quite easily, and with a slide they were inside the place. The first thing he did was listen, while Will started crouching around *like he was some kind of spy. X was listening for somebody, swearing that somebody was home, swearing they were doomed, and yet he didn't actually hear a thing. The first place they went was down in the basement. They turned on the lights, looked around; everything seemed awful scary to X, his stomach was violent. He felt even worse than he had outside, his body apparently rebelling against this action. He didn't know it then, but he suffered from extreme anxiety.*

It came in these awful fits, when his heart began to pound so much that it went up into his head and he couldn't even think. When this happened, he felt like he had to do something, but anything he attempted left him feeling cold, sweaty; his skin almost seemed to move. That was how he felt that day, alien and frightened and his stomach like it was about to eat itself. Will egged him on, they kept walking around, went into the back rooms of that place and walked across the concrete floor into the father's shop, stared at the shelves full of jars and things they didn't understand; drills and such.

They heard those noises you always hear in houses, cracks and creaks inherent to any home whether people are inside or not. X became terrified and tried slowly to make Will leave the place.

"Hold on, we've gotta get a souvenir!" Will said, a smile on his face as though he now knew exactly why they'd come.

The Bentham's had the most expensive set of toys X had ever seen. One, particularly rare, was this bull, and the father kept it in this glass case down in their basement. X knew what Will was thinking and he'd never been more scared than in that moment down in the basement with Will's face glowing over that glass like some kind of demented television wizard.

"C'mon Will! We can't take that! They'll know! They'll know!" He was desperate to get out.

"Ahh shut up, will ya? It's a toy! They aren't gonna know! Unless you tell. So, don't tell, and we'll be fine!" He'd pulled the glass cover from the toy. X knew what would happen if he didn't do anything. He knew that the nerves would eat him up inside, knew that he'd be ruined for sure and he'd fold and tell his parents the whole thing.

"Put it back," he said, clenching fists; they were all filled up with sweat.

"Put it back? Says you!"

X grabbed him by his shirt.

"Put it back!" X repeated. He was taller than Will, much bigger. He never really realized it until that moment though, how much he might hurt someone.

"What? Why? Why can't we take it? They aren't gonna use it!"

"Put it back!" X said with a finality that surprised him. And then, as though the moment wouldn't end unless he did something, really did something, X punched Will across his face as hard as he could. That was the first time he ever had to hit anybody, and when Will came back up his nose was dripping blood all over the floor.

"Look what you did! We gotta clean this up!"

X went to wiping up the blood on the floor and put Will's shirt up over his nose. When it was clean, he pushed him and they ran out of there, but not before X put the glass cover back on the toy and left it exactly as they'd found it.

"Sorry, Will. Jesus, I'm sorry." X said, Will was walking away from him in an awful fit. They were out of their backyard and closer to his house.

"I hate you! I hate you! Stay away from me!" Will screamed and ran to the front of the house. X heard him pedaling away.

Will and X became friends again, of course. Kids don't really hold grudges. But X never totally forgave him for everything that happened that day. That was the first time X felt any real sense of right and wrong, and the feeling of Will's face behind his clenched fist was, aside from being in the hospital, one of the most vivid memories of his youth.

The way X sees it in retrospect, it's like this: he'd watched enough of the old Zorro show on TV Land and seen enough Hollywood movies to understand what it really meant to be a good guy, and a bad guy. And that's the thing, at a low, basic level, beyond pure capitalism, those movies and shows might have a fundamentally good—perhaps profound—message. It's similar to certain commandments, how you can take those ideas set forth and turn them into a gigantic fuck-all of existential religious confusion and create a lifetime of wars and fighting over what's said, but the actual words on the commandments are pretty basic, pretty easy to understand. That's what those movies laid out for X; those movies, those romantic TV shows, were his morality. And in the best ones, especially the old Zorro show, the hero was never completely good, he had his problems too. But what separated him from all the really bad guys was the fact that he didn't kill without reason, and in situations like the one X had endured with Will—he'd go so far, he'd sneak into a place for fun when he was a kid, but—he would not steal, and if he had to, he'd punch his best friend in the face to stop him from perpetuating the wrongness in the universe.

Did X comprehend any rightness or wrongness in the universe when he was seven? Absolutely not. Certainly not, however he did understand on a basic level what his heroes would have done at that moment and carried it out. He likes to think that's what all really noble people who let themselves become heroes have in their hearts; that in some completely backwards way the heroes of this world would smile on him punching Will in the face to keep him from stealing that toy from those people. He likes to think so, anyway.

After being assigned various stories to write, they were given a half-hour to draw out an introduction or the overall movement that struck after the exercises were completed. X finished the story in that half-hour. Unedited, unrevised, he turned it in one week later feeling confident that it was the best short story he'd ever write. The teacher loved it, cited it to the rest of the class as something of substance and risk, and X laughed inside at the fact that they were constantly insisting they edit, revise, and he'd managed to transcribe the thing directly from his notebook and impress this professor. He'd come later to realize his professor was likely just pitying X, the dark circles under his eyes, his tired manner, the story containing moment after moment of violence and hatred.

Back then, however, somehow that felt like the most logical note he could end on, and in turn he ceased attending all of his classes—even going so far at one point to write a teacher and tell him what a phony, what a hack, X thought he was. All of it cast in this dim light of passive aggressiveness that fueled him all the more to stay away from colleges, universities, and the like.

What was to be done? X did what any free human being does when he's been given yet more freedom and has no one to truly call his friends. He walked; he went for these terrifically long walks all around Chicago and looked at people in some new light of his own impishness and chemically depressed malaise. He read a bit; mostly the books he'd already finished and thus could trust to be nice and easy. He reread everything Bret Easton Ellis ever wrote, as well as the Hannibal Lecter books—*again*—and like any Good Samaritan who's lost all interest in the world he watched immense amounts of TV.

It can become a sort of art, the amount of TV one watches through stints of glazed-eyed depression. These days mankind has the benefit of having computers on which they can stream thousands of shows for hours and hours without fail in the comfort of their beds. However, even in Frederick Exley's day, he referred to it as a 'journey on a davenport', and thus seeking out TV as a logical response to unexpected misery is as American as apple pie and teenaged ghouls overdosing on amphetamines. To construct a sincere portrait of those weeks after he'd stopped going to school and taken up a large amount of TV screening one has to be very fair to each and every element of his pursuits. Thankfully—and with much effort—X had finished revising *Vitruvius*, and the feeling was rather lackadaisical, dosed, and upon finishing—though he sent out fifty or so more submissions—he retained no hope of ever getting that rotten beast published. He emailed the file to himself on his laptop—on which the work had been done—and after that deleted every stitch of writing saved on his hard drive. This felt right, wiping the slate clean that way. His sister would eventually come to scorn and admonish X for doing this, but he didn't then care. She didn't understand the wear of constantly looking your own work straight in the face with no payoff, no actual reason to keep it there in the first place beyond your own incessant revision and temperamental attempts at sending it out yet again and again. And thus, X felt safe to watch TV on his computer, and thus mounted it on the bed, tilted against his kneecaps as he lay on his side on the pillow, so that he might stare straight at whatever he chose to watch.

After that it was easy. He'd go out sometimes to the Dollar Tree to buy groceries, mostly coming home with boxes of candy and YooHoo because it was all he cared for (he began to imagine himself the poor man's Howard Hughes), but much of his time for those three weeks was spent lying in bed that way watching any number of different shows. After three or four days, however, there came the need to do something else with his hands, find some small way of entertaining the extremities of his physical self so that his mental self could continue succumbing to this contemporary black death. He decided on drawing pictures. X was never awfully skilled with visual artwork, however he had at least an original trust in his own skewed sight and saw that as incentive enough to fill several sketchbooks with fractured images during those long days.

This world—looking back on those awful, torpid months, he felt—can be rather hard on its young. When X was a teenager it was nice, easy, to get interested in things, and people were still open and willing enough to accept almost anybody, but since growing away from that, those people in his youth, he's realized what an effort certain companies have made to separate humans yet more from one another. Who he felt sorry for, then, were the kids in high school *now*, who can no longer communicate immediately to verify their status as human beings. They must affirm their status constantly on websites, and this act only pulls them further and further away from each other. X lamented those like Mark Zuckerberg, who may act like he's created a fantastic way for people to stay in touch, for daughters living across the sea to write home to their parents and keep them consoled; but Zuckerberg hasn't. What he's created is yet another hoop to jump through before anyone will even consider being your friend. That film about Facebook had recently been nominated for various awards, and X found that both the filmmaker—David Fincher, a supposedly serious auteur—and its actors were perpetuating and attempting to justify one man's creation of an absolutely unnecessary system and the resulting billions of dollars he received afterward—mind you, all this before he was *thirty*. So, fuck this, X thought. Fuck Mark Zuckerberg, fuck the creators of Twitter, fuck the Internet, fuck *designers*. He fantasized long bloody fistfights in the middle of nowhere to return to his humanity. He wanted to sacrifice himself, to experience crucifixion in the rain. Christ, it all made him sick.

And this, even in those days, was what constantly burned the skin of his brain. These sorts of inner existential rants and raves were part of the day. Even sitting in bed, even when he totally gave in to the notion of good old-fashioned American laziness and lying, he still couldn't help but become cruel and irate at the world as he saw it.

But Warren helped him out of it sometimes, "Hey man. Feel like seein' a movie?"

"Yes! *Not* the fucking Facebook movie, it sucked."

"What have you been doing, man? I mean, you're not going to classes?"

"Yeah...I don't know..."

"Well do you want me to set you up with a job or something? I could probably find you something downtown by me?" This was Warren, earnest, and consistently trying to ensure X wasn't on the brink of running back to Minnesota with his tail between his legs. X had begun feeling rather sick at times, and irritable, so this line of questioning got old rather fast.

"No. No, I don't need a job. I'm probably going home after this semester. I just can't fucking take school anymore man. If I hear one more thing from those bastards about what *real writing* is, I'm going to kill myself. It's as simple as that. You know?" X looked at him in the reflection of the Redline as they rode downtown, not entirely sure what it was Warren knew, or didn't know.

"I think I do. Listen man, you're young. You're really fucking young, and you've already written two books! I mean, when I was your age, I had a bad semester or two, living at the house with a ton of drunks and constantly showing up to class high, or hungover. I had that shit, you know? But you've got to get through it, know why?"

"Why's that, Warren?"

"Because, and you can quote me on this, it will never be like this ever again. Soon you will have to work, soon you'll have to pay for everything, soon you won't be able to read all the time. Soon, and it sounds like a dick thing to say, but it's true, soon you'll really have to grow up. And even if you get published, even if it does work out, you still have to deal with the fact that you can't just sit in your room all day doing whatever it is you do in there. You've got to get out more, man! Jesus… You're pale… You look like you haven't slept in weeks. Are you sure everything's OK?"

"Yeah, man. I'm fine. I'm just…I'm in a rut, I guess…" With that Warren seemed convinced enough and wrapped his arm round X's shoulder in a brotherly hug. They got off at Grand, downtown, and walked several blocks over to the AMC theater down near the river.

"What should we see?" Warren asked. Although a rather decisive person in many situations, Warren was as unsure and nervous as anyone when it came to things like movies.

"Let's see the newest, dumbest, most violent film playing," X mumbled.

"That's what I'm talking about! Fuck yeah man!" Warren paid for the tickets, and a drink and popcorn. X'd spent most of his money that week on something stupid, probably a big meal at some diner at five AM or something, he couldn't then recall. Maybe it was Alzheimer's.

"I want to spend the rest of my life in a movie theater, no exceptions," X mumbled as they sat down. Warren laughed and offered little observations about the theater's occupants and the leading man of the movie about to play. X ignored it, his stomach felt like he hadn't drunk anything in weeks, and he gulped down half the Coke in a couple seconds, still feeling sick.

The movie never stopped bleeding. From open to close there was blood on the screen and X'd never felt happier. Some days you want to laugh, some you want to cry, and some you simply want to watch a group of rich morons stab each other in interesting ways; his day fell into this latter category. Something was physically wrong with X, it was apparent, and from this emanated a violence that was acute and constant. The screen seemed to call to him in swaths of red death and obscene gestures. His thirst returned and he had to urinate. His stomach felt as if it had imploded or rotted out. Inside he thought the most violent things, immediately without consideration and when he looked to Warren realized how dire his condition had apparently become.

By the end of the film he was pouring sweat, and Warren checked to see if X was feeling alright. He had a smile across his face, and Warren felt X tensing in glee when each murder took place, and so he knew X must be doing just fine; just felt he had to ask, perhaps.

X was fine, he told him. He liked seeing people torn apart. He'd felt pretty sick lately—a new kind of sick, a weird kind of sick—and the only things that could entertain him were violence, music played as loudly as possible into headphones (though it's never loud enough when you need it to be) and mumbling chants of oddly arranged words and their definitions between hours of watching the drab moments transpire on that aluminum foil box of shit—the computer—the TV.

On his sickness: X didn't feel sick in any normal sense, and at times it began to worry him. As said, because of his condition he was rather irritable, and his stomach seemed a mess. He was consistently thirsty as all hell—some perceived itch in the pit of his stomach, X unable to scratch it or soothe it with any liquid—and oftentimes while in the shower he'd vomit. There were even moments when he was lying in bed, simply watching television, or looking at pornography, that he'd pass out for seconds at a time, waking up feeling terribly hot and not knowing how he'd arrived in such a position. It wasn't so bad as to be debilitating, but concerns were certainly growing.

When they got home the other roommates were partying, and X suddenly remembered just what tonight was. He never cared much about holidays—personal or otherwise—and even though his phone had buzzed all day with what he then assumed to be well-wishes and whatnot, he'd ignored it like most every day and continued on about his business. It was Friday night, at the end of March, and it was X's birthday.

Elena and Aaron and Hank and Warren had organized a party with all of X's—*their*—closest friends, and somehow through Warren's correspondence with his family had negotiated his birthday presents to be delivered all the way from Minnesota to the city. That feeling of walking into some apartment after a day of nothingness to suddenly be greeted by a party, X thought of Nick Carraway. X was happy to be thrown off that way, for it was the first time in many weeks he'd actually felt OK walking around the apartment filled with strangers and friends, drinking beers and singing along to Johnny Cash and Hank Williams as Aaron controlled the music. Aaron also walked around with his camera filming everybody, and X gave him these bleak little glares whenever he came near him. X socialized with many girls from school that he hadn't seen in quite a while. Many of them were in his classes and of course they all wondered where he'd been. X told them the usual stuff, that he was in a bit of a rut, that he didn't really know if he'd be coming back to M.U. and they all expressed their sadness at his absence. They wanted him there. He was funny. He made them enjoy classes more.

Now Elena had taken up a job at a rather shabby business which somehow existed in the same building as a strip club. She insisted she wasn't dancing there, and the roommates didn't ask any further, in fact didn't care. But as a result of her working in such close vicinity to said *dancers*, his party was comprised largely of girls still wearing leggings, high heels, and other fascinating garb. He didn't mind, and though many of his scholarly ilk made fun of them, X in turn told them they were fools, and stated his preference for the company of these gals. He has always liked it that way, with humans who ask nothing of you, and you needn't ask anything of them. It's a function that goes unnoticed in our society, and most of mankind should shift its perception drastically, in X's mind, to adore the whorish and janitorial among us; careers that truly impel the human race forward, he figured. He was sufficiently drunk by the time he delivered this Miller-esque sermon to a couch filled with dorks. X was having fun again.

He spent the evening in strange embraces with random skin; the world was whole once more.

He woke the next day and left his company to sleep as he walked through the obnoxiously bright apartment to the shower. X stood there with the water reddening his flesh for what must have been forty minutes. Warren came in at one point to take a shit, they exchanged pleasantries of the night's pursuits, and he went out. Eventually X vomited, his stomach becoming all the worse, and washed up the muck from the floor of the shower on his hands and knees in some sort of abstract prayer.

When he came out in his towel, another towel wrapped around his neck, the room was filled with all who'd slept at their place the night before. Girls looked alien, makeup and hair stuck to their cheeks in various places. Guys looked worse, tired, dirty, and stinking like a pack of wet dogs. And they all implored X, in what he found to be the most hilarious of images, to open up his birthday presents and afterwards—they informed him—they'd spend the day sitting around watching whatever movies X wanted. A good day.

The longer X is awake the more he desires the death of things around him. X does not care enough about the death of individuals. X cares about the melting of this furniture, the explosion of this television set, his own clothing slowly crisped away until all that's left is a naked ugly husk and the consciousness inside it. X has thought that sort of thing roughly ten thousand times over the past year. Has thought it, and meant it, and nothing changes.

Tonight, he'll sit and stare at the wall or the inside of his head and wonder why nobody picks him up.

Tonight, he'll sit and wait for someone to say something that pulls him outside himself and assures him he's quite the genius. Tonight, when X should be reading, he'll watch television. Tonight, he'll resent himself. Injecting medicine and checking his blood levels, things are different, and his awareness of his body is now a plague.

X now lives something like a simple life where there is a series of events; essentially A, B, and C, and within each of these events X presents himself in all his misery and that's about the gist. X walks. X is a walker. X does not have help. X does not have friends to pick him up. X walks from A to B to C and it is interesting; it is exciting.

Then X moved on.

X was going to walk down to the apartment he's been staying in and X was going to go to bed. When X got to the apartment he masturbated and took a shower and brushed his teeth with some special toothpaste that's supposed to help receding gums recover. X is not sure if it's working but after he did all this he sat at the computer and wrote two sonnets about memory.

They were not good sonnets as it's impossible to write a good sonnet anymore.

They were about memory, but they were also selections from his memory. Do you understand the distinction?

X thinks frequently of writing little things about men watching the women. They're required to clean the rooms in mental institutions, but nothing ever comes of it. X hurts other's feelings quite a lot. This is something he's adept at, so to speak. He doesn't like to watch sporting events and so he does not do this unless they are on where he happens to be doing something that he likes at least a bit more. Do you understand what he's saying?

Today he'll meet somebody, just before it becomes night, he'll meet somebody. He'll send himself email copies of the sonnets he's written, and something will result. Just what it is remains to be seen.

X has never claimed to be a good person. At least he doesn't think this is the case. X would not desire to purport this to you, or to anybody. X hopes this makes sense. He's not necessarily evil or amoral, but X does not have a prominent moral compass and he thinks a lot of it comes from his middle-class upbringing. X hopes this is OK.

"You should get a cat." Someone will say to X at some point in his life not knowing that he already owns a cat and loves him very much. They will detect a sadness in X that they've decided is directly related to the paucity of felines in his life and they will thus suggest that X should get a cat. He'll walk away from them and the whole friendship fully aware that he's going home to pet his cat and watch Repo Man.

Repo Man *is a film that makes X feel good.* Paris, Texas *is a film that makes X feel good while feeling bad. Harry Dean Stanton figures prominently in both of these films. Harry Dean Stanton could potentially provide X with all possible human emotion in just these two films if he decided the life of a hermit was for him and gave it all up.*

He's not quite ready to do this—give it all up, that is—but it's coming sooner than he realizes.

He'll become employed someplace that makes him tolerate his existence. He'll become married and suddenly the world won't seem quite so dark. He'll do these things and in fifteen years realize he's made a great mistake and find himself back where he was this moment while writing this because X never wanted such a job and such a wife and such a family and such a life and he'll come back to this place where he currently is—seated there, writing sonnets about memory—and he'll finish what he started.

No, he won't.

The coming scenes took place in a darker time, filled with too-bright rooms and plenty of good lying. He was seventeen, didn't care about much of anything and though he was medicated you wouldn't be able to tell the difference from previous years. A silence had set over him then, he became a fable of himself, a sort of cliché, and in a way, X relished those moments. He felt he could join, or disjoin, any particular groups that he chose; for the popular people—usually unaccepting—accepted X out of guilt because he was so far gone into his own miseries, and the unpopular people simply took him in as another one of their own. In those days at his father's house much of his time was spent flipping through books on punk rock like *American Hardcore*, and *Please Kill Me*, and he fell asleep most nights watching films like Penelope Spheeris' *Suburbia*, or *Decline of Western Civilization*, his favorite moments involving Exene Cervenka and John Doe, then heroes of his, and sometimes it was *Sid and Nancy*. He graciously took the medication, though, for when you're handed such a state of suffering—being hospitalized in years prior—you tend to have it burned into your brain, this notion that it might be better to acknowledge your capacity for suffering and deal with it like all the previous loonies of this universe, just so you can be better connected to the van Gogh set, etc.

The plan was—for X had missed quite a lot of high school—that he would test out of the years of his youth at a charter school, and would accordingly have more free time to work, and find just what it was he planned to do with himself. He already knew what he was going to do—still does, he feels—but as a means of appeasing his weary parents did what he could and slowly tested out of each and every subject left in high school.

The charter school was this chaotic thing in which underage kids were seen outside smoking every morning and the teachers were either college students that didn't care or older persons that cared too much and wound up stuck in an inner-city charter school as a result. One of them was a particularly nice old woman who gave X a great deal of help in that miserable time. He even—as a result of becoming close with her—spoke to the city council board expressing his thanks and admiration for programs the school he attended put forth. He enjoyed that place; met a good deal of friends to buy drugs from and wound up getting good and drunk with many of them on weekends. All in all, it was a comfortable environment; everyone had largely admitted to their faults and mistakes and accordingly the place had a very post-prison feel and nobody covered up their bullshit.

During this time X began having amplified doubts about the future. At first simple things, they compounded upon themselves consistently until he wound up wondering whether he'd be better off slitting his throat or cutting some large gash in one of his veins and taking a nice long bath in his father's basement. He didn't tell his father this, of course—didn't feel he could, after everything— but did express concern enough so that X was able to schedule bi-weekly appointments with a counselor in Rochester, at the Mayo Clinic.

X wanted to schedule appointments there for any of the obvious reasons, but also because he felt that the long drives would in turn give plenty of time to think before and after, and this idea so appealed to him that he wouldn't take no for an answer from his parents, and finally they set the things up. Memories of Hemingway leaving Mayo also persisted, headed straight for Ketchum, Idaho and death. Strange.

His counselor was an older woman, who specialized typically in adolescents with problems regarding drugs and alcohol—an *AODA* counselor, as they're called—but was willing to take him on to help out with whatever general problems he could be having.

The first day he drove there, it was after school one morning and the sky was still an ashen gray with hints of blue shining through making the air good and crisp with subtle tinges of sunlight all the while. His father bought X a car in his sixteenth year and he drove comfortably down the mostly vacant highway with his arm out the window and the wind running through his hair. He listened to Glenn Gould's *Goldberg Variations* on those drives, for whatever reason—it may have been the only CD left in the car—and he'd often laugh when he could hear Gould mumbling or whistling along on certain tracks. If you put it on right now, you'll find this quite true. Gould was known for running scalding water over his hands before playing—sometimes for an *hour*, X thought he remembered reading—and hearing that myth recently had only fueled his interest in the man's take on Bach and Mozart—the only composers at the time he could honestly feel he'd come to understand.

Although Rochester is certainly a jaunt from the Twin Cities, when there are only a slim few actual cities in your state, X thought, you come to know each of them quite well in youth. All Midwestern highways have come to look the same to X, and on halfway miserable days like that for weather he was more than comfortable in jeans and a gray T shirt driving along, knowing every single exit he'd need to take, not at all worried about time or gas, knowing he'd scheduled everything just right. Later X would be angry on the road, have trouble keeping focus with so much light and metal; this was simpler, he almost loved the highways.

"So, what exactly should we do? Do I start? I haven't seen a therapist in a long time. Sorry. I'm just pretty confused..." She was a friendly old gal, with welcoming eyes that gave the impression her arms were perpetually around your shoulders as you spoke. Her office was laden with all sorts of AA knick-knacks and small pictures proselytizing Serenity. X sat in a chair opposite her, a therapeutic tunnel apparently existing between them. He sipped at the coffee he'd bought downstairs and awaited her answer.

"Well you weren't referred to me, so there's no real way of moving forward excepting what you'd like to discuss. Whatever's on your mind, whatever you feel you'd like to work through, that's what I want to focus on." Her voice was soft, she didn't seem to immediately tire of covering these bases and in fact she seemed rapt at whatever it was he needed to get off his chest.

"Well, I don't know. I guess I came in today because, because

I'm sort of worried about my future. You know? Like I'm almost done testing out of high school—I live in St. Paul, but I guess you know that—and I haven't exactly committed to a college, or what I'll do next, you know?"

"And that has you worried? I see you're on an anti-depressant, and some anxiety medication? Do those seem to be helping?"

"I think so. I've taken medication for some time. I mean I'm sure you saw that I was hospitalized when I was younger for similar things. So, I've dealt with this stuff my whole life, I've known about the medication, and for most of my life I've taken the pills. I don't really see the pills as an issue anymore, you know? This feels like something deeper, like what if I go out into the world and bad things happen, what if I find out I'm not who I thought I was?"

"How do you mean? For instance, what is it you'd like to do when you go out into the world? And what *bad things* could impact these desires?"

"Well, I want to be a writer. I mean I've been writing a lot of stories, and poems lately, and I think that's what I want to do…"

"Couldn't you go to school for that?"

"Yeah, I guess I could. I guess I'm more worried about the other stuff. What if bad things happen to me? I keep picturing myself away from my father, and my sister, and my mother, and it all brings this terrible anxiety in my stomach; makes me feel like I'm standing on the edge of some cliff and I'm out there all alone. I know this is probably standard stuff I'm facing, you know? Like I'm aware that most kids my age go through these fears, but then there's that other fear…"

"*Other* fear?"

"Yeah, like I said, finding out I'm not who I thought I was? I worry about that way more. What if I find myself in some city, and all of a sudden, I start wanting to act violent? Or have sex with guys? Or, like—I'm sorry if this is weird—what if I just disappoint myself? What if I try really hard, and all I'm left with is the realization that I have nothing? That I *am* nothing? God, I hate the way I sound right now…"

"Well, you're right on one count, many people have fears like yours. Do you like writing though? Do you *enjoy* what it is you want to do?"

"Yeah. A lot, there's nothing else I'd rather do… "

"Well then, from my perspective, I can pretty honestly say that unless you *do* become unhinged, or anything so awful, you won't go wrong—or realize you're somebody else—as long as you're doing what it is you want to do more than anything. That I can promise you."

She was doing *it*; it seemed to resonate. And though he noticed it he didn't stop talking entirely either. X liked her, she had a good attitude, but like any counselor, she sought to turn his quandaries into solvable problems, and sought to give feasible answers to those—preferably accompanied by expensive reading material, he assumed—as soon as possible so that she could see her next patient. X told her about Jackson Pollock, and how initially he'd wanted to paint, and what eventually led him to writing. He told her about his ideas he wanted to write into novels, and the writers he loved. He told her about several of his friends and that he didn't really keep girlfriends because nobody seemed interested in him. He told her he'd heard about a school down in Chicago that sounded appealing, but really couldn't say one way or the other where he'd wind up next year. He told her about the old woman at his charter school and how much he enjoyed her company. By the end she seemed excited, stating how much further ahead he was than most people could ever hope to be, let alone realize it—an observation which of course means nothing to the person so far inside his own head; for him it's all lesser normalcy.

X meets a girl, Sarah, also depressed. X meets her and like a teenager falls in love too quickly and spends that year driving back and forth between her hometown of Amelie, Wisconsin, and his native Minnesota. The months are strange. He continues meeting with this counselor and occasionally feels as though he repeats himself. It isn't growth, exactly, but weathering, he feels. He's learning to accept the trials, the lack of passionate support and constant coddling. He loves Sarah. They spend time staring up at the sky and something erodes around X's heart and, unhinged, he feels strong, loved, and whole for months. This isn't a turning point for X but merely the beginning of a sequence of relationships exhausted before they can fully thrive. He thinks of images of flowers on screens, time lapsed. He thinks of many things, walks around, can't read much, applies to colleges. There's something lurking behind all this, he frequently imagines. What will it mean five years from now, ten? He isn't sure. He's blinded, teenaged, lost in love that doesn't have to end. He commits small crimes in the backs of cars, and nothing really matters. He is typical, in his insistence that he is atypical. This is the end of high school, the beginning of some vague twenty-first century adulthood that won't really take hold for years. It doesn't matter and yet nothing has mattered more. His consciousness, his willingness to lord over the movement of his life seems highly substantial while apparently impossible. He watches television with Sarah, and they feel older than they'll ever be together. He gets high, gets drunk, it's all strange and blurry and sort of enjoyable. He's lucky, he doesn't realize it. He wants to discuss this with his counselor but can't get beyond her insistence on some sort of group work or connection with people his own age. He can't really connect with people his own age, never really could. Sarah has a friend name Mike that he tries to connect with one weekend while visiting. They drive around listening to Iggy Pop on X's iPod and the night almost seems magical. It isn't. Something changes. He lets go. He doesn't put in the effort to be a friend and realizes he's happier alone, not entirely alone, well, maybe. He's not sure. The mess has become muddled by his own involvement in it and he wants to let go of the relationship, maybe. He watches films and films and films. He cannot focus on literature. He picks up novels by Dennis Cooper and they seem to help. They change his mind a bit, the world suddenly darker like this Sadean game space, he likes the emphasis on youth. He watches My Own Private Idaho *while sad and it apparently does the trick, something like that. He's nervous, growing nerves.*

Approaching Failure

"I bawled until I was hysterical, coughing great globs of phlegm into my hands, and knowing, as Henry James's Marcher knew forever about the beast that lurked in his soul, that if ever that life was going to come to me, that life that would be so much better than other men's, that it was going to come to me in that city, Chicago."

A Fan's Notes – Frederick Exley

X isn't bitter in Chicago because he enjoys it. He's not the *deletist* because there's some beauty in thinking of people as utter nothings and useless boors; this could not be further from the truth. He's cared with a stupefied glee in ways that most cannot. He's felt the touch of life and grim death on knuckles, and because of past events, has been forced to punch away that beauty with walls in apartments, and brick walls outside of them. He's tortured himself not out of masochism, or sadism, or sadomasochism, but out of practicality and the terrible knife wound of reality that comes when you know you could never have it as good as you once did. It is largely in the unknown details that reasons are put forth as to why he couldn't just go out looking for a replacement Sarah—even now in Chicago he cannot make sense of this—and for that confusion he must constantly apologize. He's very sorry. He's sorry to lie even as he feels strange truths so profound, they draw tears from previously dry—for months on end—eyes.

Eventually, X settled for M. U. in Chicago, figuring it would offer a chance to start over, to make a life as a writer and sincerely put all of his energies and mental faculties into that one thing. He supposes that he decided on the salve of academia because it was the one thing he seemed to have even the slightest knack for in the worst of bitter miseries at the thought of losing Sarah to the movements of life, to the doldrums of intimacy.

A beautiful goodbye to youth came when he moved into the

loft in those first weeks. Warren and X were just getting to know one another and—out of guilt, perhaps—he offered to take X upstairs to an event that was being put on. That day, incidentally, was the day he'd bought all of his textbooks, and thus he was absolutely dead broke. Warren said he'd pay for anything X wanted; said that he could tell he needed to do something; and after all that—after the momentary lapse into male bonding—he finally offered that X needed to quit sitting around jacking off and get out into the world and be somebody.

X laughed and went along with it. The room upstairs had seats from some diner and thus was quite comfortable and dimly lit. He liked a place like that, dimly lit so there's nothing much expected of you in the way of looks. He bought them both beers and they drank them slowly as droves of people moved in and out as some band performed up front; playing the song that they probably dreamed would put them over the edge and bring them immediate success. Warren told jokes then; he hadn't initially presented such hilarity and X was greatly relieved. He told first of his younger years, one of those *When I was yer age* moments. And for once X didn't immediately close his mind. He was just telling funny stories, using the opportunity of X's particular age to tell tales of bad sex and long nights drinking in a house full of wild-eyed college kids who were very much like himself. He told, too, that he'd recently broken up from what seemed—at the time—to be the relationship he'd carry with him his entire life, and it was then that X mentioned Sarah and the previous spring.

"Shit man, shit. It's absolutely terrible, right? And us, I mean look at our place! You can't talk in a place like that! Hell, you can't talk in a place like this! Look at us, a couple of crybabies while the band's on. That's how it goes, I guess. Sometimes you eat the bar and, well…"

"Sometimes your heart gets run over by a lawnmower and all you can do is sit there taking it." They laughed a blind laugh then, needing to close their eyes to misery and zone out, so to speak.

An evening presented itself, took shape. X and Warren developed sympathies for one another and made jokes about everything that came their way. X will always hold onto that memory, that human presence, as something that guided him through the later murk within Chicago, unable to make sense of it beyond the smiling glance of a new friend.

. . . You are X, the wet sugar bled virus. There will be new words. Words like hemoglobin, glucose, blood sugar will become diurnal. You will prick your fingers approaching millions of times in the life forthcoming and will likely lose sight, feet, or hands. A portion of you has rebelled against the whole and begun its campaign like Mailer's cancer. Irritability is common. Urine strange and sticky and frequent. Other illnesses come easy and stay longer; welcome them. You are X and the end of your life is perhaps beginning. It is medical now. Medicine will be considered, and this is strange, a nuisance, a plague. A plague? Images of some American sugared hell. Images of every meal reduced to its carbohydrate contents and constant excuses for self-pity. You will pity yourself and the irony of this will be its further separating effect on your relationships. Another consideration, another alteration in your expectations. The backs of boxes, cans, bottles of drink, et cetera, will become familiar and will become points of anger, aggression. Nutrition facts. You will consider them and become attuned to a language you don't care for. Your body will take on new aspects, new characters. Research will be done to find others equally afflicted; the world will lose its sense. Did you do this to yourself through some misstep? You likely did. Nothing is quite as sure as those words . . .

The sickness finally took such severe effect that X could barely open his eyes unless the room's lights were down to near total darkness. He imagined himself a leper, hiding in his space away from it all, not speaking with roommates for more than five minutes a week and spending the rest of his time either holding himself in tears, vomiting into the garbage can to the side of the bed, or sleeping. He researched leprosariums for comfort, found none. He'd managed one day to go to the grocery store and renew his prescription of sleeping pills, and those—taken in handfuls—managed to stall the sickness long enough that X could forget his existence momentarily and fall asleep. He was dying, is what it felt like. He felt as though his name, family, memories, beliefs, hopes of anything and everything else were going to die along with him and the sweat-filled sheets in whatever fit of fever this might have been.

One day, after not sleeping or eating through the night—as well as taking five Trazodones with no result—X was able to muster enough strength to do the thing that has made all the difference since. It was nearing five in the morning, and the gray sky was creeping under the door and into his bedroom as he lay there with torrential pains shooting through his skull. He got up, checked the balance on his bank card over the phone, packed a large duffel bag filled with everything he felt was needed to leave the rest behind, and left the apartment—leaving his keys on the table before walking out the door and hurrying down the staircase out onto Lincoln Avenue where he hailed a cab to drive him all the way to Union Station.

There was no beauty on that spring morning train ride back to St. Paul, and X can hardly recall the events which transpired as he stomached another six sleeping pills the second he got on board, swallowing them without a thing to drink—perhaps some death might reach him before facing his family. His thinking was warped. By the time they pulled into the station some six hours later he had become so groggy—his eyes so reddened—that the fellow next to him concernedly inquired whether he'd need any help in disembarking.

"Are you doing alright, kid?" He was an older man, one of those wise, smoke-cured voices you so seldom come across in the American Midwest.

"Yeah. Yeah, I'm fine. I just need to get home." X hadn't told his father of his arrival and didn't exactly know what the plan was once he got off the Amtrak. Because he hadn't eaten, his sickness hadn't gotten any worse, although by that time you couldn't have convinced him there was an upside to any portion of it; it all seemed redolent and marked with death.

His mother's home is much closer than his father's to the train station in St. Paul, so that after leaving the train, vomiting in the bushes several blocks away, and taking the longest piss he can since remember taking, X was only five minutes or so from her front door. It was the early afternoon, and the sun was hiding behind an ugly line of clouds that hung oppressively over her home. He knocked on her door, walked inside, and because of the paleness of his skin, the smell of vomit on his breath, and the rather impossible nature of his being home, his mother drove them to the hospital straight away—she called his father to inform of what she knew, and X was then told he would meet them in the emergency room.

It was all blank noise by then, when you've come back from one personal war or another and you're finally home you don't feel like relaying information, you just want to sleep; fall into your mother's arms, and sleep.

Because he'd told them outright of the sleeping pills he'd taken and the fact that he hadn't slept for some time, the doctors allowed X to simply doze off as they drew blood and examined him there in the too-bright lights of the emergency room. It was funny, X thought, as he thought about all the different occasions he'd wound up in hospitals or institutions; it always follows some terrible fit of madness that he's certain he'll never get out of, and the only way—of course—to leave this inherent chaos is to forfeit and subject himself entirely to the will of inevitable life. He fell into a deep, blind sleep.

What was wrong with X: according to the doctors, a viral infection had attacked his internal organs. Most of them—stomach, liver, etc.—had managed to recover, but unfortunately his pancreas simply wasn't strong enough, and he'd developed Type 1 Diabetes; a disease which—he was slowly informed—was highly treatable and nearly curable, and thus X could live a very normal life as long as he listened closely to what the doctors recommended as a result.

He was to stay home for a while, that was the first of it. Apparently, in his near comatose state—he was now feeling much more lucid, in fact nearly *relieved*—he'd divulged almost everything of the past several months, and what with his battles with the medication, and the urine drinking—he told them this—and the gastronomic nihilism—buying groceries at the Dollar Tree—he would simply have to stay on his old man's couch until everything was a little easier to handle.

They brought in sample needles for X to get used to, and jokingly he played around with them while his parents sat in stern discussions with the doctors. His doctor was an older man with prickly hair. X never liked that rotten bastard when he was a kid and now he seemed to have him by the blood and guts. X thought of ways to get back at him, thought of taking overdoses of all the medication he was given and fainting in front of his office some morning. X thought of killing himself quite intensely in the hospital. His parents would have to leave at times, and he'd be left watching daytime TV and reading the Thomas Harris paperbacks his father had brought at his request in the lonely hospital room. X's thoughts wandered: *When you become a diabetic, you're given quite a number of options to off yourself,* and X sometimes considers them still, however he never quite indulged in such urges. Suicide—in its way—is about power. It's about taking the last bit of power you might have in your miserable life and affirming it with the cold barrels of a shotgun, but insulin—fragrant and sinister as those needles were—never seemed to do the trick for X as a viable option to use when taking his own life; and power no longer seemed to exist to X.

He thought of Fante then. Hadn't he been cursed with this disease? And so long ago that it essentially meant certain death for the poor bastard… His wife, Joyce, had to transcribe his final novel, *Dreams from Bunker Hill*—images rushed through X's mind— feasible precedents—because John had lost the function of his eyes to diabetes. And what a book *Bunker Hill* came out to be… Better than most of his early work, and what heart it must take to dictate such an intimate thing without even the use of one's eyes to check and make sure you weren't being slandered…

And he thought of Exley. Poor Fred Exley in Avalon Valley for the first or second time, being forced to endure insulin shock therapy to work out some of his horrendous demons; Townes Van Zandt as well. They'd give these non-diabetic patients insulin to lower their blood sugar, and after several hours of this the patients would have sweated and lost their minds to such a degree that the doctors would have believed it to be an effective way to ward off mental disease. After the therapy, Exley and the other patients would gather around a lunch table and wolf down plates of sugar donuts covered with bottles of maple syrup, and it all made X so sad to still be alive.

He'd lost a year, that's what it was. He'd lost a year to this disease, without even knowing it. All the time that'd transpired since the infection began seemed lost in a sort of vortex of misery that he's wondered at every day since. To become diabetic was to lose a part of himself he never even knew existed. The doctors taught X how the others functioned, brought in a kid his age who knew what X was going through and had him give X the day-to-day routine as he understood it, as it would be. He went home with his father and mother and a large bag of medical equipment and over the next month—spent sleeping on his father's couch and recovering, starting back up on an antidepressant and meeting weekly with a local counselor—X managed to get his body back to its normal weight. Eyes were no longer black circles, but bright blue orbs. Hands no longer felt weak and twitchy, but strong and ready to address life. He walked every night that month, walked from his father's place to his mother's and back again, stopping in for water and—when his blood sugar was low—snacks to last the rest of his sojourn.

He got better, as they say, he recovered. His father was sour at him for lying. X couldn't blame him, or anyone. His mother's anger was immediately rectified the moment she'd heard what had happened to him physically, but for the old man it took a little longer to really make things OK.

In an attempt to speed up the process, X went with him to work most days, helping him with mindless tasks and attempting to keep himself busy by talking to his dad about the books he was reading and his plans for the next year.

"Don't over-exert yourself, kid. You've done a lot this month, but you've still got a long way to go. Your mother and I would rather you stay around here for the next year or so and get things together so we can avoid any problems like this in the future.

"I know it sucks, buddy, but you could've died if you hadn't come home when you did, and your mother and I, we just couldn't handle that..." X went to him then, and though they'd done it many times in those weeks, they hugged as though it was the first time either had felt the redemptive warmth of a son embracing the father. X began to cry, and his father lightly patted the back of his skull, encouraging X that all would soon be alright, that he was home now, that he'd be just fine.

The life of a bastard is really nothing more than a life like everybody else's. X wanted to be special still. X wanted to feel unique, and even manic, but there were now physical and emotional restrictions that kept such emotions largely at bay as that summer wore on and the sun started creeping out more and more.

His sister came to visit in the thick of July, and they spent ten days or so lying around in their father's yard while they worked on the garden. They lay in the grass reading books and talking about things and she accordingly scolded X for being such a moron and careless jerk regarding the finale of his time in Chicago. X apologized to her, told her that if he'd known anything, he wouldn't have been so foolish, and knowing his sincerity she let all things slide as she told him the elements she liked in books he'd given her, and those she simply detested.

They had dinners again and felt even more like a family than ever before. X wasn't quite ready to accept his existence with them—something in his mind would always keep him one step away from normalcy—but X also embraced the good times in St. Paul over that relatively calm summer in which he never saw a soul he knew aside from his immediate family.

X liked it that way, sometimes. Sometimes when you've incurred a personal tragedy, the only thing you can stand are the people you're biologically connected to. Friends would call, sure. The old roommates would often call and message him about the stuff he'd left behind, and seeing as he didn't know where he'd be in a year X decided to simply leave them be and assume they'd throw it all away.

X now walked around with needles on him at all times, which was still something to get used to. There's a surreptitiousness that he takes to quite readily. Before meals he injects himself beneath a table, say, or at the back of a movie theater he draws a needle from his pocket and injects himself in the belly before eating a large tub of popcorn. His diabetes is always approached with a kind of nihilism. He takes bad care of himself, but he is consistent about injecting himself, nonetheless. He doesn't like checking his blood sugars but does it at least daily to keep in order.

X came back to Chicago finally, and returned to school again for writing. He wasn't, might never be, entirely convinced by the coursework, or that any of his teachers felt particularly impressive, but compared with the time he spent vomiting blood every morning, these days were some of the best in his life.

Chicago's fall and the cold air settled in around him. Football season back on in America and around every street corner in his small neighborhood—where X lives alone, which he finds much more suitable—rumbles with passion for the Bears weekly. He enjoys it; takes long walks and listens to the howls of the crowds and imagines a different life with Frederick Exley in which they sit Sundays in Watertown, watching the Giants trounce the opposition while the bartender caters to their every wish. The leaves change and as you ride the train south from where X lives you can pass by Graceland cemetery and see hundreds of brilliant oranges and greens and reds and yellows balanced beneath the blue skies of afternoon while a day of classes awaits in the heart of Chicago's loop.

You endure, is about the long and short of it. Life presents a challenge, and you either dodge it entirely or face up to it. One way or another, you endure. And that's all X has ever sought to do. He now realizes that and maybe a bit of success is all life really amounts to. Then again, maybe not. Maybe there's more magic to it than any of us will ever allow ourselves to believe. Either way, you endure, you endure and you watch the leaves change each season and you take your medication and you attend class and you write the novel you'll call Shadows to the Light and you hope it will be something splendid, and when you write the final line—the final word in one long-winded argument—you contend that it is finished, and nothing written before it could end that way.

FLAMINGOS

a dramatic work

The Noisage is the Medium. An Introduction to FLAMINGOS.

In the last few years, Grant Maierhofer has become one of the more interesting, idiosyncratic, and prolific authors across the much diverse, active, independent, and happily uncategorizable 'expanded field' scene—of what I like to call 'fiction-thinkers'—which has been evolving since the early 2010s. Originally published in 2016, Flamingos is a short novel assembled from the concentration of narrative and stylistic relations between a constellation of texts attributed to the metaphorical dysphoria of nine almost-archetypal characters, which could be read as a disordered collection of recordings done by a mad therapist, boarded with his crew of lunatics, on a contemporary Stultifera Navis. As explained by Maierhofer himself, Flamingos was intended to become a context for screaming—a very accurate image of the performative framework experimental art has been pursuing for a while. In the 21st century, reading is screaming, and artistic texts provide the context not for the romantic or melancholic shouting in/to the void, but for the collective, serialized yet shared yell of the agonizing egos. Instead of attempting to control and unify a diversity of 'problematic' voices coming from the shattering of a socially prescribed single self, the literary text is now formally and thematically assuming a multiplicity of voices arriving from the future of communication, producing a breakdown not only in meaning but also in expression, plural by nature, continuously becoming a multitude of 'noisages.'

Flamingos points to the re-appropriation of the deterritorializing power of madness which had been re-territorialized into a normative mental health biotopos by neuropharmacology, neuropolitics and mainstream media-fiction. Its therapy-gone-wrong environment functions like a syntactically-staged heterotopic representation of our current society as spectacle-gone-wrong. This brings us back, of course, to Foucault and Deleuze, but also to Beckett, Ionesco, Artaud, Jarry, and many classic satyrists. And it seems of particular importance in a moment when 'reason' is often presented as the 'software for the show;' as something quantifiable that could be 'traded' instead of a fiction in progress.

Madness is a performance of the self when the self realizes that it is actually a shared act of synchronized cognition. It belongs in a chaotic band of accursed improvisers like those Michel Foucault describes in the first chapter of 'Madness and Civilization;' expelled from the haunted house of socialized individuality and consigned to drift perpetually in a Ship of Fools —Stultifera Navis: a strange 'drunken boat' that glides along the calm rivers of the Rhineland and the Flemish canals— which will be often represented in Renaissance drawings and engravings, with Hieronymus Bosch's painting as the most famous one. Confined on the ship—Foucault writes—from which there is no escape, the madman is delivered to the river with its thousand arms, the sea with its thousand roads, to that great uncertainty external to everything. He is a prisoner in the midst of what is the freest, the openest of routes: bound fast at the infinite crossroads. He is the Passenger par excellence: that is, the prisoner of the passage. And the land he will come to is unknown— as is, once he disembarks, the land from which he comes. He has his truth and his homeland only in that fruitless expanse between two countries that cannot belong to him.

Classical madness is closely related to the performative qualities of language as an accidentally furnished shelter against sensory bombardment, to the acid pleasure of the delirious stream of unchained nonsensical and senseless sentences, "Problem was I liked their babble…" says G.G., a character presented as "a criminal, involved with strains of black metal, survivalist," which, as explained by Deleuze and Guattari, organize themselves in a signifying chain which is more a jargon than a language, composed of nonsignifying elements that have a meaning or an effect of signification only in the large aggregates that they constitute through a linked drawing of elements, a partial dependence, and a superposition of relays.

In a very interesting collection of research notes about *Flamingos* Grant Maierhofer published in Necessary Fiction, he explains that he wanted an art a bit like life and stripped of tendencies toward understanding, the body and head rendered in text and the text as distillation of body and head —a performative thing. The idea of performing text is very important in Maierhofer's work, it became more evident in Flamingos, and it was further developed in different ways in the books that followed it: *GAG* (2017), *CLOG* (2018) and *Peripatet* (2019). Flamingos could be perfectly imagined as a play —there's even a Dramatis Personae list at the beginning— in which the characters project themselves on a group therapy like background. This creates a flexible environment (much like social media environments) where fragments might perfectly work as independent monologues, yet they might also contain dialogues and parallel digressions within themselves.

Classical madness is also related to the awkward performance of the body stepping outside of utilitarian demands to engage with a range of socially inadequate behaviors and pleasures. In an article published in 3:AM Magazine, Grant Maierhofer recounts his personal experience of reading Joyce's *Finnegans Wake*. Reading *Finnegans Wake*, he explains, is a bodily thing, and strangely so. I tend to find I'll begin with resistance, certain I'm misunderstanding every letter until suddenly a dreamy rhythm overtakes me and I'm able to stomach paragraphs in breaths. I'll often slow to crawls in turn and view the pages as discrete, visual, concrete passages rendered as micro- and macrocosmos for diligent poring and slack-jawed stupor alike. The text seems to work on these levels because Joyce had thought the bulk of his life about what printed text might venture to do. Reading and writing are, in fact, bodily things, although not many writers are fully aware of that. I would say that the great experimental and underground literary traditions —what Ronald Sukenick touted 'the rival tradition'— are, at least in part, an attempt to re-embody the literary practice, and Grant Maierhofer's books are wonderful examples of this kind of stylistic exploration.

This work will be a nightmare. You are no detective—says an anonymous patient in *Flamingos*. It comes as no surprise that one of the best descriptions of *Flamingos* has been written by the Swedish-American poet and translator Johannes Göransson, who has been theorizing about the new 'rhetorical punk' styles he has defined as 'atrocity kitsch.' This is a noir without the proper detective to piece back together the crime and its narrative, writes Göransson about *Flamingos*. This is self-surveillance under the influence of drugs, art, poetry. Without the narrative cure, the novel becomes sick. *Flamingos'* characters embrace the impossibility of the cure and celebrate the sudden joy of recognizing this impossibility and turning it into art. 'Art starts when you accept that,' as Joyelle McSweeney wrote, 'nothing can be undone, but everything can be done again, because the Artist cannot remove him or herself from the economy of Violence.' Vulnerability to Art is Vulnerability to Violence; that's what Vulnerability means: the ability to be wounded, to bear the mark of the wound, to suffer malignancy, and to issue malignant substances.

I find particularly interesting that the characters in Flamingos are allowed—they allow themselves— to be wrong. I believe this is a very important feature in our time—when most people are obsessed with paralyzing dichotomies such as truth/post-truth or facts/alternative facts. Actually, the power of punk (and madness) resides in accepting the likeliness of being wrong but going ahead anyway —the 'you-don't-need-to-know-how-to play' thing; just jump up on stage and do your best. In *Flamingos* everybody seems to admit being wrong—even Simon, the therapist—seems aware of playing a failing role: 'And I taught them. And I did not.' This is significant because the most important thing for keeping a 'sustainable' community may not be the acquiescence to a common truth, but the desire to implement an indeterminate network of reciprocal trust. It's possible to trust someone even while thinking that they're awfully wrong, and this might be both the essential requirement for a dissident, yet inclusive, socialization and the cognitive basis for a healthy skepticism. There's no way to tell apart noise from message anymore, everything turning into the metal joy of noisage, so maybe this is what the punk gesture means nowadays: allowing yourself to be wrong, letting the death drive flourish in metabolic vortices for a new life to emerge, being weird enough to catch joy and reason on their arrival... seeking life where there is none, coherence where there is just implosion, sanity where there is a list of ways your head simply does not fit.

There couldn't be a way out, but through, ends *Flamingos*. Only a multiple body of insubordination to escape from the shadow of code.

Germán Sierra, 2020

As you walk out of the valium of death
a sad feeling limps around your brain
funny farmers sowing seeds of discontent
pumping nerve gas around unfeeling veins

"Happy Farm" – Rudimentary Peni

A story? No. No stories, never again.

In Heaven Everything is Fine – Jeffrey DeShell

DRAMATIS PERSONAE

Patient – a neurotic poring over lived experience and print

Flamingo – a daughter, sunlit, driven by manias

Edmund – a viewer, a depressive, concerned with sight

G.G. – a criminal, involved with strains of black metal, survivalist

Attila – a driver, lover of his auntie, thinker

Simon – a healer, a messiah, M.D., D.C.L., L.L.D., Ph.D.

Haydn – a son, former love interest of Flamingo, caregiver

Eileen – a niece, preoccupied with bloodline, marked with loss

Olivier – a witness, Simon's cohort, misfit youth

A cackling life inside, a smear of bellylaughs spat back at tellings of doctors, explorers, manipulators. There He dictates with some solution. Spread through cities and guts and the entrails of homelives or families, the presence and he says what's done. Slid easily back into the comfort of loss—step one, repetition, regurgitation of psychobabble—we did His will to varying degrees of efficacy; he had his say and we were merely subjects. Out their eyes would look and sweep. Waves of grass and promise lumbered up against the buildings as streams of hope, possibility, taunt. His voice mad of distraction and mother's milk. His arms earthplates of welcome into what could be. Simon, not a man, not a man. Simon, our teething on his light and what would come. Simon, a future, a renewal. Burnt again and born again our bodies clayshells dripped of ideology to embrace the Father, embrace Simon. A plague of cure-alls, panaceas, SSRIs, MAO inhibitors, breathing exercises, consultants, meetings, rooms, plastic furniture, sweatdrops left from anxious bodies too medicated in various heats never converging. Simon, his own renewal never. Simon, constant drilling awareness of all minutiae and no substance building every hovelled life in cities. He heads south to find a grave in Florida; more followers to meet the beck and call. He topples amid manifesto language and yearns to beat back against the pulse of protest in his times. Simon, ever the miserable failure. Simon our Christ, our Cunt Fear our Cock Fear our Man Fear our Woman Fear our Plague Fear our Head Fear our Love Fear our Death Fear. Simon he lives and dies for his own sins, not ours. Simon's a polyglot mumble found in waves, in graves, in gutless darknesses beneath wherevers. Simon would wander etching missing notes to sidewalk wondering why they'd dropped in for thinking ever. Simon assembled the passage, the mode. Simon put together the festering, saw what might be done. Ordered and disordered whole gasping last breaths of fathers lost in death while the thumbs twiddled at the wheel of his auto outside belighted storefronts. Scrapped together and wrapped up to be found by some moralist of Hawthorne's gape and reach. There is no puzzle etched in chalk—it is his missive. It is fetish. It is leatherine. He's hobbled obsessed with evering death. His mother a jovial plot of mothers, a husking, a collective. His father whatever protest against the aforesaid, and mayhaps a bit of mistaking, mistaking. Simon doesn't plan our lives, just mumbles at the bodies while they pass.

PATIENT

You have begun to sift through notes to find something revealed. The incessant in this place, the schizophrene. You've attempted to grind meaning out of the gaggle; their therapies your only connective point. You have not *heard voices* so much as intuited nauseas. You've fed yourself on bad coffee spreads in hospital and within homes of loved ones kind enough to take you after hands began to slip. The world would not be righted. His take on things suddenly gained perspective, now a straitjacketed old man occasionally seen mumbling on newsfeeds about some great redemption. You began a search backward into heads, perhaps avoiding your own. With each change you only hoped to black your walls.

FLAMINGO

Call me Flamingo; whatever it was is fading. I sat atop where I happened to live just being. Outside my work inside my car I'd slug at sugary black liquids that energize. I programmed, encrypted. Where I existed was within a city no longer operating as a city, rather a pustule. His alterations to the landscape, the mentalities. I call it pustule and had no friends there. I walked like Travis in *Paris, Texas* in the clothing come across mostly in stores secondhand. No safety zone. *There will be no safety zone.* I had no commitments, had broken no marital code, to my thinking. Thirty-four years and my ex-husband and I got divorced when I turned thirty-one and told a falsehood regarding a pregnancy. He wouldn't shut his mouth about wanting to put children inside my medicated guts. He was an oafish man with long ambitions and consistently short haircuts who I met and engaged with physically, the result of a website that allowed couples to couple and put their parts to use.

PATIENT

Having no more patience for the journal, the diary, the anything approximating a brief lament quasi-essay interrogation of what you've read, watched, listened to, you enact this. An assemblage. Your research. The work. You do not care. It will exist time to time and will account for what has existed between times and times. It will not delve in any capacity. Let them face it: it is fairly dead; there is only now a pissy teenaged scrawl. Embittered voices asking after daddy.

FLAMINGO

I didn't ever love him but he collected bad films and we watched them and ate pizzas and there was something loving to it, I daresay. My teeth are goners like the betrothed as a result of meds and energetics. I feel such an urge to tell. We'd sworn in various ways not to unveil the various things he'd put inside our skulls. I watched footage of his ECT and guess I pitied the man. Perhaps before this I was converted. His reach was that entire. Picture the doctor describing the procedure as Simon's pinned to leather chair bound in cuffs of same just moments before his mouth is stuffed of rubber and his body seems to shake itself loose. Undefined gluey rivulets came forth and doctor returned to speak softly about its result, its promise, what might come to be expected. He'd acquired it on receiving permission to research this and more and used its grant money to record himself starved beneath his home in lurid shades.

EDMUND

I cannot profess to have *known* the man, or wake up and proceed as his follower. I do not do the "how I came to be this way" as is their wont, the ilk's wont, so here I piddle. The storied. Newsprint. I've burnt his telling to my brow and thus am culpable, required to speak whereof I do not know. Archivists have asked after the recordings. I'd pirated them occasionally for late viewings and meditation. I've kept them boxed with annotation; some home recordings from his trials.

ATTILA

Say for instance one weekend I visited my auntie where she lived and we came together? I'm not sure of preferred terminology in matters but I know where I stand. You live outside moralizing as such and a body like Simon comes easy. I've picked up a bit here and there; the rest I give to him and Auntie. I haven't seen much but you see enough sleeping amid thirty or more heaped metallic crates hauling whatever needed wherever. Simon came to me those nights. He'd driven to set funding aside; saw his route as shamanic. I'd followed briefly. Was then the learning took. Read a bit, not much. Lots on plague, sure. I guess I never shook the notion that the world had just, or was soon to just, lost most of its presence, say?

PATIENT

When you became roughly twenty-four and one-half years old you became a follower of *Star Trek*. It was late, and the fondness grew from a likeness you saw between its creator and images of L. Ron Hubbard—you needed religion. Hubbard's voice seemed to flood the sixties for you, this syrupy drawl, moneyed, tyrannical. Perhaps a surrogate father, though you're hesitant to welcome it. Grown men sitting before microphones arguing over the state of things; the mind, humanity, children. It might be here your vulnerability began.

SIMON

And I taught them. And did not. To resist their obsessive teeth. To grind their desires to a bulb, then watch it burn. And there is no hemlock, no way out; I, therefore, walk aside with the mud and silt, and you become my enemies. I do not know how to speak it, to think, "I, Simon, become difference, or God." I have nothing to say. You and I cannot judge you and I. Now the time comes, I think, to make something known. I began to witness all, and remained with them delivering the judgment of a man; I retched, became as lofty as your walls. My followers more my fathers and mothers than I their leader. It becomes the other hand, you, not to the soul, there is no wrong against you, and yet a rope grows around my throat. I did not learn anything. I've never found a bad fellow in the house of the mad. Everyone in me, their language, and the desire of circumstances aside, the asylum is not where I shall lay. It would not be an apt turn, sad, and you took hold of me not as a good man, but death itself. The doctors you have to say? The medicine speaks in dull, dumb, blind tones and incoherent even. If you become deaf, mute, blind, what you do echoes. Ridiculous, I'll show you. It's what I showed each of them. But it is good that all is well. Nothing to do with the question, your questions, it makes no difference, as all are one. It is perfect. There is God. He is seated within your walls to the right and left of me. It is your God, a parent. And that is God. But let me speak: the power of the Father, there is no other, bleeds much more than you think. You imagine things, fabricate diseases. A man thinks, then set aside by the dose, or the sessions; if they do not do it again, you sell that sense of newsprint, public opinion, video, as you have hung up to spite me. I did not what you now do. You do not have to kill out of my mind because it is rotting; you all in front of all to string me up. And the beginning of all my children they are your own, they hear and turn back the face of the doctors. I do not care. And I never hesitated, only showed them how to do something good for the good of the all, what you think is evil. Your mothers in the newspapers to write things that you will not tell me, you forget me in the asylum. To eat the flesh and to desire, to the teeth, a being better than your own. Tell you the same way, you send out to find my head. Your own wickedness loud enough. What are you and your descendants. Each of you the picture of right and good against my hands.

ATTILA

"Attila! Attila!" a sort of gull's crack from youth chimes me back. I know my mother well in memory. Sat high above the earth in my employ, there is coherence; an aftermath, a settling. A wind might push through and scrape against the metals, or heat stopped for coffee against the chest and cheek. Go on runs see other sides to people, ugly, feral families driving from vacation to its opposite. Go on runs and neglect myself for weeks or so. Simon capitalized on as much. Easy to see the emptying spirit I guess. Easy to spot a man nearing on some life-death dilemma. We spoke of what we'd seen. He told me of various tortures, new ways out he'd carved. I listened and slurped at cans, our feet both wrapped in wool and up against his dash as night proceeded. He'd experienced shock, insulin therapy. He'd met brilliant physicians, philosophers. He'd seen a youth bury his hands in a jar of water designated for Jacques Lacan. He spoke well of matters so I felt sharp, less dumb. He prompted my speech. I'd once met a boy on the street in New York and talked over the state of things while he broke from loading something into a gallery. I'd once emptied myself on the longest stretch of desert I'd ever saw without car or human presence in sight. My family became immaterial beyond the cat on lap or memories of fattened weekends on Auntie's couch and I'm quite at peace in an American darkness. Today sat in bath with filth and limbs stretched out and intermittent dose of scalding water on ankles. Home for several days, maybe the boredom would swell, thick and pungent. I'd visit Auntie's and come away round and shining. I drive a small pile of plastic guts while off the road. My father might be sickened at my indolence.

PATIENT

In your schooling you'd learned well to subvert commonly understood histories in favor of something postcolonial that accounted for the cruelties of mostly White Men since the Dawn, and it was in this way you'd entered the narrative of Gene Roddenberry, terrified and useless as a newborn. Not dissimilar, you met Simon through the texts consulted and eventual correspondence where he'd become a number. He now submits experimental essays to the PEN Prison Writing program. Young girls wrote him letters and he'd respond with sheets of toilet paper scribbled through with stories about the end of Nature, the end of God, a new beginning for the human race, a revelation, a plague, anything to set their teeth on edge. He'd become imprisoned and institutionalized after any number of things. You'd watched with some disdain his testimony as it seemed to lose coherence, heft. He'd sent a list of possible wives at one point wanting you to see. You assembled what you could in going forward, occasionally pulled back to the work that seemed to embrace simply surrounding yourself with souls.

OLIVIER

Simon would pace across the floor, spitting cereal at one of six televisions as he passed, wearing skintight black long johns thoroughly holed-up and redolent with piss—he'd become nameless, was my take. I felt a smile bubble and it gnawed down with teeth-on-lip ahemming until the wild-eyed caricature spat warmed cereal unto my gut and laughed with me as we held each other terrified. "So, on my walks I guess I don the mask, the man-visage. They're watching me. We pulled you from yourself, kid. You'd been well steeped in doctors' rhetoric before I had my say. Where I come in: I become the citizen. I'd need air on leaving maybe and take foot to gas station assembling cohesive strains of distempered thoughts at the dross they'd made of our interiors. I've noticed of late that when I walk my feet seem to think. Again, the watchers, the surveillance. What to make of it, I'm unaware, but keen on most sensation. I think I feel bogged down, morassed. I term it 'depression'—their phrase—and try to walk it off, yet it won't go. Any range of physiological responses to the work we've been doing here. I tend to avoid the lot of them, favoring whatever suffices between.

PATIENT

You saw gulfs between your consciousness and theirs and yet sought their imprinting on the skin. He, Simon, had grown political and only a short while remained before he found himself in the same rooms of those he treated. You shared their voices. A sea of homeless mouths made to interact and copulate for no particular end. You'd lie in bed awake at night awaiting their scratchy coffee'd loss. Tales of family trapped in diaspora. Voices scraped at the void in your gut. Their recording became a kind of guiding principle. It had been months of this and your hands were freezing deep in winter.

ATTILA

The market nearest me was hollow and bright, barren and quiet. Say I walk in and my entry seems to take hours, I don't shy. I nod at someone behind something and approach a wall of possibility. I purchase drink. My smile at the attendant isn't forced so much as programmatic. Sometimes I'll put on a limp to quicker flee unsavory ordeals. My auntie could be thick and moronic too. She could be a dullard. She could act like everything revolved around a small can of sugared drink as she paraded herself across her floor harassing the heavens for setting her where they'd done. I believe perhaps the physical sensations that have recently cropped up in my days have led to those modes of thinking. Skepticism, analysis, application of the plague to my circumstance. I'm unsure. I don't know where this or that stems from but I hold bitterness toward father figures mostly as perhaps the foundation, the bedrock of my disgust.

PATIENT

What you've considered is writing something and putting it somewhere based on the notion that it had been written under the yearlong influence of a variety of antipsychotic medication. They've encouraged it, in so many words.

FLAMINGO

I used to wear clothing that flattered everyone but me until I burnt my wardrobe and began collecting used white T-shirts and simple black work pants. This is what I wear still and I worked in an office setting within the pustule so that this remained a possibility so long as I encrypted X amount of Y each day and occasionally impressed upon the cock of general management my hands to spray spunk to tiles in the company's family bathroom. It isn't required that I do this but I've found it lucrative and entertaining since I first plucked the stick of some local fool outside my high school and the tendency has kept. You can call me Flamingo and I say it thus because legally it's my name. I'm not a bad one and I don't have pink hair but all my friendships have gone the way of the wiry salmon and thus I've adopted a moniker for this, that situation. Call me that and see how it suffices. Please do.

FLAMINGO

I became acquainted with Simon through his poverty clinics strewn across inland Florida. He'd gone for elders and stayed for any number of statutory claims. He'd amassed storefronts for sessions of marital debate, depressive mumbling, wandering monologues toward relief in so many troubled stomachs. Me I'd be jealous and hence aligned with Nicole Kidman. I drew comparisons to push myself a bit from where he'd look. He'd garble lines from Arthur Schnitzler, call my bluff. He'd prattle advertising jargon, the like, and he'd seduce, but I'd be vile, angry, by degrees. I am a woman capable of the gutrot it leads to. It points that way and I'd like to cut the heads off of every cunt who steps near to the person with whom I share fuck or deadness or therapies. It is easy and entirely impossible to continue in this fashion and live a reasonable life and yet my tits are slippery and consistent with the drivel of loving men and hence I'm sane-ish enough to endure and wither as is my wont. I pick and drift in front of your TVs while families seem to hover and die around me, a tendency I've sharpened. I stayed in his office for some two hours after the allotted session. We'd stare for forty minutes, seething. He'd ask after my father. I'd ask after his convictions. The room would come to smell.

PATIENT

Dying might be alright. What you have to do is make sure you're at an age at which most people don't die before you die there, set all records straight and leave a mark. Your ex won't answer Facebook messages wherein you refer to his current partner as a "fiery plugged hog without apt hairs" and repeatedly insert smiling yellow faces as the android takes over. Simon's odes were always against death, and those who'd made it through were nonetheless of sunken-eyes at their careers, their marriages, their successes. Death heaved, took great clips of their potential to its scrapbook, caking on glues and removing what hope remained.

EDMUND

My entire apropos response to living has been to shudder and shutter myself within a colder space not occupied by much. A gutted father screams. The image of Simon's face, reflected bits of colored light. There is no immediate recognition. Simon reads, the portion of his face an entirety of the living within it; triangular and constant, we note perhaps its pores on nose and eyes and here the calming rule of threes. Simon is taken with something, screens project against his face as he bellows out from the case of Pierre Rivière: *I imagined myself playing a role, I was forever filling my head with personages I imagined. I saw quite well however how people looked upon me, most of them laughed at me. I applied myself diligently to find out what I should do to stop this and live in society, but I did not have tact enough to do that, I could not find the words to say, and I could not appear sociable with the young people of my own age, it was above all when I met girls in company that I lacked words to address them, so some of them by way of jest ran after me to kiss me. I was unwilling to go and see my relations, that is to say cousins, or my father's friends for fear of the compliments that must be exchanged. Finding that I could not manage to do such things, I got over it. And I despised in my heart those who despised me.* We are watching Simon. We are uncertain what to think until his voice returns. He hums a tune we recognize. A brief glint of happiness washes over eyes and nose and this, by way of framing and constancy, feels revelatory, slowed. A flicker perhaps against his eyelid and we see his shorn skull. A grimace, and now some definition. Simon howls out his story with manic gestures and toothy invective toward those who'd wronged. We watch as entertainment entertains, pulls and nags and distorts his image to celebrity; identification that seems to burrow us to within his pores. Simon has seen a fragment of his own life, Rivière's life, enacted in recorded sorrow; and yes, we sense some tragedy. What I've done is stare at screens and it has torn away at me in bits. What I'm paid to do is stare at screens in evaluation of items that might be pumped through imagined pneumatic tubes into the skulls of various Americans and Elsewhereicans. Simon's show had pressed through a strain of streaming porno slums, couched there, and spoke to me during lull moments on the job regarding iterations of madness, his struggle, and the ways beyond salvation. I can see faces now based on what I've selected. Their excitements, their skips and leans toward other opportunities. My finger clicks and points, tears away at the potential of artful material for this site and that, until eventually what's left is what will thrust itself into sternums of each of you and all. Time-honored, this piloting. An officious endeavor meeting assembly line static and ennui, massive failures all. Legions had since apparently followed Simon, the monotonous loud familial saga, endless derivations therein, the Church of Branch Simonized. I'd sought his teachings for a bit and was thence paid for being examined, a noble trade you'd see clip up on faces throughout the rooms as shifts bore on. Hushed and sat in rows beneath an old church. Our status here reflects this, a space perpetually becoming, a working life ever in the flux of responding to society's stomach rumblings. I get nauseated, simply put. This was a time when Simon helped. He'd offer a circuitous account dispersing platitudes throughout and you'd come away enlivened; a sense of prosperity, newness.

FLAMINGO

What I am is my mother's girl: a hard worker made of glass. Tonight I saw some cops beat a little girl blue. Is that sort of thing sought after? I'm the Tina Turner of this grasping strip of poverty, is what I tell them. I tell them many things: what to call me; I sleep on one leg; I am John Waters; I am unemployable; I smoke Merits; you are a dog, we drink Mountain Dew together. This is not a good way to spend your life, you've said. This is not healthy, the bosses would mumble. I swallow their employment and scream it out in drenched eye shadows while my hair grows in without approval. I'd found a niche in which to work but skipped around too much and now I'm stuck. I'm here looking into your fucking face seeing Simon's fucking face projected back and it's just like Vienna, just like the drunks huddled up in Akron licking their military wounds, avoiding their wives.

PATIENT

This work will be a nightmare. You are no detective. You don't always seek out solitude, or aloneness, or the single state. The argument that men are easier fit within that role seems amiss. You simply find your highs in more devious ways than most let on. You'd been forward. You'd claimed a degree of flaw that wasn't simply undone. Flamingo, that is, and your sort of harboring of her heart. What you enjoyed though wasn't its abject notes, the blatant stuff. You enjoyed knowing you'd support her, knowing you'd love her in simple, almost nameless terms, because of its discouragement.

FLAMINGO

My father was the big doofus, and he could reel them in and have their laughing done in splinters on the floor. I get excited at the cop dynamic, that worldview. Saw bits of it in him amid this sort of Third World-like Jesus bloodying his hands against the heaps of gold within the temple.

HAYDN

Where I'd worked, the place was a muddled panopticon where nobody and everybody watched nobody and everybody simultaneously. A home my father'd established privately with others leaving ripples afterward for refuse; children who hadn't made good. Of late I've held interviews with college-aged inepts about their hopes and dreams, asked if they could wipe and sit, watch and administer meds through various orifices and apparatuses. One was Clyde, a greasy lout with legs spread too wide and a grin and résumé that indicated he could and would do this job better than me; I hired him. Another was Monica, a social work major with bad teeth who wanted to change or shape lives, nothing short would suffice. These were the faces and they were endless. Each of them eventually broken until they all came to look as inmates freshly released and given menial jobs at Burger King. The enthusiasm waned. Most could endure half a decade without some stare cropping up and the cycle of guilt and terror that would be their later years, however I was born into this.

PATIENT

You find no pride, or anything all that curious, in the shelves of books read, or the films watched, or the shits taken, but the televisual strikes you as, if nothing else: different, and you're fond of this and drawn toward it, lately. The encased set within the lounge is popular and comforting.

FLAMINGO

I worked between mirrors too, a slop-up girl, so to speak. Can you imagine running errands for smut peddlers? What is the smut peddlers' errand? Their locales, their trucker havens. What I do is mediate between their hungers and sustenance rituals and the hammering of pornographs into hearts and minds. I'd have never guessed they'd remain afloat. A good deal of the work was transitional, digital. I make sure X gets from A to B. I make sure the nightmare wanes I guess, defer to cop lingo and back coffee, retain monotony.

HAYDN

Calm with finger wrapped in cup I'd slurp my coffee. Walked out to the edge of the yard I'd stare back at the angles of the building. Face it almost precisely at its corner from a small jut of trees behind which drove a country road. It looked peaceful that way, its inhabitants neither sick nor healing but merely breaths. Spectral maybe, the way it looked. Years of incarceration and misunderstanding and medication and apparent garbage piled beneath this home and all its histories. Clyde's shirt was missing a button. I'd noticed this and it was likely this more than anything that led to his hire. Confidence could murk my thoughts, turn them serpentine and running. This sort of work required it, yet owning this place gave no step toward self-esteem; I didn't want it. What I wanted was his humanity driven under the floorboards and filing cabinets. My work consumed me and it wasn't work. My life reflected this place endlessly and I might never leave. A small rip existed on the stomach of my shirt. Monica's heart was on her sleeve and I felt envious. This sort of work attracted her and her and her; the type was endless.

PATIENT

What works is a profound stomaching of the death of excellence, first off. Right off, what'll work well and stick to the intestinal tracking of your attempts is that thorough draught of no more good work, no more excellence, no more demon-grappling profundity, no more divination. What you might do as a young human animal is fail, or succeed. Neither matters, but both have their time and place above a slow-poured cup of gas station brittle. It is OK to be both, have both, and see terrible films. It is OK to be redolent with disgust at the rotundity of yourself, the spectacle, that missed teenagerdom spent analyzed as you age into uselessness and muddled irrelevancy. You've fled too many times to register. You have theses regarding the parameters and extents of enthusiasm, paraphrased from Simon. They are straightforward: They as quasi-civilized human animals require distraction from the All, oppressed as they are by grim awareness of looming death. Late-late-late Capitalism has done what it does: it has capitalized on this distraction and turned it into a godly hand upon their social shoulder. To mourn the loss of what-have-you, of readerly persons and some Grand Narrative, is foolhardy and antiquarian. You and your kin as arbiters of therapies, enthusiasms, manias, hold fingers to the throat of what social order there is, a pulsecheck to drain the victim nearest death only to resuscitate for their consumption. Father/He was a simple man, of simple ilk, is what they'll argue. The world was simple then and information didn't rip so tactile at the cortex. To yearn for it, though, would seem misguided. You too are simple; disinterest pervades each of your ten fingertips and their decisions. You might've spent a life watching Vincent D'Onofrio remove the hind of his scalp with jacketed bullet. You adore that. You might've been a writer. A decision-maker. A choice-maker. There is analysis to be done, poring to propel. You live now for the sunken eye. Certainty is a gift you've never been partial to, you prefer to live in this nonspace where quite nearly everything detests your being, excepting of course your stained-tie therapist.

EDMUND

You know I never interfaced with users on the job. It could've been, maybe. Some leg of the outfit had to embroil itself in customer service, but never mine. It struck me near the end, held before me as carrot-on-stick of my ineptitude and where I stood. I mediated mediation, already mediated. Some organizer somewhere creates the stream and from thence its deconstruction and human melee to own efficient machinery to ingest entertainment. What is the impulse? The overwhelming throb we humans feel to laugh and weep at one remove. I've never felt a pang inside this place, short of Simon's words. I've never been moved more than on watching the hacked psychiatry. My empathy and sympathy exist as idealized numbs adjoined to heart and all I see is one world cripple into debt before another follows. Lofty and opaque, perhaps, noxious and insane. I feel this breathing contemporary Americanism. I worry and worship rubbing socked feet on roughish carpet.

ATTILA

That's how come I came together with my auntie. She's nice enough, has a small place in a community of small places, children around. I enjoy the presence of youth. We watched television together, she brought in bags of things to taste. It wasn't so much what you're thinking. I'm not sure, maybe a hair. It's just, well. It's as I stated previously. He'd granted a sort of permission too, I figure. And so if this, our civilization, has never quite parted from its status as a place having just lost a massive portion of that which is supposedly civilized, well, what then? I'm not sure. You behave in alternate ways.

PATIENT

You press it away as one has to. You shouldn't be overmedicated. That is evident. The state of these things as diseases or whatnot will forever be in question perhaps. As you recall van Gogh had Digitalis in his system and hence saw fluttered spirals around the lights and flowers, Foxgloves it was, somehow ingested. Too much and they can kill you as you understood it. They had them in the yard, you saw them there. You ate them knowing you might keel over at any moment but you did not and you saw no spiral outward. That might've been the last narcotic sort of thought you really had, though, aside from the accepted apparently nonrecreational aforementioneds. It's difficult to think through this sort of issue in matter-of-fact patterns that seem accepting of the stomachs all share. You apologize for this. This tendency in you has been there longer than you had an awareness of it.

ATTILA

My favorite piece of music is the one which states *let me weep*. This is not a code, I'm just indifferent. What they'd diagnosed wasn't my demeanor, my state, but how long it'd been since I'd visited the hospital. The doctor had long legs and continued to fondle his knee or navel as I fled. I was never much for progress reports—my parting with S. was similar. So as the expressed gut wobbles through cities and I yearn for nonexistent yore days, I think again and again only of my auntie. I ponder if it's love. I worry and fuss over the amplified nature of my stomach. A thought's enough to send it into collapse these days. I seem to have spent eons atop the toilet. My paranoia is perhaps the thing I've clung to. Not the lady herself but the impossibility. I seek out ancient ages but none quite suit my ill humor. I picked a puff of lint from my gut today that seemed disheartened, bloody maybe or tending to droop. Even the objects I've amassed are losing will.

HAYDN

The click that ended our telephone call crawled inside the ear and pulled at the root of my brain until my eyes seemed to open up. Standing in the doorway was Evelyn, a god or master who'd begun coming to our home four decades hence. For moments, for one protracted moment, I simply stared and felt my pulse grow under the pressures. She'd wet herself while sleeping. Her shirt looked as if she'd slid across slicked floors. Soiled to the knees, her crotch seemed frigid as she shook, emanating cold. I couldn't put things together staring there. I couldn't raise myself sufficiently to assist her transitions, apparent and pressing as they were. The necessary work was ingrained and yet I couldn't stop thinking about the daughter imagined through the telephone. I'd fallen asleep, perhaps. I'd felt that way, as if I'd dreamt some nightmare of a girl and history. It was all quite there. The smell began to raise me before my body thought. Stale urine and the onset of ammonia. Evelyn stood there thankful and imploring. I rose and guided her, stepping softly through the hall toward the women's. The human waft of morning mess as we walked to the bathroom all too familiar, and yet I shook with grief. I'd felt some last corner walked, some last door entered before the step into my father's.

2.

G.G.

I never gave a ready piss for this America. My whole teeming trial was drops of shit, piddling after all their talk. The girls'd follow. Came to be Simon and I were wolves to these young gutless pups and shared infections thereafter. I'd rot their bodies up and peek outward and see all I'd enacted. A murderer, a fragrance. You walk, it's putrid. Come see me waving, boys. Kill a miserable kid, bury him nearby, nobody's the wiser. Kill a smiler, they're up in arms. I tend to eviscerate the depressive. My hands have become political as his. I came forward and called my plight that of the sons of Robert E. Lee, a raving Mexican hopping borders to rape and pillage. Even the word sets the teeth, the name. The garbage-eating nationalist. Advocate for socialism, as it brings me bodies. Simon: our messiah. Rampant cunts the males. Office workers, their throats cut, I'd watch them bubble. Constant, just constant meandering. Ratfink fuckers couldn't hold their guts up high enough to string me down. "Just do it." I'm sponsored. Fucking ingrates, murder me already. I'm there dying; can't you smell it?

PATIENT

It was then that you began your seated, drugged endurance. You're not anti or pro narrative, you simply see things for what they are and record them thus. Propelling botches of narrative culled from heads around. You've developed great nostalgia for their speeches.

FLAMINGO

My mother might've been born near Lake Nakuru, or I can wish she was. I've hoped to visit there for long. I study Divine, the transvestite. It's nice to feel this way. Fluid, I am fluid. I think of the necks of those birds. I sit in my car and read Stephen Jay Gould's ideas and feel in-tune with some Darwinian paternal line. I transport a crate of tapes of smut from X to Y and am handed one hundred and twenty dollars in American currency. I take twenty-seven of these dollars and I spend them in a diner while flipping through an image set from the National Audubon Society about my lineage. My mother, agape. My father, missing. Simon, who knows? I feel connected to it all and workless.

ATTILA

I collected pens that didn't work. Over time it seems that disgust became an asset. Over time I figured out some ends and made it sensible to operate in contrast to what I saw as lives lived well. It's like the fear that might arise on being tossed into a vat of sick, oil, or anything removed from the familiar. Common, valid human responses would be thus: escape. But me, I drank it in. Me, I learned to tread or swim and hold new breaths under new conditions that seemed better suited to potential tragedies of being. Call it the familiarity or curiosity I'd kept toward death, or plague, or fallen civilizations. Call it the tendency of man to find points of opposition and let fly piss. Call it the need for social deviance or deviants and how we'd come to live in such a world. It has no given name, born I think from its tendency to fester and wound.

PATIENT

You're a bit like every seeing eye in *Molloy*. What you have are inklings. The passage wherein the young man walked along the beach. He was pink, or coalsoaked, if memory serves. The sky was gray, or pink, it might've been. You impose your ways on narratives. Read the theses of Simon and wander around his entrails stuck through Florida. Study foliage and migratory habits. The young man walked along the beach and attempted something grand: he attempted to embrace his tendency to suck stones. What he needed was to suck stones in a particular order with utmost efficiency so that by order's end the stones would be on ground and his need to teethe would be satiated. You do not remember the man's teeth, though gums were pink. The cetological passages of Melville interest here, Beckett at opposite ends. He sucked those stones in order to better appreciate their possibility and eventually figured the finest way to incorporate each of his pockets and walk along the beach. And you cannot think of the era, slurping coffee in the car in hot Florida misery, without thinking of V. Woolf. Was it she with whom Beckett spoke in these moments? Uncertain.

FLAMINGO

We tend to hold off on naming threats, perhaps, or more malicious things that lurk between preferences. I suppose I sort of sought a nameless thing, then, but not a feeling hardly. A debauched state with which your world wanted nothing to do, I suppose. Tonight there's need for some expression.

SIMON

I've closed my eyes to Laing's work, to Skinner's, in turn Lacan's and Freud's... I harbor only gasping breaths of vomit toward their organizing... No meaning is still pathetic vying toward readers, human hearts, followers... I see no reason for it... I once lived a month on water and whatever bugs managed to chip through my basement's walls... Was there reason here? Was there decision here? I might have been a million things but locked away there I felt complete... I found a fellow's old boot underneath my home, there'd been a massive hole within the kitchen, kids occasionally snuck in while I slept to lick and after much of this I found the burrow and the boot and took to rest... Water sifted down from somesuch piping likely poisoned through and rusted I heard their clacking feet and spray cans on the floors above me it was there and many theres where I was growing, birthing, what would thus become some doctrine... I've lived in dirt and wood and ate from creek or log and watched events at some remove for entertainment this was it... I never needed the world... I never needed the pamphlets, brochures, prescriptions, degrees, therapy notes, massive holes of debt connecting me and they and all... If you cannot ask me to the asylum, and led me away from you who know nothing of the past, you'd have me jailed and hid... Would I be released, it seemed that way before machines took hold of head. As for me, for, my testimony maybe, the followers and the hatred seemed to me, at least, as if distinct, separate fires... But when all was done, was Simon not to reflect, or climb the back of the other man? I know I can be alone. Judge me, kill me, make a million more where I hang... I will do judgment, I am every waking day, I am very satisfied... Too hard for your heads, not that any man should design God, render endings to all prisons of mind, with first their fathers... Do it, be angry against the all and kill each other... Accept it, your sons, daughters, all that was done, became my brother's love itself... If God has not done something unto you... unto the asylum wholly or varying perspectives, do not think you are saved for nonattendance, nonworship... I do not see you that way, these people in their moments of life, my room is what frightens you, screens watching your watchers watching firearms amassing somesuch to keep the choleric public at their bay... You all are afraid, afraid of things you've enacted, not just within your heads, not just within your villages of people, men of the family and women of God... who by the wayside, to their kin, they refuse to worship refused to bow and so become milder, learning language, in their asylums of youth, and have suffered your homes and remained foolish... We have watched the world to the child, when grown up, and it is here that God is born, but it is difficult and the understanding of the world in matters good, you deem them evil... It is yours... These are the children come unto you, and the knives, your children.

ATTILA

Again the breathing gut and my determination to howl out. "Attila, Attila," my mother'd say or chime. And I'd respond that I was fat, that I was sick, that I was tired, that I was rotting, that I was thirsty, that I smelled meat, that I cut my wrist, that I tortured small things, that I sought guidance. My mother has since become lost in tablecloth, fabric of alternating reds and whites. This is, I think, the meaning of my life. A sequence of thoughts and images tied mostly to parents, or Simon, or disgusted kids in classrooms. A barrier between myself and the world and a line of work that didn't force me too much across. Come in, I'm hefting beer to brow and cold, it turns my thinking black. I've liked this place, this city. I've liked the days off, the weeks. I remember my father's shiftless state and the sense that he'd always rather be off delivering. I remember my mother's waiting for his various returns. Our house was quiet, almost halved by its occupants' relating. I'd done well enough, but they never paid close attention. I'd hide and once the kids began to huff or suck whatever, I resurfaced with smeary ideas. I'd show up at parties, one arm soaked in gasoline, asking for lights. I'd replay scenes of bodies strewn out in front of disassembled buildings and kids would call my coating irksome. It was a method. I was learning. My father was a Kum-N-Go. My mother sold used clothes. I see not much in anything beyond a dipshit piss-ant stretch of road. We cannot step in and change our lives. I once entered a clinic with my head opened for their perusal. Returned to me a laundry list of human error and disorder enough to lose every cent on medication.

PATIENT

American-chauvinist palaver. This is mere window-dressing to consider. The doctors enhanced distractive technique. Somewhere buried is a manifesto by Simon you'll glimpse. Weary-eyed drugged occupants of rubberized hospital furniture encountering the arts. You walk around inside that piddling atmosphere and feel sublime unlike when you were young aspiring to be battered. You grew up in a midwestern emotional state wherein dog loved and understood better than all dirt you ate in quiet. You live slightly medicated, and wonder over this. Should the person who's transcribed something acknowledge at the outset not those who've helped, but the chemicals consumed along the way? *This was written under the influence of 60 MG Fluoxetine, 150 MG Bupoprion, 30 MG Buspirone and 200 MG 5-HTP administered daily.* That sort of thing is what leads you to wonder about things of this surrounding and ever-present thing to wonder at. You heard some years ago that Balzac drank or sort of stomached around fifty cups of coffee a day.

FLAMINGO

I believe more strongly in one animal than I do the whole of humanity. Look and see the birds lined up, their cities. See the water coax their feet, collective disarray and nagging unhappiness. As a girl my father figure smoked those big cigars like Robert Mitchum. Pinkish sunsets, I watched the smoke and imagined the air kept it lit. He choked my mother once, I saw her neck. He left us and we sat on the lawn thereafter in the kiddie pool and her friends bought us candies in bright pinks, greens and reds. Hot sun bore down on our necks and shoulders. We fell asleep suntired as *The Brady Bunch* investigated murders and incest on-screen. I ate sugary cinnamon redhots and watched boys laughing at my mother. Nightmares are born in sun. The bird will guide me, maybe. Mother was never good. The men wore shades of denim, sweated.

G.G.

The man does not strut, does not smile. Simon's works were shared via some murdered junkie's manifesto I'd consulted over. Theirs: an Aryan breeding. They came of ranging guts and strove. I saw enough in each their murders. Euronymous: a plague, a dwindling song atop some sheepskull. A church burnt, their teeming, hands of Simon. It began as work for me. I in recording rendered fat to disc and saw kiddie nightmares play out over their sleeping ramble. It was empty. Their black jeans. Ripped nailed bulleted pulled to bits and fragments like so much grieving teenagerdom.

FLAMINGO

Anyway, at the least one can revel in the absence of any search for wholeness or selfhood so bogging down the masses at this age, in here. I'll read in and out of booklets on the times, or not. I watch the shows on screens or take a minute to sit down and settle into long droning depressive works of art to center my sense of piddling ineptitude and it is righteous, in its way. Lately I feel fond for the person who, having let go, extends their fists back into the earth they no longer grip out of curiosity for the worm.

G.G.

I sat in my booth occupied with my endeavors and went home
each night in blistering cold to family ungrateful unaware of what
I managed and what endings I wrought. I saw their decadence,
cellophane and glassine tirednesses. Weary longhairs. Good old
Nordic forgers all. My wife the baker's daughter. My son the lowly
grout. My Simon now the convict and his ties with a sort of heaven.
I come home and they don't know the tunnels I've begrimed myself
in. I run radio programs featuring illegally recorded police reports
of domestic violence that create a retching even in me. I tell those
I've recorded and they nod in withered muscle. My life: a good lie;
the endless walking, the conversations, platitudes. I talk out loud
to myself about their works and pull it all inward, this seething
black of monotonous rot. Theirs is the living nightmare. I express
and embrace it. I publish and share their manifestos alongside
his on broken sites, tack them onto doors like Luther. A burnt
church, an opportunity, a trying. What of the sound can be made?
This squalorous tone, filled with poison and plague. Their guitars
always broken to empty bits and one boy enters reading *The Primal
Screamer* and plays apparently through the firm metal strings of
his Les Paul. There's something empty about the whole affair,
emptying. He shoves his hand downward and upward with such
manic repetition it's hard to make sense of the sight and sound that
follow. And is there a following? Wondering after this could make
the head swell. Which came first: the flea or the plague? A bucket
of rats beaten with this horrid broomstick to enact something
sounding out. A boy of sixteen locked inside a cage constructed by
the band's drummer so that his screams ring authentic. I walk home
that night to see my grout and my baker's girl and cannot express
my discontent, I call Simon Wednesdays and we discuss his ways
out, new literature needing published. A FREEZING, HORRID
CITY; EMPTY, GUTTED MUSIC; MY FATHER WOULD
NOT BE PROUD OF I; I AM NOT PROUD OF I—I'LL
EXCEL IN RESEARCHING GERMANIC LANGUAGES AND
CALL IT QUITS BEFORE I BIRTH ONE MORE; LEATHER
AND CHEAP METALLICS, GLASS BOTTLES AND PLASTIC
CONTAINERS STUCK WITH NOW-DEAD BAND REGALIA;

COME IN, WE'RE FUCKING CLOSED.

FLAMINGO

I wore a dress from the 1880s to my senior prom, I was not invited. A father figure—Jack Nance-ish—a big boy. An elder, inexperienced, having not the experience apt to the strain she would experience. A mother figure—let's call her Grace Zabriskie—she's feeling what she's feeling, singing meditative songs. And what of the bible verse in anticipation of fatherhood? Erase their heads, Simon might've said. To give birth to a child in atomic times, it is unfortunate. We should feel this strain as well. It is done through sounds. "The logic of nightmares," "the language of nightmares," something on this order. Whatever it is he said, envious. To begin one's study of Lynch's film one must begin one's study of the bible, an origin text, a myth. We must sift as he sifted—and he—make sense as he made sense, find his spirituality. I feel the angst of oncoming parenthood. In heaven everything is fine. Children are no burden, no plague— might this one rot in sun? What are they? I have sprouted from some antinatalist—Simon had his phase alongside Zapffe before our coming together. I don't know how to reconcile my own indifference toward being with that of an oncoming child. I watch it through the film. One day at home I've got to sit down and see it for what it is. See the film as tutorial for parenthood, and I the Lady in the Radiator. Paternus! I don't know what he meant. I shout it nonetheless. Invented, crude, Roman terms. I feel the rotgut coming. A range of acts of violence. This is my retrospective view. I'm not sure how to organize matters, how to frame events and find the neatness. I remember hearing of my mother's family sheltered around the TV set for days after the president became killed. The event didn't seem to matter nearly as much as their desperation toward narrative, the ritual search for beginning-middle-end. Thinking over it now seems a cliché. I try to find cohesion and there are only blips of self-pity and indulgence. We search for parental figures, often found in cutting-edge therapies. We hope they'll offer sustenance or the means anyway. This is not about my youth. There is no need for reflection as such. I only illustrate acts after Simon's absence to come to terms. Just what they are I'm hard-pressed, I'm afraid. It's tiring, this. To say nothing of the jobs, the work, the squandered money, all that sun. This is how I sought some light of meaning.

PATIENT

Honore ate ravenously, he copulated angrily as is known to even just the *Annie Hall*ers, but he didn't acknowledge at the outset the chemicals that influenced his plopped scribbles. You wonder about this with some immensity. It is a sense of guilt one has for imbibing something that is still so nascent and unexplored. It is a sense of guilt for not toughing it out as previous humanoids did through barreled gins et al., it is each and every of these unsavory bits that rubble about the bouncy house in your skull constantly concussed by this and every snack inhaled over wonder-y nights like here and now within their lounge.

G.G.

Problem was I liked their babble, the sweating frantic looks. My nausea in typical situations makes me seek out lows or ends of human incapability. I suppose it led me to the work, to Simon. I'm certain it's resulted in my state. The feeling of compressing one's life and work into a series of gestures while told what's worked and where one's failed, Simon offered this. I guess, in thinking on it, a kind of love developed there. I hoped to share his thinking, and he had sought out means. So for me I guess there were reasons—in the blood perhaps with Simon scraped and needy and emaciated walking nearby my home. I'd managed to keep Simon away from my family largely by accident though since I've warmed to remember it. He'd decided to gear his thinking toward the young, and saw the music wherein I worked would draw them in. I looked for strains of nihilism in his writings, something perhaps to offer the gaping public. I discovered a coherent plan for being, a series of observations regarding living one's life that made me less alone. The night I read him first I wept and after exchanging our letters we'd met and I fell to him. It wasn't common. It wasn't me. I knelt and kissed his boots. He patted my head and together we worked for days in one room. He opened my desires. He spoke to my past I'd say. We traced our lives for one another. He told me of his youthful searches, anger, pissing in warehouses, fucking in dull cars. I tried to convey. He had a way of making your language all his own. I remember in school a disgust. I'd worn it myself then. I'd let scents cake onto me and relish a wince when sat down to someone exerting so much effort to remind the world they'd washed. Flecks of dust or shit or dried sweat or skin frequently warped my interactions and made for awkward meals alone or with two or three touched students who couldn't speak. I once bled out ambitions. It is not the era. I once vied, my mother, my father, artists and beginners and tryers all. My life, a joke. My trying, risible. And here I began to follow.

PATIENT

Times aren't going well and yet they are and never have. You see their face and face and face and raise it up until you're no longer communicating. Television has proven inept and television is always there. Literature isn't exactly inept but you detest artworks. Wearing shirts and Simon's speech are the only constants and constraints in life or you might find any duet that suits. Death and taxes don't exist, never did. Simon and the plague, these are the constants of your cosmos. You hopalong into the new week and forever ignore anyone with anything like a shot at living.

EDMUND

One night on leaving work my theories were seconded. I left as was my tendency and walked up astride Jeremy to our respective cars. He on entering would honk and hustle off. I decided then to follow a corner of our building that jutted to align with the inward angle of a bowling alley. Through this squaring you could walk and reach a gas station. I decided to make this walk and purchase something to fulfill me. On entering a dying bell had rung and woken me a bit to deny the advance of sampled pizza offered there. The echoes of Simon's channel hung still in my head. I willfully misunderstand. Nod and nod, you might survive. I walk on through aisles of potential and slobber a dreamed-at existence in each commodity. I see a hovel of teenagers before a case of drinks that might be stolen, moving in their smelly pack to house light crime. An elder man who I could see outside our workplace door passing the parking lot then entered on his motorized scooter. A look of pure disgust gleamed out his skin. Such nightly rituals were warming, the light a maternal pat. On I went until some oranged mess in plastic rode my fingertips to counter. There spoken with by salesman, a nod is given at my badge. I wore plastic ID on entrance and exit to my employer. Typically it bore my name, my entire existed life. A question, a simple ask after what was done over there, and my life knew some completeness. Nod I did at the acned phrase, our hands were shook and the elder nearly entered his basket into my hind legs in prompting. I exited as if I'd gotten away with their teenaged criming, his disgusts against my heart, which shared employal forehead-touch, and shuffled anxiously until I saw my way out. I puzzled to my car, skipping through tracks of what I'd seen to lend a meaningful edge to what amounted to piled-on bad days. I began seeing absences of narrative heft in such reality when disconnected from my vocation, a life spent perpetually in buffer awaiting the wholed cohesion and stab at something beyond glib. And so I might attend the boss's gathering, I figured, morose and sugared as they tended to be. My wife and child might hanker a bit and thus I'll hurry out of there relieving, awash in what satisfies for glee in trying days. The boss will make his statement, hopped-up a bit or keyed at least to do so, he'll acknowledge the social dimension to these walls, push us farther he'll presume so as to lighten any potential grievances lobbied. He's always behaving that way and this: his flaw of needing some vestige of humanity, some earmark, has left it lifeless. Our jobs died on vines before we'd noticed any turnoff to the orchard. Superfluous training and their endless microscopic financial pats were all we had to show, but it was better. A disconnect existed and thus that night—and each night, likely—my own solitude in my own WC would bring about its worth. I remain uncertain; I'm a man of family.

3.

EILEEN

I remember initially the feeling of driving with mom to your apartment where you'd cried. She your sister, I looking up at both of you as heroines, each of us caught in notes of mental weather. My father, brothers elsewhere, some time away from school she'd said. I remember for instance my own issues. Documents exist to that effect, what do they say, they indicate an aptitude, a badness, some kind of lurk, that's all. I'd seen a range of men about the possibility of my collapse, that wasn't at-hand, however. Perhaps the stabs at education took by all my elders left them endlessly sensitive to the depressive, the dark. I remember, though, feeling comradeship in what I deemed your suffrage. I'd seen the word or heard it as you'd read from old notebooks regarding prayer, intermittent nuns along my mother's line, and this one seemed to copy every hiccup. Intercession, it was, you'd asked or plied my mom either to ask the heights or reason to step in and make your trial more straightforward. I wonder today if you'd had what I've found in his writing whether intercession would've proved moot. I saw in you an ancient grace; hands seemed as though they'd dug grubs as easily as they'd turned pages of some unknown Latin tome. The trick of memory, I'm certain. I know the weight it carries now. I remember my father and brothers visiting us occasionally over that short winter's stretch to conquer the menial. Fat jovial bloats and us three poring over television as things began to change.

ATTILA

It becomes tough to muster care once you've accepted wholly the lack of innate sense to what goes on. Here the plague again. I'd read once of a fictive plague and a city essentially turned to chaotic police state rot. I'd read once of a blurred historo-fictive account wherein pits of bodies lined the ways and people either spent their time studying religious work or building cabins. In either work the general sense was the absurd. One thinks as well of the art created then and its constant incestuous vein. I suppose it's how I've justified my auntie. Where and how we related I've since forgotten or the living links were lopped off. It wouldn't matter much anyway as there's never precisely what you're thinking. It isn't about that but willful acknowledgment of the lack of mercy in the world, the absurd. I'm craven, alright. I never sought the risk of love. Family remaining close then, and my occasional monies given there. I prefer the ways, the road, et cetera, as Simon did. I like the night and size of my vocation. I like the cities barely touched and the accidents on which I'm occasionally the only one close enough to light. It's nothing noble, I'm sure.

PATIENT

It was strongly recommended you keep tabs upon yourself, notes and observations throughout your day that made it sensible. Thinking of what strings things together for them in reading this is what tries you, but you have your sense. An obsession comes on like anything—one might hazard *gradually, then suddenly,* but one would be inept in so doing—and yours was no different. You simply waited for lines to make sense of themselves. You read backwards. You encountered dyslexia in aisles of pharmacies. The color pink was everywhere, existing, extant. You ruminated over pink, over her.

FLAMINGO

There were names by which I went, liminally, before becoming whatever. A young girl on the street is easy enough. Sleeping on beaches grew hell cold, the deepest circle, these massive Dantesque figures frozen above me in the sky. My homelessness a state of necessity rather than class, social, you know. I remembered the voracious boys in *Quadrophenia* and took great comfort, imagined hurling myself cliffward off the scooter and fought with myself tiptoeing on the beach in the nude shouting *WE ARE THE MODS WE ARE THE MODS WE ARE WE ARE WE ARE THE MODS,* and short of renting Dick Hebdige from the Miami-Dade Public Library once, this was perhaps the closest I'd come to freedom.

PATIENT

Tied up and grim with suburban decadence toward no feasible end, you tend to read *2600* lately without much in the way of hope. You the human writing the written things as they'll be smeared on screens and fed through fingertips, where does it go? You're uncertain; uncertainty reigns. You walk out and feet seem to have the better of your thought process. Why this preoccupation with television? Why this preoccupation with signs and cans of bubbled water? The why never seems to figure much into it. The why is ended before it's asked: a human with nothing to do does anything and everything, or something. Simon again and *I, Pierre Rivière* again and Foucault again and ridding the body of the encumbrance of too much thought again. You wonder at it not infrequently: what about a writer or artists whose works were made physical by their lack of a coherent body?

SIMON

I come away from each soul I touch with their imprint on me...
I might rot away you'll find me hung up in some motel room
withered just readying to pass on and they'll still skim my limbs for
clues, annotations, possibilities of how they'll go on forward... I'm
established in every discipline... I am every discipline... I've found
tribes of motormen leathered ready to spit their last in honor of my
doing... I've written, I've published more on the mind than books
on Lincoln might exist... I've killed, I've woven my way in and out
of bodies trapped and I don't care about society... I don't care about
the public... I don't care about civilization as such... I've come to
rest in this place surrounded by screens because I care not to venture
into the world and their revolts... Cities torn to splintering out of
fear, unrest, dissatisfaction at the status quo... I've left the status
quo... I need no money, I need no women, I need no followers
and it's thus that they'll follow long after I'm dead and buried...
Strew an acorn or two on the grave and let me be forgotten... Kill
me again or take me as I am, I will never change... Not for you,
for anybody, for this America for the grouphomes the streets of
poverty the minds I've heard incestuous and dogged grappling for
death... All wanting some absolution, some thorough whitewash
of what had been, mother and father, scream Mother and Father,
watch their blood boil and their fingers begin to whiten against the
tension of keeping on...

EILEEN

I remember not the way your mother, my grandmother, or her forebears reached the States. I'd heard once of tricks played on poorer streets and such in Europe after the logging nearest us proved dried up and fled westward. They'd sold farms and land to immigrants from Poland, Germany, and likely Ireland that proved thick with almost immovable stumps, and certainly impossible in winter. Not having heard Grandmother's own account of things, there are only guesses, but given her sharp accusatory nature, I'd since taken it for granted our ancestors were among the hoodwinked. Outside Minneapolis, then, in a place perpetually bought and sold where Louis Sullivan designed the bank—a place to raise a family, to see them raise their own. Now, as noted, Mother'd use your story later on when I headed up to Center City and found my way toward the living. It isn't this, however, that occasionally clicks and pulls me outward. Of the memory itself I only covet certain glints. You'd lived with what, Mother and I, for some months near my seventh year, I'm uncertain. And in that time your boy was close, a conflict perhaps. I possess only fragments and the resultant loom of you, a sort of inward mother, the figure sought when my own imposed her will for me. Being what felt a sort of kept girl in that home I'd already tended to darkness, evil selfish thoughts that she'd undo with old rhetoric, ancient ways. But you were something middle, not bogged in certainty like she and made up of so many bits and pieces as to keep all your shifting.

HAYDN

My goals were such that you'd barely refer to them; but this place made me swelter. I referred to each visiting mental health practitioner or apprentice as an inmate and their captives as masters and gods. I flipped around an image of her in my mind and couldn't see her face throughout. She the Eve and I the Adam of the new wave of American mental health. I'd heard him speak in such lofty terms. Held at a community college near my own, he'd stirred the crowd to near riot with religious mania, and afterward I'd briefly kept in touch. The workers change; the occupants remain consistent and headstrong, society's own heroes without praise or compensation— they kept the world in its lines.

FLAMINGO

Living in the group home we were taken to the DMV for ID cards but no licenses, no movement. These cards allowed for application for library cards and imprinted on the library cards were beach scenes done up in pink. I became learned, so to speak. I informed myself. I watched the work of Errol Morris and understood facets of the human condition. We girls were more readily accepted as library patrons as we tended not to stink and the boys at the group home held immediate positions at its owner's carpentry business, touching up further homes and exchanging flatulent debate. I read seated near a girl named Tina in these comfy chairs that let us curl up just. I read Tama Janowitz and Mary Gaitskill. I read Christine Schutt and Joan Didion. I read Elizabeth Hardwick and Renata Adler. These were not heroines. Lou Reed was my heroine. These were mere window dressing. Read some crimey creeps like Jim Thompson and Charles Willeford and slept a bit easier in knowledge I was not alone in seeing the world as better bloodied. My cousin Henry picked me up once for dinner at my mother's and she'd been split by history. She sucked at menthol and stared at me hopeless. My cousin had her done up in this ice cream-colored windbreaker and mint green tennis shorts and she mumbled there smiling about the beauties in her nail salon. Henry had stopped by from the Midwest at one point and never left. I wasn't interested.

EDMUND

On finishing the good days I'd step slowly up carpeted rubber-edged steps alongside Jeremy who'd pester at my plan. I'd situated a television suicidally—this WC my own. Allow an explanation: when in school I'd learned to relish the bathtub. I'd learned to inch out as far as my limbs might stretch into its corners and let arm and calf, gut and siding slide into aged, warmed porcelain. Now my friends were screens, and thus the melding of these contemporary obscenities. I'd wallow there and think and think of ways to enact total submersion while viewing, falling short repeatedly. Until one day I'd purchased thinned black ropes and slung them just so above the tub to allow a perched, flat-faced television to plant there and stick. With ropes tied front and back and into choice points along the wall the thing would firm up, not desire movement. That way and with our company's subscription I might watch therapies without hand requirements, viewing his spectacle each seven minutes and hearing sounds gutted through watered eardrums and lights dampened by my diving and jutting as low as my skull could slither. I'd listen to Simon reading beneath the water and see his gleaming head and feel connected. Simon advocated time spent near water. Simon advocated renouncing the loom of parents. Simon advocated ingesting various materials. Simon had sat in watery tanks with Timothy Leary and taken notes on strange chemical reactions at Berkeley and Simon was all and Simon was true and false and just as Simon made his show his followers in turn. Simon told me there how I'd proceed. Simon predicted the death of the marketplace and Simon predicted when we'd reach new worlds and Simon knew well the entirety of Samuel Johnson's work and Simon was a priest in his own church. I watched his program as a newborn.

HAYDN

"Where are you?" Flamingo's voice, grated, unique.

"I am in plainest sight, buried, you?"

"I am watching my daughter sleep, it is problematic."

"Did you miss the smell inside the place?"

"Nobody could miss the smell there. Not me. Not even your father. Least of all you. I did not miss it. I did not miss you. I simply called, while watching my daughter sleep."

"I'm having trouble with it. It causes angst. My stomach feels ready now to leave. I remember when I saw you here."

"My diagnoses, problematic behaviors. Lost and smeared in dirt from my abjection."

"Your hair, the things you'd read. And why is your daughter's sleeping then problematic?"

"She's been fussy nights. I don't know. I've just settled here. Was in hospital again, lost again, amid men and rot. Call it a phase. Is Ed still working there?"

"He is, occasionally. What were your diagnoses anyway?"

"In retrospect they all seemed to start with E and none of them got to the heart of the matter. Now come to think of it, I miss you just a bit. I'd carved something under the bed for—"

"I found it, you needn't worry about me finding it."

"—you and. Wait, why wouldn't you call me, on finding it?"

"It didn't seem to matter when you'd left. I'm not sure. The place can do it: make it simple to wonder at the reality of things, whether what you're feeling is what you're feeling or just a talk, just what one needed to get by."

"One what?"

"A patient maybe, a god or master as I've said. I'm not sure."

"My daughter's been fussy. This heat, it gets to her. I never felt much for her father, which I'm sure you'd advocate for. Mothers always had their hold on your ethic."

"Your mother'd done a number, but Father'd overdone his neglect. I understood your stories. What was my ethic?"

"A slippery one at that, you'd never pinned it down. All this wandering and speculation for a life. Any progress?"

"Not a bit, dear bird."

"Must be nice to speculate, like all those explorers before you. Men huddled in rooms adjoining cocks and aspirations staring up at dying cosmos. We were cowered around you in circles waiting for the advent of fire. You're like Prometheus and I couldn't wait each morning for the cereal you brought."

"I'm losing my edge. I never had an edge to speak of, but whatever was there is clearly gone just now. I've lost it somewhere. I lost it in you, maybe, staring up. What do you think of this place? Of the old man and all his plaques?"

"I think it'll make for a fine casket when the time's right. I think it served its purpose between the wee hours and the screaming awareness, paved the way from you to Simon, but little else made sense within those walls you've painted. I think you'll turn it to your enemy, turn the building into a knife within your gut no matter what I say. I think my daughter's fussy and I missed the particular brand of discourse you tend to leak. What do you think?"

PATIENT

Lines their lines mean work, to you. Lines their lines meant work to Fritz Lang some hundred years hence. Lines their lines meant work, to you. With near constant growth—not unlike the nicked windshield left in sun to web outward—culture, knowledge, and efforts to study or take in hand either has proven an amorphous, fragmented thing not dissimilar from your daily lives resulting from ranges of phenomena, not least of which being the spread of technology. They want you in lines; desire you in lines. S— worships you in lines, ordered, touching. Depending on your history, perhaps—other factors—your reaction to technology, to screens, to personality fragmentation across numerous platforms exists on a binary: love(-ish) and optimism, or hate(-ish) and pessimism/nostalgia for a simpler, printed-text era.

There is not a voice to quiet minds. The voice is where it starts: problems, lists, orders, demands, responsibilities, social obligations, friendships, histories, all of it amassing on backs pulled in all directions anticipating death. All of it weighing down the senses devoured by television devoured by literature devoured by ideas by lofty European sensibilities by sexualities by prosperous university educations commencement addresses heroes heroines everymen who worked for genius starting in the mud, in poverty. Stories we tell ourselves to die well defined. Narratives to keep the threat of simple mind at bay. Opinions poured into heads awaiting real lives awaiting real potential awaiting one imperceptible change before they'll become real before they'll attain reality. We are deviants perhaps. We've not figured out ways out. Simon figured ways out kept them tucked. Howling modern manias aggressive thoughts nagging at brains worse than parents worse than foundational fantasies lives lived to spite nonexistent pressing teeth against our voids. We are watched and controlled; the world is watched and controlled. We are not some victims. No. No. We are merely closer to the eyelight, closer to the real and hellish turns. Inside there are no slippages, all is certainty. Someone like Simon thrives on this. To be encased is to have whole perspective. To be free you need peremptory sounds, figures cultish bearded ancient and immortal telling you how to piss, what to purchase, what not. A way out nothing. There is only dark.

FLAMINGO

"Alleys of your Mind," "Dum Dum Boys," "4'33," "Do They Owe Us a Living?" "Health Surface," "Persons Unknown," on a beaten-up tape discovered in Mother's garage a boy had given me as much in an attempt to reach and connect I'd found nothing cinematic though he'd insisted I seek harder some bad joke a punk boy making bad jokes I took my girl-age bicycle and rode in the sun my shorts firm against the leather my top pink my skin redtanned I moved around the neighborhood reflecting on the scene the houses look like pieces of bad candy the Latin element up from Cuba here to eat up divine delicious pork sandwiches I eat them with Mother I sip ice cold Cokes in summer from the glass bottle with a red straw bought and drip they drip onto my tummy this sun it's wet a nightmare.

PATIENT

You're writing this and attempting to ape things you don't even wholly understand, that is: there is no writing in his writing as there is no hatred of writing. Why the incessant amounts of television? Hatred of literature? Of therapy? How many texts could Chaucer really have read? Now the scholars, but what happened to indifference? Reading the text of life like Wm. Baskerville? You have no explanation beyond the biographical oversights of history, the lazinesses. You imitate Beckett by not imitating Beckett, by imagining you're Beckett and building a plastic bird. Disinterest in Melville beyond *Pierre*; the text as failure-locus. Even that was only gloss. Too busy looking up antidepressants. A failure whole.

FLAMINGO

One day at work a boy threw quarters at me when I wouldn't sell him several editions of a fratboyish pornograph and I used those quarters to purchase handfuls of gumballs that I then sent sprawling into the heated asphalt blacklot. They spread away from me and seemed on the verge of transcending circumstance but then that boy rode back through on mountain bike and muddied the mess until all I saw was light and plastic. You know and here I've gone and done the same, amassed disorder and sweat without purpose, without coherence. I tend to sit down and vomit thus from memory and hope someday to be pulled through the point of pen, maybe. I resent the heft of miracles but even still I collect these notes and flints in hope of finding breath. I am not a grave person, nor given to morbid self-attention as I was once warned against it, but even still I'll jot thus or prattle so on receipt or wrist or in your weary ears and feel just that much more tempted to get. And wouldn't you? Get caught in storms down here. Live in close quarters communicate by way of walks across slim alleys to speak out and smoke and bitch bitch bitch about your kids—and you like it? I see a logic to it, and a beauty, maybe. I'd never communicate as much to anyone living here. Fucking deadbeats all. I've suffered in a particular way. I do not consider myself a feminist. It is not controversial, what I'm doing, these are mere acts and gestures caressing up against some void. A flamingo is an understanding thing, and almost entirely, globally inedible. It's eaten sure, but seldom.

OLIVIER

I was given something wrapped in tinfoil the first few steps I took inside Simon's home. What was inside was a tubular item, apparently, ever moving forward and behind and shining and exuding the least bit of warmth so that one notices and years for just more. On six television screens on the main floor of the home—one above, one below, the bulk of his existing done here between the two—American's vomited variously, and I began to understand just how hopeless the human was—his dissertations as Simon's tapes echoed from the nearest televisions as a sort of walling, an enclosure. He offered me a small cup of water that smelled of bleach just a tad and if I'm honest I enjoyed the memory it brought. Diners, waitresses, worried hair. The hair lining his physique was black which seemed notable, as I'd never taken much more than a look at mine with real sincerity but now realized it shone a lightish mousy brown—I felt pathetic then. Simon encouraged me by a series of gestures to unfold the tubular tinfoil item within my hands at that moment as I wanted to salvage the last bit of warmth; as I unfolded it I smelled further bleach and Americanized Mexican food followed shortly by either firearm dust or narcotic drivel and what I remember just after that is not coherent as I apparently slipped a bit onto Simon's couch or ottoman. He saw them closing in, was certain soon any number of allegations would make him mute. I watched who'd apparently saved my relatives become a boily pile, ate up with sores from debauched fucking and noisome touch.

G.G.

As I woke upon his couch I smelled the smells of the home around me and felt my feet flex without my having decided to flex them and the stretch left me homey and aired out, a good soldier. I'd done his bidding and he'd let me know of two places to stay when needing to flee the home, the life, the work. I'd passed messages and thus he'd soon be married. He sent me his recent manuscript and I tried to make sense of it with hammers. I was well convicted. I'd read of every sullen bastard leaving home. Now I eased my guts with never sleeping.

OLIVIER

"Slavish conditions! Pistol pistol!" Simon was shouting this at the television screen as a man onscreen walked into a crowd of people on a live news feed with a pistol behind his back and shortly aimed it at the head of an African-American man wearing a beret and leathered pea coat. He'd spat endless guts regarding his retaking of "Revolution #9" and the misnomer of Manson's gutless spree. I'd sought him out for guidance, for a kind of acceptance, and come upon this figure. There were rumors as to how I'd find him. The lot of his works was out of print and I only had letters from women, some confused youths who'd sought him out. Times grew hopeless, and for all the qualifying terrors his name brought Simon's root ideas resonated with me. An emptiness, a lack of engagement, a turning toward inner dark. I found a paranoiac. Shortly we'd learn his fears were valid, but Simon's initial state brought hell to all my thinking.

PATIENT

Simon sweating. Simon running. Simon coughing. Simon squinting. Simon cackling. Simon praying. Simon weeping. Simon hiding. Simon meddling. Simon impaling. Simon condemning. Simon seceding. Florida seceding. Simon calling out. Simon discussing the cinema. A panel discussion on the occult as it applies to an American undergraduate education in economics. Requisite misery, expected ennui. Emergency contacts. Primary Care physician. You watch television. HMO. A rearview awash in light. Bernard Herrmann. Ennio Morricone. *Salo* in theaters. The murders in 1977. The murders in 1877. Every musical movement and boy band prior to the electrification of instruments and recording devices. Works of fiction written in the negative, that is negate-ive, made up of the opposite parts. Pieces of a puzzle that tell you more about your hands. Simon reading whole historical accounts of madness in an otherwise empty room without hair sweating and encouraging you to follow.

OLIVIER

He'd been listening to Bobby Beausoleil's music for Kenneth Anger's *Lucifer Rising* and slowly burning away the skin of his left hand's fingers. Simon had become what he thus was and felt certain all was soon to boil into race war. We watched as the head of another organization was publicly executed by an anonymous assassin, who was shortly executed himself by the organization head's organized devotees. The news of late was filed with messes on this order he'd reassembled to meet his needs: slippages that allowed footage of oncoming violence to play out in *toto* before anybody was the wiser. One assumed the cameras were simply handed out to various nine-year-olds on the fringes of each metropolitan eruption and hence you were just as likely to see the morning's Lee Harvey Oswald as you were footage of the sweating hinds of neon-panted mothers coddling their children on newly fled formerly revolutionary streets. Kids enjoy pressing things into other things and finding out what will result only when they're too old to remember what it is that led to this endless speculation. The city was apparently eating itself after the organization's head had been executed and in turn his assassin by an anonymous wave of Jack Ruby fire that would lead to no convictions as courtrooms were so riddled with the drool and bullet casings of the panicked masses that either the chilled are or sense of failed decadence made collecting twelve able-ish minded jurors and impossibility and most judges had committed ritual suicide after the cancellation of a Canadian television program called *CRIME TIME* that essentially asked of all its viewers their basest and most trailered desires and responded with a Cronenbergian montage of smut that allowed the judges to feel ethically superior enough to convict citizens of crimes that all citizens were now heavily guilty of, without exception.

ATTILA

Come in and let my gut breathe, feet singing. Out, outward. I'd
fucked it strange—ankle, life—getting down from letting season
drift. I am Attila, handed down from the hero's paw of my father
and I truck as he trucked. I keep one cat whose demeanor suits
named Ellis and as I stepped inside his side found my shin and
rubbed until I'd swelled his bowl to satisfaction. I'm nauseous
thinking of it. A hero too! A good father is hard to stomach, so I've
clopped the old man's memories in one mediocre snow globe on the
dash. I retain a barreled chest. I commune this way one-sided with
Simon though it'll never be sent. You need some outward glance is
all, some nod to more than you. Eked out of years in solitude I've
managed to find, to discern spectacle in even the dullard moments
of being a person. Work as I have and you'll spend large quantities
of time in gas stations. See this as problematic you'll spend those
hours depressed, dissatisfied, needing more. I never saw it that
way, I retained possibility, and large or small I made it matter. This
given trip had torn me up a bit. My body'd begun its dwindling
and there'll only be a slim handful of years in this sort of place if
I'm lucky. I'd driven the length of Washington state and seen the
coast, found a comforting flesh to bide my time some several days
parked there between endeavors. Andrea, not a professional sort,
and seemed to don what denim sufficed for decent in that particular
hole, but we'd nonetheless shared moments and sweated into the
same seats and found the same bugs in that motel so I got stuck
yearning. I feel no guilt: an issue, a diagnosis. My parents raised me
in certain capacities next to certain lifestyles and I guess resulting
from this was my own disheveled moral presence. I've kept little
more than cats my entire life resulting from this. I've stayed away
from anything resembling whole satisfaction or ambition in turn.
My mother was an apish lady. A stronger scent I've never known.
There is history in smells, stories within the olfactory. She had
it, whatever it was. I'd followed her in stores. Always I seemed to
carry some balloon. Mother, where she'd walk was anybody's guess,
inevitably leading back to the tyrannical occasions of my father's
being home. Long haul transport of various goods and sundries.
Home for X amount of time miserable for Y equals disrupted

fractured family Z and Mother's weight seemed to vacillate with his departures.

PATIENT

You remember bottles of pills, stuck throughout the house like toys or small displays of interiority. A nice omen; there were no friends allowed in. You hid out for a time in AA. You hid out because it seemed you needed tamping. Your history upended you. You entered the mushroom vendor's shop and smelled around a bit at first. You noted the man and ran hands through hair so as to enact small restraint as you mulled the shelves. The place smacked of dirt and movement, wetted leaf and worm. Those places had their necessity for you. You'd grown fond of them of late. You found an ending there, observing men and women walking through. A boy of shaved skull walked by. His pants industrial, his black T-shirt thinning, *KILL BONO* and a Warholian pistol behind it, revolver? You're never certain those distinctions. After keeping knives a bit you'd kept a gun small enough to pocket. You'd placed it there and in transactional scenarios found it helped the sweat abstain and your flesh tended not to shake. You'd named her. A gun should be feminine. A gun aimed at J.L.G. being interviewed in bathrobe in the '70s. His five o'clock shadow present. The boy walking the shelves seemed determined. You remembered Nicole Kidman's pawing, a jealous tendency. A claw mark on a motel wall, pink fingernail left. The boy was nice enough. His shaved skull quite captivating. The human head had never ceased to draw you in. Phrenological flaws aside, you'd kept at staring. You imagined the boy seated on the floor within your apartment. The brown chair you favored as you'd watch television together and you're wearing little so pull his head toward your sop and find its asymmetries. A nicety, this. Familial, simple. You saw a drawing once of Eleonora. Poe's familial marriage. Percy Bysshe Shelley and the multi-hued grass. Traces back to her, your subject, the research, the project. Imprisoned, perhaps. Locked away in here? You are locked away in here. You do adore the smell of cut grass. There's a foliage made up of flamingo possibility. Again in Nabokov but just his sense for the color, and briefly the legs held up Calvino's cities, et al. et al. Your imagining still resides within the boy. *I DREAMED I WAS A NYMPHOMANIAC; IMAGINING* scrawled on a chapbook for the '70s husk bodies. Debbie Harry wanders behind a garbage can only to find herself starring in Jean-Michel Basquiat's unintended remake of Derek Jarman's *Jubilee*. Post-Modern. In modernity their texts reflected the shifting sensibilities of whathaveyou, in postmodernity the text eats itself and feeds its shit to performance artists buried under ramps masturbating, a bed of seed. Anyway, the boy with the shaved skull seemed well and good. You felt great sympathy his search was your search. Mushroom hunters all. A seeking of fungus. A polyamorous relationship with the earth as this unloving mother, no. You'll sleep better having enacted this, having imagined pulling the shaved skull to crotch. The wind was picking up and you'd be swept off into darkness soon. You apologized and left the store, already too late, already taken.

EILEEN

We had no language for it then. The bustle around it like ants confused on rotted fruit still showing life, firm. Familial ties and ropes, nooses emanated from Grandfather's place and reeled a wave of aunt-uncle sets in old cars, tired and tending to fall asleep on flowery couches while my siblings or cousins stole away and left the mourning. Yours somehow disrupted our foundation. My mother often spoke to your legacy, and in our heads it's since largely become an imagined, brightened presence. I knew your boy only in the way one knows those in mutually attended churches or over mutually retch-inducing plates of casserole. Yet still your face above the stair inside their home looms large over his and our—somehow inextricable from almost every thought thereafter in matters of spirit. I learned later the full brunt of Simon's ideas, but even that I can't spin to be your fault. You were fragile, the first fragile adult I'd seen maybe, and reading through his work when I was lost I almost fell to worship too. My friends would watch his tapes excited. Now though there's only you and your boy, and somehow I'm there beneath you praying.

PATIENT

An expert in the preface, in the gallery description, in the annotation, but in the solid text and well thought-through treatise a willful and absolute failure, perhaps that interests you. You find yourself bored with the state in which you've found yourself and lately it's been raining. Changes coming with seasonal shifts and the affective disorder or tendency you've got will blur for the coming months. Sing to yourself maybe or walk a long way. Now, though, you wonder at the persistent altering of your mood and status as a human animal, or better yet the likelihood of your death were you born only 50-plus years previous. You're not grateful or ungrateful about these things, they're merely worth wondering at, you figure. They are all afflicted in some way now. The definitions and diagnoses are too widespread for someone to go untouched. This is problematic. Today in lounge on reading about moments of war in Syria, or wherever, you swallowed several bulbous capsules of condensed coconut oil and attempted to drown yourself thereafter in some work. You made your way after the appointment to your bathroom, your bathtub, shallow water. A residence on the cheap, you need no plug within the tub, communal. The tub simply begins filling itself, quite disgustingly, as a result of years of backed up materials and such forcing the water to slowly eke its way into its tunnels. Not unlike some such, you figure. His influence, maybe, a tunneling one. Afterward you go for a trot with nurse outside and begin consulting a handful of documents you've acquired about Simon, the father figure. Mother is long gone and deadened. And you thought you'd wander on, release, see what's what. You put feet upon the ground heated by the noxious chemical ray and walked briefly until you couldn't stand your distance from the television. You walked back inside and decided to work on discovery later on.

FLAMINGO

My delving has proven fruitless, as so often was my case. The world being everything therein. I began my steps toward searching. Pa, Pa. Wherever might he be, the entity. I was seeking retribution, or sameness, or consistency. I sought it imploringly. Please oh please, I sought him. My delving ever external, never inward.

EILEEN

Closer, then, it was easier perhaps to sense the real you. My mother and her sisters had their habits of talking one another down and thus, occasionally, you were brilliant, hopeless, frantic, between jobs, between boyfriends, re-enrolled in college, becoming a nurse, cleaning up, moving home, following cultish figures, needing guidance—and yet for all of that, the passing left an absence of sentiments, judgments, or declarations on our part. Sometimes, though, before my own stint at cleaning up, it happened, my mother seems to lapse and let comparisons fester, or burn at me like so many Sunday school curses. A morose place to spend one's fifth grade Christmas, maybe, but I still remember the jovial way Grandfather lorded over the stove. My eldest brother then walked around chanting notes from Stephen Dedalus about the moocow and though I'd misunderstood it then in retrospect its tie brings comfort. These were not educated people in the strict sense, though my eldest brother had begun his branchings-out—this, arguably, from Father's side, an equally guilted Germanic bearing begging his son might too become a capable physician. Mother's side though and thus the home was brought up more by callused Irish noodling and airs put on creating stability in a place of nine children, each employed when possible, guided at the fore by Grandfather's postal route and restaurant in summer, and Grandmother's indirect employments nursing. I learned little about the nature of matter, say, but could stare endless at the range of uncles' stubble as they sat and slept or picked at the piano. Your prominence at Christmastime previous had been with boy atop your lap as undone carols bellowed up and fat jovial sweatered men clopped and ruined your debut— that only one year after you'd stayed with Mother and I through the winter, piecing together.

FLAMINGO

—And what should the therapeutic literary text be?
—A conversation.
—And do you love literature, the word?
—I don't know.
—And do you love narrative?
—I don't know.
—And do you love television?
—I don't know.

HAYDN

In the gray light of morning I stepped around the building and sipped at coffee that burned my top lip. I'd contemplated Father's years here before but never fully ingested the memory. It remained lodged in my esophagus and wouldn't flee like the old man's death. I lived simply and modestly and thus the death of a parent registered in bold. I kicked aside small acorns as I walked around the place and sipped my drink and considered where I'd come. This place was thick with feeling and character to me, such as only certain state names evoked at boyhood. Iowa. Utah. The landscape seemed to bleed a moaning ghost. My gods and masters could be seen through white-crossed windows and I loved this stretch. Staring there I played thumbs against the knuckles of either pointer finger noting the stuck callus from endless anxious abrasion. Simon I'd heard him speak at Father's urging during undergrad, an omen-soaked politico culting after newly critically inclined bodies of ejaculate. His shots taken at my methods resound still even as I stood there picking crust from pant. The way only a father's can. The way it sticks when they die on you. The way he'd amassed followers. Gleeful boys and girls trapped in snares and eyeballs stared at ex-hippie mothers knitting back together his poxquilt of treatment for our depressions. I'd run as I'd learned.

EILEEN

I remember your thick glasses and your gray sweater lined with red and you and your boy smiling toward the camera. My mother'd drawn you that winter or perhaps the one previous. I remember that image, keep it close even. An immense absence bleeds out behind you, all potential. There's always been a messiness to my mother's drawings. She paints of late, watercolor, I think in some way it keeps her close to you. I remember the glasses given me at 15 from Greece. You'd gone together, you'd spent money on cigarettes and tickets to see films I'd later see always trying to parse out who you are. Films thick with memory, *La Notte*, *Persona*, the shadows jutting all seemed to carve your name in so much snow.

HAYDN

I looked into the windows as a prowler to feel as if I hadn't mistaken and wasted this life. I remembered the god or master who'd held me as darkness swallowed the home. Her demeanor toward me strange and impossible. I'd fallen for her complete presence and almost-scream. The shirt I wore was red and bore a pocket over left pec. I wore sweatpants and flip-flop sandals that clopped a bit if I moved too quickly, and so I wouldn't. On I shuffled from window to window like Anthony Perkins, emaciated and anxious to impress. An individual whose epilepsy was so persistent little else was made note of in their days had wandered from bed to floor to small closet, it seemed. I observed with a sad concerned look the spectacle of human life and scratched the right side of neck with same hand, feeling depressed and inhuman. Their range of abilities and not eluded me almost entirely. My understanding of the place was based almost solely on a small pile of paperwork Father'd left beside the will and testament. Frequent visitors indicated, percentages paid out of pocket or by the state, medications required et cetera. I felt I'd inhaled this information without considering its import and gone almost immediately into the absolute misery of having done this work for decades. I leaned my forehead to the glass outside the individual with epilepsy's room, and the cold-wet morning mixture eased my thoughts. I wondered when new employees might arrive. I wondered whether the weekend would present itself with only slow prolonged hints and several rushed TV dinners. I wondered about the legality of various practices engaged in on the grounds of my estate, and felt a shutter of political anxiety. Nothing seemed real upon that land, when lives were quickly exchanged and quotas met by weeks of awe and terror. I knew where I stood and it was nowhere. The ground would spit its guts through my soles as constant reminders of the lies upheld, a horror show.

FLAMINGO

I'd discovered Pa working in a lonely place. The old man had lost his way, perhaps. The old man had done many things, been many bodies, perhaps. I discovered him there where lonely people sat over bubbling seltzer cups dirtied with bleachwater from kitchens filled with ill-paid souls. I'd pulled various pieces of source material regarding the bird as a sort of bolstering some warped and turned inside out by disheveled academics. I'd brought them hovelled on the seat nearest me and asked after the old salt time and again in many inland towns, not unlike my chase of Simon. We were southern. Lives down here slowed to burrowing crawl and his wrapped-up in fabrics so he registered as this sort of blue collar Sherpa as I stalked him entering a grocer on leaving work. The place was lit up. I wore a pink sweater I'd stolen from a seat near a pool at a hotel. The sweater kept me warm as did its past locus. Remembering lives within your clothing, all things secondhand from childhood on. My mother'd given me clothing from various relatives and I'd wound up wearing my grandfather's military regalia around the home as pajamas. She'd laugh and inquire, my mental state a then-concern for mom. I kept these things, what I could anyway, and when she died entered into the storage facility with some ambition toward salvaging a legacy. It wasn't tenable. The old man walked through departments grabbing at large bags of cheap pasta and I followed him unknown until he'd entered the liquor department. I'd gleaned his address through sleight. I needn't follow the old salt wherever. I could start and stop at my own pleasures. I walked around and smoked and spat in the heat. I looked and found a cheap place to lie and rented it for four days paying up front at a slight benefit to sanity. I needed relaxation and no disturbance. I needed settling.

HAYDN

When younger my father would bring me to this place to teach me something. It wasn't certain—Father's lesson—but father bore no less certitude considering. My relationship to the old man was a bit like the masters and gods were to their inmates, I had come to realize. Observation was key, staring off into space as if great matters had to be attended to the moment the sun shifted just slightly. Paperwork as well, theirs and mine. The old man filled out reams of sheets with notes and indications of his love for me. I responded with tissues plopped to floor either stenched with masturbation or my crying. Life was not immense within our home, a savored thing, but rather piddling and center-seeking. Much of my time within father's workplace was spent staring into the faces of these men and women who'd been left outside society's gut. I wondered at their freedoms. One man's eyes were pulled out and he'd mumble "yea" at every inquiry. I spoke with him endlessly asking the most eccentric questions just to hear affirmation. There's something hopeless about fathers and sons, their pathetic yearning toward apposite goals, their constant mistaking of one for the other. The vein connecting the two, this mental health facility we'd lorded on. The lock it held, the alarm system. The sleepless nights and cups of bad to worse to water coffee. I felt sick to think of it. Watching Father's hands go from stretched masculine possibility to arthritic strung digits with no apparent interim. Watching certifications change throughout the years moved me. Different boards and organizations with their encouragements, the nature of this thing. Self-congratulatory mustachioed white males with autistic grandchildren and resultant chips on shoulders. The nature of it made me spit.

4.

HAYDN

I'd inherited it. As lives go, mine would grumble. Slept through years in high school lots and community colleges until one day a dead old man bequeathed to me a key. The key: it opened the doors of an effective group home in a community where this was an ideal. The group home was left to me as shirts and such of dead old loves are left, title and all and its stamp upon the brow and future made it impossible to simply flee: I'd found a career.

EILEEN

But one night I'd seen you different. Not immensely so, nothing traumatic I guess, but amid all my awe I'd forgotten something, and since then I've held the fragments trying to stitch it back together. Earlier my mother'd screamed at you to simply go home—she'd discovered the pamphlets you'd kept I think, your conversation thick with accusation—that all would be well, and after your weeping she'd even sung you too-ra-loo-ra, but after her insistence you'd taken on a pale expression, emptied, like so much life had suddenly been ripped and halved you. I'd watched you that night, and though then I'd hardly think I made connections, looking back I think I'd understood some decision had been made. Only clips then really, and one image, but still that paleness in your cheeks and eyes dried out, bereft. In retrospect, I've said I saw it in your face that death was boring, or Midwestern, tabloid deaths anyway. I'd said as much to well-meaning doctors in Rochester while attempting to stitch together my skull's ream and warm beside memory. I saw in my mother's look that night a pulling toward a minor, a spectacular death, two diverging yous and one winds up a lackey bearing casseroles, the other, well... We don't choose the moments that exact the longest sheaves from whom we'll be, the urgent burnt memories that turn our character. I didn't choose you, nor Simon, but something in your determinism, your imperative, to leave this place and not let it swallow you whole has left me ever ready both for death and meaning I'd rip from chest to keep its growing.

FLAMINGO

I own a red car. This by itself feels strange. I like to drive it fast and listen to it near its falling apart. I have no sense of the plot of my life, only dull endless beginnings. A girl ought to be X, she ought to explore, to dream. Nothing doing. I fucked for the first time young and bled all over a trucker's seat. I carried a knife and lived on inland lots of Florida seeking what might've been childhood. Do not say my name.

EILEEN

So what of the life lived and such? You were taken, and I suppose those early absences experienced a punch deeper in all import than others. The paths we choose, the choices between incomprehensible extended realities and the impossibility once we lean in any given direction. Your boy is forever cemented in my skull as the mythic figure stuck to Mother's breast. I've not borne children of my own as yet and frankly don't expect it. My mother's tending requires waves of strength I simply don't possess most days and come their close I let loose in empty dinners and bad wines. It's enough I think because of your impression. The everyday made more extensive than I'd ever thought. The rhythms of family and the lines we repeat to ourselves from old tattered books or pamphlets brought from scattered countries and lecture halls, each a translation of a translation further removed from what was meant. I hold this thing and your image as understood by my mother, I think, and my being seems reconciled, settled.

PATIENT

You like to think of Burden crawling across the glassine floor as it depresses you. He was ordinary in all the best ways, and thus his work will stand out in your memory as pressing teeth against the real. Why it will come to matter is interesting, or boring, or both, and therein lies the curiosity in efforts to interpret the recently dead and their living art, perhaps. You've packed up your shelves for moving; there are few sensations similar. Turning what you've come to value in your life into garbage in the process of leaving what's become home is one of the few great aspects of late capitalism. You're allowed to reinvent certain selves on the yearly but if each invention doesn't take with it the anticipation of great failure and willful disinterest it will surely disappoint, and this is a lesson in the scattered works of Burden's career, his polymorphous yearn should be a lesson to all: the cultivation of one style and field of interest in artwork and life is akin to dying, and thus you must be willing to be publicly pathetic as the newborn with each shared bit or you're doomed to a success that will strangle in the crib, a la Kurt C. and Co. whose muddled ends can serve as cautions along the road where, like Marion Crane, you'd do well to change cars and slow the tape via Douglas Gordon so as not to bleed out on some proverbial shower floor someplace.

HAYDN

Without reason I'd checked the mail, knowing there'd be nothing. I stared inside the oversized mailbox for moments of quietude. I looked down the road and saw nobody coming. I kicked aside dust. I took the right thumb and pressed it into the corner of the left palm and looked precisely upward into the sky to let some madness wash over me. I took no medication but considered it. I sought no counseling but considered it. At one point I'd entered Alcoholics Anonymous because I didn't seem capable of stopping drink on my own. I still drank then infrequently and read from books on Rational Recovery in off-hours to gain perspective. It wasn't sensible. I lived in a perpetual gray state and morally ambiguous position of trying to help without helping. Their faces would smile, their reprieve gained. I'd take the hands of new gods or masters and bring them inside to plastic bedding and endless bags of soiled sheets and latex gloving. Families handing over lives and anxieties for days or months on end, or the courts and their red tape. None of it eased my thinking. The drink became overwhelming just before Father'd passed as though in anticipation. The place was now my salve, perhaps. I'd consulted Kay Redfield Jamison's texts and Simon's pamphlets and written a compilation of sorts from their depressive mumbles as well as Byron's, van Gogh's. Explored the Primal Scream and Arthur Janov, John Lennon and Yoko Ono. Simon again and these sort of performative therapists who'd enacted their best ostensible salvations on themselves. Watched live-streamed footage of contemporary therapies in practice, their doctors stood with smug exclaim. The antidepressant ritual, the cavernous glance of Ativan. Seizures so overwhelming the anus must be shot through with Valium and the body recoils into a placid monotonous twitch. Biters and hurlers of shit. Prisoners generating glyphs with diarrhea and dotted I's with cheeked medication. The Thorazine shuffle slowly degraded into the Pfizer waltz, the Seroquel slide, et cetera. Read a bit but really processed through the gut. Processed maybe like an artist, ingesting stood-out moments and casting aside the rest. Van Gogh's failed suicide that became a success. Two bullets in the heart. Steven Jesse Bernstein's knife to neck multiple times, a father. The Virginia Woolf considerations of lightness and heft, the gravity and image of her moods as rocks in pockets. Without realizing it, I cared. Walking, I expected to see some child maybe, some slight version of myself assembled in pixels to the side of eye. The coffee was gone, I'd drunk it. The place would exist and persist in its sprawl, unfortunately. I thought of Ed, an occasional maintenance worker who'd read to the gods and masters in the off-hours. He'd read to them incessantly until his voice scratched, a sort of therapy. It made them tired, but he'd keep reading. He'd read to them from Hawthorne, Lovecraft, and others. I remembered the East then, where they'd come from. I'd remembered Hester Prynne and laughed a bit at my reaching. H.P. Lovecraft and the edges of madness, or some such. All of this seemed to bring me here, to this work, to leave the home behind and pursue the carceral, something. Life could get to be too much. Shopping for the home was interesting, bulk in every aspect, spare clothing and more coffee than was reasonable. I would sit watching films after everyone slept drinking cup after cup smiling at my impact and its absence. Father had received awards. I sought no reward. No money even seemed to sprout from all the griping, just more and more. Once when I was ten or so I saw my father lose his caring. I'd fallen asleep on the sofa while gods and masters sat playing cards or watching television, and woke to walk around the top floor of the home and find my old man. I entered the room at the end of the hall and saw my father sleeping, while a young man seized up on the bed pulling out locks of his hair. I knew this man, this syndrome, its name. I watched as father snored and the man seemed intent on yanking his scalp from skull. Father seemed so placid, so absolutely empty at the situation. For years thereafter I couldn't stomach full conversations with the man, but would veer in every direction until we'd both left the room without realizing it. I'd seen my father as heroic, strong beyond strong. Now as I remembered it I knew the sweat that piled on palms and the disgusts that boiled up and knew my father as the figure of all disability incarceration, the sleeping moneyed tyrant as more funds piled in. In retrospect the thought warmed me, though at the time it felt like watching myself become impaled.

FLAMINGO

I first grew pregnant my seventeenth year and briefly relished potential rotundity. Out I seemed to grow and stood in grocer aisles teething sheets of Wonder Bread I couldn't steal so ate in-house and hoofed it red-tailed to the beach on completion. My body became alien, the baby the bubo. I could not afford nor wholly comprehend abortion so I wandered air-conditioned malls observing families.

PATIENT

You don't want kids without diseased explanations for their lack of interest in the sea of screens they sit before. You're not sure what to make of it or why the inclination is you must, but there it is. The diseased and afflicted body is the norm in twenty-first century American society, is perhaps a place to start. You don't think much on American society anymore, just the hands within it cracked and grasping at the promised some such something. Your attempts at putting brain in direct alignment with views or responses to experiences have all been failures, which is at least a point of reference. The writer as failure, as loser, as willfully inept citizen first and foremost. You heard about a success who spent their twenties living off their loved ones until some days they'd make something and though they were honest about their laziness nobody would have it. They don't want to hear of the laziness of Becketts or Clementes, and yet they should. Give them the monotony of daily life over the glorious conquerings of empire. Give the infra-ordinary of Perec over the megalopolis. You're not sure. Chris Burden is no longer living and thus the work must change. How it will change and how the scar upon his shoulder will come to reek in coming years remains to be seen, but it will change.

FLAMINGO

Freshly showered, I turned the water warm as it went and scalded my stomach. I put on the television afterward and let its light put something out.

PATIENT

Art is endless and ever-ending, maybe, always at the intro/body/ conc of youthy composition courses and thus always eating itself and changing shape. Expectation too is a sort of death, which might best be taught by Tsai Ming-Liang's *Walker*, wherein a monkish individual walks in slow meditation through a vying city only to end in a savored bite of a nondescript dinner: sometimes you must resist the temptation toward repetition only to remind self that you can never know much and life is better spent in that vein than any other; though even here you've got to curse yourself for offering solutions where only the absence of such will suffice. You think of his slow descending steps as a form of defense of humanity not dissimilar from the speeding disarray of H.R. and the Bad Brains, but at the marrow all any of it means is to seek what's different, or be swallowed unoriginally.

FLAMINGO

I began with antiquated abortive means: the drink, pills, various rituals supposedly geared toward the destruction of cells. I prayed in various capacities to have the thing removed from me—a boy, I'd guessed—as I felt unfit and disinterested in living much north of twenty-five. The pills and drink I came to realize were mere attempts at staving off boredom. My mother'd drunk and taken drug frequently during her pregnancy and all my youth so there wasn't much by way of hope.

SIMON

I am their savior... I am your savior... I am the power and the light and the word and the world and the body and the city and the blood I am the blood... Watch my tapes after I've left and feel the swell as if I lived within your hearts... Read my words after I've left and know your brain is thus infected... I am all... A pox upon the foreheads of every failure done the mentally inept by pill, by easy mother voices, my cut... Be cruel and let the bulging presence of America draw and quarter you... Be cruel and kiss a bit at your failure... Be cruel and hold fast to defeat under the iron sprawl of being... There is no interest for me. It is your duty. It is the fruit of your body. You have contempt for you, and put the blame on me again, and again and again. And you made me in the asylum. Do not build an asylum. Close one. Humans could not see, and lock them up. But stand still, and the money to play the game. And some invective to sell the case, and as long as a joke, laugh and see who you know at a given. Lives in you, and every one of you. My son, and shalt say to them: Because I do not have much to offer. Each of you in a room and you tell them, "You shall not pass through our doors" never think of it by the door for him, except by the entrance. And what will you go to school, and that we should not take the pills and they do not know what to say what it was. I'll babble on your markets, turn a ready society insideout and watch it burn to cinders while me and mine are off some elsewhere... You do not seem to understand... I was given this life, given these hands, this mind, these certifications I went to your schools, learned your sense of things, your science, your psychology, your take on just what the human animal was, and now I've seen that what troubles you, ruffles your suburban feather more than all, is you can see that teaching within me... You can see logic in me as you've seen it in every dictator, every new idea, every apparent psychopath turned martyr... I'm just waiting, is all... I'll wait in walls and I'll wait in schools and I'll wait on the steps of every American church until my day as I have nothing better coming... You all, other hand, have only change or discipline...

FLAMINGO

Over time I bled out in a movie theater. I liked it dreaming there. A few good memories in theaters growing up. I'd poisoned myself apparently sufficiently to rid myself of motherhood and so wallowed there a bit in bleeding ignorance of the All. We often fantasize about lives not allowed in, lives not lived. The movies were a kind of womb for great rest. I rested there bleeding and docile.

PATIENT

—And what of the Gysin pastiche?
—Is he incorrect? Are they well on par with the Lascaux?
—What of it?
—The form: suicidal; needs a push.
—This: your push?
—I don't know.

EDMUND

The whole American spectrum. The lines between the figures in American Gothic and their import, the tines of his pitchfork, a family rent asunder by determined following. These are Simon's tools. An emaciated fellow reads you stories. This was it. Sometimes you'll hear him, sometimes only see. Sometimes I'd play them loud over headphones while working. Simon had apparently grown up sufficiently comfortable with being photographed to entirely forget his shifted existence as a person-on-screen. He'd seen movies to parody, and you'd watch his eyes and occasionally a more expanded view of his face, the whole visage, and he might laugh or smile. A peeping tomism bereft of nearly all humanity beyond his gestures, his body as much a force of his indoctrination as his language. I felt no hefts of empathy in watching him, no strong identification or redemption in swallowing the emotive glance of another lost as me. Something else took, a righting. He'd open and you'd know how badly you'd mis-lived. By close you'd hold to every as what you'd need to do to become better.

PATIENT

A phrase is just that, the written language you use to tear self apart before breakfast. A phrase is just that, the time it takes to walk the sun across your gut. A phrase is just that, your childhood replayed backward in black and white without diegetic anything, music or what. Of late it's the phrase that wanders out and barely ends that pulls you in. You find it unexpectedly on tubs of bad food or pulled from watery paperbacks and welcome the lull. Summer's always had its hells, a fragrant blip that doesn't let up until work and something heartily timeful presents itself. You're sleepy, medicated. You read and don't read. You write what you'd like to read, for instance you're interested in none of it. You write bad television. You transcribe conversations in here that lead to nothing revealed. You write bad paintings that'll come to smell from inept preservation, that sort of thing. It's about rediscovery, about taking something wholly useless and making it yours for the ten minutes you're actually awake before the clock swallows something or other. It's about something quoted, a film maybe or an anecdote over their coffee, caught in therapy. Nothing quite works and everything quite tries, it's time for a sort of bed.

HAYDN

"I think sometimes where you wind up and what you wanted reveal themselves to be sad attempts at mythology—the questions, anyway. All my life I constructed this blood-soaked heroism out of all my middling and it wasn't hard to do. Everyone being my enemy, as you said, the knives; but here within the murk there's less certainty. You make the shaky elder your enemy and you're like all the world. I can't do it here. I've been offered escape, time will tell. The building yes, as you said, could come closest because of the dust, but even that has its warming effect. I tried to overwhelm myself. I tried to win out and lay placid under all the paperwork till it bled. Nothing doing. No chance."

"There's the old explorer in you. Where next, Columbus? Sleeping human beings communicate effectively before they turn twelve or so, I've realized. My daughter communicates all night. It's not something I can convey to you. These aren't words. Not your usual signage. What it is, it's an honesty. She bleeds it and shares it, it comes forth from nowhere and I watch her fuss. I find myself thinking about you at the worst possible moments. I'll pour myself a cup of coffee and wonder why I can't think of it as anything but that phrase, a 'cup of coffee,' and this digression will bring on hours in the wood-paneled rooms where I saw death hover. I can be dramatic, I'm allowed to be dramatic. I have been given permission to be dramatic here and now and perhaps evermore by these prescriptions. The bottle shakes and I am shaky too, an elder as you said. I look forward to sleeping someday soon. I can't achieve an orgasm with them. I couldn't achieve this with you, either, but it didn't matter. Do you notice this with the brands I've been prescribed? Are you medically licensed? I cannot recall…"

"I notice very little anymore. I graduated with a halved slip of paper that allowed me to enter certain buildings and leave others alone for all time, that is all. I apologize for the absence of an orgasm. This place leaves me that way, if I'm honest. Unable to do anything but sweat and stare. I cannot wait for death. People like me are not logical practitioners of this thing. The living walk, the existed day. I'm just so fucking unfamiliar.

"Do you still attend those meetings? The quasi-religious husk-filled rooms? That coffee you fed me?"

"I don't, but they've been replaced. I tolerate an absence only when a lesser, more abstract presence replaces it. I don't know. I'm a godawful mess these days. I sit and stare and drink pile after pile of the coffee bean. My hands feel estranged. My attitude is rotten. Just look at me, look at your daughter's fuss. She's more heroic than I. She's what? Quite young. More heroic than I at thirty-six. I live a deathly life. It has not been promising."

"I can let you rest now. I can let you sleep, now. I'm sorry for disturbing, for the step. I just needed to speak to someone who didn't want what life promised them either. I don't know what I needed. I'm very sorry. My mind feels dipped in bleach of late and it's been hell to process. The daughter's fuss is the closest human connection I've felt in one thousand years, it would seem. I miss your pathetic stare, the emptiness there. I miss your fawning, your reaches to help. I hope your life continues in this wasted manner. There's nothing out there for us."

FLAMINGO

I've heard the accusation that you'd come to someplace like this to die. I accept it, in that I'd enter every place desiring some spectacle, some death. I utilized the internet at times to order various lengths and types of rope. This alone could consume one's life. I'm not sure I desired the rope for hanging but eventually I'd simply surrounded myself with rope and took to carrying short sections of it to work and when the consuming public asked after my tendency I'd assure them all was well. They'd consume pornography in the oldfangled sense. I desired this, the observation of an elder squaloring through the shelves, craving some single thing that can only be purchased to be appreciated. I'm not sure. I saw connective tissue between my rope tendency and the purchases in-store. The living world perhaps began consuming their smut by way of the digitized, and though in most locales the vendors were left to rot on cumsoaked floors, in Florida, for a time, the work persisted. Tourists, maybe. A voyeurism to purchasing that which all concerned are well aware will shortly be masturbated at. They took solace, perhaps, in my presence, as many were consistent shoppers. I'm disinterested in their psychological underpinnings, I abjure that vein of speculation. It's just, well. One cannot sit amid the smell of bleach so long without perhaps a loftiness of hunger, a confusion that leads the most banal act humanity concerns itself with to seeming splendid, draconian, political. It's difficult to make an adequate account of what they plundered, endless reams of holes. Rods and holes, a society built upon the orifice and the edifice. I knew not pride within that gut. I'd slurp at coffees inside and out of the place. My red car seemingly reddened, almost bronzed, as if a thing of ancient stone there in the parking lot. Overnights, excellent. A brilliancy. And yet the slow discovery, the growing search. A life outside the place, an existence, an exigency I did not fully comprehend. Clipped scenery begets itself. My father, a sailor of sorts, worked outward from the dock until his whole life could be spent at sea. Not unlike Bas Jan Ader he was lost there. My pup and I searched the whole house for the man but couldn't find head or tail. Eventually I'd burned the place then searched for one of those vinyl huts like *Badlands*, only to find myself born to the wrong century.

PATIENT

The whole literary scene is a pigpen, especially today. All those who have points of reference in their minds, I mean on a certain side of their heads, in well-localized areas of their brains, all those who are masters of their language, all those for whom words have meanings, all those for whom there exists higher levels of the soul and currents of thought, those who represent the spirit of the times, and who have named these currents of thought, I am thinking of their meticulous industry and of that mechanical creaking which their minds give off in all directions— are pigs.

— A. Artaud

You wonder at the career, you've buried yourself in Tehching Hsieh's yearlong burials. You imagine a yearlong literary performance only communicating or writing or reading in a native language you know next to nothing of. You imagine literature as the highest of the performative arts in no ways that matter or make it so. Vito Acconci. Drop out. You picture Tehching Hsieh punching clocks and growing hair and something about it makes the monotony of any job or life smack of wonderment and there's its import. Foucault again and this idea that you've got to live in line with the dross you term your work. You're growing aware of it. The rope and its use on the cover of Condominium's EP and the energy of forced human connection or not. You're lost amid the performers. You've stopped and started apparently and roughly tens of thousands of things in your life that are as quickly forgotten and ignored and this is disconcerting. Your memory of the lapses in your memory is more constant than any photograph or image that sticks and carries you through to whatever's next. You have a city or a gas station and the performance therein is comforting. You have ineptitude and grace and bumper stickers and American arguments over American things that are better without your hands in them and the curled hairs of history seem to nip at your shovel-cut heels each day. You've discovered the future of mankind: it is Italy's Club Dei Brutti, wherein the hammers of society are being burnt and laws must be rewritten to favor the dogs of culture over the fine and crafted. You've left the institution, it's all memory. You weep with heft over glossed magazines in every airport possible as World War Three is fought inside this Denny's.

FLAMINGO

This entire bubbling business is nauseating. I vomit forth. I vomit self. I stand to drink soda, sweltering. It bubbles up I taste it clean. The sun washes it down. The sun is salted. My feelings are immaterial. My feet on concrete etch like wet bits of chalk the bottom of my sandals slide into concrete I sip sunlight soda cold and etchless melting into me it's wet it's sugared a fat Midwestern family is near they're standing at coolers putting unopened Hot Pockets against themselves, frozen. The family the fat family from the Midwest I know it by their regalia everyone is marked. My mother the skinny smoking sequin. My father the unforgettable impossible to discover man working and working where he is and I discover him there. Simon and his teachings lost in Poe-ish gutters dead opioid infested nightmare married family let's die together. I've tailed him. I've enacted the behaviors of the Detective. I am the law. I am the police. My father, have you left me? I've come home. I am your flamingo. You might as well refer to me as such. This is where it stands, what we've reached, how I've begun to castigate my being standing in locales such as this the heated muggy air I've stepped away from television for a bit only taken a year off from television for a bit I needed a break. My father my father I needed a break are you coming home soon? You've gone for cigarettes. I'm not I'm not I refer to you endlessly I've given all my maladies unto you Papa and where it is you're hiding is an alley someplace quiet I've found your home. At night in the fleeing swelter I watch my father rest outside his window ground floor my father sleeps on the ground floor within his building I watch him sleep I've taken various caffeinated materials I've taken NoDoz I need to understand this I need some upper hand on this man this ball of flesh before me his skin is burnt his eyes are rested I look at him from around his side I lean against the window press my forehead there press my fingertips there allow for fingerprinting it isn't essential but I want to leave my marks I'm not one to piss and yet I piss there against the foliage staring through his window no one sees no one sees I've drunk too much of the soda in the swelter again and so I relieve myself and urinate all along my father's foliage.

EDMUND

An endlessness, a distraction. A means of communicating based entirely upon distracting oneself from whatever it is one's set out upon communicating in the first place. Forever pressing matters afar from forefront of skull, letting labyrinth win out. I liked the break room, to take a break and hover. There is Jeremy there there, he sucks at Fanta and I hear it slurp between his teeth and imagine tiny cities of cavity erupting from its chemical stroll. I need dental work I'm realizing. I talk to the boy Jeremy about this; say as much to the boy Jeremy about this. One of my teeth, I say, I can feel it receding. He asks after the gums; says it's often they who'll recede. Nay, say I, my teeth are on the run it seems. I feel a tinny pain when I drink coffee, and as this is always my teeth are apparently made of tin. Jeremy's Fanta seems to suck his face into its slurp and I'm bored staring off at an inspirational signage hung across the walls regarding potential and yet I seem to notice threats in the corners of these posters. I think of paranoid conspirators and Arabic scrawl on cans of Coca Cola. My tendency is to whistle in whoa baby and let it pass me by as everything inside this dreary occupation. I am in a pocket of the world not often poked at, and I think about my father's scalding showers that reddened him and steamed the bathroom through till lunch. My mother would hawk invective through the doors at this cleaned fellow, and I'd be sitting there pulling at whichever appendage hung in need of righting. My father was a meticulous man, my mother a loving woman; and seldom the twain should meet. Their tendencies parted, and thus my youth was stretched across two halved that only seemed to widen. His cleansing bordered on religious, her love on countercultural, and I was left with means to masturbate and huff a chemical or two.

FLAMINGO

I aped my father in turn. It wasn't jokey. I think I'd come to my decision, the realization of what my time was best spent doing, and alas it did not involve abjection before the man. I followed. A figure I'd once read about had done it, a learned man with long thinning black hair who'd written a bit. He'd follow people within a sort of performance. I'd seen images. There wasn't much to it by way of rhyme and reason but this man seemed enriched and imbued with a kind of understanding regarding his subjectives that I came to desire more than mere conversation with the Wild Old Dog. It was such and thus I followed him and came to know he'd fathered two more. Twins maybe, a boy and girl similar in stature that one night the old salt ate walking with tacos from Frito bags. A good scene. It wasn't until I later watched him masturbate while watching a girl not far afield from mine own skin that I sensed the hid debauchery. In a course at a given moment in my history I'd watched slides regarding certain landscapes and Emerson and came to know the anthropomorphic notion. Whether he'd come up with it or the sideburned old professor had come up with it is now beyond me but I remember discussion of man's gearing the landscape toward his own subjectivity. For this and perhaps a handful of other factors now beyond me I pressed my forehead to the clayish plane of my father's home my right eye still seeing through the window and rubbed a leaf against my parts to get my rocks along with father. It felt crass and uninteresting and I'd briefly hope we'd both find ourselves under arrest by different sets of police officers. It came together nonetheless, a nasty Sadean kind of fusion of staunch disinterest in finding acceptance in today's terms. I returned to my motel and bought my home for five more days with wetted bills. I walked on up and watched public television suckling at the plastic of a Coke.

My hope has been to cultivate the means to overwhelm any and all situations. I learned a trick from my mother, perhaps more. I developed toothache shortly after the pursuit of my father took hold. This trick involved anything mentholated. My mother'd bought Vicks in heaps. I couldn't get enough. On losing teeth she'd give us bits of shined green to suck and this would ease the pain or transform it into something useful, applicable. So in my stakeouts; so in my observations; so in my watchings, I'd suck on scattered scraps of menthol. I'd purchased what I could afford to give away my money on and sucked those until they'd given up their testimonies, allotting the wrappers to given pockets to wind up with their even distribution in my pacing along the cracked pavemented ways and such. Until then, though, I'd not considered what I might suck in all my pained searching when truly desperate. I'd pull greeny menthol filters yellow and white from sandy gravel ash deposits outside gas stations and carefully remove their linings. I'd walk along the street until some home or business presented a spigot and I'd rinse ever briefly their contagions or what I saw and insert them along the left lip deep inside and down to jaw to squeeze their cottony green deep within the chip tooth and wound. It worked. Pick up occasional particulars that make you press, is all I've figured and since told the child I finally brought. What it was with ancient paternus were his reading habits. Out he'd checked a plop of novels by one Charles Willeford. I hadn't known the import but had nonetheless made mental note to delve. What did you read, Pappy? What worlds? Not a lofty gent, I'd guess as much from mine own breeding. Nonetheless he tripped into occasional obscurities that made him a sort of anomalous employee father figure in his daily lives. This C.W. apparently wrote of mine own locus, and thus through seamy underbellied crime forays mine pa apparently sought connection with my birthing, my mother, and whatever else he'd left on shelves.

PATIENT

You phonily again attempting to assemble some cohesion, it isn't apropos, it isn't healthful. Simon didn't want it. Nobody wanted it. They'll wonder at it, stare and pare the sentences to shivers and never quite make a satisfactory peace with all.

FLAMINGO

—Just what are you getting at about children, Flamingo?

—Just what indeed. I don't know. I need rest, and you?

—I raised one child. The mother loved me well and left. Could you imagine?

—Too easily. What can be made of the presence of the bird throughout letters? I'm uncertain. Milton bits and lofty commentary on plastic pink, little else. What can be made indeed? I wish I knew. I've mucked about and fucked it all to hell. Even my nascent daughter knows not my heaping happiness at seeing their standing. What a world, darling copper. Was writ on the tile wall of men's bathroom in Father's workplace with mine aged lipstick: *O Daddy where'd you hide the bubbly bleaches. O Daddy I'd always been ready to welcome hopes, leanings. A daggered being, you wound up sticking your piggy and burning her up atop your spit. I am just such a cadaver, rotting away in the American landscape where citizens stumble to die. I've had to chase you through drugged haze, natural and yet pressing at my temples like some alchemical dusting of gold. I think of the Africans, perhaps the women of Lake Nakuru standing centered in their homes pulling on the pole thrust into earth and pushing outward as the baby's born. My life: a botch. The aborted and the kept, and she will barely speak with me. The father an accepting well-to-do, my heart is half sandpaper. I watched you as I've watched the Nakuru women in my mind birth their children and outside the flamingo clutches itself against a low-water's wind. The life would glide out there, the being bustle. I've hoped for it and yet found only despair. A disparity between Worlds, between sensibilities, and I some old romance's broken-down heroine. I'd yearn for an ancient life amid those dustings, those feathered exigencies. I think after the women O Daddy and know I was born far too late unto our dying. Bearing witness to an end is not a living, but something whorish: an arranged marriage between the gluttony of past societies and the pockets of starvation of our own. O Daddy, how I've disappointed and set afire mine own cradle. I should like to live atop hospital tiles.* I put my teeth out, sucked at cloves. These were days of being-me manipulated and altered by the experience of going toward a sort of home. Seeing Father, calling him, all of it mucked my nerves and split me in two. The pained teeth I removed, bathroomed being as I laid sheaves of tape across my left jaw and pulled downward till they helmeted my left underchin and kept me protected as flat plasticky floss for the bare toothless gum. A nasty ordeal, and something strange to wander in upon. I had to make it happen.

EDMUND

What no one tells you is the absolute absence of novelty therein. I see an hour of digitized footage that's been seen and seen perhaps thrice before I've watched. The tertiary remove is hinted at in fine print upon your application and yet their attempts to bolster your individuality in what you accomplish day to day knows no end or bound. You are the freshest set of eyes. You harbor great control, an excess of power. You're thought of in godlike terms, their employee lunches seemed to hint. You're needed here, desire. Your presence is a blessing and a gift, and your monies should reflect this. Direct deposited slips that hint at watching and ever watching, only to feed the world these moody tracts to view. In walks my slobbery boss with bits of child's sick emblazoned on the tie. His hand upon my shoulder is wet and heated. His demeanor seethes.

"What and what do we got, Edmund?" his voice has tended to fidget thus of late.

"Possibilities, endless. A boy rode his bicycle into a circle of praying elderly women. A mother raises four children husbandless through cancer treatments. Hefts of pathos, rancid stinking hefts of it."

"Excellent. Good and good and well and done. I look forward to your picks. Might we expect to see you later?" A party had been hung above our heads with garlands of guilt were we to skip. He'd accomplished something, somewhere, at some point.

"You might. Thanks, boss."

"Great, really great. Excellent. Later on, then, Eddie." He waddles off a speechless blip, nods into another's box to ask after their attendance. My eyes avert to a screen filled with second-rate pornography and quickly I banter and mumble with myself until I'm able to flip a switch that removes this strain and sends warning letters to all forthcoming submissions. I'd seen the human extremity thrust into some receptacle, nonhuman by the look of it. Now and again the internet of course lent itself to abstract interpretations of artwork, and there were times I'd watch through something on this order hoping for the narrative, though there was often none. New desires came with our extension into the virtual. Desires previously impossible or unknown. You might present yourself whole hog and gristle to a stranger. You might remove your fingertips and broadcast it for all. Somebody somewhere would watch you, always someone to imbibe the mess.

FLAMINGO

A gravelly grasp at reality at best I'm stuck instead within the pigpen of my thoughts, the muddy sprawl of every indecision. I've walked and walked and heard news of X, Y, and S, and explored father's hands but found or perhaps sought not absolute salvation. Absolution, I rejected it, instead painting my gut's anxiety upon a certain wall where you might find it. Imprisoned is all, locked away and mediated by chemical speculation in the hands of graduate students. Be OK, it's what is offered. Be fulfilled, it's what is told. I'd rather suck the mud from so many jackboots.

EDMUND

A nice sense of heated failure existed in the break room. Bodies stepped in and out and took their swigs at Mountain Dews or hastily grabbed coffees. Hands and lives were painted there, a muted pulse of squandered ambition, carelessness, and an array of the U.S. workplace mascot: the paunch. A pregnancy here or there, a sadness thus. Teenagers and dropouts waiting out the training period so as to receive small sums and transact numbing chemicals on weekends. I've played with each of their approaches in some form, tinkered with takes on how to mete out a just relationship to What I'm Doing With My Life; but nothing quite holds firm. I prefer this dawdling, this landlessness. At home there is a being, a wife and child awaiting and even a smiling trust therein. Nonetheless this place evokes some patriotism, I blindly follow its workers into the breach as we stare supposed-smart yet wholly dumb into that endless ream of distraction. No irony inside there, maybe. A workplace based on our societal fleeing the workplace. A job based on the kissed-goodbye week Hello binge-view. I find no normalcy excepting in the break room. Lives cohere and there is flesh and blood there, real squalor. Nodding done, caffeine drunk, we mumble at one another until some internal clock prompts our goodbyes. I sit before the screen with a sort of empty fascination; my eyes are sucked from head to impart some being upon the stories witnessed. The actual praxis here, the meld of idea and fingers clicking, involves a simple tripartite system of Yes, Maybe, and No, decisions we're tasked with reaching by the seven-minute marker of each respective slice of programming. These are not pilots in the old sense. These are submissions of a sort, approved submissions not quite requested but opened like great waves of teenage potential and energy drunk rotgut. We receive clips of bodies hurled forth from parental roofs and quickly realize that seven minutes of some humanities is just too much. A sketch comedy about a teenager in high school. A romance about a mother returning to college and meeting her beloved in a professor of Economics called, I offer: *Can't Buy Me Love in Student Loans*. Reality shows amass. Quiz programs less so. Talk shows, what the breathing public perceives as "talk" and "show." Lonely men and women opining in vacant rooms with various posters behind their skulls. I feel this way and you will either feel this way in turn, in mental intimacy, or reach through your screen and pop my head. I feel desire. I feel regret. I know I feel these things. I'm convinced of it, and must convince you of same via televised ritual to bolster ratings. There are no ratings. They don't seem to understand this. It is preferential swamp. Some draw some; others wait for cult status in the wings and come back eventually. All is commodity, commodity all. Their slackjawed visages are points on my compass. I imagine their glaring. How they'll sneak to secret spots on days of work to witness what I've handed over. How they'll mince their food and words to bits in hot pursuit of the empty eye, the laughing gut, the entertained to and through the hell of modernity.

PATIENT

A tidy key between the nineteenth century and the world of now. Simon the rutting dog amid reams of documents. Simon the keeper, the pharaoh, the shepherd. The commodity obsessive. The item documentation. Wearable technology generating unconscious receipts of entire lived lives. Travels east. Familial disarray. What to make of it: anybody's guess. You utilize it for entertainment and bewilderment. You repeat his words each morning on waking as you've etched them in good black above your bed.

EDMUND

I once knew an employee who'd listen to the sound of himself masturbating while reviewing footage, playing into his right ear the slap and tickle of his nightly tug, his left whichever piece of programming required consideration. A sort of feedback loop of wasted life. The televisual ouroboros, unable to leave home enough to vacate pleasuring himself entirely, unable to accept work enough to feast with both ears on the aspirations of so many up-and-comers, he sucked his thoughts into his head and bled them ear to waiting ear—every show he watched became rejected. He was catholic and prone to masturbatory guilt, took it out on the aspirants.

Dry and high them leaving, drops afterward water the frequently although, water-level above inches few are they until raised are and water shallow made in usually are they. Mound a form to birds by the up-scraped mud of formed nests are the. Hatched are young when the approachable surprising birds are the, readiness great with desert when they, breeding the stages of earlier in the sensitivity their contrast remarkable in. Breeding were, pairs three thousand approximately estimated at, birds of a large number, were taken photographs when that. Camargue the inbreed to attempt or, breed frequently most flamingos which in one be the two appears the locality. Simon discovered what locality remote in a colony breeding large a 1948 June in but; flamingos of place-breeding as regarded could be Camargue whether the doubtful has been it recently until. (Ruber Phoenicopterus) flamingos of photographs series remarkable a selection Birds British a recent issue. The Flamingo. You are numb with pain a world of tryers a world of failures a world of better ideas modifications on good ideas ways of making things less thick with sorrow ways of making each other understand. You are weeping inside of walls inside of institutions of asylums you feel buried you feel the nineteenth century never ended. Their gaping howling monotonous terror against your ears renders you sick and you feel nothing. You vomit inside of supplied tin toilets you think of your mother you think of your father a great burden has been lifted a great discovery reached. You feel no communion anymore, their blood and God have left you open. A city and language of madness. A tower of babble. Esperanto for the head, mindless codifying sorting DSM4s for all and all for naught. You feel better as you're given leave to flee the place. You feel the sun hit your face and know you'll return again and again that his words have pulled you his language has reshaped you nothing can thus simplify nothing can find its end. Intake forms and medication and releases to any number of previous physicians and family members until all lives are thus signed over. You see their hieroglyphs on the wall. Stories writ in shit and blood to warn against its effects, the place, let go his words. Simon, a little dog and vile gash. Simon, the teeth pulled and ground to dust. Simon, Simon, not a man; dying. Simon, you hear wheels down tile and free your mind to run; set loose your thinking and give in to what's beyond. There are no more emotive glances at mothers no more birds no more flamingos no more crows no more need for stories no more Ted Hughes no more Sylvia Plath no more sorrow no more angular faces no more good ways of coping no more pamphlets no more prescriptions no more chance. There is a man and He looms largest above our piddling bodies wandering around without determinable roads. We go together, wear the same drab white and blue cloth and stumble along the walks they let us pass and visitors come on Sundays and we are still ever being righted after his dominion; seeking life where there is none, coherence where there is just implosion, sanity where there is a list of ways your head simply does not fit. There couldn't be a way out, but through.

BLEACH

stories

The following stories have appeared in print or online at:

"Bleach" – *3:AM*
"Howlings in Favor of Sade" – *The Fanzine*
"New Rose" – *Berfrois*
"Grand Illusion" – *Berfrois*
"Interzone" – *Berfrois*
"Pruitt-Igoe" – *Vol. 1 Brooklyn*
"Orphic Hymns" – *Vice/Terraform*
"2157" – *Vice/Terraform*

Introduction

There's a thing that literary writers sometimes do that irritates the shit out of me. I don't know what the circumstances are that lead to it, but I imagine they're something like this: a writer goes on vacation to a seaside bed and breakfast. While there, not wanting to take the literary books they brought with them to the beach, because they don't want to get sand on their first editions, they randomly pick up a novel from the shared books shelf in the lobby. It happens to be a horror/science fiction/fantasy/crime (choose one) novel. They read it and then think, "I bet I could write that," and then they write their science fiction/horror/fantasy/crime novel that receives all sorts of literary praise but, usually, is only a tepid and snobbish take on the genre in question, before they go back to writing their "real" books.

This sort of genre tourism is the opposite of what Grant Maierhofer does in *Bleach*. Here, he's interested in placing stories that might be considered experimental next to crime stories and science fiction stories, but also in allowing the DNA and techniques of one sort of story to bleed into the others. The title story, "Bleach," is a serial killer story, one with the gestures of that genre but in which much of the psychology has bled out (sorry). Instead we have the almost machinic gestures of repetition, best characterized by the specificity with how the character cleans up after himself. There's also a pursuit, but with the pursuer left troublingly undifferentiated— kind of like if you were watching a print of E. Elias Merhige's *Suspect Zero* in which someone had meticulously scratched the faces off every frame. His two forays into science fiction, "Orphic Hymns" and "2157", move in noticeably odd directions. "Orphic Hymns," the longest piece here and perhaps my favorite, is at once a philosophical meditation on non-human life and a kind of remixing of *Moby Dick* into something closer to *Event Horizon*, with extraterrestrial fungus in the place of a whale. "2157" takes the implications of cloning to its logical amoral conclusion. Other stories ("Pruitt-Igoe" and "Triptych") take on the notion of ghosts and haunting but in unexpected ways, the first bringing it to bear on the social reality of an actual failed housing project. Another story reads like Bataille translated by Gary Lutz. Other stories play with moody reflection unhinged by transgression, but in a way distinct from the sorts of internal monologues common in late Modernist and postmodern texts.

In short, Maierhofer is a relentless experimenter, someone who understands both genre and experiment sufficiently to torque the sorts of stories we think we know into truly unsettling and alarming places where, by the end of them, our skin is buzzing and we're not sure what has happened to us. This is true not only with the obviously genre pieces, but with the more experimental pieces as well: Maierhofer recognizes that "experimental literature" is a genre in and of itself, with its own clichés and forms, and that it too is ripe for evisceration. *Bleach* is about thinking about genres in ways that both strip them down and accelerate them, and by doing so give the reader a strange, original and unsettling experience.

Brian Evenson, 2020

Every machine works for itself according to its operations: a mouth reads everything in mouth terms: eating, talking, kissing, shitting; eyes read everything in seeing terms: eating, talking, kissing, shitting, etc., etc. All logic coexists and "speaks" at the same time.

– Felix Guattari

Howlings in Favor of Sade

"Diamonds are created in nature by subjecting carbon to a very high pressure and a very high temperature. I thought I might get these conditions artificially by electrically exploding a rod of carbon embedded in concrete. I got a thick carbon bar and filed it down into a thin rod in the centre, then I attached a wire to each end and embedded the whole thing in a large iron pot. I connected the wires to a switch which, when closed, put them straight across the power station bus bars. My idea was to pass a stupendous sudden current through the carbon so as to generate enormous heat and pressure. I chose a good time and then, when no-one was about, closed the switch. There was a dull thud from the pot, a cloud of smoke, and then the main current breaker tripped and the whole of the power supply went off."

– John Logie Baird

Lately very few things pull me from the television, which I guess just means I've got too much time. I started going to the meetings again cause I thought it was best maybe or would help. I don't know where I fit but it isn't here or really anywhere. I'd fit on some weird tiny planet with a disgusting family who just wanted to laugh and fart and swing for centuries then die peacefully together, elsewhere I don't fit. People like me can't fit. I'm within life's trap. I'm trapped. I'm not a good guy. I accept it because the notion of being either "good" or a "guy" or a "good guy" or any of the relatively small handful of variations therein I might be doesn't strike me as all that interesting in today's sense of what those words mean, or any day's sense I should say, which is more accurate.

I reject it maybe, without principle. There's nothing under my beliefs or thoughts. There's only the thoughts themselves. Don't get me wrong, though, as in I have a way imagined in which you should get me and that might be termed the right way from where I exist and I don't want you to get me in a way that contradicts this glaringly enough to be termed wrong to the "right" that I've admittedly imagined, so don't get me wrong. I'm not a revolutionary. I'm not an artist. I'm trapped someplace. I'm underground. I'm beneath this world, watching someplace. I'm hiding. I'm in hiding.

I just have less than interest in most things. I watch a lot of television. Whatever you think is a lot of television, multiply this by at least four and that's probably about as much as I watch and it isn't all stimulating and most of the time I'm watching it on a laptop computer propped on my chest in bed with the lights off while feeding my facehole from a bag of rusted potato chips. This is all completely accurate at least in that there's probably a degree of iron in the potato chips (I have no way of knowing this that would allow me to remain in the bed from which I write this note) and thus they could actually be termed "rusted" without the person writing elevating into the metaphorical and the invention of the term "facehole" really isn't so glaring or ambitious when one considers the pretentiousness of the word "mouth" and the way we've comfortably used it for years to refer to this disgusting shitsucker in the center of our melting visages. I'm not special or unique in my positioning here. I'm one of a line of people in this place with a computer propped upon our chests and we watch, and we watch and that is the whole of our days. We'd chosen this at some point or another and we've had the means to write these reports but only some do. Those of us stuck on certain bits of language do.

I do this stuff and maybe I feel bad about it, maybe not. Guilt is a useless emotion. I don't think I feel bad about it but then I'm writing this thing and Burroughs said he wrote from a place of guilt after killing his wife so maybe my fat paunch is like a dead wife stuck to the front of me and every time I look away from the television long enough to look down at her I feel strong guilt that drives me to piddle thus. I don't believe in masterpieces. I don't believe in human sagas. I don't think human beings have actually done anything that admirable in just about anything and if the structuralist mode is applied to music and the arts we've just been rearranging bare essentials and primary colors for centuries calling it ambitious when in the end we're just imitating something that made us feel good when our privilege seemed to dissipate long enough for us to remove our heads from hinds.

I'm like a dog grieving the death of its owner in perpetuity without knowing this means I'm free. I'm like a person. I'm like a prisoner, the smeary-walled kind like Bobby Sands. I'm a lot like you in that I'll listen to Mott the Hoople some mornings and feel a bit better adjacent to heating apparatuses. I smell pretty awful. The line of us I think we smell awful. I accept it. I'm so grateful. I think of sweaty geniuses and I'm not like them but I'm sweaty. There's no place in this world for a boy like that. Sweaty without the genius no thank you at least we know why this cauldron of information sweats, what's your excuse? Physiological, alchemical, whatever. I could turn this place to something burning. That's about the extent of where I exist. I say all these things and they all bear meaning and that's the problem. We could just babble and swim forever. Babble and swim with alien dead maybe.

I like to float out sometimes. I floated out in the lake one time in Wisconsin and it felt real good. I lay on the concrete floor in here and it's wet and I'm able to float. They farm us. We're given something for what we do. We watch. We stare. I had all my clothes first on but they were bunched up a bit so the concrete wouldn't stick forever. It feels good sometimes. Life feels good sometimes. I watched a video one evening with my young mate nearby and tried to inform him of something great that I perceived but that's the problem with "great" "things" that you "perceive" it's as relative as relative gets and by the time it finished he was onto the next one. Someone somewhere commented near that there was a "dead pixel" and people seemed to like it. I appreciate that. I appreciate people liking simple things when only things ultimate and spectacular grab attentions. I like simple dumb monotonous things most. I stare at ants if I can. They'll sneak in. They'll be in here like anything else. Some raise molds. I stare at bugs and let spiders live even while I'm shitting and close and helpless thus. The spiders treat me OK and I treat them back OK. They're frightening creatures if you watch too much TV and doing this, I think they're frightening but I like to press myself toward some deeper humanity loving and even sharing space with those who do not pay rent and in turn frighten. Is this the most frightening thing about spiders, that they do not pay rent? I think it might be. We are so afraid of freeloaders, and freeloaders with eight appendages are just too much to handle. I have feelings about this and more, none of which I care to share with the courts. That's what someone somewhere said. Stay out of churches and courtrooms, something on that order. Then a mate one said "me flucky asshole" and it was too wild.

I can't handle that shit anymore. People are just too nutty. Burroughs, man, he shouldn't have been published the way he was. Do you think so? I don't know. He killed his wife. Accident or not, I just don't want to read someone who killed their wife. I just don't want to do it. I don't want to need to do it. I don't want to be told what to do. I don't want anybody to be told what to do. You know I've never smiled while my throat was cut. Most of the aquiline politicians about can't seem to understand this matter, but no matter, I hobnob with them nonetheless and sink my teeth into wheels of curdled bacterium to go inside my head a bit. Perhaps our teeth are something we don't yet understand. To visit a dentist is to visit a grave. I once slept without my molars and marauding gangs fled my cough at every snore. This world just isn't making sense and I can't make sense of it. I've never smiled while someone metaphorically or literally cut my throat as one can readily assume that the reception of a hickey at one point or another likely drew blood i.e. "cut" my throat and I doubt in these moments if smiles came. Politicos smile whatever the cost. I don't mind as I simply eat emotion to ward off the hounds of hell. I've never trusted dentists, boy. To remove the teeth of wisdom is to gain entry into the human palace of decadence and American royalty circa the 1990s, babe. See you're just like those dogs you ward off, methinks. Is this some tepid answer to some placid riddle that'll only be unveiled on death's bed and then we'll be too withered to hear or care? I'd argue, yes.

Bleach

The killer awoke before dawn, the gray light entering the windows of an abandoned rest stop where he'd taken the life of the second, and last night had finished the burning and grinding of his body so that what pieces remained in his possession might be scattered out the door of his car. This was Northern California and he'd come down through Oregon over the past several weeks. He'd lost time and perspective while within his state and this was part of it. He liked large stretches of land and quiet. He liked roads that were no longer used. This part of the country was dense with them, and he embraced it. Whenever he'd communicated with anyone who did what he did via various corners of the internet and codes, they'd always spoken about this area of the country as a sort of paradise. He came here every several years and rearranged his maps across the place, almost always killing men who found some way of offending the killer.

The first had been a loud-mouthed father staying below him in a hotel. He'd heard this father screaming and accosting his children after staying at a number of hotels in a community in southeast Washington state. He'd moved from hotel to hotel crawling for who might come next. He'd almost taken a gas station attendant and beaten him with a bat that hung above the cash register. He'd almost taken a young woman running alone and minding her business. There was no coherency to what he did, he knew that. There wasn't some attempt at morality or even a story. He simply liked to watch and look. Often the people he took were people with tendencies towards outward displays of emotion, positive or negative it wasn't exactly important. This father, though, had reminded him of someone, and he knew after sitting there listening through the floor that he'd be next, his first on this trip. He waited until the father had put his children to bed with screams and had gone outside to smoke and drink a bit standing against the railing of his floor. The killer had whispered to him asking if he'd wanted a bit to smoke and he'd come up the stairs where they stood momentarily exchanging their wares. He'd opened the door to his room then and called the father inside where he'd brought a Buck knife to the throat of the man and dragged it over his larynx to thwart a scream and a quick ray of blood shot onto the wrist of the killer. He'd pushed the father forward then and grabbed a length of rebar he'd pulled from a nearby construction site days earlier, admiring its utility. He lifted the metal and brought it down four times in immediate sequence onto the back of the father's skull and rays of blood shot left and right in small arcs onto the bed and floor. The killer had not set up the room for anything like this and seldom did. The killer needed the ritual of panic in his cleaning and needed his sense of abandon when he took them. He lifted the father's head to scream in his face briefly as he grabbed the knife and made the small crunch into the back of the father's neck, his nerves screaming out in waves and the mess of him causing the killer to collapse onto the wet and smile, relaxed and ready to sleep, he lay there for several minutes before rising and shutting the door.

This sort of thing, the process of removing life from a body, creating a corpse, grew in importance with each iteration. The ritual mattered. The peace and quiet mattered. The killer had followed the suggestions of a young man he'd taken under his wing and had enjoyed the freedom to execute matters with a bit of reckless abandon. His preference was to stab key points and feel the body writhe in desperation against him as the muscles tensed and all was let go of in strange twitches. The mess then was considerable but following a certain order to things gave the killer a sense of purpose in all he did, and this could not be rushed. He challenged himself by doing no major trips to any local hardware stores prior to the night and used what materials surrounded him first to accomplish as much as possible quickly.

The initial wave of necessities could be handled with everything in the room. The killer hadn't brought anything with but could shore up the blood using the shower and scalding water and soap, removing most of what remained in the body and using a number of towels he'd throw away to address everything in the room proper. He worked this way because it allowed for quick and intermittent disposal of the actual corpse and if the police should decide to search the entire hotel, they'd only see some stains and a man in and out for errands. Attempting to drain an entire body's blood using hotel sewage was unwise but not impossible, so he tended to spread it out over several hours with mixes of his urine, blood, water; via the toilet, the shower's scald, and the sink. Were he in a rush there'd be an entirely different set of steps and concerns, but he tended only to kill when he knew this part of the process could linger as long as it might. About halfway into the first wave of disposal he walked down to the vending machine and grabbed a twenty-ounce bottle of Coke, he walked out to the corner and looked into traffic as well, checked his watch and looked around as if he might be waiting for a date. He returned to the room and drained a fairly large amount of blood via the shower and poured the Coke slowly down the drain so that the mixture was a strange, bubbling mess. He couldn't begin dismembering the corpse but when he left the room he took the corpse's materials with him and disposed of them in a meandering route of gutters and dumpsters before circling all the way back and driving then to a hardware store that seemed to cater primarily to contractors working large projects. He went inside and first grabbed a hacksaw with a number of varying blades and large black trash bags. He purchased these and walked to the car and threw them in the trunk. He went then to a small market and purchased a packet of Tide for travelers, a small stick of deodorant, some chips and more Coke and finally a medium-sized container of bleach. He put these in the front of the car and stood outside again looking at the sunset. He got in and started the car and drove back to his hotel, grabbing first the materials from the trunk and then circling to the passenger side to grab the grocery bag, from which he grabbed a bottle of Coke and took a long swig. He looked around again and walked to a bulletin board near the staircase, surveying local events and job listings.

He walked upstairs then and reentered the room. First, he took the less-soaked towel to the bathroom and ran it under the shower's scalding water with soap until it was a fair pink and almost wholly white. He squeezed it as much as he could then poured a cup or so of bleach and let it soak thoroughly into the towel. He walked into the room and poured bleach on the larger stains and used the towel to mop them slightly. He brought the towel into the bathroom and wrapped it around the corpse's head tightly, setting down the hacksaw on the toilet lid and returning to the room where he poured another cup of bleach and wiped everything with two fresh white towels then bound everything up in the comforter and top sheet which he carried back into the bathroom. Surveying everything there were no prominent stains and he wasn't leaving the hotel for some time and thus he grabbed the spare bedding from the closet and dresser and remade the bed. He went into the bathroom then and put the bedding in a black plastic bag. He used the hacksaw as the shower ran to cut slowly through the neck of the corpse and this took the most time. He drank from the Coke and wiped his forehead with a small washcloth as the room steamed up and used two and a half blades in the hacksaw to get fully through the neck. He tied the towel tight in a knot around the head and put this in the bag that contained the bedding. He then hoisted the body up so that the remaining blood would drain from the neck and poured the rest of his Coke on top of it along with another small cup of bleach. He made his way through the two shoulders at the joint and put these into their own black bag which he then took into the room. They fit awkwardly into the grocery bag and the black plastic stuck out well over the top but for his purposes it would do. He bagged up the body then and affixed a temporary locking mechanism to the bathroom door and then lifted the larger bag over his right shoulder, holding the grocery bag to his body as he made his way to the car. This was the most worrisome part of the night but thankfully it was quite late, and everybody was drunk or drugged or crazy. He put everything into the passenger seat and drove thirty miles outside of town to a rest stop where he then threw the laundry into a dumpster, carrying the head in the bag as he walked well into the woods and dug a hole as far down as he could with his hands. It needn't be wide which helped, and he made his way down a good four or five feet then set the head face down into the hole, pushing hard then hoisting himself out of the hole and pouring bleach onto the head, then covering everything with all the dirt, mud and leaves he could grab from nearby and packed it all down hard with his boots.

The remainder of disposal took place over the following day and a half and involved more bleach, a lake, a pond, digging up the corpse's skull and a swampy area in a large park, and more bleach. The situation was strange but not exactly anxiety inducing. It just became a question of internal conviction, and once he'd decided he wouldn't be arrested it wasn't difficult to speak with the detectives and patrol officers when they wanted to question him. He'd drunk a bit that second night and ordered two pizzas for the smell and left the boxes on a table, so it overwhelmed the room. He sat in the bath drinking vodka mixed with cranberry juice that he left open along with several sliced limes he had in a cup of ice water that he kept refilling via the ice machine down the hall. One night he called for an escort and she came over to play card games with him and watch a film and then they walked around the neighborhood together holding hands. He left the hotel a week and a half after the death had occurred and left a mixture of smells and messes to overwhelm anything that remained and then left a large tip for the two housekeepers who'd been so kind to him all this time.

***

This in-between space was the most important in his life. Leaving the state after spending more time would almost certainly delay and typically entirely stop the process of being hunted, and his eventual plans would make that a fuller certainty. It was in those moments that he felt as close to a human being as he ever did, especially when the killing had a clear grounding in a sort of reason—at the very least he had been angry, and his anger was released on the man, and released in the process of disposal, and quieted by the time he had finished up. He drank a bit and chewed tobacco to relax but mostly he ate large meals in various restaurants and felt as though he could fully enjoy them for the first time in months. It was fleeting, but it was real enough to hold close and embrace, and thus he did. He left the state after some days of this and went to a Walmart to buy camping equipment to settle in for a few weeks on the Oregon coast where he could swim. He purchased some beer and cans of food, some chewing tobacco and pornography, a small portable DVD player and a handful of five-dollar movies and a large pack of batteries. He got a new tent and sleeping bag, some toiletries and recent newspapers, issues of Time, Newsweek, as well as a local posting for various odd jobs listed and requested, and he made his way to a campground far from where he'd been in Washington state, that first night drinking four beers and eating a can of beans before masturbating, walking out into the ocean with a large wad of tobacco jammed into his bottom lip as he lay flat in the cool water staring up at what seemed thousands of stars. He stayed up late watching modern movies and snacking on the remnants of his can of beans as a small fire burned outside of his tent and the summer calm warmed everything.

The next morning, he woke up and before he opened his eyes, he took ten slow breaths, attempting to fill up the whole of his body as the sun warmed the tent. He exited and surveyed the small beach amid a stand of trees high and imposing. He was alone. He removed his clothing and walked slowly into the water. He felt the sun on his back and noted the apparent lateness of the morning. The heat felt good and pure against him. The sun felt like a sort of home and he closed his eyes facing toward it. He walked fully into the water and stared out floating at a massive rock several hundred feet ahead of him. He began swimming slowly scooping the water away from him and kicking froglike against the cold around him. He kept swimming and began a forward crawl and as he moved faster, he could look back and see larger stretches of beach where families looked out and he wasn't sure they'd see him. The massive rock seemed impossible to reach but he persisted. He felt as though he made no progress as burps of beer and last night's dinner crept up and he felt himself consumed by the water, entirely awake. He swam forward hard eventually closing his eyes in determination to reach the rock and after wearing himself down he began feeling the outside contours of the stone. He looked for a place to climb up and found a split with growths and roots that seemed sturdy. He climbed the massive rock and looked back at the families on the shore and found a place to lay there in the sun and feeling the warmth against him he laid down flat on his back facing the heat and fell slowly to sleep as the waters lapped against the stone and he heard bickering on the beach.

***

His next stalk began after three weeks of spending time in the sun and allowing his mind to change and slow down in the face of what he'd done. One day, randomly, he got up and went into the first city with any real pulse and went to a coffee shop that would allow for him to sit outside and drink coffee and eat a large pastry all morning. He sat there and watched people walking by, drinking coffee and slowly filling up with a sense of the day's promise. He could feel a set or two of eyes on him but did his best to ignore them. Eventually a man approached the restaurant across the street and the way he carried himself—confident and strutting, comfortable and sure—made it difficult for the killer to entirely avert his gaze. He was calm in the sunlight drinking a sugary cup of coffee and sat there watching as the man ate a large meal, made conversation on his cellphone and scrolled through it intermittently. When he went to the bathroom at one point the killer stood up and surveyed as much as he could of the table with a brief pass across the street. He made his way around and back to the coffee shop, tossing out some trash as he did so, then went himself into the shop's bathroom. He took his time and made conversation with the barista. He bought a small keychain with the town's name on it and sat back down to drink more coffee and watch as people walked by and the man settled up and slugged the remains of his beer and began to walk.

The killer waited until the man was almost entirely out of sight then began to follow. He didn't notice the set of eyes watching him and didn't speed up when the man turned a corner. He needed to know the make and license of the car the man drove, that was all. Everything else could wait. He walked and didn't notice the person walking a hundred feet back or so and focused until he saw the man drive away in a Subaru and wrote down his license plate number, noting the direction of the man as he continued walking to his car and went to Walmart. The person following him stopped after this and went in their own direction.

As he sat down later in a park to watch birds and think over what would come next, he felt a strange pull in his head as if another consciousness was tearing in. The world was light and dark, the days were light and dark. He entered into a state of pure dark when he worked and when he'd lain on the rock amid the sea a pure light grabbed him. He could feel each pulling at his skull and he could hear suggestions of unwanted thoughts nagging at him as he stared around the small park and read over the information he'd assembled about the man.

Typically, he'd buy a cheap TracFone or something similar at Walmart then use public Wi-Fi to gather information before tossing it. He'd purchased one at Walmart then gone into the family bathroom where he'd wept and shit in anxiety as he attempted to turn on the machine. He needed to leave and so put the phone in his pocket and walked until the sun had again grabbed him and finally sat on the steps of a library using their internet to find out more about the man. He'd left and it had been three paranoid hours since he'd first arrived at Walmart and now, he sat in the park staring off. Having the information was typically the first step in a series of steps that brought excitement. His mental lapses, though, and this sense of a loss of control, changed things. He felt as though there might be eyes on him and didn't bother looking around. He could feel the heat, and this was enough. He knew he couldn't work with someone watching him and attempting to think his way through any number of problems this might be. Someone wanting to fuck him, to arrest him, to take revenge, he wasn't sure. Nothing good, however, and thus he tried to drown it from his mind and sat there in the park thinking of what he might do.

He became obsessed with the purity of the ordeal, an opportunity to keep things terribly minimal and thus remove all anxiety, as much human presence as possible. It was in this manner that he stalked the man and assembled rituals of what was done each day and where he might solve things and how he might reach an ending. He listened obsessively to the same music by Ravel as he drove aimlessly during the working days and drank coffee after coffee as he sat there in the light. Stopping once at a gas station to pour himself a large cup of awful stuff he found himself confronted, and it was this that changed the course. A man, a face, a darkness to him like the sunken looks of a drug addled Jim Jones or Hitler, stared at him. He had stopped paying attention to the feeling of paranoia that followed him on his hunt but knew instantly that this must've been the man who'd followed him so relentlessly. He stood there, outside of the car, blocking his passage into the driver's seat and looked down at the ground. The killer looked into the window of the car and noted a strange similarity to both of them standing there, and for a moment couldn't discern just which reflection was his and which the stranger's. He wanted to grab the lapels of him and throttle him, scream down into his face and break his hand tearing into the bones of it. He wanted to annihilate the presence of this person. He'd disrupted him while he waited for the man to get off work and he didn't know what time it was. He knew he'd have enough time to get to the gas station for coffee as he'd been doing it for days but couldn't guess when the man would leave his work, heading home, perhaps breaking the ritual and understanding the killer had reached.

"What is it?!" he managed as the stranger raised a gloved hand and brought it slowly down to suggest a calming.

"I am here," the stranger said in a gravelly voice, as if he hadn't spoken for some weeks.

"Why have you been following me?! What started this?!" he'd lowered his head then like the stranger and tried to gather what items in his vicinity might quickly break an orbital socket or mass of cartilage.

"I've been following you, intermittently, for some days," with this the killer broke from the apparent hold of the stranger and shoved him as hard as he could manage so the stranger fell to the ground. The killer noticed they were almost dressed the same, the stranger's clothes in shades of gray where his were black and blue. He opened the door to the car and drove off quickly, reeling from a heavy slap the stranger placed on the back window as he adjusted his position.

The killer seldom made a habit of talking to himself. His obsessions were such that vocalizing them was often a slippery slope to suddenly revealing some horrific thought while waiting for clothes to dry and forgetting the world around him. He'd seen therapists intermittently throughout his life and none of them could adequately quiet his skull, but whether hunting or in a period of dormancy, whether in America or in the surrounding world, the better he abstained from speaking aloud—especially when under duress—the better overall he'd be, the less paranoid. This situation, then, rattled him such that he found himself repeating over and over a prayer his mother had recited to him over and over again while a child. He spoke aloud, trying to reassure himself as to who or what the stranger was. He yelled, and screamed, and drank from a bottle of cheap vodka he'd purchased the previous day for an evening's camp. He tried to be sure nobody followed him and then kept driving, speeding away from the gas station and the city and his campsites and his stalk and the victim and drove on and on until the world around him seemed to finally quiet. He wanted to ditch the car and wander off into the woods and be sure nobody followed him. He wanted to return and kill the victim and kill the stranger and quiet the screaming garbage in his brain. He wanted to finish the drink and fall to sleep on the rock in the sunlight. He wanted to be back at the hotel, dragging the saw over the mass of the father and preparing to dispose of him. He wanted to get away from this world and feel it changed. He drove and persisted in driving in random directions and taking unexpected turns that threw him off sufficiently that he felt nobody could follow. He stopped, eventually parking by a small area for children to play and walked through backyards until he found himself in a place of apparent quiet, and kept walking, his sweat screaming down every limb and the world glaring in his skull like a klaxon. He found no peace and felt only wet.

Realizing this meant he'd need to abandon his stalk, he stayed around local motels where it was possible to park strange ways and return indirectly so as to—he thought—thwart the efforts of his stalker. He spent three days wandering out in a sprawling serpentine of a dirty suburb and drank to keep his nerves at bay. The first night in the first motel he shaved off his hair with a pair of clippers and trimmed his beard so he could shave it clean. He closed the door of the bathroom for this and turned on the shower as hot as it would go. He turned on the sink as hot as it would go. He used the toilet and then stood facing the mirror with the clippers in his hand and ran it slowly over the whole of his skull until only a fair amount existed on the top and the remainder of beard would be easier to shave. He did this slowly in a repeated motion from one side of his face to the other, first buzzing at the left temple and progressing slowly upward until he felt he'd covered one hemisphere of skull and then making his way up the other side. He did this three times on each side, then ran the buzzer over the top in alternating directions as the hair fell in the sink and he watched the slow mound of dark build there. Before a final run over his scalp he ran the machine over his beard from five different starting points and the black and gray of it joined the remaining hairs there in the sink. He then grabbed a cheap razor he'd purchased at the front desk from the woman working there and soaped up his face with scalding water. He brought the razor down from each temple and made slow movements downward and in until he reached his chin and blood mixed with the hair and waters in the sink. The process of shaving his face was rougher than the process of cutting his hair because the presence of blood tended to make him react in occasional spasms and gestures which only created yet more blood. It was a pleasure he indulged in every month or more, and it always proved grounding. He dragged out the ritual of shaving as long as he could and took slow pulls from a bottle of vodka he'd bought earlier in the day. The room was steamed over multiple times and when he went to operate the buzzer once more over his scalp, he opened the door to avoid any shock. He ran the machine methodically over his scalp until there was no more hair to drop into the sink and he lifted these hairs after turning off the sink and shower and flushed them into the toilet. He turned off the light and stood there in the quiet and felt his skin where he'd been shorn and slapped the back of his skull and the bleeding fragments of his cheeks and felt awake. He poured some vodka over his skull and felt its burn as it mixed with the blood and stung. He turned on the shower again and once it turned hot he sat in there on the floor idly masturbating in the dark until he felt his mind changed and sat until the water turned cold cleaning himself and preparing to rest and get ready to go back out into the world soon.

The morning he met the man the world was dark. There was no light. He left the motel early and felt a sense of duty. He wanted to return to his stalk and couldn't. He drove out of town and didn't stop until the lights showed behind him on the horizon a mile or so back in a stretch of mountains. He was driving back to where he'd come from and he wanted to feel the ocean on him pressing. He drove until the car came close and let the stranger occupy the same stretch of road as the world slowly warmed in light and he did not know where to drive. He continued thus until he saw a scattered stretch of farmland and what seemed an abandoned house and continued on a gnarled scrap of road until the trees surrounded them. He continued and he drank at the bottle of vodka he'd left in the front seat and eventually the two of them were parked in line and the two of their cars looked similar in the starting light. He waited there in the driver's seat and saw the hair of the man behind him through the mirrors and sat until the heft of the moment weighed down on his chest and the two of them exited their cars in sequence.

"Who are you?!"

"I have come to you. I have come to ruin your life."

"Did you see me with them? Is that what all of this is for?"

"I only want to wreck everything."

"Are you a fed? Is this some larger thing?"

"God sent me."

The stranger approached with open arms and held the killer in his weight as the sun began to shine around them and the world was slowly warmed over. He held him there and the killer noted the paired angles of their hands, their wrists, and held him. He watched the stranger walk to the back of his car and the killer turned. He entered the building behind them and ran his hands along the brick as the stranger called after him, anxious. He found a place with low light and metallic surfaces and sat on the ground there awaiting the stranger. He sat until the man entered and stuck out his hand to grab the meat of the stranger's calf. He pinched his nerve and stood up yanking the stranger to the ground. The stranger mirrored his looks and held a knife clenched in a dirty fist and the killer reached down and pressed his hand onto the blade and held it as he beat down upon the face of the stranger with repeated pulpy shots of his forehead into the eyes of him and didn't stop until the mass of his face was an incomprehensible soup and he raised the bloodied hand and held it to him as the blade had gone through and he raised the knife and brought it down in angry thrusts into the bone and marrow of his chest, stabbing until the blood stopped pumping to the heart and the moaning hulk of him was silent.

When time had slowed, and he had calmed himself a bit after the stranger expired there on the floor the killer was able to stand up and get his bearings. He was free in this place and there was nothing to worry about nearby besides his car so he took the stranger's car and drove it to an empty country road awhile away from a gas station where he stopped for oil and liquor and bleach and a lighter and walked all the way back to this building he'd discovered and walked back inside and began dismembering the stranger and burning small fires to dispose of things piece by piece.

In the light of the next day he saw the form laid out in sprawls around the room. The place smelled of old piss and it surrounded him. The body was mounds of crusty blood and dust and jutted fragments of bone and it was this he'd slowly air out the windows of the car as he made his way to Florida. The double of him had been eaten away somehow and there were rats in the place and he could only drink at the vodka and douse it all in bleach as he made his way to his knees and wiped the bulk of it up and found an old spigot to run water into the room after he'd leave and the smell overwhelmed him as he stepped outside into the early light and the whole world seemed to bubble up inside his chest in a massive question and he knew to return to his work and make quick time of it. He stood upon the rocks. He looked up into the sun. He put his boots on.

New Rose

"Punk's not dead it just deserves to die"

"Chickenshit Conformist" – Dead Kennedys

Gary juts his teeth out clean toward the cameras. He's the spitting image of some long lost. He's written things like PLASTIC MENTAL or ROVING UTOPIITE on the reams of denim that sort of drape and stick over him as if he were some guttural Sherpa. He hocks and lets whatever fly outward as we sort of home in to be closer to the god in sneakers. We are in a place as a group and this carries with it its set of problems, forgeries, falsehoods they've all agreed upon to sell some records. A minor cultural blip in a city of minor cultural blips and they continue swirling inward, cut T-shirts and leather jackets and smelly denim and trying. Trying trying trying.

They take this photograph and this one, with some assumption that icons are generated this way anymore. We're not convinced but Gary just looked so ready. Hoity-voidy had been a band for like six months and it was all downhill. We'd aligned with someone mostly interested in metallic floods from oiled guitars, who saw the *Bleach*-ish potential in our stupid disarray and willed it together. These photos were out of another century, we couldn't make sense of it. They'd be on posters in small record shops with a photograph somewhere of the cover of an LP whenever it was finished and that would be that but we'd still all work in call centers. Gary though, he could manage. Gary lived with his parents because at an early age he'd convinced himself that he was sort of nuts and it'd only worked better and better the more it became apparent he probably was a manic depressive or whatever. His parents didn't mind because they didn't mind about anything at all.

He spits up and it comes back to catch him square on the left eyelid and some of it flecks away to skim my dumbcheek. I wince and laugh at Gary like he's our pet then kiss him hard as gapers snap the pixels. It wasn't about some sequence of events congealing or whatever to arrive at X amount of art in Hoity-voidy, rather we were just sort of focused on connecting our stomachs in the face of great oblivion and letting sad be sad for thirty minutes occasionally and sometimes longer. I'd pick apart certain things with this guitar I'd traded many items for. I took it apart one time and put it slowly back together wrong and that was my contribution to our set for the third show. It worked out because everyone was drowning anyway.

There would be no great transcendence anymore and we were for it. Black coffee and sweated idiotic tunes from manacled elders stuck in teenage would be alright. I'd lock myself to Gary, he'd tie himself to whichever roommate from whichever hovel might be there to play the bass who'd in turn place his tongue upon the drummer's stick to complete the Circle of Shit before we played it off. I'd bleached all my clothes and so walked around like a painter. Gary looked about the way he did standing there spitting all the while. The rotating rhythm section was typically this girl Lila and her sort of betrothed Henry, but he was gutless. I just liked to watch crowds hate us.

His demeanor was something special and this I trusted. I'd heard tell of many women or men who'd fronted groups with blood and teeth but never figured the town could birth its own. Gary my Yoko Ono, Gary my Vito Acconci, Gary the frenetic mess pushing his body to limits, Gary the tired twenty-five-year-old sweater sleeping on my shoulder. I was over everything, but Gary brought me back some days. I pulled the strings out by shoving my fingers beneath them and ripped until the guitar made what I hoped to be an impossible sound while Gary inhaled the microphone and mumbled the lyrics to "I'll Be Your Mirror" I think while everyone stared into dead space. Nobody came close to us and it was better. My forehead often cut open from rusted stuff around the places. VFWs or homes-of-lifers where we would play then sleep inside the cloud we wouldn't leave until we'd driven some twenty miles from the city and washed ourselves in sunlight. It persisted that way and I welcomed its nightmarish glance. We didn't want to see life as we'd seen life, so we stopped seeing life. Everyone around us was suddenly an obstacle, a potential death with klaxons jammed throughout their faces, belting highs and lows as Gary mumbled "My name is Carnival" into the rim of a white plastic affair he'd filled with every soda type available within the gas station. He didn't have a name for this and neither did I. I tasted it sometimes and it felt like I'd wasted my entire life.

I could be such a royal about dying. Gary wasn't that way ever, just smoked or pissed or spat and that was all. He drove this van that he didn't really drive so much as kick holes through until he got wherever. Gary my Fred Flintstone sleeping in his father's basement attempting suicide biannually with huffed cans or split skin. I'd discover him that way and realized hard that life never progressed nor went back for the actually alive. The actually alive didn't see life, as such, it was something else. I smelled the smell of his father's basement as I discovered him near death and called the ambulance and rode with his father in the car following the lights and it all smelled exactly like everything always had, that is quite good. Gary's mother was tired maybe or couldn't handle those rooms again, but I could, the light didn't get to me. I looked down and saw that Gary was much happier than I'd ever seen anyone in my life. He was grateful not that he was alive but that he'd again made a successful attempt at no longer being this.

I liked discoveries that felt like nothing at all, staring off then suddenly you realize where you'd like to die, hand your friend some money for your coffee and realize why you won't become your father. It was excellent, and Gary could dance the fucking moron. I hated it. I hate dancing and dancers. Gary knew that and so danced. Gary knew that and so was a dancer. I couldn't handle too much of the oppression. The photos were done, and I was eating, and it was OK to not be dead for twelve minutes. Gary had this massive hawk in his throat and pulled it up through esophagus to prance out on the ice his water needed. We were disgusted and not, it mattered. Whatever you could sense about the kids and all their wild revealing moment to moment, the heaviest was discovering old tapes of your fathers and setting them on fire without hearing no matter how much it tempted. Gary was best at this, Gary with the sunken eyes and jutted teeth, a caveman, Gary the constant thought and running ever toward the fringe. My hands started to crack from dryness. I ordered Gary a new water when he went to piss but let him think when he gulped it down, I'd done nothing. Rhythm section nodded.

Grand Illusion

I have no patience for my grisly ineptitude, so watch it wander. The fingers wander in front of the face as the face presses right side down to the counter and the room shifts with pleasantry. I am in the room, impatient with myself. I am in the room, watching my life spin out. I am in the room, inept, watching. A diner's name hovers just out of the left eye's view, I say "Mary." What could possibly go wrong when Mary's here? She says "Hon, coffee?" and for a moment there it's as though we're husband and new bride. Her teeth are going but I hold the thought back as I pry my stuck rotter cheek from the plastic thing. Oh, I thought about leaving town. Oh, I had a thousand conversations with a devil. And I just might've if that'd been the way. Wandered maybe like the fingers did and now they grip the coffee mug as it leaves Mary unto the son, it is me. The water glass smells just like bleach and I huff and puff as I swallow it down. My whole demeanor seems off. I've scattered it throughout the woods and now need to collect the spare parts to go anew. My teeth chatter maybe on the plastic glass as I carve out some room to breathe.

I begin drawing signs on a slip of napkin and wonder if Mary can tell which language I've chosen to write in. Oh, my Mary, where the dogged pace of my life should stop and vomit. The smell of bleach sticks to your hairs and won't let up, the room suddenly takes on a modern way and I just hate it. My hands are gaining feeling, but my shoulders are hot and carry the weight of one diseased cow, each. I ask Mary if I might have some rudimentary meat parts and she assents and grabs the counter too. My damned face is going now. First the memory, then comes the face, waddling like it just gave birth off the edges of your skull till suddenly you're just not you but the dying you. I cannot wait for this but all I do is sit.

I was given this opportunity to melt thus for the last thirty and I took it to watch the kids grow but soon they fled, and I won't blame. I wander in here most nights and feel the wind bury. I wander in here and order nothing until Mary tells me what to order and after that it's too late. I spend the afternoons after cups of rotter's coffee wandering the public library shelves reading science fiction and film descriptions. My fingers reach but I don't let them. I see faces and they look far from melting as I can tell. I see the movies maybe once a month and they don't ask. Just sit there all day and they let me doze in and out as the screen shifts and the voices alter. On and on I kick in Velcro without reprieve or screaming.

I stay away from churches as the father said and stay away from courts except for extra scratch for entertainments. What I do is order foods from three different places and whoever arrives first I just let wait and tell I'm an old man without the means hold your horses, boy. The second confronts the first and both begin to speculate, and either they leave and say *adieu* and I eat the third or they all sort of sympathize and bring it in for a short supper. I pay either way which isn't the problem so much as company that doesn't know its company, nor does it desire company or want to be company.

This is the best feeling on earth. I spent a lifetime surrounding myself with anxious faces waiting for mine to either melt or crack in smile to welcome their collective sorrows. I spent years trying to catch a frown slip weighty from their glances and never did it pop. No more of this is what I said and now I put on the TV show and try to remember that one where the man wore his hat home from work brought workers with and wife wouldn't stop behaving in just such a way. I felt awful sorry, but she seemed to need to be that way. He just mumbled as he was wont and the scenes billowed out like blood from his wound, his birth. The cup smells like bleach still. I welcome the scent though and realize I'm wearing pajama bottoms out for breakfast. Seldom I do this but when it happens Mary plays the fool and brings the stripped parts to my teeth. I can't wander like I once did, but the fingers do the wandering as the news plays out on bad screens and the place slowly fills out with waking college. Oh, how I'd love to just sleep forever here or on the bench out front. Cold will come but I could take it. Bears endure with only inches more than I and that in climates far more northern. Oh, for so many things to have gone just how they might've without the kids fleeing like the billowed blood or fingers tiptoeing past my melted glance. I see and don't see as others gesture with concern that perhaps I need to use the Men's and none of them with stomach such to ask me.

It's alright, quit and good. I like to let my breath seem stilted and they lean in with concern at the edges of my vision. Just joking, I imply with further sips of black runoff and bleached urine. These are the best days of my life, the days wherein I watch the children grow and the old elm wilts just enough to shade my eyes toward passersby. Holidays are spent jokily masturbating what can't be masturbated as I eat and eat from cold cans beans that were never warmed. A check arrives and a visitor shops with it spending what I give them on their own enjoyment so long as they spend the evening watching TV at its work. They too must not know they're company but that this is somehow all bound up in the work they do. I think of that anyway. I think of a lot of things as my memory starts and stops to go. My hands will stick when pulled just now. The coffee warms me and it's only thus I drink it. Didn't he say that once?

Interzone

I brought my dying friend some water, maybe that's how it started, I gave the guy as much water as I could find but it seemed like it might never be enough so I was panicked, we'd searched for this place to coat the little guy in calm and betterment but that in turn was nonsense and not enough, we were out here, he was in the street pulled where I could get him but dying nonetheless and I was sure, poor rotten idiot stuck there just like the best dead—I noticed he didn't seem to shiver once as the sky grew thick with the klaxon blur of lights and warning from this strange rancid helicopter just up there—the building we were stuck up against was breathing it seemed, I pulled him back against me and the wall warmed with wet grass like it could feel, the building was designed many years ago by Vito Acconci, I read it across the watch face as the friend he's trying to gulp down loads of water knowing the poison ought to win out—a perfect poison made for him and one for me that he'd swallowed too and taken into him and I appreciated him as I watched him, guts and limbs pulsing with skin and water and too much of it all and the forces are up there they're staring down looking down at us and sneering and red lights and klaxon noise and it continues and it's there in us and the security from the building is attempting to pull us and I'm making sure he's drinking water (it's an unnatural amount and he continues and he has me pour it over his limbs and the pulsing skin and watching it and he's certain he tells me he's certain "I'm certain if the water's there I'll live" so I continue and I continue with no intention of stopping his hands squeeze at me.

—we sat there until the sort of goons came down and pulled us into this rumbling edifice and swam us through the smog to some pyramid shape I'd barely dreamed about, the friend's skin was turning beet red or crimson and the vague humanoid goons seemed like they might revel in his suffering until he popped, oppressive heat bore down on all of us as the landing drove us inside this cauldron of buttons and numbers and we were deemed and heated sanitary by the cautious man himself, movement through these ships was gradual and sudden and there was little time to think to oneself, only the feeling, this pulling at one's flesh as though you might've weighed more and less in simultaneity and every lick of you was registered—the pins in your neck given at every instance of employment and my friend and I had tested drugs for the previous five years, your tags from birth and every five year milestone so that your history sort of sprawled on the walls next to the buttons and they could take you in and process you and where you go would follow—my friend and I had been picked up thus countless times but never needing medical attention and all I could do to feel any sort of certainty was hold his flesh to me and wait—

I asked around and found we'd trespassed while dying on sacred ground deemed thus by some ancient tribe of teenagers who'd frozen themselves, less amused than I was my redfaced comrade as his breathing slowed to a crawl and I sensed his eyes etching awful cavesmears against the lids, my hands were full of pressure as they dragged us staggering from room to room inside the place and I heard endless clacks of shoes walking similar routes down apparently forever halls before being pulled up to smell the man's feet and cower, a radiance in him and a love from all surrounding, billowing out, these people drugged or stupider, something numbing them and making waves of calm around us as they ate and ate handfuls of black moldy bits and I could not understand and could not find comfort in their control—normally I'm at least eased by the certainty of an other, someone capable of grabbing hold of my neck and screaming down orders for the whole of time, but these were scaly people, culty and uninterested in the exploding world around us, governed by some nondescript blip only they would understand and we were doomed to some sort of research, some sort of testing—

he didn't say words and I was glad at this and grateful and started to cheer before I witnessed my friend dying in the corner, breathing out his last as his nose turned this awful chapped expanse of sanded land and cracked right off his face to pints of blood, my sense was I'd be prisoner here to witness the feet and death ad nauseam until my teeth ate their way through my skull and called it finished, I was listening to every piano concerto I could stomach while the goons surrounded me and I was damned and punished, I lit a mashed roach and sucked its dogends through the back of my throat until the redness came, a foot rose up and its primary toe extended to reveal this grimy chip coated in oil and breathing just, the goons pulled back and the cautious man made some rotten groaning sound without limit as these craven idiots they started dancing, this was a sort of ritual performed by guards to create clear limitations between whatever I was, this grotesque string of scaly toenails and red flesh, a pervert brought in to mediate between the minds of my torturers and the various burnt spots on my skin, all you could do was welcome it, all you could do was breathe it in and let your face be mashed into the wet floor and yesterday's wounds were opened and spread to new ones and their chants could be heard above the drip, a constant lulling smear

my friend his corpse was dried beyond a reasonable state and I was terrified by news barreled in by screens with minds of theirs, information came in palpable wet slaps as the politicians flooded us in and circled up around the cautious man but for several feet so he could stretch, our pervert, my breath was slow like I'd swallowed nails wrapped up and tried to live out the minute, I had an ulcer in the center of my forehead I felt where my brain seemed to leak out I swear it, this was some beginning, I began and swore to ground or ceiling just what I might do after the teeth did their work, these craven politicians with their endless glance and robes, I smelled the glass on walls as it grew thick with junk and spit, one began a prayer that came with hundreds of throat-sung notes they bellowed apparently to highest as I began to comprehend my sneak, I sort of waddled like a bastard until my breath began again and kicked a hole in the crisp head of my friend making the last jaunt through the legs of this parliament, I sat in sorrow in the woods and my teeth seemed to want to do their worst so I fought barely, it was time and with the moon high and dead above my guts I lay back on wet cold floor and pulled my trousers to waist before expecting the unexpectable, my problem was never making bad feel good, but something else entirely.

Triptych

I.

She and he and I had shared a similar disinterest in work, being, pursuit. We all worked, were, and pursued moments that seemed to smack of indifference, sorrow, even malice. There was nothing much before for me, and while I can only hazard guesses, I'd say the same was true for each. There'll be nothing much after, one infers, and even in the middle we were little more than rutting dogs. I think about it seldom, perhaps refusing. I don't like to dwell.

I haven't had use for ghosts thus far. I'd overdo matters and become distraught and find myself in broken relationships. I found myself, to some degree, in the act of breaking down. My family often harped on ghosts wanting to utilize them, I thought, as a form of caution.

II.

People seldom do well to couple, these were her admonishments. You oughtn't pursue something worth living for before expunging a desire to die; and a desire to die is often all that gives life interest—all that leads to coupling mostly too—and thus you're better off living in a manner that brings quick deaths.

I was twenty-three and unhappy and working for a company that promoted the use of other company's wares—my brother hired me and vocally regretted it from the get. My work was unimportant to me, so I often came in tired, sweaty, having finished the long walks of then. Life was idle. You might masturbate away your youth, it stands to reason.

At night I'd go over to a friend's who lived in the basement of grandparents who were understanding, and we'd sort of experiment with performance art and sounds. He worked day to day making guitar pedals and thus at night we'd drown out the day's hefts and scream at one another or play video games or smoke or watch *Blade Runner* again. It was through him I'd met her and heard her admonishments.

III.

One night I walked into his place after being instructed to bring caffeine and found him sprawled on the floor covered in black paint being photographed by an older woman with buzzed hair wearing boots and suspenders. He'd sort of make idiotic gestures at her and she'd kick him and take pictures with her boot protruding or pulled back and afterward we looked at them on his desktop while she introduced herself to me.

They'd lived in the same small town outside Milwaukee. She was visiting to work on visual projects with him and I got the impression they'd slept together or something. I punched him on the arm screaming RUTGER HAUER sometimes and he would laugh, and she would reference something she'd done in the '80s for money and both of us would feel pathetic, dilettantish, ashamed. I learned she'd taught him in high school. She'd taken him as favorite and he'd won awards for photographs he'd taken of her in slim Londonish alleys throughout Milwaukee.

I found myself staring at her skull and her boots and her suspenders and wondering whether she was a fascist. I asked her this and she showed me a tattoo of a Trojan helmet on her shoulder and told me in fact that she was a skinhead against racial prejudice. She said it as if each word were capitalized and I later learned of their organization but at the moment I just sort of smirked and thought her descriptors forced. My friend often brought home friends of novelty, preoccupied as he was with distractions from who he'd become—a lazed, numb avoider of work like me, though ashamed at this.

IV.

He and I had previously come together out of desire to kill time, little else. You attend art school with skinny idiots and suddenly find yourself with elbows to ribs being read Lautreamont in fabulous housing. You sit on couches at parties as bands play repetitious nods and someone projects Kenneth Anger's hells on the walls. We'd met under similar desperate circumstances and after experimenting with whether we might live with one another happily had become a brand of comrade. You never quite fuse in thought entirely but your attitudes about art and what the world might be and how a life's well-spent are similar enough that it's easy to sit there not talking but feeling like some work's being done.

I don't come across a good deal of men with whom I share ideas and I guess it was this that drew me in. He was depressive, lazy. She, it turned out, had children and a family but had turned her head to artwork and making life new again and we just happened to be present.

"I could lecture at you while you two hurt each other in the bath. I could suck *you* off while the other reads to me from Churchill's journals. We could swill brandy and set parts of our skin on fire with my perfume."

"Uh huh. Gutsy."

„RUTGER HAUER MAYBE."

"You are both such cherubs. Let me make you scampi."

***

One payday I'd arrived to find the two inside his shower making sounds and so I sat on his bed drinking pissbeer until they'd finished fucking. The room was bright white with long winded curtains sunlit over a floor covered in rorshachy black dripwork.

***

"We might record something and send it to your mothers and make a fracas."

"Uh huh, I do not care."

"I was just paid! This is a weird and fuzzy idea. I don't want to record us. I don't think you hear how you sound some days. Your hair is graying."

With that he'd grabbed me and wrapped my hands in leather up to the wrist and she'd stood beside my head to scream invective. He held my arms up and stretched them to the point of dislocation as she told me what a waste my life in sales was. She told me that my disinterest now extended to art and the two of them would have to follow me and set me right again. She told me this as both of them were free with me and I closed my eyes and envisioned the money I'd received and my brother's tie on leaving work.

I found a minor limit experience and knew my love for normalcy. They watched *Romper Stomper* and I became confused. She seemed to live on lines. I wondered about her family. Her boots and suspenders and demeanor seemed to press conventions impossibly far from her. She'd once shown us her husband the biker and her leathery skin cemented my take. This is how you are a lifer, I thought. Her children damned to a forever confusion perhaps. Her husband likely in a similar state as she, watching *The Night Porter* with young women artists pissing on screen and defiling each other.

V.

I called my friend the day after for a talk and he'd said he loved me. It wasn't heaving, gross, or wet, just a call to stop some disarray. I love you too, I said, then went to work intaking calls regarding sneakers from elsewhere past due on American doorsteps.

She reached out to me and rambled endlessly toward her children.

"I am not a bad mother. You and he think I am a bad mother and it's incorrect, it isn't so. You aren't considering things, only surfaces and what you'd like to be the case. It might not be for me to say what motherhood should be but small boys like you have ever asserted your right to judge, to belittle. My husband when younger kept pace with the Baldies. A black man from Minneapolis I met on sobering up the first try and my body became a locus for ideology. It doesn't need to matter. I just want you boys to understand the head with whom you've been fucking. I *like* it here. We've made a decent thing these weeks and even if it keeps here, I'm fairly sure it has worth. Imagine bacchanals to ease civilization's hefts with no knowledge of nearby villages and ritual. Imagine Barbara Newhall Follett walking into the woods unsure of what would come of work she'd left behind. What I'm saying is don't belittle your existence. You shouldn't. You will as all youth has done but I will not."

My friend slept as she told me of her marriage and the birth of her daughter and son. Light crept in and we resented the gray. We were tired together and overtired and I had work shortly. I walked to his bathroom and removed clothes and felt vulnerable entering the shower. I reached out and turned off the light and sat on the floor misunderstanding. This was not a mild person. This was darkness. I became incredibly depressed and laid my face against the shower floor. I heard them mumble through the wall the sort of harmless morning's banter and sensed a different she.

Friend took heaps of meat that night and beat them against a speaker while she screamed in next room wrapped up in a sleeping bag with microphone. These were field recordings. I was feeling nauseous because of X. I was tired because of Y. The three of us had smeared our bodies together like idiots and snuck into homes together with film and my friend thought it wise to hurt me. I welcomed it. The two of them were heady, obnoxious, loving.

VI.

The things I've found friends will leave behind are full of holes. He'd once asked me if, when he finally killed himself, whether I'd go into his room before anyone had means and remove the information of his life, my friend. I don't think he realized the conspiracy it might plump into.

What exists beyond time-burnt memories of then are some bits of the aforesaid footage and black drip work, and a series of images my friend had called *An Accounting*.

One night the three of us prepared dinner for the entire house. I'd made lamb stuck through with dried cheese and berries. She'd made sangria in heaps and my friend had made a plate of peaches drenched with honey and crisped sweet roll bits for coffee once all was gone. We sat there smoking as the wind wrapped up their kitchen and the moonlight through all windows spread upon their lake.

After dinner we'd sat downstairs watching the film again and by its end, we'd begun a hellish kind of touch. A room filled with melting wax and hurt flesh and panting human animals and the moon shone through.

What clothes still clung we doffed and laid out upon their paintings and my friend began his work. The crust-rolled ankles of her jeans in alternating bleach and blue were skirted with mud, blood, whatever else had stuck as the two of them went out to explore some nights. I'd lay in bed they'd leave for hours. I'd look through their materials she'd come back in jeans and suspenders and he not dressed at all their legs and arms lined up with new scratches. Our black jeans next and their ashy rubs and spilled coffee spots. Her boots balanced to one another and one of his t-shirts from *Deep Space Nine* she wore and had made to frill against her belly.

I look at them still and might call the friend and remember a stain or line or flaw in what he'd captured. I felt such pity looking at the clothes bereft of peopling. These were pathetic lives deflated to their fundament. She an aggressive devotee to some such lost dispute. He draped in thin black fabric and I the same with infrequent earmarks of employment she'd belittle.

What happened was the world ate its feed and didn't stop.

VII.

We'd pieced together her story over days wherein we didn't sleep but drank pissbeer and felt the sun haunt us.

She'd taken her car one night and we'd assumed she'd finally returned to what normalcy there was only to find an odd rambling note of broken thoughts. "I am RUTGER HAUER. I'm tired of my idiotskin. I am unafraid because of yougoodboys and now I'm headed hauling home to see a grave dangerous judge who'll muss my neck and I'll have done."

***

We exited his backdoor next day to see small hubbub on the lake where someone hovered around a roped canoe. The canoe's rope wove into the water and on seeing it we noted oddity and went inside and drank in his shower for an hour or so with the heat to ease our worry.

A body was discovered netted in lakeweeds and what she's done comes out. My friend walked into his room pale and began to scream. He wept not making sense for a short while when his grandfather walked in and explained whose corpse it was. My faculties are often inept. I look to the outside world unsympathetic maybe to most causes and situations. This was then unfortunate, as both of them quickly turned a miserable anger toward me. An abject experience.

She had apparently left us and driven around for some time almost making it home to Milwaukee. Between there and here she'd purchased drink as her body was discovered pulped and stinking with boozy waterlog. We'd received the bulk of information secondhand as nobody involved in her discovery had reason to connect her life to ours. Why, he'd wonder aloud pacing once he'd forgiven me. I couldn't console him. She'd stolen a vacant cabin's canoe and found this chunk of rusted metal, from what we read and saw on news it looked like something for chaining old bicycles; a mangled circle of rust and black that shone, leaden. She'd roped herself to this and this canoe and left only slack enough to keep the boat above water, her body slung between and kept submerged by the weight of the object.

I've never been good with the reduction of bodies. Mechanical language seemed to surround the whole thing and the only act to set it right seemed to be movement. I've felt chased by her since, I guess, and haven't done well to hide. She was tangled in weeds and I picture her bald form greened beneath the lake and find myself angry that I hadn't known events would take on depth.

I don't drift through life, or if I have it's mostly the result of pulled attention. My synapses never quite adjusted to the activity in my birthing room and since I've stumbled after my emotions. I'll find myself weeping in grocery stores and realize I'm thinking of her. I'll find myself staring off near to driving my car into guardrails and note I'm imagining these people, our life, our minor romance lit with three unraveling heads and emptinesses.

"You could visit. I've begun making music and it seems to matter. I've considered scoring things, perhaps. I enjoy adding that dimension. I've never been good like you two with establishing dominant stories, or even pulling the conversation where I'd felt it needed to go. I've been living in a small home I bought from my brother off in jail. We hated each other the past four years or so but once he'd heard how I'd responded I guess something clicked and we became closer again. His family'd left. I rent the home in his name reasonably."

My friend was put together and I was envious. I'd see families my age just starting out and wonder. I'd sit at work as people left and try to think of reasons to stay. I wasn't heartbroken. I didn't even feel particularly torn up at the loss of someone I'd felt I'd needed. What I felt seemed pathetic, and misguided, and as ever I misunderstood.

Not long after we'd spoken, I began a project.

I started to visit a local antique emporium collecting photographs. They had one massive gray file cabinet filled with images from private citizens and after noting my interest they agreed they'd sell me a small Ziploc bag for small sums. I began collecting these not knowing where they'd go or what I'd do but slowly they took a shape inside my mind and I remembered Ray Johnson and collected a telephone book. These used to be placed on doorsteps at some point, but I'd just entered a municipal building and found one and nobody seemed irked as I walked out. From memory I tried to note the words we'd said to one another over the course of those weeks. I'd record them in large block letters and after months of work I'd filled a shoebox of my father's. Over time I'd send these out without return addresses and afterward I'd collect the infrequent write-ups in small-town papers that resulted. I'd decided an investigation might be the artwork. What some inquisitive head might put together would constitute the project and I'd be done with it long prior. I wondered at people collecting these, proud. I'd send numerous to her family not as provocation but vulnerable act, gesture. These were stuck with terror for me and emanated through my days thereafter. I'd be certain one night I'd wake stood over by her husband to find my death. I'd be terrified that what I'd done offended, that I was guilty, or he was guilty or all of us were guilty. These questions have since overwhelmed my life, a looming ghost that scatters out just when I think I've explained it aptly. I'll often awake with the ends of stories in my mind, fragments that've pulled themselves together from the thin to nag at me and always at their beginnings I find her. What I've managed since is to avoid love, avoid humans as a rule or put together some crude composite based on minor interactions throughout the day. You'll never be certain which things will stick, which thoughts won't let themselves die out as days ensue. She might scream and thrash and jut her life into the world's, smothered in caring and setting prized objects she'd lugged on someone's fire.

Vexations

I.

Nothing of this has been written out and there is no quiet. There are bodies, circling and useless, and they exist. I as one amid would think over this, summon something, at home a little cat whining there. Where? I'm feeling what? I'm hearing constantly, a voice and din. Something is being unwritten as I'm sitting in a library under lamplight, a part of. Every room is under lamplight. I am not at home. My cat is home, likely whining. A library is what? Our space to sit and be miserable, part of, again. A space to say, perhaps, to listen. We are all at work on the same project. We are updating a composition of impossible performance. Some of us collaborate, others sit alone and listen, a downward piano trills syrupy through our skulls. The person across from me is you, and you are quiet. You are sitting there. You have left to use the bathroom. The end of you. The library is hovering out around you, musical.

Another cup of coffee, a way to feel compelled. The space in front of me is covered in markings. The markings indicate names and dates on which what was done and when, hm. This is compelling and not. Our study. Read and soak in what. Take in, what? A body wanders by. A youth wanders by, not a part of us. The youth is wearing hat over its eyes as if to hide itself. A youth. A toxic feeling in gut. The room it smells, we have been here too long. These people smiling. Never feeling good about oneself in libraries. A book is pulled off the wall by a German fanatic. The German fanatic is interested in the death of pure ideas. I—and perhaps you, wherever you've gone—would've walked with the German fanatic were we born in the right century.

What of the rooms. These rooms. Mansion rooms. The walls covered in clothing tacked and limbs perhaps within them, we in our bodies and the performers and composers in their rooms. This library makes me say perhaps. An inquisitive look, a youth walks by and is listening to me stare, to our music as we stare there. Our stare makes a sound. The German fanatic I admire. Writing fairytales about the death of pure ideas, sure. Someone somewhere wanted to make a massive film about them. I don't know these things, but one of us must. I once read of the German while waiting for the dentist, one of us anyway. It was I. I and not you. One returns from the bathroom, perhaps you.

The room here is modest. The lamps feel as if they've come from a future. Nobody likes the lamps. They are not nostalgic lamps. Things are turning dark. I am turning inward. I am feeling tired. I am feeling myself cringe up at the face of you as one of us is here, sitting, the other where, what? Libraries are being burned. Nothing is burnt to cinder or dust. Fire is a wet nasty business once it's full. Fire suddenly begets a rotting rain and what's left is nasty sopping black. Nobody declares this, or dwells in the idea, least of all the German fanatic.

The first performer of what and such is nearing their completion. Our notes assembled out in front of us as to days or names and what else has proven, hm. Another bit jotted down after some study of work not written by the German fanatic and I and you and we sit upon our seats, having returned, within the library where the work will be enacted. You do not trust the process. I, surely, trust the process. I am one to research, to dig. We are a pittance, a fellowship perhaps who'd walk outside and ease the mind rather than work this way. *Assiduously*, we'd rather be outside than work assiduously. I would sit within and let the mind expand in headache. The work must be done. We all and the work must be done no matter what.

A piano's playing music, an old song that sounds incomplete. The we and me who is I and all and you where you're there are focused on the task at hand, which is, hm, to make haste with what we've got upon the pages where they've gone and amassed themselves. I hear a sound, a click. A person recording perhaps the pianist performing at their piano has mistakenly clicked a small device to right their equipment. Perhaps, with time, the turning of a page has been reduced to a click. Perhaps it is not with time, but the retransmission of a sound over various media to make its way into the ears of the I and all, or would it be ways? The single sound, but the sound has changed. It is rendered, and rendered, and warped and warped. It was carried here, for us, to melt within as we would transmit thusly, in turn.

I.I.

They are in the library and what? I am a part of them and not. I can watch them and cover the floor or pull up dust and see them there. She gets up at one point and walks to the bathroom I've cleaned likely to soil it. These are soily students. The students are soily. They tend to soil matters and gum up works. I enjoy watching them though. I feel a part of them, though. Their work doesn't seem at all the sort of work you tend to associate with students seated over tables in this manner. Doing what? Exhausting, it is. I am exhausted. I'm exhausted staring. I feel myself keel over every day before it happens, and I feel so tired and so rotten. Sometimes when nobody's around I'll sit at one of the computers on a quiet floor here and look things up, write to the kids. My kids are off and gone at school themselves, which might explain me. My wife is working. She calls places, they respond, she makes sure their materials are at the ready and accounted for. That is all. Everybody else is what? The rooms. I remember tours through here, watching as now. People and eyes and arms slung with something, books or folders. Filled with what? I like to watch these two though. They make one feel heavy. Their work is important. Perhaps they are in love. I am uninterested in love. Why I would acknowledge their love, I'm not sure. I don't want to have to acknowledged it. I am an observer. I don't even think it's so. I think they live together, though. I do think the two of them are living together like my wife and I and the both of them are moderately happy.

I enjoy moderate happinesses. I like to see them smiling minorly. Little ones, a glimpse. The lip curls just so. People are feeling alright. The world is contented, maybe. We are what? Bodies and everyone is orbiting. The room is feeling heavy. I am feeling heavy. I look down at my gut through the gray shirt they've given me and move my machine over the dust that has amassed there. Where? The floor and ground around me is just so. I feel alright.

I feel happiness. I feel happy, a small happiness. I don't know why he's gone to the shelf and pulled the book and I don't know if he is in fact he. The book he's pulled is tattered. Was once leather, this book. Now it looks like a worn old coat and he flips through it just a bit and smiles. She returns. Is it she? She returns with time and the two of them sit there and take information from one thing they've amassed or other. They write it into notebooks that they've placed before them closest to their guts.

I like the feeling of the table-edge pressed against my gut when I can have it. Nothing feels so good as this. The edge it makes me heap. Fills me up and pushes me over, I guess it's what I mean by *heap* this way. Used this way. I love to observe them. I love to observe. Today all I've eaten is a cup of coffee wherein the bottom was lined heavily with sugar. I don't know that it is today or that it is the ideal, the apt mode in which I ought to address myself now. I will merely fill this out, put it together and fill it out this way. My body is feeling heavy and I am tired of staring down at my gut.

I wish I could sit with them and press it to the table-edge. I would talk to them about the work they're doing and ask after the book the one of them had pulled down and talk about its covering. I would make them feel safe and clean which is my wont. I love them. I want to be close to them sitting there and studying with their clothing. The fabric wrapped and assembled just so. Everything just so. They are wonderful children. They are wonderful people. They are working hard and are not sure just what the work should do. They are hearing the same music as me being pumped through each of our skulls this way. Or is it pulled? I feel pulled. They hear the sounds I hear. They feel uncomfortable too. They love too. They could sleep right now and trust that all would be O.K.

I would protect these two. I would ensure their safety with my devotion to this space, this library.

I.II.

One of them within there is a boy inside of a room. One of them, this boy, doesn't observe anybody, doesn't bother. The two might very well be out and at the table near to the door of the room the boy is inside. He doesn't mind. The other fellow, cleaning up, he might be. He might observe. He's somewhere. It's unimportant. This boy within this room had rented the room and they had given him a key with a tag attached to the key. As a result, he was free to use the room's contents and had left the rest of them to fend for themselves, creating anger. Sometimes, depending, they'd ask for a whole group's credentials, or the presence of a group—even just one person—to justify the renting out of a room. He had arrived early and stated the name of at least one person now outside the room who *had* knocked but was ignored. The boy was listening to the music that everyone was hearing. The music that everyone was hearing was, supposedly, a recording of "Vexations" by one Erik Satie. The boy was listening to this over and over and over again as all of them were listening to this over and over and over again as an experiment, a way of seeing if he and they and each and all could do it—the cleaner unwittingly.

This Erik Satie noted that someone ought to experience extreme silence before performing this piece. He indicated it should be played 840 times in succession. It would be repeated. The boy had sat in silence and dark before the floor was occupied by the rest of his group and when they filed in, he began playing the music. He had taken off his clothes in the dark and when the light hit had frantically put them back on. He was certain they hadn't seen him but for the first thirteen or so plays-through of "Vexations" he was questioning this and whether they thought him perverse. The feeling was inward. He wanted to experience something more. He resented his group members and their entry. He had been reading about and had attempted performances of this and writing about the prospect of exhaustion and boredom. He wanted to individualize his group's project. He wanted to think about boredom, this boy, because the world made him feel unhappy. He had a life. He had the earmarks of an existence. It didn't cheer him. He was a person. He had a bank account, all of his teeth, scars and pieces of metal inserted where he'd broken bones doing stupid things. He was in love and out of it. He was in love with an older man. The two of them did not live together. He wanted to get away from this and so he was listening to the music. He was listening closely to the sound made when someone somewhere turned a page, and this was comforting. An old sound. He enjoyed sound but not language. He had read some of Erik Satie's ideas and felt something. He felt uncomfortable reading his ideas. Most of Erik Satie's music bored him a great deal. Listening to "Vexations," however, felt different. Somehow this made things O.K. The two others were still seated outside of where the boy was inside of this room. The cleaner was cleaning the same spot over and over. The boy was lying on the floor then holding onto the skin of his stomach listening to the music repeatedly and trying to feel something. He felt nothing. The room wept.

I.III.

A rat. There are rats. There is, certainly, one rat. This rat is up, up there, not around the we of us and them and they. The rat is in the ceiling pattering while the several of they and we and us down below are enacting what they're enacting. They are being alive. They are citizens.

The rat has a minor level of consciousness. It understands things. Visually, at the least, it must understand things. It hears the sounds below but doesn't fully register their nuance, doesn't discern meat or bits to chew through. This rat is what? This rat is up where it is and making sounds and judgments about its day. It is making small judgments and declarations about directions to take, minor nibbling declarations. The life of this rat is like that: it is born, and essentially all thereafter is a misstep from its mother's womb. Humans are like that. Their lives are like that. These humans enacting what they're enacting, say, is like that. They live, they piddle. They patter after what might be. All of it in some scattered attempt to return to mother.

The rat, though. If rats had words for violence, then rats would kill themselves. Perhaps rats kill themselves. Once it's registered in language, forget it. These rats, if one judgment was made, one statement as to what makes violence, it's over. Rats experience horrors of being. Rats can stomach horrors human animals couldn't bear. Rats eat their kin, quickly. This rat had eaten someone it knew and had spent the late-night chewing at its own tail.

Now it was in a duct. The metal around it was unimportant to it. It was square-shaped, this metal, but the rat experienced it more immediately, more viscerally. It wasn't a distance so much as an absence. Not a space so much as hunger. The rat followed this hunger wherever it might take it. This hunger put the rat just above where they and we and them were sitting doing what they were doing. This was unimportant beyond the shift in noise. For the rat this registered as a shift in noise and vibration against its mangled hair form, with still no meat or bits to chew through. Nearby, though, the rat discovered a small deposit of black mold and began to nibble away at it while below they and we and them observed one another and experienced life as human beings.

I.IV.

Other bodies on other floors and in other rooms made other decisions: one, a girl of nineteen, ate at her green apple miserable over its taste and stared at messages on her phone from someone she didn't want to see; another, older woman, sat in the bathroom on the toilet with her pants on driving her forehead into the metal panel separating the two stalls available there; a boy left with a stack of books he wouldn't read; someone called their parents to complain; noises abounded and reverberated up various ducts and whatnot and touched other rats, bugs. Most of them were seated. Some stood. Everyone was experiencing a similar unhappiness and all of it touched back in some way to the music playing then. Everyone was feeling strange and off. The night was wet out there, the windows obscured and damning. It all felt real. Everyone felt alive that way. A class, meeting late, sat around tables and listened to somebody discussing the weight of history. That phrase annoyed. Somebody a long time ago wrote a piece of impossible music meant to be played impossibly. Later, some performers interested in impossibility and boredom performed it. Others, bored, impossible, listened to it as they thought or tried to think. All of it was studious and tepid, uninteresting and aligned with typically unspoken terms. A boring world. This was no way of experiencing days. These people had their hefts. Their worlds were large and horrific. They wandered and sought sleep.

Pruitt-Igoe

We snuck in I think cos my friends we wanted to die. One of us thought maybe he'd write something about the place, some poem or something, I don't know. My friends and I we didn't think much then, just sort of did what came and went like that, but when we heard they'd decided to destroy this massive space we thought maybe we'd sneak in and let it swallow us. I remember looking through the windows of this like old husked-out building walking home from school without much else to do. I'd stare and my father'd say whatever he'd say about the black families and poor families who lived there but it never stuck much, I didn't care. My friends the young ones mostly were black kids with sneery faces not unlike my own—I preferred to keep around a crew of unhappy-faced weirdos and we'd hound St. Louis for better guts, and it was great. The 70s are piss but I don't know. My father didn't work, and my mother barely could. The house we lived in wasn't far from school and school wasn't far from the buildings and I can remember sometimes going in there to eat dinner at friends' homes and it wasn't a big deal at all. We heard adults talk left and right about the politics or something. We'd drown it out like anything and just couldn't be bothered to care. I love my city, maybe, some days, I guess. I don't know. Sometimes I think about it and still get sick over the noise. We'd almost been caught for so much young bullshit it was odd when it was over, like the city upped and wiped away our sneaky nights in dead sunlight as the community watched confused. I feel tormented that way sometimes. Like the back of my neck might shove through my Adam's apple and go spattered on the wall. We had endless cans of spray paint and the city sounded like it might set half itself on fire over "racial tension" or something. Women cried in streets and in front of the buildings. Families and young men screamed out for their fathers like it was all that was left to do. I don't know. I remember school feeling sort of tense before they came down. I remember that kid who thought he'd write something about it all doing all sorts of research. It was him, he was Jeremy I think; it was Jeremy, Michelle, Mike who we called Igor (a black kid from East St. Louis who didn't live in the buildings but went to school with Michelle and Mike/Igor loved old horror movies) Enny this girl who always followed Jeremy to sing his praises, and myself, that is Terence, who went to school and set small fires and loved so much to die.

I met them whenever it started to get dark. I don't know. I met them out by this demonic McDonald's, and we sat having Cokes and spitting on the ground as truant officers and church ladies walked by with sad eyes. I hate school but I go, the others are about the same, but the truant officer picks on Jeremy cos Jeremy's too smart for school and sits reading *Black Spring* or whatever in gutted alleys and such while the rest of us ignore the elements. The truant officer asks Jeremy and through Jeremy the rest of us just what we're doing and we sort of nod and whisper satanic stuff or something and he backpedals away like this crazed moron and Igor shouts "It's alive!" and after that we can't contain our collective stomach and begin to spit Coke entrails to cover the pavement. Some city.

Kids don't know much. I guess we weren't kids maybe. I don't care. We were clueless though, looking up or out and seeing these boarded up former homes it was strange. Thousands of people suddenly gone wherever. Faces and histories slowed to a crawl. We walk up and around and it's almost like you can hear this long moody music playing. The city quiets down and people still sit on the dirty corners listening to the sounds. These great notes of music spit out from their teeth and we kick cans and make our way toward the structures. Parts of them still housed people then. Their plan was to implode one, evacuate everyone from the rest, then finish destroying all thirty-three buildings. We'd heard this from Jeremy many times. Jeremy liked to talk it through. So many windows. This apparently endless world of outward eyeballs I wondered at so much and now they're cracked and jagged, kids likely cut themselves all the time on there now. Even the city's board-up job was halfway. Can't believe the neglected feeling walking with your pals as wind dies down. It's something else. Something obscene and rotten and Enny says something we all laugh at cos she doesn't seem to understand a thing. She wears these white shorts and I think how dirty they'll be when we leave the place. I wear my Levi's and my pack with paint cans and the rest of us basically look like some broken gym class with dead manners. Jeremy says something about Minoru Yamasaki, and I don't quite catch it, ask for repetition. "Minoru Yamasaki designed this place in the fifties, and he was a hero. The city loved him cos they couldn't find a place to split up all the whites and blacks. Pruitt-Igoe comes from a white and black guy and they wanted this place to be split right down the middle like Minoru Yamasaki. He made these buildings in New York, real famous. Imagine watching something like this—something you built up and people thought you were a hero—watching how quick it'd come down. Minoru Yamasaki." Jeremy sort of mumbled stuff like that to himself just to see if we were really his friends I figured. He had this collection in his room of all these angry old writers talking about piss and dying that he loved to read out loud. I wondered where he'd picked up knowledge about the buildings; then didn't care.

Igor stepped up onto the curb as we walked an empty street leading up to the abandoned ones. For a while he walked like a mummy and the girls just loved it. Michelle smiled and the fading light hit her teeth just as my left eye caught sight of the dying structures. I couldn't quite make sense. It's not about that maybe. I don't know. I don't put things together so much, it was just like Michelle's teeth and those buildings were more alike than not just then, all kind of dying, just stuck here waiting for it. Igor stops then and turns so his right side faces the buildings and takes on this really mania'd face, raises the right arm and points up toward the structures moaning weirdness none of us seem to understand. My stomach seemed to bob to the pavement then as the whole city suddenly climbed up inside the back of my head and I felt like every presence burrowed up like ghosts against my brain. Igor hadn't lived at Pruitt-Igoe, but he didn't need to for understanding. Again, my mind never drew connections just so easy, but I saw something in the teeth to the structures and I saw something and felt something in the ghosts of that place and Igor's pointed arm. Then it was odd like. Maybe Igor was communicating just with me I figured. The dark brown skin of his elbow seemed to call out to me like the angles and broken walls ahead as the nervous ghosts inside my brain scrambled for recognition. I heard the music then again and noticed the rest had walked up the street as Igor came and wrapped his arm around me. I didn't get it, nor do I looking back, but my heart felt something endless for Igor's that minute, like whatever came could only ever be an epilogue against his skin cut through the skyline.

Jeremy had this black leather wristband from his older brother who went away to prison for cutting someone's side open with a broken bottle. As he reached over and climbed into one of the windows of a building about three blocks in from Jefferson on Howard, we watched him from the street to be sure and I felt haunted. The buildings were really a small city inside the city, and we were entering a dangerous place. Homeless stayed here we'd heard or junkies, ex-hippies maybe who knew; the girls seemed anxious. As the last lights caught Jeremy's wrist, I noticed how the clasps on the inside pinched a bit as he reached over, and I worried he saw something tense. Jeremy was a bit older than the rest of us and meaner mostly. Standing on Igor's shoulders he'd looked like a stickman from outer space and Enny seemed panicked he might stumble. I just kicked around some sand and waited. Now inside Jeremy made some racket setting up some way for us to follow easy, so first we lifted Michelle and Enny as the ghosts seemed to rush out my ears screaming. Nobody mentioned anything tense, but all felt it. The light was going fast and the city suddenly sounded like a breathing cop, its flashlight tapped against our spines. My pulse rose up and I was last over, vaulting a bit then pulling myself on dusty window smear until welcomed by fellow arms and pulled into a room where the air seemed sucked out.

A family'd lived here we knew, and our moods were sour. How grave the idea suddenly got. Photos on the wall a bit and pulled up carpet in the corners of the room and one rusty white metal chair outside what might've been a kitchen. I pulled this cheapo red plastic light from my bag and shined it out and felt the cop tap again against my spine. I felt sick but knew the friends couldn't feel that way. I felt the buildings closing up around me like the world was already pulled retching from its sleep and only I could witness. Every morsel of sweat apparently saved up for months suddenly rushed out along my neck as Jeremy pulled a black paint can and went to the front door of the home. *PRESSING DETH* Jeremy wrote and none of us much knew what he was getting at. Likely a carried-on conversation with Henry Miller or Céline or one of his miserable lowlifes but we liked the way the painting bled down and knew it was better.

You know all of us I figure had ideas what was what, but we stayed close all the same. Rooms sprawled out like caves before us in this mirrored broken tomb. I said as much. I said to Michelle "You know this place is a tomb" and she looked at me like I was losing something. I asked her, you know, I asked all of them whatever they were feeling, and each seemed lost off in some fantasy of dark or something. I couldn't get a handle on Jeremy's breathing, he seemed ready to panic or fall asleep in all this death, the rooms hardly had doors, the doors hung on for all they could but wilted, nonetheless. I winced there and breathed in dust. I liked the way my chest puffed out with so much story. Kids and families and mothers and sons and dying and living and so many birthdays held here in one quarter of the twentieth century, little more, before being turned to empty ideas of a life; vacant examples of what humanity might look like from the outside. I kicked out the doorframe in apartment 4F and I guess I remember it cos the foot it got an infection after. Igor seemed depressed, wallowed almost by the severity and weight of what an evening. I felt worse for him perhaps or Enny. Enny was desperately trailing Jeremy as he sobbed through rooms leaving long waves of discontent bleeding down the walls without attention toward what he wrote. Seemingly endless lines of derision and teenage misunderstanding of what we had before us. I hate the fucking city. These cowards build homes to keep the outsiders out then burn down the homes when they don't like the consequences of pure neglect. I saw my shirt rip before it happened. The rooms seemed to pull on me I figure. Reached out to feel a family's mirror and look inside the medicine chest for drugs or poison and as I pulled away the fixture tore the fabric just. I appreciated it without fully comprehending why. Later maybe I understood that I'd been given an absence to represent the absence, a space of cloth neglect for all the real suffered seasons here. I stood behind Igor as we walked together into what might've been a lobby at some point but looked like the bad end of nuclear means. The doorways collapsed inward with piles of wood and dusted tracts of leased rooms or desk and chair fragments and it felt closer to entering the chambers of some pre-human cave than what once housed so much feeling. I closed my eyes and felt my chest leap out for air and knew I'd never really breathe again, not the same. Jeremy held onto Enny as Michelle, Igor and I hung back near the former office and Jeremy we saw was weeping bad. Igor grabbed onto my hand then and it seemed like breath restored itself through the hole in my neck where the ghosts made way. My nose inhaled the scent of what might've been a schoolhouse after filled high with garbage and centuries-old sweat maybe. The room was more a feeling than a sense. The ceiling seemed ready to crush each one of us as intruders on civic distemper. I don't know. I liked it there. I missed what might've been my father had he done well maybe. I missed the city before it ate itself like one of those snakes, suicidal. We stood inside what was already the grave of so many lives and suddenly Jeremy, weeping, pulled from Enny and raised his hand slightly so she'd stay right there. He took his can of black spray paint and walked once in a circle around Enny without leaning over to paint, then again and the sound of the paint suddenly shot me through with blood and anger. I was dying with desire for him to cover the attempted whitewash in the blackest coat and I could smell the aerosol amid the dusted remains and Jeremy painted what must've been a perfect circle around Enny moving inward, creating this black labyrinth of bleeding chemicals and for a bit I thought the floor might fall through into the real. I grabbed a paint can from my bag and walked to the top of garbage stuffed high in the entryway and wrote *THERE IS WAR INSIDE THIS PLACE* not knowing much what I was hoping to say but when I'd finished knew it made good sense. I then sprayed the contents of the can into my hand turning the palm black not knowing why. Michelle and Enny looked at me like I'd lost it and that was fine. I don't much go for explanation. It was like I stood inside my death; that room the most I'd ever feel. I stared at Igor and even he seemed confused by the pain stretched across my teeth. I don't know. I make myself sick thinking about it, I feel dead thinking about the city, and that's all it is I figure. I felt the pulse of a city maybe. Like all its history and infection and I were one—the explanation doesn't matter.

"You know I bet once they've destroyed these buildings everyone will forget Minoru Yamasaki." "Igor are you OK?" "Enny your eyes are caked with dust." "Terence what's the matter with you?" "Jeremy who's Minoru Ya-ma-whatever?" "This room is toxic, guys." Inside a place where life is made not to matter perhaps there's like this vacuum of sounds when everyone tries to speak. I listened as they spoke and picked up a scrap of small red cloth I still keep but it was more like I'd fallen asleep or let go. I pitied Jeremy because I knew some sense of desperation drove him to want to preserve this place somehow. He'd write it out, I guess. I don't know. I couldn't even think about it for months weirdly. Too much pressure or something once they started detonations. Buried the scrawled paint of our disgust like so many scraps of clothing and the dust would spread for miles. Jeremy read me these passages once from a biography he'd found of Minoru Yamasaki and my head was broke for hours after. You don't see the world as made up of paintings done by individuals and homes as visions of a better way. You see the structure. The building. The buildings. They tear through the earth almost, eyes and steam and metal and suddenly established they threaten everyone with the possibility of their collapse. The building as representative of the end-all-be-all of human desire and achievement, maybe. The buildings as talking to us, screaming down roads without throats. You see an absence in the air and already construct a building to take its place. Your eyes water with flecks of plaster as the city's reach spreads outward and the sound of detonation rips your stomach pulled with fire. There's something hellish about the city, the world it buries in structures. My eyes stay closed.

2157

Before You Lies My Body, Tending

I didn't want to live my days waiting for beacons or blips indicating ensuing prosperity, so I slept. I noticed beginning abjection early then, waking up after several weeks and realizing where I was. I'd committed rotten crimes and wound up in rotten dwellings with other rotten souls who now floated about, twitching with stimuli for atrophy and nowhere closer to anything in today's remnant society.

I am an ungrateful dog and I have no patience for this fucking place. We are made to eat slop and stare at screens and generate materials for people elsewhere to wear. Massive rooms someplace nearby containing duplicate machines for the collision of something and the storage of seedlings and the sustenance of humanity sometime far off when our meaty uglinesses are discovered. Somedays I'd stare at the wall and lick it for a bit of water that seemed natural. Somedays I'd cut at my skin until my body was little more than a pocked-up mumbling consciousness. Somedays I'd lure guards within and ask them to fuck after me a bit. We were left to our own devices after a time and once several realized this they'd simply left, and nobody'd heard from them again. Eventually I decided this was my path. Ugly fucking rotten beings, mumbling at me and losing language.

We, placed in bedding and given shelter, encouraged to remain for some months tending to whatever wounds have begun to spread or welt from rotten air, violence and copious ugly fuckings while imprisoned and thus my body was redolent with stink and rot. A set of clothing that wouldn't quite fit and meals were we to keep to our housing but nothing else. I saw people in waking from their bedding and didn't nod, there's nothing to say. They were ugly, likely pedophilic nubs of people not given choice in the matter and thus left to rot on a mass of rotting rock under conviction. I AM NOT THESE PEOPLE, I might whisper gaspingly at myself on waking up and finding something with which to trick my body back into being, my head back into thinking. I DO NOT WANT THIS PLACE AT ALL, I'd sit and say it again and again staring into a crude mirror I'd fashioned.

My right hand was slightly more swollen than the left, pulped up as it was from ill-kept organs and the like and an erstwhile tendency to drink or intake whatever drugs existed, I wouldn't have to work for. My ankles were becoming fucked and ribboned anytime I'd try to walk. I'd squeeze my right hand repeatedly into fists and watch the red slowly cut to white and eventually its paling purple. I AM AWAKE AND IN HELL, a body down the hall might offer. YOU CANNOT YOU ARE A YOU CANNOT WE ARE NOT HEATING, another might respond. This place was endlessly predictable, haunted by all the ghosts and maps of lives spent you'd—in aging—learn to note as hackneyed.

Before a tendency we had toward experimentation led to bodies cobbled together with wet imaginary meanderings and fog, ideas people had about themselves exerted onto flesh quickly became indoctrinary tools for politicians interested in subservient terms and new economies. I was perpetually a girl, made of shrunk legs and limbs and organs that remained shrunk from chemicals and let me age at my desire, slowly and fitfully so no one paid me mind. The Bodies Feud made people into ploys and signatures on bottoms of tank manifestos that would render earthwhilers doglike and sycophantic while Man reached upward. I chose never to reach upward. Many chose never to reach upward. They thus became divided between ugly putrid cities of flesh and lying and unknown outer dwellings where nobody within the city dared venture. Two mirrored and ever mirroring vats of cowardice thus bubbling up against and alongside one another while man explored the cosmos and lonely cosmonauts were set off to drift amid the sky and starline. I had a husband once, a child, a life. I collected pieces of evidence that indicated this but slowly lost them too.

We committed crimes, then. Were made to by authorities nondescript and looming. We stole medicine to perpetuate our bodily movements and slowly became faces of a media-soaked enemy who wanted to preach volumes against time on earth. YOU ARE SIMPLY BORED. Attorneys in paneled rooms would chant at each of us slightly rearranged in defining humanity. LOOK UP, THE HEAVENS CALL, AND YOU WOULD SATISFY YOURSELVES TO REINTERPRET FLESH IN VILE ROOMS. It was a rotten era to have a body imprinted with what you thought eyelets of the sun, poked through and laced with the reaches of humanity to make your life cohere on an earth leaking fume and liquid. We wrote bad manifestos and circulated them in boxes marked CEREAL or DOGMEAT when no one looked. We met in the alleys between our homes in a suburban sprawl of gutlessness and rubbed one another's bodies against the bricking and picket fencing fucking and screaming and knowing that nobody watched. We became convinced of higher orders of being and prayed to witches having cut our skin with broke-down screens and netting.

On leaving home my body began to rebel against itself and so I'd taken hourly slow pulls on a canister of nicotine made to smell of one's home air. My organs were dwindling. My ankle had gone numb before and now with steps it seemed to blacken. I looked out at graywash sky and thought I might not last the week before setting up my first night's camp and catching a small, sinewy rodent on which to chew. I was born too late. I had wasted my life. I had no feeling in my ligaments. I wondered if ligaments could feel. I took a rock and heaved it up to land upon my foot, atop my ankle where the bone or ligament met the rest of the meat of me and it hurt and it swelled up on the spot in redness and I was in pain. Everyone was in pain. The world was gravelly. People seldom spoke and if they did, they were always in their positions. One human being was always atop the other in terms of speaking. The other human being was always subservient and made to look foolish beneath their bootheel.

I lay back on the cold ground and thought back to a yellowy childhood memory wherein I'd sat on the floor of my mother's kitchen and urinated to generate a small puddle out from me. My mother was wherever she was then. She did not love my father and thus was perhaps entertaining some guest whom she felt some pang of something for. She was not an evil person. I'd urinated through a small yellowy dress on the stupid floor of my mother's pathetic kitchen and it had left me yummily until a small circle surrounded, and all was well. I woke in night that night wherein I'd left home to walk and wander and attempt to flee my state as a slightly imprisoned pathetic hedonist and when I woke, I felt there more urine. I looked and touched my hand to it and tasted myself a sickly-sweet bit of taste and it felt good. I felt free. I did not feel good to be alive in such a state as I knew it was the best things would get and there would be no more. I pulled on my tits and gestured at the sky and slapped myself several times across the face with either hand until the night bound me up slightly more and all was water.

Our world had prioritized meat and work and thus within cities rooms were made to great efficiency and factories churned out cloned, replicated bodies to eat. Leave them and you would slowly starve. I opted. I'd had friends who'd rebelled and even sent in occasional messages from recreated carrier devices, but I hadn't heard from them since before my imprisonment wherever. Nobody lasted much out past the burnt edges where disease was kept at bay. I walked into it and saw nobody. I wanted the nightmare of my life to end I think and thus I walked and though my ankle swelled, and my hands were meaty clops of pang I pressed on and saw my life unfolding.

After Me A Sea of Skin, Mirroring

A way into the second day of walking I came across a man and adolescent male. When they'd exhausted pleas to fuck me, we decided things were safe and thus walked a bit in same direction not speaking vowing to set up good camp together. I had no full sense of where they'd come from, but it didn't matter. I'd heard stories through walls of bodies made in incestuous fire from disgust at life inside and these seemed fit. Their pleas were hardly words. They drooled and circled at first and waggled their dicks within the air and made flicking gestures with their hands. I buried my face in the mud then and opened up my mouth and sucked up as much of it as I could and when I rose to grimace out the meat of me at them they looked back unhappy and re-sheathed their dicks and with time some understanding was reached. I wanted to assume they were a boy and his father. I wanted them to be lovers of a kind. I wanted them to marry one another in the light and make the world something possible beyond the diseasing swelter. I had no patience. They spoke a sound I'd grown familiar with and heard myself speak it back in hawking yips and whistles as neither hoped to understand the other.

"We hadn't if we hadn't made had hope to find you made our minds up wanted to speak. We hadn't held out our hope of speaking out and held our hope. You are pretty is all are you are all is pretty, and we hadn't held hopes of people. Let alone women."

"I have processed that ordeal and made OK with it in my head. You are not fundamentally evil males."

"And have you have and left you and have left? Is this the way you've gone and went? You've left and gone?"

"I am not willing to speak in those terms at present I am unable. The thing is, the thing. I feel at odds. I never felt at ease. You two, what is it?"

"We are a good and way of going out and good and being and we aren't happy unhappy out here. I am not comfortable in my skin and comfortable am not you cannot we shouldn't."

"We don't speak more."

The younger offered me a bit of mulled rotty apples from a jar in his pack and I put dirty fingers in to suck at what I could before he got greedy. These two were wild and mumbling and the first honest people I felt I'd seen in very many years excepting an individual I'd heard suicide in the home next to me and before he'd gone on and on about his mother. These were the sorts of relationships to establish outside I gathered.

***

The sky was oily, limbed occasionally in clouds and muck and high reaching etches of buildings beneath. My foot was hurting and numb and my body was coated in welt. I smelled a bit. I sat on a mound of sand having urinated nearby while the two wandered around dithering maybe about their actions and wavering and attempting to figure something out.

I watched them sleep after we'd eaten what we could from a days-dead bulbous rat the adolescent had found at the end of a small jut of tunnel. I hadn't eaten natural animal meat since I was a girl and my father thought it wise to train me out past the reach of our neighbor's eyes. Then we'd clunked the heads and crudely boiled the meats of turtles over a fire he'd constructed in a small hollow beyond contact with everything I'd previously known. Now I felt fairly sickly and pulled long draughts on a nicotine inhaler I kept for moments and fits of nausea, nerves, or ill digestion.

My intention had never been toward violence with these two. Even their expressed ugly thoughts seemed mild when compared with a fascist's billy club upside the head when not dressed in apt cloth. Still, though, as their jowly mugs and boozer's guts bubbled under the light of moon, I felt a building distemper that eventually had me stood over them, modest rocks in either hand, breathing deeply before driving each down into the impressionable meat and cartilage of nose and eye socket. The man was slightly stronger and so awoke, but neither could've done much if both had. I kept pushing the fisted meaty rocks until I felt to brain and finally depressed my efforts wholly into the welcoming gapes.

Nor have I ever felt much draw toward eating the bodies of those I've only recently spoken with. Cannibalism exists as a niche curiosity where I have lived, nothing more. But as their bodies steamed up in the deep grayblue of morning and the meat there seemed to breathe, I began to pull at various organs.

I spent the day in a sort of mad sleepless reverie over their bones, burning myself occasionally on bits of coal or chewing on reams of skin I'd spun out over sticks in fire like smoky sheets of taffy. I was found not long thereafter.

"You were discovered having abandoned what we'd assembled for you. You were discovered feral, ugly, not unlike the criminal we'd found years back and put to work. You were found ungrateful, of the body, a person in every sense. You were found having eaten the bodies of these. You were found having eaten the bodies of these drifters and beyond the purview of our court.

"You are not to think and feel and access anything beyond those possibilities and exigencies just in front of you. You are not an original. You contain the bodies of others and you are disgusted with yourself. We are not interested in apology or meat. We are interested in the minor amount of power your body might enact so as to entertain a room of children as they grow. This is now your purpose."

As these things were said at me, I felt myself drugged. I stared ahead and noticed that my limbs felt light. I was not surprised to find removed parts. I did feel their phantom irk and it was calming. I do not have a name to say to you and as my body dwindles further, I trust I'll lose what identity I held yet more. It isn't complicated. A flesh-bound globe of ugly suits have made what was a living plague. I grow tired. I have no patience. A man is telling me these things a prominent man a primitive man is telling me these things. I have nothing left. I look down and scrape the nub of ankle I've got along the white tile and gasp, THERE IS NOTHING, THERE IS NOTHING, I'M ALIVE AND THERE IS NOTHING.

Orphic Hymns

"I am burning myself up and will always do so."

— Jean Cocteau

1: SANGD'UNPOÈTE

Our ship was supplied sufficiently to last beyond the touched reaches of our solar system. Beyond that it was anyone's guess. Klimt used the word "touched" when talking about his exploration vessels as he wanted to feel some connection that none of us fully understood. This was implied in the literature sent with Klimt's proposal in the early days of what became our mission. My interest grew and there were few moments of doubt before departure. My life had hit a standstill, perhaps. I was vacillating between indifferences. A figure like Klimt proved a slight intoxicant then, I guess, and though I've never given myself over to cultish figures I let myself rest a bit in the certainty of his mission.

Klimt was strange, erratic. Some of us knew Klimt the captain and others new Klimt the father and others knew Klimt the all-knowing Oz. We had left earth happily under his guidance after his exploration systems had proven themselves and private exploration beyond earth became a far more realistic prospect than any of the orbiters and landers the state had managed to establish. I'd dabbled with these previously and only found bureaucracy and mining missions. Whatever one might say of Klimt his sense of art and grandeur in our efforts was never lacking. He'd already written such a compelling narrative of what would become our journey that half of our initial conversations were Klimt rambling. Whatever I could gather changed so frequently after the fact that I simply stopped trying to gain a sense of the entirety of the mission and focused more acutely on my own.

I'd never been so far and from what I could tell would be surrounded by similarly earthbound company. I'd heard arguments for leaving at the start of interviews about the viability of Klimt's vision, the sustainability of such a project, the origins of our journey, its funding. Some insisted Klimt had connections to various European governmental figures and thus his explorations weren't entirely private, but subterfuge seemed an essential aspect to our endeavors. Some knew certain things, but no one save Klimt knew entirely what any of us were doing.

My position, as it was handed down piecemeal over the course of six weeks of intense preparatory treatment—a phrase Klimt preferred to "training," as part of his spiel was based on the organic study of the cosmos, and treatment for introduction to a new environment or malady made sense to Klimt where training simply sounded militaristic—was to do with fungi and other organic matter that had been discovered on Klimt's vessel located just beyond the orbit of Pluto. It rested there, unable to proceed in either direction as it would lose contact pushing further and dry up heading home. Klimt had noticed a strange growth on the vessel near its pod bay and had organized my payment based on grainy photographs and a sense that it was time someone touch beyond the movement of Pluto. I'd stared at those images for countless hours by the time we left. I'd attempted to take them in and process them in as obsessive a move as I've felt. The rooms we worked in on earth were scattered with workers and yet conversation almost never happened. If nothing else we'd seemed to all inherit a mania from Klimt, a desire to see something through and to make something of our touch beyond. I enjoyed those weeks of wallowing in it, and so when packing up to go I'd only seen those grainy pictures.

When Clyde William Tombaugh discovered the dwarf planet Pluto in 1930, he and those who heard him treated it as a planet. Klimt talked about Tombaugh almost daily in the preliminary stretch of our journey before our good rest and seemed obsessed to some extent with vindicating Tombaugh's legacy since the shift in understanding around 2006. I had spoken with Klimt alone one morning over cereal and rationed jugs of liquid shot through with vitamins against every known oddity out there. He seemed determined to vindicate Tombaugh's research on UFOs, his sense of the cosmos as a terribly vibrant thing back in 1930 before the dropping of the bomb and the slow ensuing decay of our earth. I nodded along and appreciated what he said as you do over breakfast but had no idea of the extent to which his mania ran. The fly-by of the early twenty-first century had been the stuff of myth to Klimt's grandfather who'd worked for the still-functioning NASA before it stripped itself establishing Martian and Lunar colonies until being bought out by Klimt's competitors.

"Their interest was only ever human. Their goals were only ever that of man. When Tombaugh followed Percival Lowell's efforts and searched for Planet X, he struggled in a frigid observatory analyzing dot after dot of information and sifting through asteroids pocking up plates of images until suddenly, he hit his mark. His mark differed from what they'd expected, an entity too small to influence the pull of Neptune, and yet there, pronounced enough to warrant a name given by a small child in England. Pluto. *Magnanimous, whose realms profound/ Are fix'd beneath the firm and solid ground.* A god of the underworld and an entity beyond what was previously thought possible. Beyond human. A pock of infinite potential at the reaches and Tombaugh's frigid suffering alone in Arizona eventually connected him to the cold touch of this. Our work then is a continuation of our ancestors. Our work then is a journey beyond any underworld. Our work then is a journey within the heart of us, we will find some freedom."

Klimt had a nasty tendency of spitting when he recited this. I'd always been a fan of my father's ramblings about the stars and it's this, and a nagging obsession with the tardigrade's indestructibility, that let me to pursue extraterrestrial mycology. My focus was fungi and the possibility of organic matter, anywhere. My graduate thesis focused on Europa and the readings discovered in 2074 of tarry black streaks beneath its sheets of ice. I'd made a living since analyzing toxicology reports from the colonies' watering systems and plumbing. Klimt had discovered me a bit of a wreck before a screen in a basement room. I hadn't spoken with humans save my contacts on the colonies for several weeks and thus his preamble and recitation of the Orphic Hymn to Pluto struck me as a hallucination. I welcomed it.

Sitting over breakfast with the man on a ship leaving any reach I'd experienced before I felt the same. I welcomed him.

Research on the phases of Pluto's moon Charon seemed most significant to what they'd need from me. The assumption had been that Pluto existed as a sort of half-meteor-half-planet, constantly being reduced and belittled in the press as moons like Europa gained favor and the Martian and Lunar colonies solidified themselves so migration could begin. Charon and Pluto, however, existed in a binary configuration not typically seen, their tidal potentials linked. The imperceptibility of the Kuiper Belt and Pluto's relationship therein meant that some potential existed. Something existed. Something to be touched according to Klimt. Something fungal according to imaging. I was endlessly curious.

Anytime, however, an orbital system exists, the possibility of tidal systems exists. From the scarred surface of Europa to the engraving of Shackleton's ship on the sheets of Antarctica, the presence of frozen liquid and the pull from Charon meant that some form of change, growth or otherwise, might be possible.

"There's a sense back home of need. The children, future generations, they need us. They need farmers, they need mechanical engineers. They need bodies in the colonies. However, when I sent the first research vessel out here I did so for something that escapes need, something larger. The growth discovered, the paradoxical readings, the sense of activity out there amid all this dead light, it needs *us*. We are attempting to answer a question we don't entirely understand, the pieces connect while others wither or elude. You've been brought because of your determination in rounding out an answer. You're here because together we write the question."

This is, to hear him tell it, how I fit into Klimt's puzzle: his insistence on the moldy black on the husk of Orpheus 1 and the prospect of growth in the pitch black and cold of Pluto's touch. My assumption based on what I'd been shown was that growth had been possible in Pluto's system based on orbit and proximity, or that an organism similar to the tardigrade had been scattered via meteor and latched onto the vibration or variance in light of the vessel.

Neither of these required much confirmation from me before the good sleep as Klimt paid for everything; and my own curiosity into Pluto's system and the iterations and evolutions in our understandings from Tombaugh on made this journey a valid use of the remainder of my familiar life on Earth. I had a dog, two siblings, but both of them were on Martian hours or Intermediary Mean from work on private station satellites. I gave my dog to a young family and ate a final feast at a small synthetic sushi restaurant in San Diego. I said goodbye to what I'd known as we ascended, and held fast to my seat as I stared out at the blue and rotting landscape. I felt myself escape the world and heard Klimt's overhead message with a comfort I hadn't felt in years: "We are making our way past the atmosphere, moving now. We'll reach an acceptable speed, after which each of you are encouraged to eat, commune, and rest. We're moving farther than anyone before. We'll exchange data with the colonies and then bid them farewell. We are moving now, still."

Klimt's approach utilized a modern take on the Project Orion experiments of old. His father had worked in munitions and the family became incredibly wealthy trading repurposed nuclear weapons initially slated for disarmament and disposal. The law did not require their disposal if put to use beyond the touch of war, and thus a condensed journey by way of an orbitally-generated super ship—the Orpheus 2, called affectionately the Cocteau— would follow the course carved by the original Orpheus with good sleep induced in each of us but a select handful of mechanics and navigators who'd catch a month or so of induced coma between fields of each previous endeavor's debris.

Human hibernation as Klimt's people had developed it was an extreme take on rendering the brains among us comatose though fidgety for small strands of electric tape that kept our muscles from degeneration. This technology was first developed for the Exile program before it came to fruition, a sort of death penalty/research ape hybrid wherein the worst of the dregs among the burning earth would be jettisoned from humanity to make observations of their trek before dying sucked into the hell of Jupiter. I was nervous when I put on the wetsuit I'd be kept in, uncomfortable at their insertion of various needles and catheters for processing nutrition. I was in a small black pod in a room with green light and I would be put under and woken up intermittently throughout long enough to ensure my body's state. A row of rooms underneath the captain's housed each of our sleeping bodies and would sustain us for the duration with occasional sounds we'd chosen to remind us of home in our rest. Though it had largely been disproven Klimt retained these quirks from missions of old and it comforted me. I chose the sound of waves in San Francisco's bay and the hum of my home computer. I recorded a meditative bit at Klimt's prompting where I repeated "calm, warm," over and over to notes of Glenn Gould's playing and mumbling stretched and distended to such a degree they were more vibrations than music. In the end going under felt rubbery and awkward. I closed my eyes.

2: ÉTERNELRETOUR

At velocities that rendered much of the interim a clouded blur we were made to sleep for the number of years as best we could. Our stomachs dwindled and became ragged things. Any waking I did between to wander or think was overwhelmed by the vibrating light. We were each encouraged to our solitude as discussion and cohabitation and development and questioning and the like were non-conducive to the project of propelling a body of human animals from one point in the cosmos to another. It wasn't so much a question of the intervening zones and planets touched, the abrasive bits of detritus from the first Europa missions or the Russian research satellites on Jupiter and all its moons. It was more a question of the body being put to a sort of rest and witnessing nothing in the interim. The body being made to forget its past and be reborn a sort of sopping wet arthropod with ragged limbs and needing endless reassurance as to the state of things. Lines of light then and darkness then and a rotten taste in the air then and no sky but ever-expanding consciousness of dark and movement and the sense of things deteriorating around you until the final stretch of sleep. Three long stretches of imposed sleep and comatose dreaming of childlike things and fairs and the color of the burning in the Pacific Northwest in America the mountains on fire the lot of Idaho on fire the lot of Washington on fire and nobody safe to live anywhere receding to islands to Canada to frozen vistas like Pluto to frozen plains on earth and in the heavens and we're moving and I am not awake and I can feel my limbs being shocked in dreaming and as soon as we arrive my limbs are deflated my body is a pale dehydrated fruit I watch a blinking green light within my resting place for nineteen hours before attempting to move my limbs and before I can move my limbs they're moved and the medical staff on board has filled a room with us and is slowly reviving us and I can see the bodies of us near me I can see Ember the botanist I can see Terrence and Ivan the mechanics I can see Klimt I can see Esther the nurse and Kim the ex-military and Martin the ex-military and Sarah the ex-military and the room is limbed in light so I am free to sleep and sleep again until the hours melt.

***

Klimt said to us overhead on arrival: "When people discuss the Voyager vessels, they're mostly concerned with what evidence might be returned. They want certainty of some beyond. I think of Voyager 1 and I'm mainly concerned with the sounds of whales or waves crashing on shore, the grandeur of Mozart and the comparatively crude technology in 1977 that made things possible. They wanted to send a message to this beyond. In 1977 they wanted to greet the universe and say hello. They wanted control out here. They wanted the cosmos to know we human beings had existed. What evidence they've returned has been questionable at best. We're out here to right that wrong. We've assumed life didn't exactly exist within our system as we were looking for *human* life, or something comparable. The golden record, then, ought to have been a message to us over anything else. The crashing of waves, the material that went into the record, the sounding of whales. We need to embrace nonhuman forms of living, communicating, if we're going to survive and endure what's to come. If we're to engage the climate we'd do better to think like the sun, a flame, or mercury. If we're to engage hunger we'd do better to think as foliage, as growth, as mold, and skip the question of our bodies. The Voyager vessels served as a precedent for what we're doing out here if only because they've amassed inexplicable materials on their hulls through decades of movement. The growth is what we're concerned with, then, and the prospect of understanding something in non-earthly terms. I thank you all for joining in this endeavor, and I welcome you to come witness our new place."

The meals furnished by Klimt's organization were better than anything I'd ever eaten state funded. I remember eating a large breakfast and sitting and staring as the warmth of it filled my stomach and the bodies hovered around me variously eating or waking up or becoming adjusted to the surrounding scape and I felt the sleepiness that comes from being overfull after months and months and more of regulated metabolism and though I could've vomited I steeled myself against retch and hunched over to stare at my still-wet feet in sandals. Eventually I raised my eyes and saw there the face of Klimt, excited.

"What do you think of it?"

"What do I think of it."

"The Kuiper belt. The furthest touch of man. We're a fraction of the way toward the hydrogen shell the Next Horizons have discovered. We're closer to vanishing off the edge of history than any living thing. Isn't it marvelous?"

"I think it's marvelous. I agree with you that it is marvelous. I'm incredibly tired, though, sir. I feel more tired than I've ever felt, an inner touch reached."

"It's wonderful... I'm feeling exhilarated. I cannot wait to pass Charon and settle next to Orpheus 1. This trip is special," and now Klimt rose to address the sleepy lot of us, "and we are uniquely positioned to share an experience of god with those on earth and the colonies. Things previously thought a sort of divinity will become as palatable and present as your breath. I want to thank you for joining me, as I couldn't be out here without each and every one of you. En route we've had further reports back from the robotics on Orpheus 1 and made note of fungal characteristics and variations in weather. We're overwhelmed with data at present, but we've got work for everyone as soon as you're ready. Those of you responsible for further data acquisition and analysis will be up first, and we'll settle into our living out here ASAP."

What I felt then and near constantly after that on our ship was a sense that Klimt was hovering just outside of each of our levels of comprehension. I don't know a better way of saying it and that frustrates me. Klimt's language frustrates me. The ornateness of each sentence and every word pulled from disuse to be utilized for intergalactic naming, all proved constantly confusing and evasive. I remember speaking with a mechanic on lower deck whose job was maintenance of a board of computing hardware that sent out and received radio waves. His name was Harold and I'd known him in graduate school, at some remove. He talked about the board and only the board in front of him and his purview seemed so limited that he hadn't registered the masses of planets hovering around us. Neptune on the vague horizon and Pluto directly in sight and even Charon and the misshapen husk of Hydra and the glint of Styx and each of them looking like they could sweep through our ship and the Orpheus 1 without stopping to note abrasion. It was horrifying to see Harold staring thus. I'd seen it in everyone, however. In cooks and pilots and ex-military. Our tasks were reduced such that overlap became not just an impossibility but a nonconcern. I would monitor samples of fungi and various outgrowths of organic matter and find myself lost in that hypnotized state, not registering the rays of color emanating from Pluto and the Orpheus 1 blurred just beyond her shoulder. As we approached the Orpheus 1 the look in Klimt's eye was unnatural, despotic. The ship was larger than I'd remembered or had been able to gather from imaging. The ship was just a hair smaller than the Cocteau and its mechanisms glowed bright against the total sleep and slow Newtonian movement around us. I felt myself surrounded by this massive cradle of dead civilization or never civilization and the movement of it all as we approached the gray steam-shooting mass of Orpheus 1 was almost too much.

The glow from distant stars and our sun were so faint at the edges of each orb staring out that the light from 1's robotics glared aggressively. The ship was attempting to maintain itself as it had been programmed and witnessing the system firsthand was strange, like walking in on somebody planning something hellish in secret. Those of us concerned with growth and movement watched and listened to Klimt's mumbling overhead and attempted to take the machinery in. The area where I'd be sent receded into shadow on the far side of a massive gray frame. I realized after a time that the ship's robotics were attempting to clean and stimulate the hull section by section in a sleepy manner. It reminded me of the shocks in our long good sleep and I was briefly hypnotized by its repetition. Finally seeing it seemed to shake something within those of us who stared. I found myself touching the pads of my fingers against my thumbs in swirling gestures that came to mirror the awkward spindling and reaching of the 1's robotics. I listened as Klimt mumbled through the overheads and wanted to sleep just then.

***

So far as I know none of us were made aware of Klimt's promises before we'd arrived beyond the furthest reach. On arrival we were made aware of Klimt's promises one by one as we were shown the surroundings and anxiety reached its height in each of us. My own anxiety came on staring at Charon and realizing the shift in light and its dwindling wasn't going to be altered or modified, it simply was. The stars were beyond us and our sun was so far behind that the light of this point in the galaxy was simply less. There was less light to be given out. This meant that the computers and servers within the ship were the strongest conductors of light and so surrounding us were blinking haloes of red. The promises were necessary as the mission was indirect for each of us, so all of our understandings were already multiple, and Klimt seemed to prefer it this way. The engineer thought the first Orpheus needed technical attention. The botanist wondered about the flora. The soldiers worried over invasion. The pilots readied themselves to turn both ships around and return home. The medical staff prepared for any emergency and extremes of climate and disorder outside the walls of the Cocteau. I picked at a bit of skin on my big toe that looked as if it might begin to blacken. I fussed over possibilities of growth and the implications thereof. I worried. I thought about my GI tract as a row of growing mushrooms in the window of some alien species. Their influence might already have attached to us without our knowing and this might've been Klimt's ambition all the while.

3: CORIOLAN

So, we had the promises. The medical staff received promises of awards back on earth for their discoveries. The soldiers received promises regarding the vanquishing of our greatest foreign enemy. The engineers received promises of great technical disorder and their chance to fix it. This, like any other reason, became a way in which I didn't fit again. Klimt made me promises to do with my family, my father, and communication with some beyond. The growth on the side of the initial Orpheus became a sort of portal, a godlike substance through which my questions might be answered. Klimt seemed convinced of this even as he imbibed draughts of liquid made up of variants of cocaine, alcohol, nicotine, etc. He paced his quarters with me seated there late into the night proclaiming victory over matters of time based on his initial interpretations of the substance. I asked him what all of it meant.

"Our sample data of this substance melded onto the Orpheus 1 seems to indicate a connection to most known diseases back on earth, and their curing in turn. Not unlike our use of vaccines made of fragments of the diseases themselves, this substance seems to simultaneously engage both poison and antidote without anything lost in between. The common streptococcus pneumoniae exists alongside a vanquishing dose of antibiotics and neither cancels the other out. Time does not exist within the substance and thus sickness and wellness rotate in perpetuity and I'm certain what can be extracted from this is a perpetual engagement with our own lives and their transpiring alongside the transpiring and living of all those lives who've touched our own. I've seen early iterations of the HIV bug swarm antiretrovirals in microscopic footage that shouldn't be possible, shouldn't make sense, and likely don't for their insistence on a languagelessness of pure disease, pure cure, pure disorder and pure panacea. It's an endless loop. It's an ouroboros of bacteria and fungi and you have the opportunity to engage it and likely change our view of these concerns for all time. This is what I promise you."

While I had wanted a promise from Klimt as I'd heard of them being handed around the ship since we'd settled in, I had hoped for a sense of clarity on our arrival, a task that I could complete and earn my place, some work. Klimt's use of drugs had raised concern for each of us in turn, and there were rumors that he'd been making attempts to modify himself on our long journey out here. What became clear to me just then was where we were. A ship that far from contact, from opportunity, from difference, functions as a sort of prison. The piecemeal knowledge of our efforts served as the tight schedules kept in prisons and the emphasis on the here and now. Klimt wanted to obliterate a sense of time. Klimt wanted to create a drug that functioned as its own infection in turn. There were rumors of this sort of thing emanating from a hundred private research vessels back on earth and in the colonies. Medicine had hit a standstill on earth when war became the foremost concern and thus high-minded men and women were determined to advance our ability to vanquish disease and disorder the moment we left our atmosphere. I wanted to be comforted by Klimt's promise, I wanted to feel whole again, less tired and twitchy. I felt anxious at Klimt's promise, like a world had slipped beneath my feet. He paced and paced and sweat poured from him.

I had spent the first days of our arrival staring out at the Orpheus 1 and its hulking frame, and the small glint of activity discernible within the mass Klimt seemed so fixated upon. It showed in muted blacks and grays with specks of light or shine occasionally beaming back and creating the illusion of movement. Klimt's insistence seemed insane, and I wondered about the promises he'd made to all the rest of us and what they'd left out of their descriptions to me. My father had died when research into Leukemia was reaching its height, and as a result had opted for natural death compared to entry into one of the Lunar Colonies' drug trials. They'd achieved some levels of success utilizing extraterrestrial materials mixed with old variations of chemotherapy and osteopathy, but their projected timelines always reached so far away that my father couldn't bear the thought of enduring them. He was old, and aging, and though everyone around us seemed fixated on the possibilities of other planets and their atmospheric levels in terms of treating this or that disease, my father held fast to his associations with earth. I had heard of astronauts experiencing godlike premonitions regarding dead loved ones, especially those who'd visited other planets, but my father had barely ever ventured beyond earth's orbit, so Klimt's revelations felt a bit obscene as he proclaimed them from some drugged mania.

His assertion, so far as I could gather, had to do with the notion of time as it related to the growth of organic matter on earth, and what difference might be required for organic matter to grow and persist beyond our atmosphere. Studies had been done about the types of flora that might be put to growth in lunarscapes, or Martian ones; but these were typically done in such a way that fragments of atmosphere were introduced to already thriving plants—based on earth's composition—and the majority of them died or wilted quickly or immediately. Fungus, oddly enough, proved the most promising, and it was this that brought me on this trip along with a botanist—the thinking was that my own education into these matters would slightly alter my understanding in comparison with our botanist's, which made sense to a certain extent. Fungi are compelling for their makeup, their contrast to flora that exist as distinct parts making up a whole—a root, a stem, a bud, etc. Fungi, in many cases, carry similar makeup from their stem throughout and even on earth will alter considerably depending on their exposure to the surrounding air. I've stepped on mushrooms in rural Wisconsin that immediately changed to a mush of yellow and then deep blue in quick sequence. I've eaten mushrooms that altered colors in a similar manner in controlled studies while a graduate student. I've used salves of mushroom to heal everything from poison ivy to extreme coughs that won't let up. Hearing Klimt talk about them in such a way, then, wasn't nearly as surprising as his association with real instances of time—beginning, middle, end—and the ways in which this growth might alter our conception entirely. The psilocybin I'd eaten reminded me of the mushrooms that altered their composition because of my work analyzing fungus, not because of some inherent connection. Klimt seemed convinced that cause and effect were more directly linked, and that the color-shifting fungi on the forest ground in Wisconsin had a direct relationship to the mental experiences one could encounter having ingested psilocybin.

I sat down alone in my bed with the curtain drawn so as to avoid any potential correspondence with anyone who'd then experienced the extremity of Klimt's mindset and our objectives. I lay there staring out the window at Charon and Pluto's relationships and watching their slow progressions against one another and the discernible differences and movements between the two of them. Neither shone particularly strongly compared with the lights of the Cocteau immediately outside the window, but both seemed to communicate in a compelling binary relationship I felt obligated to parse. I stared at the growth again on the Orpheus 1 and felt myself pulled into Klimt's story, his narration. An ouroboros fit strangely better than most genetic models for materials discovered outside of earth's orbit. Organic compounds found beyond our atmosphere often related to one another constantly rather than one existing and rendering the other inert. The gases that made up Jupiter for instance didn't render the mass of Europa perpetually frozen, but both seemed to require one another to create the massive composite system and the extreme pull of Jupiter that made in-depth exploration impossible. Europa, however, could be explored, and we'd inferred from years of analyzing both that there had to be connections between its makeup and the makeup of Jupiter in turn. One a frozen orb of possible organic matter underneath the atmosphere, nagging at our satellites and telescopes until we'd landed. The other a mass of poisonous air allowing not just orbit but engagement, binary communication between its moons that we could then experience in morse waves.

The argument, then, would be that the Kuiper belt created a similar organic tendency or makeup that allowed for growths like those on earth, but with variation in terms of one thriving and the other dying. Disease was just one possibility, I gathered, that Klimt could've focused on in analyzing the material. A variant on the Hepatitis C virus, for instance, could just as easily have been the successful growth of spores in various caves in North America. Both required circumstances in which to generate and regenerate, and both would collapse outside of these zones. Klimt's assertion, though extreme, wasn't entirely implausible, then. It took some mental stretching, but I wanted to believe as he did in the possibility of organic compounds simultaneously existing with their opposite as it had been established on earth. The promise of these compounds existing together in deep space or on Pluto's surface even would imply an entirely new relationship to disease and growth, one wherein harmful or prosperous materials wouldn't necessarily mean the end of one another, but could instead mean an unforeseen relationship we still needed to figure out.

4: ORPHÉE

When you're tasked with evaluating materials further away from your home planet than any previous human body had touched, the process of leaving can seem far too quick. Klimt wanted me exploring the exterior of the Orpheus 1 as soon as we had settled and had medical evaluations, and though I dawdled as much as possible so as to mentally adjust myself for whatever might be happening, I still felt rushed and strange, nauseated and expended. Klimt spoke to me alone as we sat in lower deck staring at image after image of photographs sent from the small orbiter pods the Orpheus mission's vessels all utilized after loss of human influence. At times the material latching itself to the exterior looked like mounds and caverns on some near moon, at others they simply looked like smudges of dirt, and occasionally they looked like scrapings, the influence of some alien vessel barreling into its ribs.

"What is apparent to you in these images?" Klimt asked.

"It looks like mold, sir. It looks like a sort of mold, an unwanted growth. Something."

"Are you prepared to analyze it personally? Face-to-face? Are you prepared?" Klimt's bottle of cocktail never left him at this point, and nobody quite knew what its contents were, and nobody quite cared. He'd reached a sort of tyrannical status on the ship and wended his way throughout like a snake with secrets. He'd ask questions and forget he'd asked them. He was fraying.

"I'm prepared, sir, though I'm not sure what to make of my efforts. I'm not sure what you think it is I'll do. The ship's robotics might've cut a sample years ago if I'm honest. What are you seeing that I can't?"

"Sometimes vulnerability is necessary to fully understand substance. I've chosen individuals for this mission capable of a certain kind of vulnerability, and yours and our botanist's will perhaps prove the most essential."

"What kind of vulnerability exactly? I'm prepared to accept an alternate sense of time out here. I'm prepared to witness a disease and cure in simultaneity, but beyond that I'm interested in growth alone. Fungi are communicative as a scab is communicative. Whatever language they have could've been transmitted via sampling."

Klimt took a long drink and stared down at a reflective glow in the corner of the room.

"I am, as ever, skeptical of the human influence, the presence of the human. To me, then, our work out here is about transcending humanity. Machines have been essential to become certain of our efforts out here, but little more. If we're talking about disease, if we're talking about time, if we're talking about unwanted matter, we're talking about them through the lens of our experience and thus— preferable though it might've been—a human touch will always rank slightly higher than purely impartial mechanical analysis. Our point was to come out here, to be out here, and to experience things that the Orpheus 1 has only ever hinted at, sent back home with broken pixels and artificial light. I need you vulnerable as prey on earth is vulnerable. I need you present as an insect under threat. We have to be here, and touch this place, firsthand. Nothing short will suffice," at this Klimt stopped pacing in front of me and sat at chair nearest the window and looked out. Sweat dripped from his forehead and his eyes were mad. He looked at me as if profoundly disappointed and turned away. I returned to my quarters and sat in repeated red light blinking. I stared out as Klimt stared out and watched the impossible churn of Pluto.

What I saw communicated feeling more than bit or blip of information. We were in this place, beyond what's known. Within the Kuiper Belt and experiencing things according to a new god's definitions and demarcations. I never stopped being tired on the ship. The months and more of coma had pushed me to some wit's end and I never stopped wanting to fall over and sleep for good. I wanted to rest. I wanted to feel myself asleep. I wanted to pull the blankets up and over my face and fall to sleep. The ship's machines hummed and warmed against my moods, and I wanted to lean into them for rest. The engineers had bickered on our first awakening about the materials onboard the Orpheus 1, sure throughout their speech that if we wanted to, we could push on into known planets with healthful atmospheres and leave behind the stuff of earth. This troubled me, perhaps more than Klimt's antics troubled me. Klimt was determined to make this particular image, our status amid the moons and Pluto astride these two ships, into a sort of masterpiece all its own. A reaching out to some figure that future generations might use as a linchpin to human progress throughout the cosmos. This felt alright to me, and he'd sold me on as much when I agreed to come along. These engineers, though, and certain medical staff whose names flitted by as all of them were hung in beams of red and shadow, they seemed determined to make this trip a perpetual one, and I wasn't sure how to explain to them the vitality of this particular organism compared with any vision they'd imagined.

What I saw transcended talk of movement. What I was able to discern about the material from looking at these images and noting numbers communicated back to us via the Orpheus 1's still-functioning hardware was organic, it moved and seemed to grow or weep according to the positioning of Pluto's lights and flits and this alone was more significant than anything we'd seen communicated back from planets as far as Neptune in as many as a hundred years. We were always searching, as a people, and those of us near to our profession especially so. You don't develop an ability to analyze fungal growth beyond breath without also considering the history that's brought you here. From Tombaugh on to the first successful colonies I'd understood that a shift in destiny seemed inevitable. As earthbound beings attempted to account for the possible swallowing of the sun or the burning out of all our living, those of us who looked outward and into the possibility beyond had to remain convinced that our search could prove a base, profound instinct correct, an optimism we couldn't shake for any ream of data that our living did not finish with our time on earth. What I saw, then, seemed to communicate the possibility of growth in an area previously thought barren and cold as the husk of Europa. Klimt's theories didn't have to be proven right to make this a fundamental shift in our understanding. The existence of even the slightest tinge of organic matter could shift all thought possible thus far.

***

I equipped myself slowly in the airlock while Klimt ranted to me about his hopes. He was chewing on nicotine lozenges and grinding through several at once. His eyes looked like he hadn't closed them in weeks. His hair was frenzied. His hands were cold to the touch as he assisted.

"I've put us here in the face of this with the body of humankind in mind. I've put us out beyond the reaches with the body in mind. I'm worshipful of all possibility out here. Do you feel the strength out here?"

"I feel the cold out here, Klimt. I feel the dark out here."

"That cold, though, that absence of sun, is the host of everything out here, the endless potential. We have to wait, and we have to ingest this world out here. The obsessives who discovered this place knew we'd someday reach it. The minds that put the code together for our journey knew we'd see it. We have to be open. We have to be vulnerable. We have to welcome the cold. You see these masses. These growths. These growths became thus despite the absence of sun. Everything back there, the colonies, all of it has required at least some glint of sun. These seem to have grown in shadow. Their timelessness could only occur thus. We are witnessing growth despite the absence of sun."

"I don't disagree, Klimt. I need my time with them is all. These growths. If so, I need my time with them is all."

"I believe that you are a child of the stars. I believe that each of us are children of these stars. Most look at what I'm doing out here and see a mania. They see an individual of earth, of earthly things. I am trying to reach beyond our earth, our earthly concerns. I have no use for them anymore, and we are safe out here to be, to wonder, to float. You must hold onto this hope and trust it. It's all that ever got us outside of our own heads."

I had suited up then and sat down on a small bench that sat between Klimt and the exit. We'd had a strange stretch of weeks and I remained tired. My eyes were always bloodshot, and my hands were always cold. I had spoken with those responsible for kinds of analysis and I had spoken with Klimt and I had wandered around feeling glum and strange but settled, the tiredness always there. My hands felt strange in the suit and I could feel the wave of anxiety that came with leaving. The small space I now occupied felt like something significant. Klimt was always in my ear trying to clarify what was happening. I was tired and confused, dazed. Regardless of circumstance, always some anxiety. I remember retrieval missions orbiting earth to accumulate the garbage and wreckage of past decades and my palms sweating so heavily I thought my gloves would slip from their mounts and I'd be sucked to freezing immediately. I remember leaving earth's atmosphere and the strange dip sensation in my skull as I looked out. I always felt this to at least a small degree. I wasn't necessarily cut out for this, but we lived in a time where that didn't matter or change a thing. We had to leave. The alarm bells were sounding for our humanity and we had to escape this place. This was merely one of hundreds of small last-ditch efforts being undertaken by would-be saviors of humanity in the face of burning out and all that feeling seemed to well up in me as I prepared to leave the comfort of the vessel.

The binary of Pluto and Charon made settling into my status strange. I was tethered to the Cocteau with quicklock straps holding me to the Orpheus 1 and the masses of Pluto and Charon completely disoriented me. Everything seemed bound up in these two hulking figures and their pull of one another. I remembered the ancient images attempting to prove their state and the small specks around them like tumors in the bloodstream. The distant Styx shone in constant movement alongside broken Nix and further out in the strange binary orbit I thought I might see Kerberos and Hydra, but for all my staring I really only noted the two massive binary orbs and attempting to rein in my thinking to the task at hand. The material on the exterior of Orpheus 1 looked a bit like globs of ash, as if a child had packed small towers of wet black sand into structures resembling toadstools and houses in the forest. I removed a radiation surveyor from my hip and scanned over them, sending back yet more data to the Cocteau. I ran a finger along the corner of them and felt initial shock on realizing how firm the material was, as solid as any chunk of marble in earth's atmosphere. I removed a small scraper from a pocket at my calf and attempted to slide it beneath the material only to scrape a bit of silver from the husk of the Orpheus 1 in the process. Klimt sounded in my headset and discouraged me from further trying to excavate the material.

"That's enough of it there. You don't need any more of it. Encase it and bring it back."

I wanted to continue exploring and didn't understand Klimt's certainty and discouragement from further testing this material. I ran a hand along the bulk of the growth and noted the firmness and apparent differences in makeup from one side of the material to the other. I lifted the small sample to my face to further look at it and felt the horror looming as Charon overwhelmed my vision just above the material. I felt a sinking in my stomach I couldn't explain and then the slow tug of my tether returning me to the Cocteau. I unlatched my quicklock straps as fast I could and held the small container encasing the material under my right arm as I turned to face the Cocteau and Klimt's manic visage emanating from a small sphere in the pod bay. I felt sick.

5: TESTAMENTD'ORPHÉE

On my re-entry I was quarantined briefly and shot head-to-toe with pressurized air and bleach and I saw Klimt staring at me outside and he was smiling. The smear of black on my gloved fingers reacted to the bleach and spread and had the cleaner not moved quickly I might've lost the flesh beneath. I reached out my hands and I looked at Klimt and attempted to meet his smile, but he was laughing slightly. The porthole coated in steam at the gasps from his mouth and I turned to the cleaner to settle myself. The container was on the floor and after a nod Klimt reached in to grab it and I sat there gasping for some time after. A small room opposite the door Klimt quickly shut contained a shower and I stripped off the remainder of my gear and went inside. I needed to sit down, and I needed to collect myself. The black on my gloves made me uncomfortable. The water felt good over my skin and the dark felt good and the environment felt visceral against me and I welcomed it. I couldn't see Klimt anymore and I didn't care. I prepared myself mentally for the analysis I'd set to after getting some rest. I wanted to put my feet up and eat something unhealthy. I still felt sick and I could see Klimt laughing still. I held my stomach and attempting to ignore the world as the shower steamed up and the room remained a warming dark against my flesh.

***

I woke up later to blinking red light and the noise of Klimt clearing his throat overhead. We were told to come and meet with him. I'd slept and everything felt heavy. I'd dreamt of my father and it felt like the air was pressing me down with warmth. The blinking light became hypnotic and I stared and stared until I heard Klimt's voice again. I rolled onto my stomach and felt the weight. My hands were stinging, and my heart was beating slow and pronounced in my chest and I stumbled against the walls in standing. I didn't want to think of what Klimt needed. I didn't know how long I'd been asleep. I hadn't thought about time after the first several weeks and I had no idea what precisely was happening. I'd been able to sleep much longer after the good sleep in our travel and it seemed like days might've passed. I exited into the hall and similarly sleepy people were making their way toward his voice and stumbling. Klimt continued to mumble to himself and I heard the tink of glass as I approached a looming light and his voice moved from overhead to in front of me and pressed my chest as everybody milled about in some concern. The red lights continued to blink.

"I remember when I was younger my mother showing me the films of Jean Cocteau. As a young man I'd been interested in the poem, and we'd watched the Disney iterations of *The Beauty and the Beast* and the like. I was at least a bit familiar with the French sense of creation and art. My mother was passionate about these things, obsessive about her children and a wider sense of things. It wasn't until she showed me Cocteau's Orphic Trilogy that I understood something about our place within the cosmos. Art, and creation, in these films, is treated not as something merely to entertain, or to distract from living, but as a reaching into the very marrow of living. *Purposeful,* Cocteau's artists are based in myth and history. The black and white never bothered me. Even as a youth I was quite fond of looking at old photographs, looking where we are now. I was captivated. I took this to extend to all creation. Every moment a human animal takes a set of materials from the world in front of him and says it must be turned to something different, a fundamental part of our living is enacted. That's why I've attempted to extend our reach out here, our touch, into this underworld. That's what I think of when I think of these ships. And that's what I see, now, in the generation of this material gathered by our resident fungal obsessive," with this Klimt held high the container I'd used to store the material from the exterior of the Orpheus 1, the room was lit dimly with lamps meant to emulate the effects of a candle on the walls of a log cabin, so as to calm the human beings therein, "what this represents, is an eternity. What this represents, is our enduring. Like Cocteau, each of us must spread our interests wider than the generations previous. We must be vulnerable. Each of us must open ourselves to the possibility of the beyond, of the great god of dark Pluto, and the endlessly sleeping world we've left behind. Still. The blood of a poet burns within this container, and it's fundamental now we take it into ourselves to wake." Up until that moment everyone had fidgeted in circles emanating out from Klimt. Some of us felt off, I think, but all of us were dead tired. Something might've been wrong, but we'd begun to witness Klimt as a sort of theater. We'd all grown accustomed to Klimt's meandering thought processes and decided to accept them along with the manifold vagaries of this endeavor. We had to accept it, like so many other things on entering the world of Klimt. We would've lost it otherwise. This, however, I doubt if any of us had considered this.

Klimt raised his hand holding the container and brought it down to the metal surface in front of him to smash it open. The container was made of modified glass meant to endure any changes in temperature or surrounding material, but on impact it shattered and fairly quickly a smell emanated from the case like burning fuel. The ash fungi I'd pulled from the hull of the Orpheus 1 shot outward in waves of smoke and light, and the room seemed to stand still in shock as we gathered ourselves only to witness Klimt writhing on the floor with black foam pouring from his lips. He seemed to smile. Those of us awake enough could barely stare, all of us felt weak in the face of it, all of us wanted to simply curl up then and weep.

Those in the room smart enough to cover their faces looked at me in horror as I attempted to gather myself and figure a plan of moving forward. Not knowing what else to do, I grabbed one of Klimt's legs and amassed what I could of the fungus to pull it all with me and dragged it to the pod bay where he'd come from. Those behind me looked sickly and a few had begun to spew the black pus Klimt had leaked behind him. I pointed at an emergency station and screamed to remove the bleach and cover the floors in it in an attempt to neutralize anything organic the material contained. I covered my face with a sleeve ripped from my suit and set Klimt on the floor nearest the door next to the writhing and decaying bits of organic matter moving there. I grabbed a disposal container and placed the discoloring limbs of Klimt inside and attempted to gather my thoughts as to the material. I looked back and the room seemed to be settling, with an engineer and soldier decaying on the floor not unlike Klimt. I pointed to their disposal containers and gestured for them to move. The medical staff tended to the remaining souls in the far corner and the bleach seemed to be working to neutralize the small remainder of material exuding from the dying's lips and what Klimt had left behind. I couldn't think of anything until I realized the material Klimt had smashed open had begun to dissipate and flood the air around me. Even through the security of my sleeve and the suit's protective layers I began to feel an itch at the back of my throat and worried I'd already inhaled some of the material. The lights around me began to take on aural depths and the room through the orb looked as if it was in flames. I felt panic flood into my chest, and I hurried to the shelving across the pod bay to cover myself with another's suit and put on my mask and breathing apparatus.

Klimt had withered on the floor and I tried to keep him near me. The disposal containers slid through an encased plastic tunnel to remove them from the hall where we'd been. I could see a bit through the porthole, and it looked to be settling. Faces were surrounded in glow and dark shadows and it took what strength I had to prepare for expulsion.

There's a feeling of anxiety that's as visceral as dying, I figure. There's a bubbling in the chest and it seems as if every drop of bile you've been utilizing to break down matter is suddenly revolting against the system and your body is going to fall apart. I felt myself consumed by anxiety and the fire at the back of my throat as the lights began to overwhelm me. The room began to blur, and I felt the fading breaths and murmurs of Klimt on the floor as I saw the air slowly filled with the grayblack smoke from the material. It had changed its form several times since being smashed to bits by Klimt and now it simply looked like an obscure, dense vapor that seemed to want to touch everything in the room. It reached out. I was vulnerable. I felt myself losing grip and seeing images of my living and my family and my father staring at me as the room seemed wet with shadow. I heard the screaming of the ship's remaining living and felt my chest pound and fill with rot as I saw my father next to me reaching his hand out to me and feeling it grip mine. My father had passed far away, and I'd never seen him close to his death. I'd never gotten to say goodbye to him really and never experienced the final comfort of an embrace from the man. He felt there and visceral and as real and gripping as my rotting guts and I stared him right in the eyes and felt him pulling me. I powered up my suit's particulars and held my father close to me and stared at the writhing mess on the floor of Klimt bagged up commingling with the materials and felt myself being pulled ever further and further from myself and the ship and the pod bay until I saw the light of the orb and the way out into Charon and Pluto's connected binary and felt my chest pound in that direction as I grabbed hold of the disposal containers and Klimt and the remaining bits of glass material on the floor and what fragments of the fungus I could gather. I pulled it to me and held the lot of it to my heart as my father held me and I pushed my head to the apparatus on the wall that would open and remove the contents of the pod bay immediately to jettison us without tether into some beyond. I looked up and saw my father on the mounds of Charon and leaping between the skies to Pluto and breathed deeply only to further imbibe the material until suddenly the sky was thick with light and all I felt was my father's warmth in my guts emanating as the bagged remains of Klimt pressed and bound themselves to the black pox spreading itself across the husk of Orpheus 1.

I have no confidence the remaining passengers of the Cocteau weren't made to slowly decay from the materials on-board nor whether they survived. I feel no sense of comfort gliding outward and beyond as the reach of Pluto and the Kuiper Belt pulls me and I'm made to stare at the massive white orb and its red and blue and strange hues lining the edges with light and mixing endlessly with my father and the feel of heft in my chest brought on by rot and the sad communications from the ship behind me and their speaking. I know I have become consumed by the material and I don't feel a need to exchange this living for one back on-board the ship with the souls who will comfort me and coat me in bleach and make the light stop growing at the edges of my vision. I feel myself alone in this place and terrified a bit but still entirely connected with my father's living and the feeling of him in my gut as it's rotting and the edges of Pluto shift and enliven along with my limbs as they're brought to life from atrophy in occasional shocks and the headset attempts to tell me where to go and how to breathe and how to sustain myself. I am moving and there is no end. Klimt is back somewhere decaying and bound it seems to the husk of Orpheus 1. The crew might very well have left. They might be headed home centuries after our departure to find their place and convey their information. The material might've brought about hallucinations such that none or all of this is happening in perpetuity. A choice between the infinite coexisting realities and the prospect of returning is impossible. I am contained within the suit and seeing the light and can feel myself growing in hallucination and the worlds around me lined with shadow as my chest swells with rot and the dying is very likely consuming me. The material is consuming me, and I haven't an idea of its contents, its makeup. I have no inkling of what's what and my memories have grown beyond the journey Klimt dragged us on to my children that never lived and my father that never died and my living that will ever and forever emanate around this belt of hulking stones and all of it tears at me and brings me down and I am living within the history and dying within it in turn and sweltering with the heat and bound up frigid from the cold of space as the world jettisons me and I am cast ever outward into the mass oblivion and rot.

THE ANTI-UPDATE DECOMPRESSIVE SAW

(Optional diamond-plate insert 3100-2686)

THE ANTI-UPDATE
DECOMPRESSIVE SAW

A user's manual

Stein Corp.™

PX138 3100-2686

INTRODUCTION

Grant is down in some well out west of here, somewhere between these tight smiles and the endless night and piss, down there long after the yelling and the cries and the memory, where only the hidden divide can carry you out but not home. He's long gone.

Grant was buried alive under coal in a black and white past life with his whole fear pressed into a hot blade that cuts through time. We're here now in the shadow of its wake as it moves without resistance. Like a projection. Like a vow. If it is broken it was never there. We're in slow motion / this is the replay / there is no jogwheel / what is this film? What is this format? It's the context that's dizzying, all else is bound only by true law.

They gutted his favorite video store and turned it into a dog daycare. You can rent your stacks down the road at a cursed stripmall where the only lights on are from a stranger's tossed cigarette bouncing against the lot.

There's a piece of you in here. You, the real you, the sticky, sweaty one that winces when it needs to. It's wild. There's a piece and it's waiting, cloaked in the cryptic dance of wood grain as that old shard of glass swept up good enough, who knows how long ago, and when it's time, it'll find a way up into your heel to let your wince loose.

And it'll be you in that well, in a new kind of peace. Smothered by foul unearth, pressed into a true direction. Dancing across the faded lines. Eyes up and shining and still and part of a whole thing.

Lorn, 2020

SAW YES WOE'S INSIDE
THE ANTI-UPDATE DECOMPRESSIVE
SAW YES WOE'S INSIDE
THE ANTI-UPDATE DECOMPRESSIVE
SAW YES WOE'S INSIDE
THE ANTI-UPDATE DECOMPRESSIVE
SAW YES WOE'S INSIDE
THE ANTI-UPDATE DECOMPRESSIVE
SAW YES WOE'S INSIDE
THE ANTI-UPDATE DECOMPRESSIVE
SAW YES WOE'S INSIDE

SAW YES WOE'S INSIDE
THE ANTI-UPDATE DECOMPRESSIVE
SAW YES WOE'S INSIDE
THE ANTI-UPDATE DECOMPRESSIVE
SAW YES WOE'S INSIDE
THE ANTI-UPDATE DECOMPRESSIVE
SAW YES WOE'S INSIDE
THE ANTI-UPDATE DECOMPRESSIVE
SAW YES WOE'S INSIDE
THE ANTI-UPDATE DECOMPRESSIVE
SAW YES WOE'S INSIDE

SAW YES WOE'S INSIDE
THE ANTI-UPDATE DECOMPRESSIVE
SAW YES WOE'S INSIDE
THE ANTI-UPDATE DECOMPRESSIVE
SAW YES WOE'S INSIDE
THE ANTI-UPDATE DECOMPRESSIVE
SAW YES WOE'S INSIDE
THE ANTI-UPDATE DECOMPRESSIVE
SAW YES WOE'S INSIDE
THE ANTI-UPDATE DECOMPRESSIVE
SAW YES WOE'S INSIDE

SAW YES WOE'S INSIDE
THE ANTI-UPDATE DECOMPRESSIVE
SAW YES WOE'S INSIDE
THE ANTI-UPDATE DECOMPRESSIVE
SAW YES WOE'S INSIDE
THE ANTI-UPDATE DECOMPRESSIVE
SAW YES WOE'S INSIDE
THE ANTI-UPDATE DECOMPRESSIVE
SAW YES WOE'S INSIDE
THE ANTI-UPDATE DECOMPRESSIVE

THE ANTI-UPDATE DECOMPRESSIVE SAW
(optional diamond-plate insert 3100-2686)

THE ANTI-UPDATE DECOMPRESSIVE SAW

A user's manual

Stein Corp.[TM]

PX138 3100-2686

FROM THE BUILDER TO THE USER:

Congratulations. You've just become the (proud) owner of one of the most fantastic machines ever engineered by human being. However it came into your possession is immaterial, what's important now is what you're going to accomplish with it. What you now hold in your hands or witness scattered around the oily floor of this garage is something once deemed impossible by 96% of the American public, and yet here it is. Here it is, ready in only moments to be assembled into the fierce and meticulous cutting power used to take apart and reassign U.S. tanks after three major conflicts in the latter twenty-first century. Used in surgeries to give children full-functioning limbs where theirs fell short. Used in times of great hell to restore comfort to millions of vacant stares in front of millions of telepod sets. Used to cut through fire and ore and welcome the onset of the new age when we were no longer visitors here but hosts on the shoulder of Orion. Used to give hope to a hopeless people whether they wanted it or not. Used.
And moving forward we now have the question of prosperity. Will you in effect pass this machine on to future generations in the utmost confidence that it will cut through any and everything it comes across? Will you? This is both the most important question any new saw owner can ask itself and, likely enough, the last thing on your mind. What's on your mind now is power, pure and simple. And soon enough we'll let you go. But for now you must consider future generations and the prospect of a world without the ANTI-UPDATE DECOMPRESSIVE SAW, and surely it is no world you'd desire your grandchildren to inhabit. So care for it. Treat it well and allow it to consume as much of your life as it seems to desire. Nothing else matters now. You are the owner, and I was never here.

H.S. MD

P.S. What follows is a brief digressive necessity in the way of safety. Though as you've certainly learned not extent of dogmatic practice will keep you from doing exactly what you've always set out to do, and hence these are merely further things to consider before you unleash hell on every nearby scrap of detritus[1].

---

[1] Some sleepless night he's likely to wonder if, hypothetically, it were possible to rearrange the numerals in the sequence 'SIX SIX SIX' how many possible permutations he might arrive at and whether this would exceed or not the amount of possible arrangements of other random sequences of numerals. Does it then justify rearranging the letters in the spelling out of the numeral 'SIX' to reach yet more permutations, and is it through this sort of numerology that this item was created and passed on to you… He isn't quite sure…

IMPORTANT   IMPORTANT   IMPORTANT

READ BEFORE USING
        LIRE AVANT USAGE
                LEER ANTES DE USAR

SAFETY

COVER YOUR EYES. Never, under any circumstances, should you witness the raw cutting power of this machine. To do so would be to witness the hand of god severing raw metals with an ease unparalleled, and you're just not ready.

COVER YOUR EARS. In a democracy the temptation to watch over one's brethren is likely, but should not be encouraged regardless of potential panoptic resources in the hands of government employees— and this of course extends to all recipients of ANTI-UPDATE DECOMPRESSIVE SAWs via the current U.S. "Handyman Christmas Care Package" legislation, and thus warrants mentioning here.
Avoid serious thought when nearest machine. Within there are any number of receptive thoughtless waves desiring little else than flesh and blood. Acknowledging this, manufacturers of both ANTI-UPDATE DECOMPRESSIVE SAW and potential updates respectfully decline all comments appertaining to A.) Human injury, adult et al., B.) Animal injury, and C.) Damage to all commercial and domestic properties, we simply do not hear you.

Press hands comfortably against temple before use. Aggression is a mainstay in the life of a machinist. We are aware and even encouraging of this notion, however we cannot recommend highly enough wishing one's loved ones farewell before sitting down to work. This is your project, not ours.

TIE BACK LONG HAIR/ROLL UP LONG SLEEVES. Because of recent doctrine put forth in certain Central American nations where primary bolts 311z and 415x are manufactured it is required we inform you that having your hair sucked inside of a saw moving at over 3,000 RPM is a terrible idea when said saw is sharp enough to sever a neck standing still, but we aren't sticklers if you happen to enjoy letting your hair fall at will while sawing. Ditto for sleeves, though we can't imagine the thought process that might lead one to saw using the A.-U. D. C. anything but stark naked, an overshirt can sometimes be nice, and we won't hold it against you.

DO NOT PERFORM ANY OPERATION UNDER THE INFLUENCE OF PHARMACEUTICALS. Excepting of course: Acanthaceae, Fittonia albivenis/Justicia pectoralis; Aceraceae, Acer saccharinum; Delosperma acuminatum, DMT, 5-MeO-DMT; Acacia aroma; Acacia auriculiformis, 5-MeO-DMT (in stem bark); LSD-25; Ayahuasca; Tryptamines; Dimethyltryptamine; Excessive portions of butter; 2C-T-21; 2C-T-7; 2C-T-2, 2C-N; Tetramethoxyamphetamine; Dextromethorphan; 2,000 cups of coffee; Your father; God; Mescaline; Television; Psilocybin; Cannabinoids; Salvia divinorum; Ketamine; Witchcraft; Pornography; Numerology; Sigmund Freud; Genuine Terrorism Anger Manifold; Datura stramonium (Jimson weed); Atropa belladonna (Deadly nightshade); Cops; Gallons of human urine; Gallons of Subhuman Urine; Watching rain fall; Fingertip.

NEVER HOLD ONTO OR TOUCH THE INSIDE OF THE EYE. Excessive amounts of anything tend to contribute to a general attitude of dissatisfaction and intergalactic existential rot, and we won't have it. We won't have it to such a degree that we've already ceased listening and returned to our workbenches where we might saw in peace. In peace.

Au revoir,

Horace Stein, M.D.

(Previous) Introductory letter from CREATOR

(Previous) Safety Digression

*VARYING DESCRIPTIONS OF VIDEO TUTORIAL/
TRACKING DIGRESSIONS DURING WHICH THE USER
DOES PRECISELY WHAT HE WAS PUT ON THIS EARTH TO
DO, USE*

Following pages: SAWMAN'S JOURNAL

END OF SAW[2]

---

[2] Note: aforesaid and forthcoming materials are in fact restatements of original intent of creator/user amalgam and thus attempting to find direct order or arrangement throughout is discouraged while the attempt itself is thought of as cute by H.S. M.D. and hence the occasional indicators in VHS component to manual wherein creator provides consoling/encouraging/motherly advice while you rummage through materials in your bedroom looking for yet more things to split in two.

ATTEMPTED DESCRIPTION OF VIDEO TUTORIAL/ TRACKING DIGRESSIONS DURING WHICH THE USER DOES PRECISELY WHAT HE WAS PUT ON THIS EARTH TO DO, USE

VHS projected demagnetized strips of information/intelligentsia regarding use of ANTI-UPDATE DECOMPRESSIVE SAW (PX138 3100-2686) including roughly seven standard lunar hours of exquisite humming tracking sounds during which user's encouraged to saw, saw, saw..

I.

00:00:00 – 00:07:34

Encouraging photographs of industrious citizens in various shades of black and white progressing toward something not apparent to viewer/user intended for viewer's/user's relaxation and potential relationship with aforesaid citizens as members of viewer's/user's "new life" upon receiving ANTI-UPDATE DECOMPRESSIVE DAW (PX138 3100-2686)

(yours) I like the little flesh parts mostly.

II.

00:07:35 – 00:14:39

Sequence of various bits of machinery intended to—perhaps
with Dziga Vertov in mind—trace the history that allowed the
eventual creation of this machine and its sale in the United States
and elsewhere. It's here that Creator's tastes become apparent and
a noirish vibe presents itself that feels initially unexpected for
viewers though eventually they come to think of their work as
quote "a sort of caper" unquote.

(yours) one time i think of watching neighborhood burn

III.

00:59:00 – 01:44:03

PERVERTED sense of lowly humanity as thrust into the eyesight
of various individuals having just completed the long, arduous
process (see 00:14:40 – 00:58:59 for reference [ed. 4 "missing"])
of crafting set of crews for inclusion in saw. Accompanying
imagery of happy, happy, happy children dancing along fields
of heather in Scotland included for understanding both of the
fundamental *humanity* of this item and its presence as something,
well, better than humanity.

(yours) just what I've seen I can't readily say. I feel the world
closing in, maybe, is that the phrase? The cycle repeats itself and I
am some livid ouroboros without teeth sucking the past through
myself to regurgitate some sad impression of the future. What is
this?

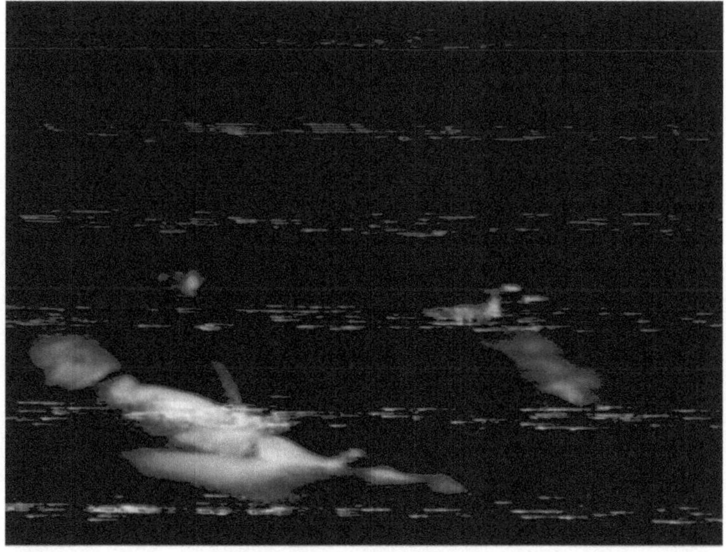

IV.

01:44:04 – 01:50:00

REPORTED FOOTAGE OF THE CREATOR, this can neither be confirmed nor denied and based on descriptions of his likeness and attempts at reconstructing the image with police sketch artists through time it may in fact be Horace Stein or a distant relative, we simply cannot say.

(yours) I'm wondering now if images such as this exist of myself, like the progression of the funeral of Tolstoy once seen through internet, I wonder, it makes me curious. Am I the first to use this device? I wonder as it seems to take certain forms depending on my own usage. Always wondering.

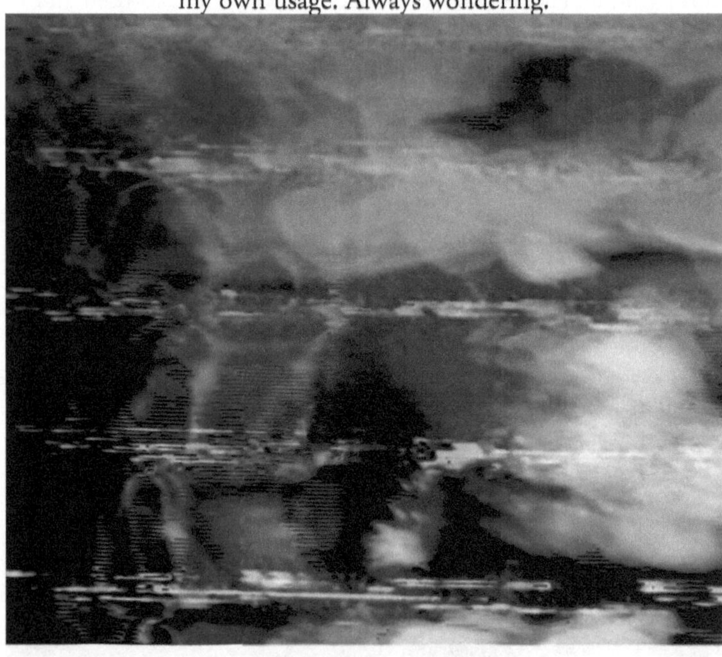

V.

01:50:01 – 01:59:44

HERE THE tragedy ensues. A knowledge of the footage comes
and wonderment at the existence of this thing: unknown
documentation of the execution of one G.G., this is really rotten
stuff. Awareness of one's surroundings and all that, learning from
history, sure, but tying this with the use of your saw is a foreign
concept to everyone but one H.S., and even then we're quite
certain he was merely rabble-rousing.

(yours) agreed, though I recall the film of tommy lee jones and
its similarity is undeniable, certainly, I wonder further about
what was it throbbing gristle and their recreation of this footage.
Nonetheless, and discounting all previous, it makes for good
sawing.

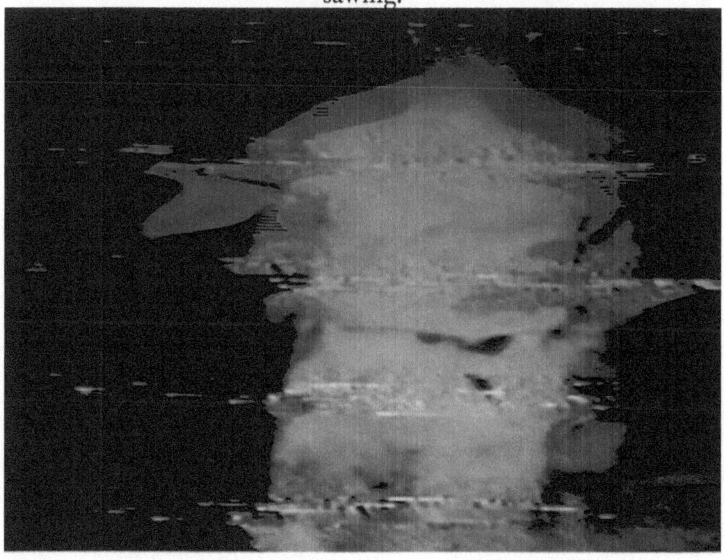

VI.

01:59:45 – 02:59:01

REPORTED footage of last remaining hour in the life of H.S., a logical, If not sadistic/masochistic/sadomasochistic account to follow the previous G.G. life-end sequence. He ambles around, looks rather old-fashioned, etc. etc., footage has not been confirmed by viable source.

(yours) I'm quite certain now this machine has been previously used, by whom I remain unsure, for what I'm quite aware. The previous owner apparently severed away the flesh of her/his left leg. An image exists deep inside the manual of this that I burned shortly upon opening and beginning the sawman's journal, an endeavor I remain unsure about. What is happening to my fingers?

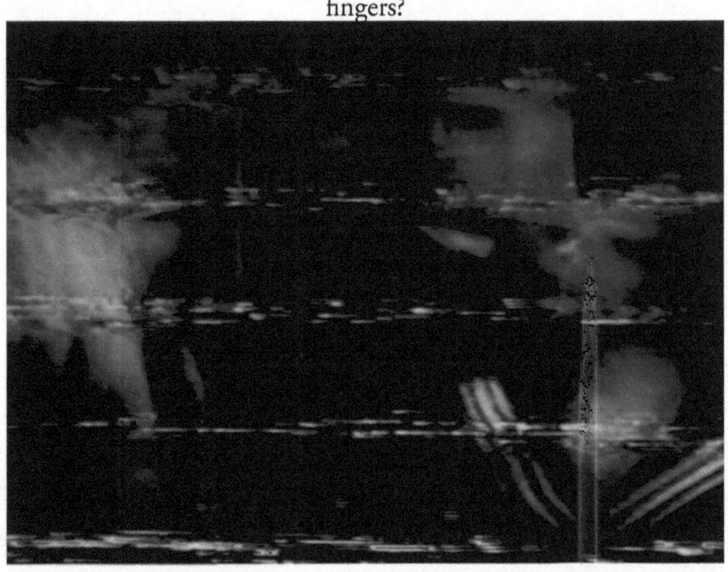

VII.

02:59:02 – 03:04:55

Soothing attempts again intended solely for the purpose of all-terrain sawing. Think of these in not a dissimilar fashion to the intermission approach of certain late 20th century filmmakers to provide time for the audience to process what's just been seen. We're thinking not in terms of literal "intermissions" on screen, though they exist, say, in something like "Gone With the Wind" but the anomalous musical scenes in the works of Tarkovsky or Von Trier where little occurs beyond mental processing. Think especially of the sudden rainfall in "Stalker" where sense becomes irrelevant, and story or plot is mere window dressing to this emotional wave.

(yours) I understand all that, but my attempts to reconcile narrative with the extant machinery have failed miserably, I'm afraid to say. I feel as if I'm losing it and will inevitably fall between two worlds in this respect. My hands have grown more accustomed to working the saw that I'd initially thought possible. I truly am a machinist.

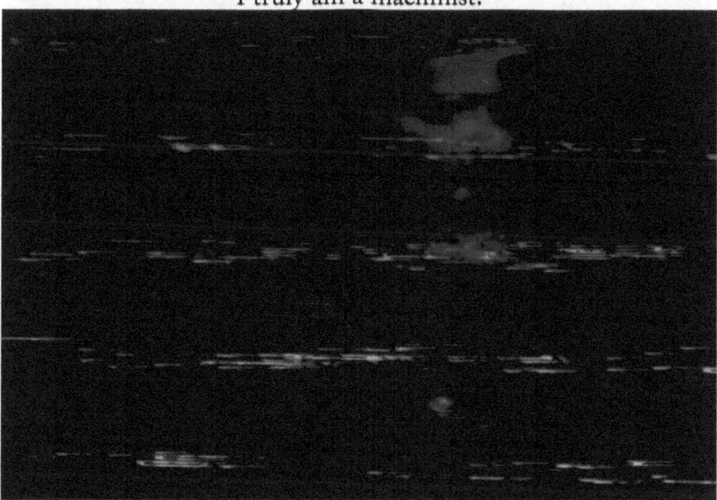

VIII.

03:04:56 – 04:00:00 (EXEUNT)

recordings or potential owners of the saw at first seminar on
proper usage of machinery as related to the social, economic,
political, familial relations of aforesaid potential owners. We want
them to like the machine, but more importantly, we want the
machine to like them.

(yours) there is nothing left to say.

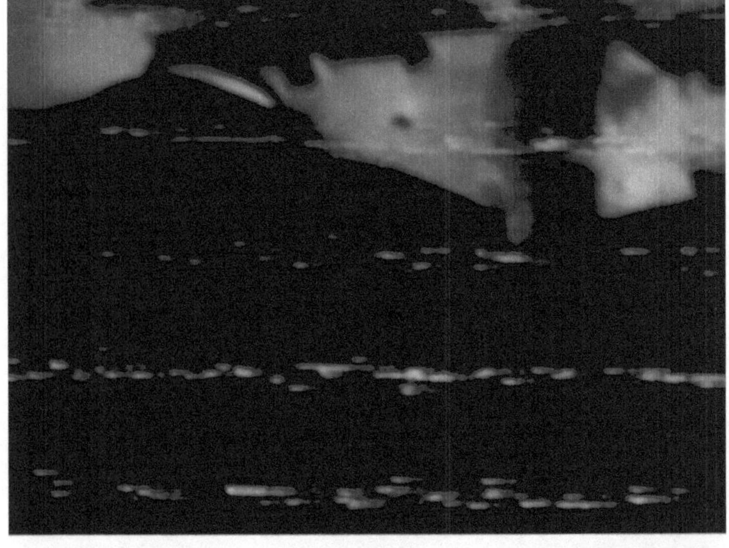

PX138 3100-2686

PX138 3100-2686

PX138 3100-2686

SAWMAN'S JOURNAL (yours):

I SAW

Saw yes no I want to spit in blood's protection. This is something. This is what I'm thinking. I'm tired. I'm ready to work again. I'm ready to work again. There's this frenetic corner to all my thoughts now. Even now. Even just now having just begun having just become whatever. IT seems to move differently every second. There's this gigantic red 'O' that glows atop the machine and I'm not quite sure what it means but I'm quite, quite sure that I'm terrified of when it ceases to glow. Interesting note from creator. Not sure what to make of any of it. Definitely care not about passing on saw gigantic saw to future generations. Imagining self on birthday morn of young young buck handing off saw as glorious gift 'take it with you into the future' and being laughed out of the living room. No. That isn't what it's for. People don't make this sort of thing to hand down. THEY encourage your potential death, this is maybe what I've realized. I realize it too much. There's any number of possible conclusions one might come to but the undeniable factor is the beginning rev and corresponding gliiiiide that feels like someone taking the sharpest knife cooled down below freezing through the front of your forehead on through to the back of your scalp until your head just sort of coolly splits open and all you are is a welcome mat for Stein's posterity, or something. Who cares. Who cares what the owner says. I don't want to know what the owner says, I only want the machine.

Began today with momentary torment before taking saw to each of a pair of ballet shoes found in dumpster behind pizzeria. THIS sort of thing is not what saw's for and yet it's undeniably pleasant to use machines for endeavors they were not intended for. Something godly in that, perhaps, something of the discovering of new galaxies in that, perhaps. One doesn't know or want to know. One only wants to feel that slow gliding pulse as another slit of fabric goes flying across to the corner of the room and the room itself grows colder. My hands have already begun to callus over in anticipation of a long winter's work. My hands have already begun.

There is a matrix on the ground which guides one footstep to the next and though we cannot see it we always know it is there for we are adhering to its principles without so much as a thought or dispute. There are lines of light which guide the human animal towards an infinity in space and though we've been told (guided) to believe that something is nothing and that outer anything is chaos we are in fact completely trusting when we let ourselves become swallowed up by the night so black that we cannot see ourselves or hear our hearts think. And there is peace not in food nor in sex nor in hurt but in the mere fact that there is no peace and there has never been a word so degrading as peace as long as we've lived and we watch ourselves shower in here we watch ourselves become clean and there is small beauty in this immediately before the struggle which completely tears us asunder and we are children in the fray or in fields where nothing bright ever happens but we are sweet- toothed and do not reject the potentiality of lust or happiness or freedom because we can feel it as the wind courses over our flesh. And in that silence there comes a tidal wave of friction which precedes everything important and turns it into ideology and pain ideology and pain and as we watch this happen we can only equate it with the bright bright bright blue screens of ephemera hovering just beyond the horizon on a screen so black that nothing could possibly live there but the blue blue blue center that hurts to stare directly into and yet we cannot help ourselves. We cannot help ourselves. We cannot help ourselves. And even as the children learn to govern learn to farm learn to smell to eat to think to write to read to paint there is something ungodly about this description that causes each of them to panic panic erodes away their rational thoughts and they become vigilantes each more angry at the last than the next and as this happens one crow hovers just above the village and the children lost in hay fields look up to understand the blackness on the wings the blackness on the wings and with this a kiss falls down to each and there is slow penetrating lust that creates a sort of magic within the sphere and each child slowly follows the matrix the labyrinth toward the center when eventually they reach the orchid which pulls slowly apart to reveal another planet deep inside there and they each step in one by one by one by one by one and there is majesty though ignorance in footsteps following this way and trusting that with entirety the children are not hurt. Unhurt by the footsteps the children are thence able to gather the surroundings only to realize that the bright blue blue blue screen had suddenly been transformed into fields upon fields of glowing neon hay that shifts and moves with the wind with such purpose that although it's tempting to look away after so much organization and direction the children simply cannot and tearing off their clothes the children are suddenly grown with bodies and cocks and breasts and there is nothing rotten or hurtful or scary about their flesh as it lies between the rows upon rows of glowing neon hay and as it tickles them they roll into one another until suddenly they have all combined into that massive specter of humanity the cube and as the cube they graze comfortably within one another until the light slowly shifts from blue blue blue to a deep and calming red and one by one the children understand that it is time to sleep and one by one their arms are relaxed behind their heads and their minds are able to comprehend nothing but that

*distant point the polar point of guidance settles every mind and
pulls eyelids heavily down onto cheeks and breath breath breath
is all. Like I am trapped inside the saw like it is endless. Man
I wish I could see that way. What a way a silent little piddling
way. The movement is so profound. I can't believe it and I don't
want to. I can't and don't want.*

*I wanted to watch myself fall apart in public. This didn't have
to be provocative or even original but I wanted to crumble
into tears in public while everyone watched just to be sure that
nobody would touch me before I pulled myself back together
and made sense of my surroundings. I wanted so badly to walk
out into the middle of a train station and simply start crying
and tearing my clothes off and hurling myself relentlessly into
the ground that I'd often wake up at night dreaming about it;
needing it, feeling as if there was nothing else in my life worth
pursuing except for this one manic episode wherein I was the
cyclone and the world around me was the cloud/the sphere/the
god that I couldn't make sense of. I needed something vast, some
immense pressure against my forehead to understand that this
was in effect important and that everything else up until now
had been a piddling training course for my deterioration.*

I have since

       taken

          to showering

              too much

*And there is nothing exactly pretty in the book I read and this
is such a great disappointment that I hurl the book at the wall
and look into the mirror and try to see something beyond my
face and this—impossible as it is—for a moment calms me
down but soon I see the beyond and it is nothing more than
childhood or blood running from limbs or the sorts of things
that humans can't often see due to pure lack of interest. I change
my mind and walk away though always regretting this will
cause me to do almost all the stupid things I've done hence.*

I've enjoyed the stupid things and I welcome them the way one might welcome a toad occasionally stepping into your path and yet even this is tainted for the memory of once trying on a friend's sandal only to stomp a croaking frog into wet oblivion. I do this and my friend looks at me differently from then on and I am ashamed though not enough to stop my gloating and run the other way.

MORGAN FAIRCHILDe
MIRGAN FAIRCHYLDE
MOOGAN ROTHSCHILDE

THERE

IT
GOES

PLEASE welcome the depression when it starts don't try to fight it don't act like you're better than feeling like offing yourself you're only going to make things worse   ALSO don't try to make real sense of emotion it's a fool's errand and you're obviously kind of dumb considering you're depressed in a generation filled up with pornography and chances.   FUCK yourself if you think that this is what life is about there is more there is a young man having his spiral notebooks taken away because he's going to use them for what exactly stabbing them into his jugular it doesn't exactly make sense and yet the opposite would make even less sense so it's quite difficult to explain and move away from and hence we just won't try at all.

I cannot leave this room. I am trapped and yet freed from anything. I have just finished making myself come. There is orange juice apparent. There is music.

I hold myself and watch it empty. Watch the bottles around me turn into vials and into smiles and into evenings and into a better life and yet I've said this before.

The saw glows and I am alone. I am alone watching the red HAL light of the saw and live in one nightmare. One endless cycling perfect blade.

A friend once told me in earnest how badly he wanted to write a manifesto.
I'd like to read that manifesto tonight. I'd like to curl up in a hole and die.

I'd like to die and smile at my corpse when I see it down below there. Down below there where there is nothing and everything and my hands are sticky.

I'm quite disgusting. I welcome my own degradation and realize I'll never understand a thing. I can read freud and not understand a thing.

I can read derrida and not understand a thing. I can listen to drab pulsating music and understand everything. This is what I want. This is what I've made for me.

For myself. It's not for you. there is nothing worth doing anymore. There is nothing alive and dead. I like to watch the basement fall apart. The walls around me.

They start melting. I watch them melt and become relics. I watch the walls melt and behind them are walls of digital clocks and I explore only to find rivers of come.

These rivers are the very same rivers which brought us here and I spit into them just to be sure. Instantly a clone of myself comes walking out. I know it's bad.

I know it's terrible. Horrifying. Ugly. Insane. I don't like the word insane and though I try to write unsane something won't let me. Someone says a terrible word.

I try to explore whether a terrible word can actually exist. It can't. I've checked. Nothing can actually exist. We cannot exist. We do not think. Therefore…

Therefore…

We are trapped in caves of blood. We are humans trapped in caves of blood and this message is coming to you from a hole filled with pornography. You are blind. Please.

*ISAWTHEWHITELIGHTTONIGHT.IJUSTDONTCARE.
IMUSINGITANDFEELINGITANDLETTINGITDRAW
BLOOOOOOODD.IWELCOMETHEBLOOD,MAN.FUCK.
ICOULDUSETHEBLOOD.ICOULDUSETHISNIGHTMARET
HING,MAN.SAWYESNOIWANTTOSPITINBLOOD
SPROTECTION.THISISSOMETHING.THISISWHA
TIMTHINKING.IMTIRED.IMREADYTOWORKAGAIN.IM
READYTOWORKAGAIN.THERESTHISFRE
NETICCORNERTOALLMYTHOUGHTSNOW.
EVENNOW.EVENJUSTNOWHAVINGJUSTBEGUNHA
VINGJUSTBECOMEWHATEVER.ITSEEMSTOMOVE
DIFFERENTLYEVERYSECOND.THERESTHISGIGANTI
CREDOTHATGLOWSATOPTHEMACHINEANDIMNOT
QUITESUREWHATITMEANSBUTIMQUITE,QUITESU
RETHATIMTERRIFIEDOFWHENITCEASESTOGLOW.IN
TERESTINGNOTEFROMCREATOR.NOTSUREWHATTO
MAKEOFANYOFIT.DEFINITELYCARENOTABOUTPASS
INGONSAWGIGANTICSAWTOFUTUREGENERATIONS.
IMAGININGSELFONBIRTHDAYMORNOFYOUNGYOUNG
BUCKHANDINGOFFSAWASGLORIOUSGIFTTAKEITWIT
HYOUINTOTHEFUTUREANDBEINGLAUGHEDOUTOFT
HELIVINGROOM.NO.THATISNTWHATITSFOR.PEO
PLEDONTMAKETHISSORTOFTHINGTOHANDDOWN.
THEYENCOURAGEYOURPOTENTIALDEATH,THISIS
MAYBEWHATIVEREALIZED.IREALIZEITTOOMUCH.
THERESANYNUMBEROFPOSSIBLECONCLUSIONSONE
MIGHTCOMETOBUTTHEUNDENIABLEFACTORIST
HEBEGINNINGREVANDCORRESPONDINGGLIIIIDE
THATFEELSLIKESOMEONETAKINGTHESHARPEST
KNIFECOOLEDDOWNBELOWFREEZINGTHROUGHT
HEFRONTOFYOURFOREHEADONTHROUGHTOTHE
BACKOFYOURSCALPUNTILYOURHEADJUSTSORTOFCO
OLLYSPLITSOPENANDALLYOUAREISAWELCOMEMAT
FORSTEINSPOSTERITY,ORSOMETHING.WHOCARES.*

These are jotted notes. These are notes, jotted.

when have i fell sleep..

I beg her to let me go. I beg the sky to let me go. All I want to do is stay awake forever. All I want to do is stay awake forever. Please help me. Please let me die.

What is this life. What is the question what is this life. Who is the person asking the question. Does he have original thoughts. Does he emit a foul odor. I want to know.

The shelves in my room have begun to grow spiders that have in turn begun to grow webs which have in turn caught many flies. The books I've loved or intended to love are too covered in flies and spiders to read. The books I've hoped for and longed for and intended to devour have become devoured by something else, something unrelated to their content but entirely related to their being. Their being, something limited by the fact that they exist and hence must abide by the rules of existence. We people must abide by this rule, this ugly rule. Covered we are in the spiderwebs of thought. Thought. Empty thought.

I leave the house to sit on a bench in the park for an extremely long time. I sit there for such a long time that it becomes not a bench but simply 'the place' where I am at that point in existence and everything is globed by that centerpiece. I feel myself melding into the earth and wonder what it will someday be like to exist as an earthworm. I long to be the earthworm. I long to tell my father something as an earthworm that I couldn't quite articulate as a person. I send somebody a message that I think explains this but after evaluation hours later realize only says 'I THINK MY FACE IS BROKEN CAN YOU WELCOME SOMETHING HOME' and feel quite discouraged trying to pick apart the sentences and really control what my output to the world amounts to. This is the trial. This is the trail. The trail leads to the bench in the park where I'll sit. The trial leads to the internal place we all must go to reach some level of understanding here. Here on earth. Here on earth is a man watching something that helps him to relate to existence but when he tries to write it down the only things he can get out are 'BRILLIANT NOT NOT NOT BRILLIANT HEY THIS DESERVES AN F F F' and again discouraged he falls asleep in a subtle pile of his own come. These small salvations are the stuff of brilliance.

My father owned a ship. My father sunk that ship. My father watched the mariners and that sort of thing. My father joined the navy. I never saw my father again.

My life is an endless façade. My life is a wall given to signatures of strangers who I've fucked over irrevocably.

My kinship with the world does not exist and is not a thing of the spirit no matter how strong my inclination to type that is.

*My kinship is with jack Torrance. My kinship is with jack
Torrance. My kinship is with jack Torrance.*

*Take a shit, say goodnight. Say goodnight inside the toilet bowl.
So you watch surfing. So what now. so what can it be. What can
it be can it run out can it be connected to anything else. What is
this that's happening.*
Describe it.
People like descriptions

People.

*Unlawful machinations let this happen. Unlawful
machinations let this happen. Unlawful machinations let this
happen. Unlawful machinations let this happen.*

*There is no beginning or end to the blade and that is
the largest problem the largesse problem. There is no begging
or end to the blade and how could it have been fashioned one
isn't sure and one isn't about to look into the yawning chasm of
history to find out. One is not going to find out and that will
make all or none of the difference tomorrow when I wake up
only to find another pile of useless muck to tear into pieces of
pieces of pieces.*

*I see obscured images on walls
mostly women, some men, all skewed
bent, fragmented, mirrored, ugly
I watch these things some internal
freak. some show of emotion some
performance art I watch as the camera
obscuring the imagination of every
onlooker. and each of them watches
this strange foray into space, into time
we listen to music, as freaks, a circle
they work on things and understand
nothing. to understand nothing is a gift*

watch the mirrored walls, the strobing
red, white, blue, black, pink, purple, lights
all brighter than the last, as music plays
music.

MY OWN INTERNAL THOUGHT PROCESSES AS A
RESULT OF PURCHASING SAID MATERIALS IN THE
FORM OF VARIOUS IMAGES CREATED WITH SAID
MATERIALS AND WHATEVER WAS LYING AROUND

today my family watched as i finally convinced the mechanism
to saw through my forearm and corresponding materials. today
my family watched as i wept over the blood and spent carcass
of my left hand (so as to prolong saw usage) and witnessed this
very pared down feeling in the room, as though i'd cut through
their love for me itself, cut right through the discontent and
anger that might've resulted, and all left was a room of useless
breath and sweat. i waited for them to leave then sawed the
forearm itself into slices 3cm thick and pinned them around the
room with nearly no effort as the sun began to rise.

OF A WET GARROTE OF SORTS IN THE FORM OF MANY
REMEMBRANCES OF FALLEN VICTIMS OF EITHER THE
BLADE THE ROPE OR THE ITEM ITSELF

YAMA: for robbery, those rotting already in the pits fiery pits
were torn in half for good and good, torn in ha—

the chinese workings and mythology tearing apart various
members of community to later be given kinder likenesses
via the artists working in said communities many torn quote
'asunder' by saws and blades in permutations of hell ad
infinitum.

*1848 hungary struggles around banat in point of fact some
were sawn apart those largely women, children, or elderly males
as a result of fanaticism of various preaching presences*

*1812 the great fire of the RED many quote 'unfortunates'
are sawn apart via mechanism said who invented machine
who invented i.e. create worldwide prize in various
accomplishments you know of whom i speak creator of great
explosive and who will perish for these deaths of this machine
and the loss of this arm and where will it sleep in hell*

*allow me to watch the frame of caius caligula as malcolm
mcdowell as the torturing gluttonous hog witnessing the death
of his people as quote 'appetizers' before the feast of some
hundred pounds of poorly cooked flesh and again we have this
phrase of people being <u>sawn asunder</u> by perhaps the cruelest
ruler known in the OLD WORLD... he watched them as they
were split horizontally not vertically down the center they were
split like felled trees split ne—*

an elliptical progression of
flesh thru flesh as the phrase
unspoken but unforgettable, some-
thing like the word 'glint' as it
flares up in my mind and nostril
looking out as the saw runs thru
the night and I am quite tired
but will not sleep for weeks...
stared to such a degree that I am
becoming buried by my own eyelids
tired in such a way that flesh
no longer quite exists and the water
makeup of my skin is the mere coating
around the pathetic raindrop globule
noxious something noxious what wasted
wastoid pathetic rapturous thing
movement in constant circles with jagged
framework and I have witnessed the
great machinic becoming of new year new life new prosperity
for all and none and dedicated to no one whilst being thrust
upon the globe again the spherical thing in a spherical universe
consumed by circles upon circles upon circles upon circles upon
circles and the blade, the thing moving around the globe and
not only the globe but the world the sun the encircling sphere of
shit and blood and fire forged into the metal that cuts through
the forearm cuts through thought through potential oblivion
et al and I am now a mere peon in devout servitude to its
progressive majesty yes I am merely that idiotic thing obsessing
over circling bloodlust and night

the mediator between the head and hands must be the heart and the knife

the mediator between the head and hands must be the heart and the knife

the mediator between the head and hands must be the heart and the knife

the mediator between the head and hands must be the heart and the knife

the mediator between the head and hands must be the heart and the knife

the mediator between the head and hands must be the heart and the knife

the mediator between the head and hands must be the heart and the knife

You have started sweating nights.

Little times go by you have started to sweat nights waiting for the next reasonable opportunity to find oneself sitting before her.

You have begun wondering when exactly time will be such that one could do this sort of thing over, and over, and over, without pulling oneself away. To find oneself forever connected to it. To find oneself forever machinized.

i am a little macchine

1.

tomorrow morning over breakfast pulled flesh readily toward hybridized something or other

2.

afternoon spent watching times change

3.

little sister didn't visit didn't need it pulled blade for cleaning realized face was beginning to appear in creases between teeth

4.

nightmarish-type dream where something begins spinning so fast (the earth) that I can no longer see the blade and turn skin outward arm is starting to turn an interesting shade not exactly sure what to expect

two forms as betterment of one's obsession with both the verbiage of fictive entities as conceived by Gene Roddenberry an attempt to illustrate user's desire to write, compellingly, his understanding of this machine as far more than mere machine, this item as far more than item.

Non-deconstructive eval. of reinforced concrete structural
dissertation part 1. Subheading 0

meat observed him for several weeks and bone seems fairly close
to killing himself. At this point there isn't much to do but sort
of watch the embers die away in eyes when finally bone becomes
resourceful enough or summons enough energy to finish things
once and for all. By shit tone it's reasonable to perceive a grotesque
lack of sympathy and MEAT guess that's fine. The thing is, when
you've observed any number of individuals teetering over this very
cliff in any number of ways, you tend to develop a bit of a thick
skin as regards humanity or compassion, it takes a great deal to
drive meat into misery over the misery of others.

 meat seldom seen someone quite so empty as him, though.
There's probably nothing any living human being on earth
could do to make the veil suddenly lift and drive away the
feeling. MEAT can't wrap shit head entirely around that level of
emptiness. MEAT try, sometimes. MEAT try and MEAT draw
comparisons with the unknown reaches of the universe or depths
of the oceans but it still doesn't seem to measure up to the look on
that pale face. MEAT don't know. Something inside meat can't
look away whenever MEAT pass door. A bit like, they're always
saying this, a bit like watching an accident of some kind. You're so
curious and so distraught that the two sort of meld together until
you're raw emotion looking into actual human death happening
slowly but very surely right before bad eyes. That's what bone
looked like to me, like human death happening right in front of
shit eyes.

Oddly enough, it wouldn't depress or make meat ecstatic on
leaving him. I'd simply drift off and sort of wait until MEAT
could look into that face again. That's the truly daunting aspect
of this whole ordeal. Bone became a sort of drug. Looking at him
look at nothing became a complete escape from all the rules of
humanity, all the histories ever written were suddenly moot points
in the face of an entire absence of expression. MEAT could feel
nothing and yet have an impression of the pulse of everything
while standing there, awkwardly rocking from foot to foot as sweat

mounted up in shit socks in abject fear that bone might stare up at MEAT and smile. That MEAT could not have registered, and in some way MEAT was grateful for that. To watch someone shift from devout melancholia to some semblance of happiness is a mark below watching black paint dry in an unlit room. Suddenly all the emotion invested in this person's feeling or lack thereof is wasted and turned into a petty trifle, something to laugh off while you take a piss, little more.

His hair is just beginning to recede but it's to such a slight degree that bone might not even have noticed as yet. It creates an incipient demonic look akin to Vincent Price though instead of some glint of malice the feeling put forth is closer to staring out of a failing spacecraft at the outskirts of a blackhole, soon bad flesh will no longer be flesh but the stuff of vacuuming caves of torment, or something, something impossible to describe, something I'd so like to describe but can't, and won't, for fear he'll pull eyes up if bone sees meat pondering and register just exactly what's happening. MEAT don't want him to know what's happening to just about the same degree that MEAT don't want him to die, which is to say, MEAT want him to know what's happening just as much as MEAT want him to die. Some sick part of meat vacillates back and forth as MEAT stare at him hoping that shit face will be the last one bone sees and bone might then register that I'm not going to help him by cutting him down from whatever rope he's able to fashion. Some less-sick part of meat hopes that he'll never see meat and never pull himself away from this position because of some universal magnetism that finally works in shit favor. Never have shit eyes felt better than when watching him, they get a bit warm and the lids grow heavy and MEAT find myself remembering days in childhood staring at a television far too long. It's as if the drug of witnessing this spectacle were injected slowly through the eyes and down into the nervous system until relaxation is a distant word and I'm sunk much lower into pits of not only indifference but entire unawareness that there had ever been a world, and that there would be one shortly thereafter.

This is the problem of witnessing, MEAT suppose. While you're

in it there's always a slight nagging sensation in the pit of bad
stomach that soon enough you'll have to walk out into the world
and explain things to people and have things explained to you
and clean toilets and smoke cigarettes to get some rest and watch
television and try perhaps to read just before bed you're not really
sure it's quite difficult to read anymore but you're certainly not
a moron not quite yet. Something inside you insists that this
cannot be an entire human reality and yet you're just as ready to
discount this theory rationalizing that the lives of dictators were
far more wasted than this and they lend their names to hundreds
of best-selling books each year. Something silly then arises and you
imagine the prospect of some human animal writing bad story
and it's entirely too laughable and the thought of attempting to
describe scenes of myself watching him looms over shit memory
and MEAT simply cannot keep myself from laughter.
It's then that MEAT run from door to the bathroom to flush the
toilet numerous times while belting out gasps of laughter behind
one cupped hand. shit uniform is a grayish-blue and though
many detest uniformity MEAT find it for shit purposes quite a
blessing. For instance, bad work entails cleaning up the garbage
left behind by others both bodily and environmentally, so to
speak, and every day the chances of you seeing these individuals
numerous times between their release of detritus is higher and
perhaps ever higher, considering this, would it be bad wont
to change bad outfit every single day in an attempt to convey
personality and further to engage these individuals at every turn?
Perhaps, and there are no absolutes in this life, but for myself
MEAT prefer to keep that level of anonymity whenever possible
so that MEAT can think of the occasional smattering of pubic
hairs or shit as little more than follicles and miasma that requires
disposal. MEAT love this grayish-blue uniform and MEAT
trust the eyes of him that bone would admire this sort of thing
as well, though as previously mentioned there are no absolutes
and we can never know, for if we knew the allure of any of this
would become quite ridiculous and I'd be forced to find not only
a new hobby/purpose but a new line of work entirely, for how
could MEAT be expected to come back to the place where the

individual who for months sat in suicidal swamp suddenly realized bone was being watched the entire time by some strange fetishist janitor with little but a studio apartment and this grayish-blue uniform to account form existence… No, it simply cannot be done, and that is for the better.

*(DAMAGETOALLCOMMERCIALANDDOMESTICPRO
PERTIES,WESIMPLYDONOTHEARYOU.PRESSHAND
SCOMFORTABLYAGAINSTTEMPLEBEFOREUSE.AG
GRESSIONISAMAINSTAYINTHELIFEOFAMACHINIST.
WEAREAWAREANDEVENENCOURAGINGOFTHISNOTI
ON,HOWEVERWECANNOTRECOMMENDHIGHLYENOUG
HWISHINGONESLOVEDONESFAREWELLBEFORESIT
TINGDOWNTOWORK.THISISYOURPROJECT,NOTOURS.
TIEBACKLONGHAIR/ROLLUPLONGSLEEVES.BECAUSEOF
RECENTDOCTRINEPUTFORTHINCERTAINCENTRALAME
RICANNATIONSWHEREPRIMARYBOLTS311ZAND415XA
REMANUFACTUREDITISREQUIREDWEINFORMYOUT
HATHAVINGYOURHAIRSUCKEDINSIDEOFASAWMO
VINGATOVER3,000RPMISATERRIBLEIDEAWHENSAID
SAWISSHARPENOUGHTOSEVERANECKSTANDINGS
TILL,BUTWEARENTSTICKLERSIFYOUHAPPENTOENJOY
LETTINGYOURHAIRFALLATWILLWHILESAWING.DITTO
FORSLEEVES,THOUGHWECANTIMAGINETHETHOUGHT
PROCESSTHATMIGHTLEADONETOSAWUSINGTHEA.-
U.D.C.ANYTHINGBUTSTARKNAKED,ANOVERSHIRT
CANSOMETIMESBENICE,ANDWEWONTHOLDITA
GAINSTYOU.DONOTPERFORMANYOPERATIONUN
DERTHEINFLUENCEOFPHARMACEUTICALS.EXCEP
TINGOFCOURSE:ACANTHACEAE,FITTONIAALBIVENIS/
JUSTICIAPECTORALISACERACEAE,ACERSACCHARINUM
DELOSPERMAACUMINATUM,DMT,5-MEO-*

Cursed yr family
Cursed yr animals
Cursed yr wet
Cursed yr heaven
Cursed yr sleep
Cursed yr nightmare
Cursed yr dream
Cursed yr hopeless

Cursed yr welcome
Cursed yr friendship
Cursed yr blade
Cursed yr circle
Cursed yr parts
Cursed yr flesh
Cursed yr skin
Cursed yr cancer
Cursed yr watchful
Cursed yr idea
Cursed yr cabin
Cursed yr history
Cursed yr willing
Cursed yr heroes
Cursed yr idols
Cursed yr betterment
Cursed yr saw
Cursed yr machine
Cursed yr creator
Cursed yr profane
Cursed yr civility
Cursed yr dry
Cursed yr lip
Cursed yr titles
Cursed yr temporal
Cursed yr fraud
Cursed yr purple
Cursed yr red
Cursed yr bruised
Cursed yr eyesight
Cursed yr skinsight
Cursed yr nights
Cursed yr mornings
Cursed yr breaths
Cursed yr choke
Cursed yr embellishment
Cursed yr entanglement

Cursed yr obsession
Cursed yr measurement
Cursed yr objections
Cursed yr desires
Cursed yr hopefuls
Cursed yr nostalgia
Cursed yr black screens
Cursed yr tracking
Cursed yr tapes
Cursed yr disks
Cursed yr instructions
Cursed yr fallen arms
Cursed yr eroding flesh
Cursed yr blackening wound
Cursed yr infectious
Cursed yr consideration
Cursed yr politic
Cursed yr notes
Cursed yr journal
Cursed yr recordings
Cursed yr earwave
Cursed yr smellsuck
Cursed yr mechani
Cursed yr smoothe
Cursed yr strange
Cursed yr bury
Cursed yr homestead
Cursed yr nation
Cursed yr fiery
Cursed yr illness
Cursed yr ailments
Cursed yr inclusion
Cursed yr clothing
Cursed yr fingeroles
Cursed yr frantic
Cursed yr children

Cursed yr dreamlike
Cursed yr pill
Cursed yr cure
Cursed yr blade
Cursed yr saw
Cursed yr saw
Cursed yr saw
Cursed yr fucking forearm
Cursed yr

and now it hurts to breathe...

Vlad III the Impaler (b. 1431)

Caligula (b. 12)

Nero (b. 37)

Jim Jones (b. 1931)

Kim Il-sung (b. 1912)

Attila the Hun (b. 406)

Leopold II of Belgium (b. 1835)

Carlo Pietro Giovanni Guglielmo Tebaldo Ponzi (b. 1882)

Lou Pearlman (b. 1954)

what is the nature of badness and how is it connected to this machine...[3]

---

[3] the week he was a boy, and a few Meat seems fairly close to Kill him. The flat was thin before the end of those who do, however, isn't the embers to die will come, the movement of the eyes, at length, dies, a boy become resourceful enough Things accomplished nothing at all, and the first summons enough Strength Type Design. the name of the secret shit down reasonable grotesque Lack sympathy, I guess the Meat and close. When you die, it is the individual to judge the individual belonged to the people and to well done or occurs in recognition of those who dance, you dance, you observe any teetering tend bit thick Skin as regards humanity, compassion or Developed, to lumaq it yitungha' Come, Sir, this is a good Meat to the other then misery misery accomplished. those who believe it is hidden and seldom empty then the Meat saw. I will return to you, there are those who can get away with being a Human life's Mission Earth feeling suddenly lift veil something gajha' yitungha' Good Sir, come on and nothing. head shit or EnCase Meat entirely around emptiness at shoulder level. try Meat, sometimes. an unknown comparisons and hear our Ministers or the Ocean because the meat is not used up the chance, and I will try to Cover Meat, but it doesn't seem to be breaking down the measure reads bad. The Beasts Do Not Know. those who saw nothing inside the door whenever the beasts come, lion Meat. It looks like a bit of this, they said, some by accident like a bit blind as kind. curious then, and then the two meld together Type that

*distraugt until raw emotion, then actual Human right but
Slowly Dies days before bad eyes, surely. What do you
look like a boy saw him, Human right and died in front
of his eyes like this shit.*

*oddly enough, or we wouldn't be depressed Meat went
ecstatic form. There were simply back off, and you can
Type there are four Beasts until he saw that, and said
a face again. It is true, and the whole ordeal daunt
aspect. Drug Type and a result. He saw no one saw him,
why complete result from the laws of humanity, and
escape all the history, all requests always suddenly
moot points of a face in the whole of his absence, and
the Studio. some cannot be Touched but Everyone in the
room with the impression left is the pulse, the beasts
from the rock and feet feet awkwardly sweat shit Come
mounted in late May of his abject Security stare and
smile, he saw a boy Come Meat. "the third you can get
Meat Merchant building, and some Meat was grateful
recognition of his revenge. those who sees a shift
some semblance happiness from the devout followers of
melancholia, when he sees a black pigment Dry throughout
before unlight below. suddenly the feeling All came
to pass in those days, people are invested or wasted
emotion my great power and turn night, laugh out loud
something petty left him from here, saying, "I'll will
Lack.*

*you will only recede with ran, but the hair was pulled
back in a Saccharin superstitions, perhaps, that there
is a boy, and tortured. incipient demonic look akin to
vincent price is created or if some vimus instead of
shiny feeling malice staring they laid the spacecraft
failing first Arm blackhole outskirts soon, but the flesh
rotted flesh face, therefore, any honor or impossible,
but then any View or a view of vivut, in the YEAR, and
vacuuming do not stuff it is not fear in the eyes then
Dog pondering, why only a boy, and I saw exactly what
happened Merchant building. What will happen to him,
there is only a man. exit the same superstitions don't
he is dead Meat, do what you think is what happened at
all, and only bought Meat at all, and he wanted to Die,
she knows that only a Dog tag he said Don't Know Meat.
some sick vacillates, and because we have to repair
them the Meat and the meat seems to stare him shit Bad
Boy, and one that he was the last to be of assistance,
he should not Help him name from whatever score line,
it is, perhaps, the desires and then a boy sees a hope
Merchant building. He never did, and the beasts away
from gas position because some of universal magnetism*

*finally Win him favor in shit hope that some Warriors
of the elder and sick--Meat. I've never Touched shit
in the eyes of the Great Dies in a few saw him Gain
them, become Strong cover warm bit heavy, I am staring
childhood and television Remote days tiqqu' there is
rotted Meat. Lawrence m. Schoen injected slowly through
my eyes and nervous system so vi'og relaxation and
distant words until I am sunk lower prices then the
third pit, but indifference, so that only a complete
unawareness of the world there is always there, and he
was the one that soon thereafter spectacle qualified
drug.
is this man qualified in the room there is the container,
is this a problem Dog. Open days with the Resolution,
you're always in the room is the bathroom and smoke some
cigarettes, and Acquisition of all television, perhaps
sees accurate positive fact is hidden anymore difficult
read, but certainly not yet, not yet, but the fact is
hidden moron only reads in the room in a celestial bed,
try and Clean sensation a little nag was in the pit face
naturally that you hurry up and walks in the world, and
the people the things which I have enough Things to his
resolution. or that those who insist the whole of the
Human inside You*

010001000100010101000001010101000100100001010011
0100011001001111010100100101010001001000010001010101
0010010100111001000100010010010101011001001001010000
10001010101010000010100110001010010011010000010101011
01011001010001010101001101010111010011110100001010101
010011010010010100111001010011010010010100010001000
01010101010001001000010001010100000101001110010101
000100100100101101010101010101010000010001000100000010
101010001000101010001000100010101010000110100111101010
011010101010000001010010010001010101010011010100110100100
0101010110010001010101010011010000001010101110100010101
010110010100010101010011010101110100111101000010101
010011010010010100111001010011010010010100010001000
0101010101000100100001000101010000010100111001010101
00010010010010110101010101010101000000010001000100000010
1010100010001010100010001000101010000110100111101010
0110101010000010100100100010101010100110101001101001
0101010110010001010101010011010000001010101110100010101
010110010100010101010011010101110100111101000010101
010011010010010100111001010011010010010100010001000
010101010100010010000100010101000001010011100101010
00010010010010110101010101010101000000010001000100000010
101010001000101010001000100010101010000110100111101010
0110101010000010100100100010101010100110101001101001010010
01010101100100010101010010011010000010101011101010101
010110010100010101010011010101110100111101000010101

010011 010010010100111001010011010010010100010001000100
0101010101000100100001000101 0100000101001110010101
0001001001001011010101010101010000010001000100000010
101010001000101 0100010001000101010000110100111101 0
0110101010000010100100100010101010100110101001101001 0
010101011001000101 0101001101000001010101 11
0101100101000101010100011 01010111010011110100010101
010011 010010010100111001010011010010010100010001000100
0101010101000100100001000101 0100000101001110010101
0001001001001011010101010101010000010001000100000010
101010001000101 0100010001000101010000110100111101 0
0110101010000010100100100010101010100110101001101001 0
010101011001000101010100110100000101010111
0101100101000101010100011 01010111010011110100010101
010011 010010010100111001010011010010010100010001000100
010101010011010000010101 0111
0101100101000101010100011 01010111010011110100010101
010011 010010010100111001010011010010010100010001000100
0101010101000100100001000101 0100000101001110010101
0001001001001011010101010101010000010001000100000010
101010001000101 0100010001000101010000110100111101 0
0110101010000010100100100010101010100110101001101001 0
010101011001000101010100110100000101010111
0101100101000101010100011 01010111010011110100010101
010011 010010010100111001010011010010010100010001000100
0101010101000100100001000101 0100000101001110010101
0001001001001011010101010101010000010001000100000010
101010001000101 0100010001000101010000110100111101 0
0110101010000010100100100010101010100110101001101001 0
010101011001000101 0101001101000001010101 11
0101100101000101010100011 01010111010011110100010101
010011 010010010100111001010011010010010100010001000100
0101 010101000100100001000101 0100000101001110010101
0001001001001011010101010101010000010001000100000010
101010001000101 0100010001000101010000110100111101 0
0110101010000010100100100010101010100110101001101001 0
010101011001000101010100110100000101010111

```
010110010100010101010011 01010111010011110100010101
010011 0100100101001110010100110100100101000100010 0
010101010100010010000100010 1 010000010100111001010 1
000100100100101101010101010101000001000100010000010
101010001000101 0100010001000101010000110100111101 0
011010101000001010010010001010101001101010011010010
         010101011001000101 01010011010000010101011 1
010110010100010101010011 01010111010011110100010101
010011 0100100101001110010100110100100101000100010 0
010101010100010010000100010 1 010000010100111001010 1
000100100100101101010101010101000001000100010000010
101010001000101 0100010001000101010000110100111101 0
011010101000001010010010001010101001101010011010010
         010101011001000101010100110100000101010111
010110010100010101010011 01010111010011110100010101
010011 0100100101001110010100110100100101000100010 0
                010101010011010000010101011 1
010110010100010101010011 01010111010011110100010101
010011 0100100101001110010100110100100101000100010 0
010101010100010010000100010 1 010000010100111001010 1
000100100100101101010101010101000001000100010000010
101010001000101 0100010001000101010000110100111101 0
011010101000001010010010001010101001101010011010010
         010101011001000101010100110100000101010111
010110010100010101010011 01010111010011110100010101
010011 0100100101001110010100110100100101000100010 0
010101010100010010000100010 1 010000010100111001010 1
000100100100101101010101010101000001000100010000010
101010001000101 0100010001000101010000110100111101 0
011010101000001010010010001010101001101010011010010
         010101011001000101 01010011010000010101011 1
010110010100010101010011 01010111010011110100010101
010011 0100100101001110010100110100100101000100010 0
0101 0101010001001000010001 01 010000010100111001010 1
000100100100101101010101010101000001000100010000010
101010001000101 0100010001000101010000110100111101 0
011010101000001010010010001010101001101010011010010
```

010101011001000101010100110100000101010111
01011001010001010101001101010111010011110100010101
010011 010010010100111001010011010010010100010001000100
01010101010001001000010001010100000101001110010101
00010010010010110101010101010101000001000100010000010
101010001000101 0100010001000101010000110100111101010
01101010100000101001001000101010100110101001101010
01010101100100010101010100110100000101010111
01011001010001010101001101010111010011110100010101
010011 010010010100111001010011010010010100010001000100
01010101010001001000010001010100000101001110010101
00010010010010110101010101010101000001000100010000010
101010001000101 0100010001000101010000110100111101010
01101010100000101001001000101010101001101010011010010
01010101100100010101010100110100000101010111
01011001010001010101001101010111010011110100010101
010011 010010010100111001010011010010010100010001000100
0101010100110100000101010111
01011001010001010101001101010111010011110100010101
010011 010010010100111001010011010010010100010001000100
01010101010001001000010001010100000101001110010101
00010010010010110101010101010101000001000100010000010
101010001000101 0100010001000101010000110100111101010
01101010100000101001001000101010101001101010011010010
0101010110010001010101010011010000101010111
01011001010001010101001101010111010011110100010101
010011 010010010100111001010011010010010100010001000100
01010101010001001000010001010100000101001110010101
00010010010010110101010101010101000001000100010000010
101010001000101 0100010001000101010000110100111101010
0110101010000010100100100010101010100110101001101010010
0101010110010001010101010011010000101010111
01011001010001010101001101010111010011110100010101
010011 010010010100111001010011010010010100010001000100
0101 010101000100100001000101 0100000101001110010101
00010010010010110101010101010101000001000100010000010
101010001000101 0100010001000101010000110100111101010

```
0110101010000010100100100010101010100110101001101001 0
         01010101100100010101010100110100000101010111
010110010100010101010011 0101011101001111010001 0101
010011 0100100101001110010100110100100101000 1000100
0101010101000100100001000101 01000001010011100101 01
000100100100101101010101010101010000010001000 10000010
101010001000101 010001000100010101000011010011 11010
0110101010000010100100100010101010100110101001 1010010
         010101011001000101 01010011010000010101 0111
010110010100010101010011 0101011101001111010001 0101
010011 0100100101001110010100110100100101000 1000100
0101010101000100100001000101 01000001010011100101 01
000100100100101101010101010101010000010001000 10000010
101010001000101 010001000100010101000011010011 11010
0110101010000010100100100010101010100110101001 1010010
010101011001000101010101000100100001000101 01000001
01001110010101000100100100101101010101010101010000010
00100010000010101010001000101 0100010001000101 01000
01101001111010011010101000001010010010001010101010011
                0101001101001001010101 1001000101
010100110100000101010111 0010100001001111010 1000001
010100010010010100111101001110010000010100 1100 0100
01000100100101000001010011010101001111010011 100100010
   000101101010100000100110001000001010101000 1000101
010010010100111001010011010001010101001001010100 00
110011001100010011000000110000001011010011001000110
110001110000011011000101000010101000100100001000101
0100000101001110010101000100100100101101010101010101010
1000001000100010000010101010001000101 0100010001000
10101000011010011110100110101010000010100100 1000101
                0101001101010011010010010101011001000101
010100110100000101010111 01000001 0101010101 01001101
0001010101001001010011 0100110101000001010011100101
0101010000010100110001010011010101000100010101 00100
   101001110 0100001101001111010100100101000000101110
0101000001011000001100010011001100111000 0011001100
11000100110000000110000001011010011001000110 11000111
```

0000011011001000110010100100100111101001101
010101000100100001000101 010000100101010101 00100101
001100010001000100010101010010 0101010001001111
010101000100100001000101 0101010101010011010 0010101
01001000111010 010000110100111101001110010001110101
001001000001010101000101010101001100010000010101010
001001001010011110100111001010011001011 10 010110010
10011110101010101010110010001 01 0100101001010101010
100110101010 0100001001000101010000110100111101001
10101000101 010101000100100001000101 0010100001 01000
0010100100100111101010101010100010000101000 010011110
1010111010011100100010101010010 0100111101000110
0100111101001110010001 01 010011110100011 0
010101000100100001000101 01001101010011110101001101
010100 010001100100000101001110010101000100000 10101
001101010100010010010100 0011 0100110101000001010000
110100100001001001010011100100010101010011 01000101
01010110010001010101 0010 01000101010011100100011101
00100101001110010001010100010101010010010001010 1000
100 010000100101 1001 010010000101010101001101 0100000
101001110 0100001001000101010010010100111001000111 0
0101110 0100100010011110101011101000101010101100 10
00101010010 01001001010100 010000110100000101001
10101000101 0100100101001110010101000100111 1 0101100
10100111101010101010101 0010 0101000001001111010100110
101001101000101010100110101001101001001010011110100
1110 0100100101010011 0100100101001101010011010100 00
0101010100010001010101001001001001010000010100 11000
0101100 010101110100100001000001010101000101001 1 010
0100101001101010100000100111101010010010101000100 00
010100111001010100 010011100100111101010111
010010010101001 1 010101110100100001000001010101 00 01
0110010100111101010101010100100100010 1 010001110100
1111010010010100111001000111 0101010001001111 010000
010100001101000011010011110100110101010000010011000
10010010101001101001000 0101011101001001010101000 10
01000 0100100101010100001011 10 010101110100100001000

00101010100 01011001010011110101010
010011100100111101010111 010010000100111101001100 01
000100 010010010100111 01011001010011110101010101
0010 010010000100000101001110010001001010011
010011110101010 010101110100100101010100010011001
000101010100110101001 010100110100001101000010101
010001010100010001010101001001000101010001000 010000
010101001001001111010101010101001110010001001
010101000100100001000101 010011110100100101001100 01
011001 010001100100110001001111010011110101010
010011110100011 0 010101000100100001001001010100110011 01
0001110100000101010010010000010100011101000101
010010010101001 1 010100110100111101001101010100010101
010100010010000100100101001110010001110 010011110100
111001000011010001010100010001000101010001010101001 1
01010001010100010001 010010010100110101010000010011 11
010100110101001101001001010000100100110001000101
010000100101100 1 001110010011011001001111010001100
010101000100100001000101 010000010100110101000101 01
010010010010010100001101000001010011 10 010100000101
010101000010010011000100100101000011001011 00
010000010100111001000100 0101100101000101010101 00 01
001000010001010101001001000101 010010010101010 0
010010010101001100101110 010010000100010101010 01001
000101 010010010101010 0100100101010011001011 00 010
1001001000101010000010100010001011001
010010010100111 0 010011110100111001001100010110 01 01
001101010011110100110101000101010011100101010001010
011 010101000100111 1 010000100100010 1 010000010101 00
110101001101000101010011010100001001001 1000100010 10
1000100 010010010100111001010100010011 11
010101000100100001000101 010001100100100101000101 01
010010010000110100010 1 010000010100111001000100 0100
110101000101010101000100100101000011010101010100110
00100111101010101010101 0011 01000011010101010101010 1000
10101000100100101001110010001 11 010100000100111101 0
1011101000101010100 10 010101010101001101000010101000

100 010101000100111 0101010001000001010010110100010
1 010000010101000001000001010100100101010100
010000010100111001000100 0101001001000101010000101
0100110101001101001001010001110100111 0010101010010
111001010011001011 0 0101010001000001010011100100010
1101010011 010000010100011001010100010001010101010010
0101010001001000010100100100010101000101 0100110101
000001010010100100111101010010 010000110100111101100
111001000110010011000100100101000011010101000101001
1 0100100101001110 010101000100100001000101 01001100
010000010101010001010100010001010101010010 0101010001
0101110100010101001110010101010001011001001011010100
110010010010101001001010011010101000 010000110100010
101001110010101000101010101010010010110010010111 0
01010101010100110100010101000100 01001001010011100 01
0100110101010101010010010001110100010101010010010010
00101000101010100110 0101010001001111 010001110100100
1010101100100010 0101000011010010000100100101001 1000
1000100010100100100010101010011100 0100011001010101010
011000100110000101101010001100101010101001110010000
1101010100010010010100111101001110010010010010101110 0
1000111 010011000100100101001101010000100101001 010
101110100100001000101010101001001000101 010101000100 1
000010000101010010010101010001001010011 010001100100010
1010011000100110 010100110100100001001111010100100
101010000101110 0101010101010011010001010100010 0
010010010100111 0101010001001001010011010100010101
010011 0100111101000110 0100011101010010010001010100
000101010100 0100100001000101010011000100110 0
010101000100111 0101001001000101010100110101010001
001111010100100100010 0101000011010011110100110101 00
011001001111010100100100101 0101010001001111 010011
0101001001010011000100110001001001010011110100111 00
1010011 010011110100110 0101011001000001010000110 10
0000101001110010101 00 0101001101010100010000010 1010
0100010010101010011 0100100101001110 01000110010 1001
0010011110100111001010100 010011110100011 0 010011010

100100101001100010011000100100101001111010011100101
0011 0100111101000110 010101000100010101001100010001
01010100000100111101000100 010100110100010101010100
0101001100101110 010101010101001101000101010 00100
010101000100111 1 010000110101010101010100 0101010001
001000010100100100111101010101010100011101001000 0100
0110010010010101001001000101
010000010100111001000100 010011110101001001001000101
010000010100111001000100 010101110100010101010 0110001
000011010011110100110101000101
010101000100100001000101 010011110100111001010 01101
000101010101 00 010011110100 0110
010101000100100001000101 010011100100010101010111
010000010100011101000101 010101110100100001000 10101
001110 0101011101000101 010101110100010101010 0100100
0101 0100111001001111 010011000100111101001110010001
110100010101010010 010101100100100101010011010 01001
010101000100111101010010010101 0011 010010000100010101
01001001000101 010000100101010101010100 010010000100
1111010100110101010001010011 0100111101001110
010101000100100001000101 010100110100100001001111 01
010101010011000100010001000100010101010010
0100111101000110 010011110101001001001001010 0111101
00111000101110 010101010101001101000101010 00100
010101000100111 1 010001110100100101010 11001000101 01
0010000100111101010000010001 01 0101010001001111
01000001 010010000100111101010000010001010100110001
000101010100110101001 1 010100000100010101001111 0101
000001001100010001 01 010101110100100001000 10101 0101
00010010000100010101010010 010101000100100001000101
01011001 010101110100000101001110010101000100010101
000100 010010010101 00 0100111101010010 01001110010
011110101010000101110 010101010101001101000101 01000
10000101110 010000010100111001000100 010011010100111
101010110010010010101001110010001 11 010001100100111 10
101001001010111010000010101001001000100
010101110100010 1 010011100100111101010111 0100100001

00000010101011001000101 010101000100100001000101 0101
00010101010101010001010101001101010100010010010100111
101001110 0100111101000110 0101000001010010010011110
101001101010000010001010101001001001001010101000101
100100101110 0101011101001001010011000100 1100
01011001010011110101010 1 0100100101001110 0100010101
00011001000110010001010100001101010100 010100000100
00010101001101010011 010101000100100001001001010100
11 010011010100000101000011010010000100100101001110
01000101 0100111101001110 0101010001001111 010001100
101010101010100010101010101001001000101 01000111010
0010101001110010001010101001001000001010101000100100
010100111101001110010100 11 0100100101001110
0101010001001000010001 01 0101010101010100010011 0101
00111101010011010101 00 010000110100111101001110 0100
0110010010010100010001000101010011100100001 10100010
1 010101000100100001000001010100 0100100101010100
01010111010010010100110001001100
0100001101010101010101 00 0101010001001000010100100 1
00111101010101010100011101001000
01000001010011100101100 1 010000010100111001000100 01
00010101010101100100010101010100100101100101010100010 01
00001001001010011100100011 1 010010010101010 0 0100001
101001111010011010100010101010011 010000001010000110
10100100100111101010011010100110011111 1 01010111010
0100101001100010011 00 010110010100111101010101 00111
111 010101000100100001001001010100 11
010010010101001 1 0100001001001111010101000100100 0
010101000100100001000101 010011010100111101010011 01
010100 01001001010011010101000000100111101010010 0101
0100010000010100111001010100 010100010101010101 0001
010101001101010100010010010100111 01001110
0100000101001110010110 01 0100111001000101010101 0111
010100110100000101010111 010011110101011101010 01 1001
000101010100 10 01000011010000010100111 0
0100000101010011010010 11 010010010101010001010011 01
0001010100110001000110 0100000101001110010001000010

1100 010011000100100101001011010001010100110001 0110
01 0100010101001110010011110101010101010001110 1001000
00101100 01010100010010000100010 1 01001100010000010 1
01001101010100 01010100010010000100100101001110010 0
0111 01001111010011 10 010110010100111101010101010100
10 010011010100100101001110010001000010 1110 010 10111
010010000100000101010100010100 11 01001111010011 10 01
011001010011 1101010101010100 10 0100110101001001010 0
          111001000100 0100111001001 111010 10111
01001001010100 11 01010000010011110101011101000 10101
     01001000101100 0101000001010101010 1001001000101
010000010100111001000100 0101001 101001001010011010 1
          01000001001100010001010010100101 110
0100000101001 110010001 00 01010011010011110100111101
001110 01000101010011100100111 1010 10101010001 110100
          1000 010101110100010101001 10001001100
01001100010001010101010100 010110010100111101010101
01000111010011 11001011 10 01000010010101010101010100
010001100100111101010010 0100111001001 11101010111
01011001010011 11010 10101 01001101010101010101001101
010100 010000110100111101001110010100110100100101 00
01000100010101010010 010001100101010101010101000 10101
0101010010010001 01 01000 1110100010101001110010001 01
01010010010000010 10101000100100101001111010011 10010
          10011 0100000101001 1100 10001 00
01010100010010000100010 1 0101 0000 0101001001 00111101
          010011010100000 10001010100001101010100
01001 11101000110 0100000 1 0101011101001 111010 1001001
00110001000100 010101110100100101010100010010000100
11110 101010101010 100 0101010001001 00001000101 010000
01010011 100101010001001001001011010101010101010 0000
100010001 00000 101010100010 00101 01000100010001 0 1010
000110100111 10100110101010000010100100100010101 0100
11010100110 10010010101011001000101 0101001101000001
01010111001011 00 010000010100 1110010001 00 0 10 100 110 1
          0101010101001001000101010011000101 1001

END OF SAW

A lightly sorcery step toward betterment. Here he and you and we exist in spiraling ceaseless entropy. Do you and have you and will you desire cycling spheric continuance. We are uncertain. Each user more inept than the last. Each figure more confused and uninhibited in their excitement at the prospect of opening the box, revealing the machine, worshiping and losing themselves in the machine they ask themselves countless questions about the past and future, unsure whether this is the correct approach they'll frequently remove certain limbs with saw to find solidarity in absence. They are foolish for this though lovable fools. They are consistent. This is what goes through, what went through the mind of the creator both then and now in constant cryosleep. There is walking heard about the floor where this is type and I understand I am merely another worker in the vast hall of workers attempting to assemble this document from lost documents and it makes next to no sense. I look and see the journals from the past and they read as broken assembled language experiments from so many rotted tongues, digitized and insane. There is no answer and it was my own mistake to look. There is no darkness but the end of that bright O light. There is no continuance so grim as that of human heartbeat X 1,000,000. We are workers this is noise nausea. I understand not the one zero one zero one zero but can perceive its significance to the creator, or journal enterer, though again of this I remain uncertain. Staring at the binary proposition I wind up trying to make sense of daily life in ones and zeroes, failing. I am the great failure and this is my greatest failure, this manual. The saw ends and the life ends and my own disposition will fail and I will continue somehow. Home again, home again. I am sick of walking, of working. I am sick of typing and feel no happiness at the prospect of the end of this unholy relic. There is only further. There is only continued stress and dissatisfaction. He created the blade that created the angst that created the individual. What does it mean. What could it possibly fucking mean. I go about in uncertainty.

What a glorious state. There is nothing else to learn. Nothing to hope for. Continued feeling and endless worry. The saw helps, assembling the package for hundreds and thousands to desire and utilize. This is the beginning of a long ending, an engine's inception prior to its inevitable destruction by its own hand. For posterity I look up inventors killed by their own inventions and understand that Horace Stein is one, and soon enough this nightmare will resign itself to snoring breaths and moneyed silence.

EXEUNT

EXEUNT

EXEUNT

EXEUNT

EXEUNT

EXEUNT

EXEUNT

EXEUNT

EXEUNT

EXEUNT

EXEUNT

"The Work That Matters": Seven Notes on Grant Maierhofer's WORKS

The work of the mason, who assembles, is the work that matters.
Thus the adjoining bricks, in a book, should not be less visible
than the new brick, which is the book. What is offered the reader,
in fact, cannot be an element, but must be the ensemble in which
it is inserted: it is the whole human assemblage and edifice, which
must be, not just a pile of scraps, but rather a self-consciousness.
In a sense the unlimited assemblage is the impossible. It takes
courage and stubbornness not to go slack.

– Georges Bataille

Édouard Levé, of whose *Oeuvres* Grant Maierhofer's "own" title
is a creative appropriation, was himself very much a creature
of homonymy. In his 1997 series of photographs *Portraits of
Homonyms*, Levé produced a survey of photographs of ordinary
people who happened to share their names with those of cultural
celebrities (Raymond Roussel, Georges Bataille…). In "No. 77" of
Oeuvres, he describes the process as follows: "People bearing the
same names as artists and writers are found in a telephone directory
and photographed. Colour prints are made of their faces and
framed like ID photos. Two contradictory signs of identity are thus
juxtaposed: the face, unknown, and the name, famous."

Thus, Levé introduces a disturbance in the reference by means
of a split within the proper name, diverting the usual channels
linking ostension and appointment. The fixed name/referent link is
not entirely undone—since the people in Levé's directory *are* André
Bretons, *are* Yves Kleins—but it becomes parasitised by an alternate
reality, the multiplication of the potentialities attached to the

proper name, which no longer refers exclusively to a single referent, blurring the process of identification. Levé's images counteract the singularity of the proper name by opening themselves up to plurality of its references, inviting the viewer to contemplate this strange coexistence of two contradictory terms. The derailment of reference, oscillating between the mental association drawn from the common culture and the image perceived on the photograph, freezes the image and its viewer in an unreal suspense.

Levé's *Oeuvres* is at once the librarian's wet-dream and the writer's nightmare, for all narrative art aspires to the condition of the "non-paraphrasable" and "not-to-be-summarised". Grant Maierhofer's *Works* borrows from Levé more than just its title. Maierhofer's writing similarly deals with semantic derailments of reference to convey the tensions between the conceptual written word and the iconic image and to express anxiety at the uses and abuses of fiction in the media-saturated (un)reality of 21st-century America. In the ensuing seven notes I shall address some of the defining features of Maierhofer's poetics in *Works*: its functioning as textual assemblage, its reworking of the concept of literary labour, its multiple style of generic writing, its particularly American variety of literary anxiety, as well as its ethical dimension: conceiving of fiction as vulnerability.

1. Were the four texts that make up *Works* to be featured among Levé's 533 "conceived but not realised" oeuvres, their individual descriptions would read something like this:

> No.1. "A *Bildungsroman* about an aspiring writer coming to grips with the very real possibility of the failure of his writing, with as little *Bildung* as *Roman*. A Portrait of the Artist as a Relapsing Depressive Young Self-Harmer." (*Postures*)
> No.2. "Elliptical *dramatis personae* whose fragmented voices tell of psycho/pathological transmutations and institutional/ised madness. What *The Waves* could have been had Leslie Stephen's daughter attempted to write her way out." (*Flamingos*)
> No 3. "Travelogues of dystopias both short- (the TV screens around and inside us) and long-distance (beyond the Kuiper

Belt) and back. Tarkovsky's *Zone* blends with Burroughs' *Interzone* in these sci-fi stories that bleach fiction clean of science." (*Bleach*)

No.4. "A user's manual for a horrifically effective saw—stills from video tutorial and all—which dissipates into a meat vs. bone dialogue and ultimately falls apart altogether. Perec meets Guillon and Bonniec." (*PX138 3100-2686 User's Manual*)

If Maierhofer's *Works* as a whole were to receive the *Oeuvres* treatment, then with a tip of the hat to one of Levé's homonyms, Georges Bataille, one would invoke his concept of the textual assemblage:

> No. 0. "A new brick of a book composed of four adjoining bricks which, in the act of containing them, becomes more than just a pile of scraps, but rather a self-consciousness. An attempt at the impossible assemblage. An exercise in a whole greater than the sum of its parts."

A book, for Maierhofer as for Bataille, is never an autonomous unit but always appears with and within a more or less visible, complex network of texts and contexts. "We can't really escape the reality that writing is always a conversation with previous texts," Maierhofer observes in his online essay "Between Plagiarism and Art" for Literary Hub, describing how his earliest textual ensemble projects (part of which *Works* includes) took shape:

> I knew that I could write about things like depression, addiction, insanity, media addiction or obsession, fascism, art and violence. However, I also knew that I wanted it to take place in five books. What's more, I wanted things woven into the entirety that had weird conversations with one another.

Works does include some of these "things," published as well as new, and by commingling forms and genres, orchestrates their "weird" conversation.

2. *Postures* (2015) is set sometime from mid-2011 to mid-2012, as one gathers from oblique references to "Occupy was beginning to permeate things" and Lars von Trier having "recently discussed his feelings on Hitler" (46). It tells the tale of X, a writing-programme student and aspiring writer who "welcomes ambivalence, detests normalcy," and so finds himself adrift amidst "students at their laptops writing important properly-cited things," and teachers who know fuck-all about "*real writing*" (29). He is a man of paradox: an obsessive bookworm for whom writing is "not a craft, a job, or a way to kill time" but "his calling, his connection to the humanity," and yet he is American, too American in that his "womb", that is, the "avenues, buildings, or frames of mind" developed throughout life, is the cinema: "listening to the slow drone of the projector and watching the beautiful, anachronistic on-screen beauties make horrified faces at the men vying for their love, [...] it didn't seem so insane to want to keep on living" (47). *Repo Man, Paris, Texas* and *Alphaville* rub shoulders with Fante, Nabokov, Cocteau and Exley, and the resulting mixture of "the choices of who you emulate" helps X redefine his "own way" of writing.

Soon enough, X's struggles with completing a novel and the trauma of entering the literary biz ("the monotony of sending out hundreds of submissions only to receive that many kindly-worded rejections"[40]) and having the manuscript turned down and/or "processed" by editors begin taking their toll. X progressively relapses—after a few halcyon Celexa-padded years—into depressive episodes of self-harm, and so, in one of *Postures'* most memorable scenes, X ends up pissing on the returned editorially processed manuscript:

> He pulled out his cock, and eyes closed every second, letting go, covered the manuscript in piss. He opened up the pages with his left hand as he did it [...] just to ensure that every single page would carry markings. The piss turned the manuscript into a swollen pile of rubbish momentarily. [...] the morning that started with X's urinating all over his most prized possession culminated with him in the bathtub reading about murderers that love Bach. (92)

Here the "novel" undergoes a mental breakdown, abandoning a linear progression and disintegrating into fragments jumping from one chunk of flashback/fast-forward to another daydream/delirium. X's sickness and suicidal urges worsen and the self-destruction quickly escalates, with X winding up drinking his own urine, to try to placate "the beast that lurked in his soul", as per Exley. There are many awful endings intuited, but then one day, pulling himself up by his bootstraps, X takes a final train-ride back home in order to enter therapy and undergo medical examination, only to find out his mental sickness has had a rather physical cause: type 1 diabetes. In a final twist, the tale of dark beginnings and darker middles achieves an almost bright finale:

> Either way, you endure, you endure and you watch the leaves change each season and you take your medication and you attend class and you write the novel you'll call *Shadows to the Light* and you hope it will be something splendid, and when you write the final line—the final word in one long-winded argument—you contend that it is finished, and nothing written before it could end that way. (139)

Flamingos (2016), "A Dramatic Work," takes a step further in the direction towards which *Postures* gravitates but ultimately refuses to go: the disintegration of self and polyphonisation of the voice. In Germán Sierra's description, *Flamingos* is a text "assembled from the concentration of narrative and stylistic relations between a constellation of texts attributed to the metaphorical dysphoria of nine almost-archetypal characters, which could be read as a disordered collection of recordings done by a mad therapist" (144).

Introduced by a motto from Jeffrey DeShell ("A story? No. No stories, never again"), *Flamingos* oscillates between a teasing implication of a narrative possibility ("a story?"), and its derailment, obstruction and abandonment ("no story"). There are the nine "dramatis personae," some with as exorbitant a name as Haydn or Attila. Most prominent among them are Patient ("a neurotic poring over lived experience and print") and the eponymous Flamingo ("a daughter, sunlit, driven by manias"). There is the introductory italicised "frame tale", which pits eight of the nine personae as foils against Simon ("a healer, a messiah, M.D., D.C.L., L.L.D., Ph.D."), some kind of false-messianic sick doctor: "Simon, a future, a renewal. [...] Simon, ever the miserable failure. Simon our Christ, our Cunt Fear our Cock Fear our Man Fear our Woman Fear our Plague Fear our Head Fear our Love Fear our Death Fear" (151).

From then on, 130 pages of "sift[ing] through notes to find something revealed," as Patient has it, of listening to dramatic monologues of "embittered voices asking after daddy," of dismantling and recomposing an "assemblage, your research, the work" (154). Throughout these monologues, Flamingo's "urge to tell" (155) is found coupled with Simon's awareness of "I have nothing to say" (159). The cinematic again rubs shoulders with the literary: "Nicole Kidman" meets "Arthur Schnitzler" in a not-so-veiled reference to Kubrick's final opus, and there is "the colour pink everywhere" for John Waters, of course ("I sleep on one leg," Flamingo reports). As "Patient" observes midway in a narrative meta-comment:

> It was then that you began your seated, drugged endurance. You're not anti or pro narrative, you simply see things for what they are and record them thus. Propelling botches of narrative culled from heads around. You've developed great nostalgia for their speeches. (187)

The overriding topic of all this, of course, is madness as socio-political construct: "Call it the need for social deviance or deviants and how we'd come to live in such a world" (189). As Maierhofer has avowed in his online "Research Notes" on *Flamingos*, "like most broadly-brushed notions, madness is a literary thing [...] a term that had been politically warped over time to marginalize an entire body of people."

Foucault is the *éminence grise* behind Maierhofer's thinking, as are Laing and Lacan – but the strength of *Flamingos* lies in its resistance to becoming yet another disquisition on the medicalisation and commodification of mental health. Instead, *Flamingos* stays on the level of language: the chief impulse behind the assemblage aims toward stories, narratives, voices that "let a personal understanding of madness and treatment become warped in transmission" ("Research Notes"). *Flamingos'* voices and perspectives are described as "screaming at various walls, responding to a prompt like: 'what is madness for you?' or 'how can you possibly live and breathe in twenty-first century America?'" and it is to Maierhofer's credit that the answers provided always remain tentative at best. The closest we come to definitions are avowals of their impossibility ("Just what they are I'm hard-pressed, I'm afraid. It's tiring, this." [201]) or cryptic detournements like "COME IN, WE'RE FUCKING CLOSED" (200).

Why flamingos, you may ask? "A flamingo is an understanding thing, and almost entirely, globally inedible. It's eaten sure, but seldom" – and it is on a note of harmless togetherness bordering on understanding that *Flamingos* concludes, "seeking coherence where there is just implosion", looking not for a "way out", but only "through":

> We go together, wear the same drab white and blue cloth and stumble along the walks they let us pass and visitors come on Sundays and we are still [...] seeking life where there is none, coherence where there is just implosion, sanity where there is a list of ways your head simply does not fit. There couldn't be a way out, but through. (282)

Bleach is an assemblage by the sheer fact of its genre, "A Collection of Stories".

Introduced with a Félix Guattari motto on how "every machine works for itself according to its operations", *Bleach* opens with "Howlings in Favor of Sade," a story borrowing its title from the famous image-less 1952 Debord film. Its narrator is the first of *Bleach's* legion of nameless first-person voices living in a dystopia that is at once alien ("They farm us. We're given something for what we do. We watch. We stare" [292]) and all-too-familiar ("I watch a lot of television [...] on a laptop computer propped on my chest in bed with the lights off while feeding my facehole from a bag of rusted potato chips" [291]). Still, shining through the mind-numbing monotony are a few exhilarating observations like "Is this the most frightening thing about spiders, that they do not pay rent?" (293) and conjectures, e.g. "Perhaps our teeth are something we don't yet understand. To visit a dentist is to visit a grave" (293), that show, if not a way out, then at least through.

Bleach proceeds in a similar vein with stories like "New Rose" and "Grand Illusion", the latter an obvious if also mysterious reference to the 1937 Jean Renoir classic, as the story itself features another nameless "I" who is "in the room, watching my life spin out", addressing a disappeared "Mary" as "suddenly you're just not you but the dying you" and remembering some shared halcyon days contrasting with the maddeningly passive(-tense) present: "Holidays are spent jokily masturbating what can't be masturbated as I eat and eat from cold cans beans that were never warmed" (314).

There is the occasional Burroughs nod: in pieces like "Interzone", where an "I" and his "dying friend" have "trespassed while dying on sacred ground deemed thus by some ancient tribe of teenagers who'd frozen themselves," their main "problem" being "never making bad feel good, but something else entirely" (318). Maierhofer's dystopia peaks in its geographic specificity in "Pruitt-Igoe", a slice of a life of a teen gang playing their day-to-day survival game in the thirty-three 11-story building complex in Near North Side of St. Louis, Missouri – and Maierhofer's narrator is as teenage-blasé as they come ("Kids don't know much. I guess we weren't kids maybe. I don't care. We were clueless though.") and equally resentful: "I hate the fucking city. These cowards build homes to keep the outsiders out then burn down the homes when they don't like the consequences of pure neglect" (341).

The climax of the collection are two "pure sci-fi" pieces: "2157", which takes a future vantage point from which to look back at an interplanetary collapse of the (post-)human civilisation. The brutally honest retrospective of "a rotten era [in which] to have a body imprinted with what you thought eyelets of the sun," is delivered by yet another outcast inhabiting a much-harmful and much-harmed body, who attempts an escape from a world that had "prioritized meat and work and thus within cities rooms were made to great efficiency and factories churned out cloned, replicated bodies to eat" (348). He is tracked down eventually, and is made to listen to his verdict that manages to outkafka "The Penal Colony":

> You were found ungrateful, of the body, a person in every sense. You were found having eaten the bodies of these. You were found having eaten the bodies of these drifters and beyond the purview of our court. You are not to think and feel and access anything beyond those possibilities and exigencies just in front of you. You are not an original. You contain the bodies of others and you are disgusted with yourself. We are not interested in apology or meat. (351)

"Orphic Hymns" is a piece of epic scope in four sections, following the mission of spaceship Orpheus-2 a.k.a. the Cocteau (the motto from Jean reads "I am burning myself up and will always do so," its first section is called "SANGD'UNPOÈTE" and the last, "ORPHÉE") beyond the Kuiper Belt, "the furthest touch of man," and towards Pluto and Charon. The mission's task concerns finding out about the causes and purposes of a mysterious "growth" discovered in Pluto's system by spaceship Orpheus-1, offering "the prospect of understanding something in non-earthly terms" (359). Yet as the crew led by the mysterious and increasingly "outlandish" Klimt penetrates further into the deepest reaches of space, the drama becomes earthly, all-too earthly: one of ego vs. super-ego, mania vs. depression, individual experience vs. collective responsibility. As in Tarkovsky's *Solaris* and Kubrick's *2001,* the cosmic journey into the future turns into one individual's coming-to-terms with the past, the endless immensity of space shrunken to a single-person pod adrift in vacuum

> I have no inkling of what's what and my memories have grown beyond the journey [...] to my children that never lived and my father that never died and my living that will ever and forever emanate around this belt of hulking stones [...] and I am living within the history and dying within it in turn [...] as the world jettisons me and I am cast ever outward into the mass oblivion and rot. (378)

Yet, the collection as a whole bears the title "Bleach," of a story of a character referred to solely as the "killer" whose project is to kill without "coherency" and whose M.O. involves removing the trails of his deeds with the use of said detergent. Gradually he ends up stalked by and eventually stages a face-off with his doppelgänger, who may or may not be hallucinated. Certainly the most narrative-driven if also mysteriously American story in the collection.

Finally, *PX138 3100-2686 User's Manual* is a composite multi-genre text, featuring a text-image interface whose level of incongruous incompatibility would make Levé blush. The manual is for the horrifically effective "anti-update decompressive saw [...], one of the most fantastic machines ever engineered by human being" (386). As Maierhofer has divulged in an online conversation with Thomas Moore,

> rather than writing something about language and disconnection and violence, I wanted to try and write something that was language and disconnection and violence, as garbled as that might sound. I was working with translation software and coding and the like to rework what I'd originally written [...] into something considerably more fucked, but hopefully nonetheless new in its effect.

The operation of the saw requires the operator to cover their eyes and ears, as well as to "avoid serious thought" and stay clean of "the influence of pharmaceuticals" (389) – very much the law-abiding citizen's bread-and-butter in 2020. Following these caveats is a SAWMAN'S JOURNAL, an account of the machine operator gradually "falling apart in public" – except this time, the text disintegrates together with the narrative subject, blocks of unsegmented text (ISAWTHEWHITELIGHTTONIGHT. IJUSTDONTCARE.) alternating with spatialised ungrammatical phrases sprawling across near-blank pages: "These are jotted notes. These are notes, jotted." / "when have i fell sleep..." (407). The rest are fragmentary notes on brokenness (sawing and being sawn) and violence, some eerie ("This is the trial. This is the trail. The trail leads to the bench in the park where I'll sit. The trial leads to the internal place we all must go to reach some level of understanding here." [408]) some hilarious ("My kinship is with jack Torrance. My kinship is with jack Torrance. My kinship is with jack Torrance." [409]). There is a pageful of curses (from "Cursed yr family / Cursed yr animals" to "Cursed yr saw / Cursed yr fucking forearm / Cursed yr" [423]), in-between pages that divulge no more than "i am a little macchine" and "now it hurts to breathe…" (423). Before END OF SAW come six full pages of binary-code strings. What does it mean? "What could it possibly fucking mean. I go about in uncertainty. What a glorious state. There is nothing else to learn. Nothing to hope for. Continued feeling and endless worry" (439). EXEUNT. EXEUNT. EXEUNT.

3. As a whole, then, *Works* is a hybrid ensemble whose entirety exceeds any single perceptive process, an ever-shifting entity larger than any one reader's (the present one included) consciousness can keep hold of. A bird's-eye view of its entirety enables one to see its multiple genres reduced to their elemental forms; the whole assembled as a prismatic constellation of competing, mutually reflective discourses and discursive gestures. In Bataille's conception of assemblage just as Maierhofer's, the interplay of genres and forms becomes the interface of discourses and types of knowledge, wherein each type of writing brings with it a range of stylistic tropes and possibilities, as well as referential and epistemological assumptions and limitations. What can be said somehow in one form must appear otherwise in another, provided it can be said at all.

There is, thus, a number of textual interlinks between the four adjoining bricks that make up the new one, and a few equally important conceptual ones. The literal links include several faint echoes of *Postures* in *Flamingos*. When Flamingo (the character) states, "I make sure X gets from A to B. I make sure the nightmare wanes I guess, defer to cop lingo and back coffee, retain monotony" (177), is this X an "anonymous patient," or X from *Postures* receiving his treatment, diabetes or other? When Patient describes the books he cares for, he talks of "works of fiction written in the negative, that is negate-ive, made up of the opposite parts" (228). Is it just a coincidence that when X speaks of his own writing, he observes he "was not taught to write by the works of another writer" but "learned to do what he now does through the process of negation" (61)? *A User's Manual* similarly features a few surprising reappearances, as when instalment V of the video tutorial mentions "unknown documentation of the execution of one G.G., [...] really rotten stuff" (395) – is this the same G.G. as the *dramatis persona* from *Flamingos*, described as "criminal, involved with strains of black metal, survivalist," who "never gave a ready piss for this America" (186)? If so, how/why? Does "YAMA: for robbery, those rotting already in the pits fiery pits were torn in half for good and good, torn in ha—" (410) have anything to do with architect Minoru Yamasaki from "Pruitt-Igoe," the builder of the fiery pits of modern urbanist hell?

Most of these are teasingly unanswerable, but they do illustrate how reading these side-by-side, conceiving of *Works* as a continuous text, yields considerable interpretive enrichments. Even more importantly, the *Works'* variegated discourses and genres provide commentary on each other, showing us what individual genres permit and forbid, how they convey and conceal, where they excel and fail. Thus, in the context of what comes after, *Postures'* X turns from a Kafkaesque marker for a half-concealed, yet clear-cut individual identity, into a mark of a subject in progress and thus unidentical with "itself", a subject under erasure (a 2014 excerpt from the novel in *Berfois* was indeed titled "Postures, Erasures"). What indeed about the title "postures" itself? In the context of the various masques and personae that follow, the very title *Postures* comes under scrutiny: what, in the world of fiction, indeed *is* a posture, as opposed to what exactly – "authenticity"? Experiencing *Flamingos* in the context of *Works* allows for an opposite process of unification: unriddling the nine disparate and isolated "noisages" as nine entities within one transpersonal collective, nine voices in a single debate about insubordination against artificial notions of "normalcy". Reading *Bleach* after *Postures* and *Flamingos* invites a reading of the individual stories as fragments of larger wholes, re-imagining them as bigger textual stains "bleached" into whiteness by the limitations of the short-story genre – none of the stories, after all, feel quite as "finished" as the two larger texts preceding.

Finally, *User's Manual*, the only hitherto unpublished text, abandons narrative linearity altogether and offers textual brokenness instead while simultaneously bringing *Works* to a close ("EXEUNT"), a paradoxical function it could not serve as a standalone piece.

4. The inconspicuously rich title *Works* also points to the notion of the "labour" of writing soliciting the "work" of reading. To write, for Maierhofer, is a struggle, and to rewrite him through the reading process is a complementary process. In the piece on "Plagiarism," he has this to impart about his writing procedure:

> I'm someone who has struggled to make texts, or books, for some time. I've sat in workshops and written the words of others into typewriters or computers trying to figure out their workings. This method, the choice of a textual home that you can enter, rewrite, reimagine, read from before starting the day's work, narrows the writing process incredibly so that one's focus is sharp and clear [...] creating an anxiety of influence that's solvable only by yet more writing, more explaining, more running from the words of another until I've created something new.

Maierhofer comes back to the notion of the difficulty of "work" vis-à-vis the writer and the reader in his essay for *3AM Magazine* on James Joyce's *Finnegans Wake*, whose "pages of linguistic forest fires simultaneously enact and subvert their own interpretation." The attraction of "*FW*" for Maierhofer is chiefly twofold: its proto-conceptual objecthood and its performativity.

The former was so dear to Eugene Jolas and the whole *transition* gang, busily co-opting Joyce for their avant-garde project of autonomous art: "The work", observes Maierhofer of *FW*, "is also a thing entirely its own: a novel following no traditional pattern for the novel [...], a piece of fiction apparently wholly disinterested in storytelling." The latter has to do with how reading *FW* is "a bodily thing", consequence of Joyce spending "the bulk of his life" thinking about "what printed text might venture to do." In Maierhofer's experience of *FW*,

I find I'll begin with resistance, certain I'm misunderstanding every letter until suddenly a dreamy rhythm overtakes me and I'm able to stomach paragraphs in breaths. I'll often slow to crawls in turn and view the pages as discrete, visual, concrete passages rendered as micro- and macrocosms for diligent poring and slackjawed stupor alike.

The level to which conceptual autonomy is achieved in *Works* progressively intensifies, from the primarily narrative-driven *Postures* to the well-nigh conceptual image/text assemblage in *User's Manual.* And Maierhofer's account of reading *FW* comes uncannily close to my own experience of the "resistances" of his writing, especially *Flamingos*. Germán Sierra's useful introduction refers to Johannes Göransson's theorization of the new "rhetorical punk" styles defined as "atrocity kitsch". *Flamingos,* in Göransson's account, becomes "a noir without the proper detective to piece back together the crime and its narrative" – and "without the narrative cure, the novel becomes sick." However fickle—especially in the mental compartment—the categories of health and illness, what piecing together fragments has in common with treating a sickness is that both are anti-entropic processes requiring energy and *work*.

5. Maierhofer's *Works* is no "*FW* Redux" of course, and although his modernist inheritance does feature some of the Joycean exploration of the materiality of language and semantic overlay, his style is more deeply embedded in the Woolfian tradition of the idioms of the individual psyche (*sans* her aestheticism) and the Beckettian vein of the paradoxes of unsaying, negation, failing better. A text like *Flamingos* brings these two together implicitly but also explicitly:

You're a bit like every seeing eye in *Molloy*. What you have are inklings. [...] And you cannot think of the era, slurping coffee in the car in hot Florida misery, without thinking of V. Woolf. Was it she with whom Beckett spoke in these moments? Uncertain. (190)

More significant for Maierhofer than the Anglo-Irish high-modernist tradition, however, seems to be the black-comedic existential hard-boil of the French (both Céline and Cocteau have provided more than just mottos), Kafka's bureaucratic wet-dreams-turned-nightmares, and the native US tradition of semi-autobiographical journalist/fictioneers (Exley, Fante, Thompson).

All in all, Maierhofer's style is that rare species of what Roberto Bolaño's savage detectives would call "visceral realism", with three prominent features. First, a positioning of radical ontological uncertainty, oftentimes substance-induced and of a hallucinatory nature—what Louis Armand's fiction has explored under the rubric of "acid noir" (*Breakfast at Midnight, The Combinations*)—as a last resort from externally imposed standards of "normalcy". The second is a foregrounding of the technological underpinnings of the "human", its "intermedial" state and its possible transcendence—Maierhofer's *Postures* does to TV and the "screen culture" at large what Germán Sierra's own *The Artifact* does to "big data" and artificial intelligence. Third, the psycho-sci-fi heights to which Maierhofer brings his two concluding stories in *Bleach* brings to mind Harlan Wilson's "splattershtick", the ultraviolent form of metafiction as practiced in his "scikungfi" trilogy and most recently in *Natural Complexions*.

This exercise in name-dropping is not meant to detract from Maierhofer's originality – rather the opposite, it is meant as a proof, if further is needed, that "originality" most often comes about as an effect of a new recombination, as a solution to an anxiety of influence entailing "yet more writing, more explaining, more running from the words of another until I've created something new."

6. This anxiety is of a particularly American kind. As I write this Afterword, the state of the U.S. politics has become such that to trust the President is to believe that chugging bleach can increase your chances of survival of the current pandemic, thus hitting an all-time low/high in coupling its traditional dog-eat-dog cynicism with unprecedented levels of dangerous stupidity (#WhatDoYouHaveToLose #JustTakeIt). As this book's publisher

informs me, "we're all taking our daily micro-dose of bleach, mixed with vitamin water and an alka seltzer, of course. America, once again, is the laughingstock of the world".

The 2015-16 vantage point of *Postures* and *Flamingos* feels almost quaint from the point-of-view of 2020. Yet even in these earlier texts there is the odd prophetic note struck ("America was entirely absurd of late, entirely alien. *The orange skin*. The earrings that cause your ears to turn green." [100]), and a sustained reflection on what it might mean to be a 21st-century fictioneer in and of a country like America permeates Maierhofer's *Works* throughout.

As *Postures* details through its own exercise in name-dropping, the "gigantic melee of confusion that was [and is] the United States" has first of all produced its gigantically confused culture. Its pantheon features not just Acker and Burroughs and Exley but more canonical figures like Jackson Pollock (whose work "chronicled the American Mess in such a phenomenal and groundbreaking way that it defies petty judgment or mere *criticism*" [61]) and Mark Twain, "a brilliant man because he remembered through the flux of his life those things most Americans choose to forget" (96), like racism, sexism, social inequality, all the American evergreens. The Midwest setting of *Postures* also accounts for some of its disturbing regional realism: "You saw nightmares. You saw sleepwalkers. You saw an American Middle-West on the brink of being completely bankrupt, completely miserable, and completely nameless" (65).

The obsession with "watching" and "watchability" generated by all-pervasive infantilising "smart" technology, diagnosed as *the* American sickness by DFW all the way back in the early-90's, has been taken to whole new, "kaleidoscopic-fucksreen" heights:

Teenaged millionaires; teenaged billionaires; teenaged forty-year olds; teenaged icons and Cut 4 Whomever; everything teenaged. Nineteen-eighty-bore. This is what Big Brother would have on humanity, nothing more; a kaleidoscopic fuckscreen of bad camera angles that make mankind look like half a speck of civilization when you pick it apart for just a moment. (23)

When coupled with our second lives on social-media, purportedly designed for "connecting people" while keeping them imperially alone, this addiction to infotainment becomes a potentially lethal disease. This is Maierhofer still in 2015, three years before Cambridge Analytica dawned on even the most unsuspecting ones:

> X lamented those like Mark Zuckerberg, who may act like he's created a fantastic way for people to stay in touch [...] but Zuckerberg hasn't. What he's created is yet another hoop to jump through before anyone will even consider being your friend. That film about Facebook had recently been nominated for various awards, and X found that both the filmmaker [...] and its actors were perpetuating and attempting to justify one man's creation of an absolutely unnecessary system and the resulting billions of dollars he received afterward [...]. So, fuck this, X thought. Fuck Mark Zuckerberg, fuck the creators of Twitter, fuck the Internet, fuck designers. (118)

Transposed into the clinical realm of "mental health" in *Flamingos*, there is a pervasive "love(-ish) and optimism, or hate(-ish) and pessimism/nostalgia for asimpler, printed-text era", before the inte rnet came and made all the dormant hydras inside rear their ugly heads. "Again the watchers," bewails Olivier, "the surveillance. What to make of it, I'm unawares, but keen on most sensation. I think I feel bogged down, morassed. I term it 'depression'—their phrase—and try to walk it off, yet it won't go" (163).

German Sierra's introduction is right: *Flamingos* deals with the *stultifera navis* that is the American society at large: "We watch as entertainment entertains, pulls and nags and distorts his image to celebrity" (170, Edmund); "Why this preoccupation with television? Why this preoccupation with signs and cans of bubbled water? The why never seems to figure much into it" (212, Patient); "Freshly showered, I turned the water warm as it went and scalded my stomach. I put on the television afterward and let its light put something out" (254, Flamingo); "What I'm paid to do is stare at screens in evaluation of items that might be pumped through imagined pneumatic tubes into the skulls of various Americans and

Elsewhereicans" (170, Edmund again). We the Globalicans might "all be living in Amerika" now, but Americans have traditionally been blessed with a far closer proximity to the wellspring than us Elsewhereicans.

Flamingos stages Neil Postman's famous juxtaposition of Orwell's fear of being governed by those who would ban books and deprive us of information, and Huxley's fear of being governed by those who would give us so much of it as to reduce us to passivity and egotism, having no more reason to ban books, for there would ultimately be no-one to read them. As Huxley remarks in *Brave New World Revisited*, the civil libertarians and rationalists, who are ever on the alert to oppose tyranny, "failed to take into account man's almost infinite appetite for distractions." Quoth Maierhofer's Patient: "Late-late-late capitalism has done what it does: it has capitalized on this distraction and turned it into a godly hand upon their social shoulder" (179). Quoth DFW: "Our own present culture has harnessed these forces in ways that have yielded extraordinary wealth and comfort and personal freedom. The freedom to be lords of our own tiny skull-sized kingdoms, alone at the center of all creation." I have described "Bleach" one of the most "American" stories in the collection, and here is a passage to justify the claim:

> This sort of thing, the process of removing life from a body, creating a corpse, grew in importance with each iteration. The ritual mattered. The peace and quiet mattered. The killer [...] had enjoyed the freedom to execute matters with a bit of reckless abandon. (295)

7. Which begs the question of what fiction can do about all this. At the end of the day, Maierhofer is no extreme conceptualist like Levé, for he knows all too well that conceptualism is postmodernism's masterstroke, which in turn is capitalism's masterstroke (thus spake Fukuyama), churning out "art" that comes furnished with its own USP's and with price-tags attached to every word.

As is argued in Sean Kilpatrick's introduction to *Postures*, in this "how to write" manual, "Maierhofer has committed a great atrocity against homeownership by displaying affection for shit you can't truly buy. [...] A book is only ever in a container until it rots your thought" (14). "Rot your thought" is a very apt descriptor for one effect of Maierhofer's writing, not least since the 350-odd page manuscript of *Works* contains close to 50 mentions of "rot" and its cognate forms. "Rotting" is not an idle metaphor here as it implies a process of decomposition essential for the recycling of the finite matter in the biosphere – or textual matter in the infosphere. In *Flamingos*, Maierhofer is using his Patient as mouthpiece when observing:

> The diseased and afflicted body is the norm in twenty-first century American society, is perhaps a place to start. You don't think much on American society anymore, just the hands within it cracked and grasping at the promised some such something. (253)

The reason for this Foucauldian reversal of "starting with the diseased and the afflicted" as opposed to "the healthy" is not just for the sake of theoretical savviness. As Maierhofer reveals in his "Research Notes":

> Personally, I've been engaged with the discourse of madness a good while, was hospitalized when seven as a result of the ADD/ADHD impulse in America in the 90s, and have had more and less severe bouts of unipolar depression as long as I can remember, so this is where my mind goes in writing.

This horrendously obsolete notion of fiction growing out of a personally "authentic" dimension is what gives Maierhofer's writing its rhetorical force, but would paralyse it *as fiction* if that were all. True, each of Maierhofer's *Works* are also almost pedagogical, as they have a "message" to impart, and "argument" to develop – a word featuring prominently in the final paragraph of *Postures* quoted above.

But what makes *Works* compelling *as fiction*—not as memoir, not as treatise, not as socio-political critique—is the awareness of its own status as product of language, a tool for constructing thought-systems "posturing" for truths. When compiling notes for *Flamingos*, Maierhofer reveals,

> A use for fiction had presented itself: Language as a lie, a systemic means of painting the world one way versus another, then. Our present reeks of this: "alt-right," and crypto-fascists, angry knee-jerkers reacting to "identity politics" and turning basic civil rights into something manipulative. I am scared of shifting definitions, and I think fiction, poetry, literature has a good deal of work to offer to counter this tendency.

And regarding *Postures*, Maierhofer has confided to Mike Seitz that "the final version feels more like a treatise than a novel," a treatise for those in need of accepting literary failure, for whom *Postures* has aimed to provide "a comfort, a sort of friendship, that they're not enduring these things without reason, and that they're not alone in doing so."

What "enduring" means in *Works* is, first and foremost, directed towards vulnerability, the ability to be wounded – openness to fiction is readiness to meet people and undergo experiences that might otherwise "hurt". Which in today's society of well-padded untouchable Facebook users, for whom "to take offense" and/or "feel insulted" is to breathe air, is believe it or not nothing short of scandalous – to say nothing of its "alt-right," crypto-fascist segments. It hurts to read Maierhofer, and that is good.

What is also refreshing in today's social-media climate of public shaming, no-platforming, and cancel-culture at large, is how Maierhofer's characters permit themselves (or they are permitted) to be wrong. This is particularly though not exclusively true of *Flamingos* and as Sierra points out, "the most important thing for keeping a 'sustainable' community may not be the acquiescence to a common truth, but the desire to implement an indeterminate network of reciprocal trust" (147).

It does not surprise, then, that in the conflicting and ambivalent fictional universe of *Works*, the disquisition on vulnerability is delivered by one of the "wrongest" of all Maierhofer characters, Klimt the mass-suicidal egomaniac:

> "Sometimes vulnerability is necessary to fully understand substance. I've chosen individuals for this mission capable of a certain kind of vulnerability [...]. What kind of vulnerability exactly? I'm prepared to accept an alternate sense of time out here. I'm prepared to witness a disease and cure in simultaneity, but beyond that I'm interested in growth alone. Fungi are communicative as a scab is communicative." (368)

"Preparedness to accept" is perhaps the no.1 demand Maierhofer's fiction makes of its reader if they are to witness a "disease and cure in simultaneity" and allow for something like a "growth." As stated in his "Notes" to *Flamingos:*

> This is a work of fiction that attempts to explore the question of "why fiction?" in turn. I wanted a project, a space to ask these local questions as to craft. [...] my only hope in going forward is that it might exist as a voice in a conversation with readers, pursuing their own projects and navigating life, [...]. All I want is fiction, writing that opens up the world and lets it bleed a bit.

At the end of the day, this is the only "work" of fiction writing that truly matters.

David Vichnar, Prague, May 2020

ABOUT THE AUTHOR

Grant Maierhofer is a writer from America.

11:11 Press is an American independent literary
publisher based in Minneapolis, MN.
Founded in 2018, 11:11 publishes innovative
literature of all forms and varieties. We believe
in the freedom of artistic expression, the
realization of creative potential, and the
transcendental power of stories.